MADE IN HEAVEN

MAY MCGOLDRICK

MM Books

Thank you for reading. In the event that you appreciate this book, please consider sharing the good word(s) by leaving a review, or connect with the authors.

OTHER WORKS BY MAY MCGOLDRICK, NIK JAMES & JAN COFFEY

NOVELS BY MAY MCGOLDRICK

A Midsummer Wedding

The Thistle and the Rose

Angel of Skye (Macpherson Trilogy Book 1)

Heart of Gold (Book 2)

Beauty of the Mist (Book 3)

Macpherson Trilogy (Box Set)

The Intended

Flame

Tess and the Highlander

The Dreamer (Highland Treasure Trilogy Book 1)

The Enchantress (Book 2)

The Firebrand (Book 3)

Highland Treasure Trilogy Box Set

Much Ado About Highlanders (Scottish Relic Trilogy Book 1)

Taming the Highlander (Book 2)

Tempest in the Highlands (Book 3)

Scottish Relic Trilogy Box Set

Arsenic and Old Armor

The Promise (Pennington Family)

The Rebel

Secret Vows Box Set

Borrowed Dreams (Scottish Dream Trilogy Book 1)

Captured Dreams (Book 2)

Dreams of Destiny (Book 3)

Scottish Dream Trilogy Box Set

Romancing the Scot

It Happened in the Highlands

Sweet Home Highland Christmas

Sleepless in Scotland

Dearest Millie

How to Ditch a Duke

Highland Crown (Royal Highlander Series Book 1)

Highland Jewel (Book 2)

Highland Sword (Book 3)

Ghost of the Thames

Thanksgiving in Connecticut

Made in Heaven

Marriage of Minds: Collaborative Writing

Step Write Up: Writing Exercises for 21st Century

NOVELS BY NIK JAMES

Caleb Marlowe Westerns

High Country Justice

Bullets and Silver

Silver Trail Christmas

NOVELS BY JAN COFFEY

Trust Me Once

Twice Burned

Triple Threat

Fourth Victim

Five in a Row

Silent Waters

Cross Wired

The Janus Effect

The Puppet Master

Blind Eye

Road Kill

Mercy

When the Mirror Cracks

Tropical Kiss

Aquarian

CHAPTER ONE

Newport, Rhode Island
September 1995

EVAN KNIGHT PARKED his cab in front of the three-story apartment building and got out of the car. Moving around to open the trunk, he stepped over a pile of broken bottles and empty beer cans that lay beside an overflowing dumpster.

They had been at the hospital for nearly eight hours. Eight hours of pacing the halls and sitting in a lime green waiting room only to be told that it wasn't time yet. He opened the trunk and took out Jada's frayed canvas backpack. Evan frowned at it, thinking that not nine months ago the girl had stored her school books in there instead of clothing for a baby that she didn't even want.

He slammed the trunk shut and stalked around the car to get her out. Jada already had the door open, but she was just too big and tired to haul herself out. He took her gently by the hands and let her pull herself to her feet. It was then that he saw the tears on her round face.

"I'm sorry, Evan. I am so sorry. I was..." She began to sob silently, and he gathered her to his chest.

"Don't be, Jada. Don't be."

As he ran a comforting hand over her back, he glared at two goggle-eyed punks walking by. He didn't think he'd ever face a teenager in this town again without wondering if the kid might be the father of Jada's baby. No matter what the girl's father had threatened, she had been determined not to name the boy. "I was so scared last night. I was *sure* the baby was coming."

"It's okay, honey. That woman doctor said this is very common with first-time mothers." He took out a tissue from the back pocket of his jeans and handed it to her. First-time mother, he repeated silently, gritting his teeth. And only fifteen. A child herself.

"I wish daddy was back. Then you wouldn't have to be bothered with me in the middle of the night."

"You're no bother." He pushed her away slightly until he could look into her still teary eyes. "I don't care what time of the day it is. Until your father gets back, you call me, and I'll take you to the hospital. The doctor said you're getting really close. It could be any time."

He didn't let go of his grip until she nodded.

"You've got the cell phone number, right?"

"I've got it."

"Okay," he said gruffly, steering her toward the graffiti-covered door of the building. "I've got to pick up that Bellevue Avenue fare they just buzzed me on, but you call if you need me."

When Jada was safely inside and old Mrs. Jeffers, the warm-hearted neighbor from the next apartment, had taken charge, Evan trotted back out to the cab. As he pulled out of the parking lot, he thought about how much Ted, Jada's father, would want to be here for this. Well, he should be back any day now, Evan thought. A fisherman's got to make his living while the weather's good.

Raking a hand through his wavy brown hair, Evan turned onto Bellevue before calling in his route. As traffic slowed, he gazed absently at one of the mansions through a twelve-foot iron gate, and thought of Jada, her legs wobbling as he walked her into the hospital last night. She'd been in pain, and so frightened. And he'd been unprepared. Totally useless. He hadn't known what to say or what to do. Like the walking dead, he'd just paced the halls of that hospital for hours and waited.

Next time, though, he'd do better, he promised himself. Next time, he'd support her the way her father would.

Through the rear window of the car in front of him, Evan watched three teenage boys laughing. The one in the back seat lit a cigarette and glanced back at the taxi.

My God, Evan thought, he'd been a teenager himself once, and a wild one, at that. But he didn't think he'd ever acted carelessly when it came to taking care of his partner. He wondered who the hell the father of Jada's baby was. No doubt, a lowlife scum to hit on a bright-faced innocent like her. The kid must have seen her start to show before she quit school in the spring.

Evan brought the cab to a stop in front of the closed gates of the fenced-in mansion and announced his arrival through the intercom. A moment later, as the gates opened, he started along the tree-lined driveway leading to the rambling stone house. Unimpressed, he muttered under his breath and pulled up to the porch. Getting out of the car, he opened the trunk for an irritable servant with a suitcase in hand.

"You'll be taking the young Mr. Rand to the Kingston train station. He's got to make the 3:26 train to New York. Here is the money for the fair, and you can keep the change."

Without looking, Evan took the money from the man and stuffed it deep into his pocket.

"You're *late*," the man pressed. "We were afraid you weren't going to make it in time to—"

"I am here, aren't I?" Evan snapped. "But how the hell am I

going to get young Mr. Rand's ass to that station in time if he isn't ready to go?"

The servant's face turned crimson, but before he could say anything, a lanky young man hurried down the stone steps, and Evan slammed the trunk shut.

"I'm sorry I'm late. I'm ready."

Without sparing a second look at the teenager, Evan climbed into the cab and called in his destination. The front door of the cab opened, and his passenger got in beside him.

"Ready," the young man whispered to himself.

In a few minutes they were making their way through the downtown traffic, and Evan's mind again returned to Jada and what he could do to help her through this. She would not accept any charity. That's the way Ted had raised her. But there had to be a way that he could make things a little bit easier for her and for the baby.

His passenger's voice broke into his thoughts. "It's nice to get the town back from the tourists."

Evan made an incoherent sound and went back to ignoring him.

"Once we got stuck for two hours in the traffic on America's Cup Avenue right by the army-navy store. We had the limo, though, so it wasn't so bad. In fact, it was amazing to just sit here and see so many different kinds of people just go by."

"What the hell do you know about kinds of people?"

"Hey, I go to school. I used to go to the Priory School here."

"And you never hung out downtown?" Evan looked out the window disgustedly.

"Nah, I couldn't. Besides, I'm going to a new school now. In New York."

"So what happened?" Evan snapped. "Your daddy thought your blue blood would discolor, mixing with the poor kids here? Or did he get upset because somebody spit on the limo?"

The young man blushed and stared straight ahead.

The cell phone rang, and Evan answered it. "Jada?"

"No, it's Henry. But I'm pleased to hear there's a Jada."

Evan paused and took a look at the kid sitting next to him. Young Mr. Rand was staring curiously at him. Evan reached down and clicked on the radio in the cab before talking into the phone.

"What the hell are you doing calling me at this number?"

"Dammit, I've tried everything else. You don't read your e-mail. You don't use an answering machine, and you're never home to answer your phone."

"So?"

"So do I have to drag my butt all the way from New York to Newport just to talk to you?"

"You do that, Henry, and I'll throw you right off the bridge." Evan looked out of his side window as the cab sped onto the suspension bridge. "Over two hundred feet from the top to the sparkling blue Narragansett Bay. It's sure to kill you."

"You can't scare me off that easy. Besides, there are probably sharks down there who'd treat me better than you do. Are you working?"

Evan reached down and turned up the volume of the radio.

"I can't hear you," Henry shouted. "Turn that damn thing off."

Evan rolled down his window.

"Where the hell are you? Is that a wind tunnel?"

"Yeah. And it's just about to tear the phone right out of my hand."

"Don't you dare, Evan Knight, or I swear on my dead mother's grave that I'll be sitting on your doorstep by nightfall."

"Now that's a terrifying thought. But don't do it, Henry. I've got a frigging reputation in the neighborhood." With a crooked smirk, he turned down the radio a bit. "You'll just ruin it."

"Are you working, Evan?"

"I am. I'm working right now."

"Then show me the proof. I haven't seen anything."

"What, my word's not good enough?" He placed the phone

against his shoulder and turned to the kid next to him. "What's your name?"

"Matthew. Matthew Rand."

"Tell my boss here that I am working."

Matthew leaned over and spoke in the receiver. "Hi. I'm Matthew, and he is working."

Evan then brought the cab to a halt at the toll booth and held the phone out to the attendant. "Hey, Raz, I've got my boss on the line. Tell him I am working."

"Your boss?" the man snickered.

"Do it, and it's good for drink on me at the Pub."

The man grabbed the phone out of Evan's hand. "Hello. This is Raz O'Shea. No, I'm a toll collector for the Newport Bridge Authority, and Mr. Knight is working."

Evan yanked the phone back and threw Raz a salute before driving off. "See? I have witnesses. I'm working."

"Don't do this to me, Evan."

"Excuse me, Henry. A pressing matter." He turned to Matthew. "What time is your train?"

"Three twenty-six."

"Sorry, Henry. We're late. Gotta go."

"*Don't!*" Henry shouted. "For God's sake, you are no cab driver. I am your agent, and you're Drew..."

Evan turned off the phone and stuffed it back in his pocket. "I really hate middle management."

CHAPTER TWO

AS THE TRAIN picked up a few more passengers in Providence, Meg gazed out the window at the renovated downtown area. What had a few years ago looked like a war zone, now looked like a cosmopolitan urban center. Beneath a raised street, she could see people strolling and lounging along cobblestone walks that bordered the river. Where the waterway opened into a small lagoon, an older man and a child could be seen enjoying the afternoon sun in a paddleboat. On the far side, Meg could see a painter at work at a small easel, and a young couple—arms around one another—were looking over his shoulder.

That could be you, you know.

Meg started at the sound of Robert's voice.

You are missing out on life.

"I don't know what you're talking about."

"Excuse me?" The man in the seat across was looking at her over the tops of his reading glasses. "Are you talking to me?"

"No." Meg blushed. "Just...just thinking out loud."

"Oh, sorry."

"Don't get me into trouble, now," Meg whispered.

It's time, Meg. You've got a life to be living, and I've got to be moving on.

"Robert, now is not the time."

The newspaper rustled across the way, but Meg had a distinct feeling that a pair of eyes were glued on her.

This is it, Meg. Last year, I tried to explain it to you, but you wouldn't listen.

"You were wrong, and I was right," she whispered. "You're back in spite of what you told me."

"Ahem." The man across the way leaned forward in his seat. "Are you certain everything is all right?"

"Haven't you ever seen anybody talk to herself?"

She sounded snappish, but she didn't care. And her fellow traveler *did* crawl behind his paper again.

Well, you can believe what you want. But I am telling you that the time has come for me to go. In fact, I'm down here this year on another matter. There's someone—

"I knew it. You are seeing somebody else." Meg scowled playfully. "After fifteen years of marriage."

Ten.

"Fifteen."

The last five don't count. You forget, I've been dead.

"Not to me, you haven't. This is the same anniversary getaway we've been going on for the last *fifteen* years. I don't care what you say, you're still a married man."

"Divorced?"

"Stay out of this," Meg ordered at the eyes peering at her over the newspaper.

Death did us part. My ticket's punched, expired, gone.

"I'm not going to discuss this now," Meg whispered, watching another traveler take the seat beside the busybody across the way.

This time you have to, Meg. There is no other way. It's been selfish of me to drag it out this long. If I'd just gone away, the way most others do, then you wouldn't be in the predicament you're in now. You have to make a change in your life. It's time.

"There is nothing wrong with my life."

"Pardon me?"

"She likes to talk to herself."

"Oh. One of those."

"It's great. Just listen." The man lowered his voice behind the paper. "She is practicing for a fight with her husband. He's screwing around. His name is Robert, and it looks like he's getting ready to dump her."

"Ahem." Meg threw an irritated glare at the Nosy Parkers across the way, letting them know that she'd heard every word.

You see, you're making a spectacle of yourself.

"I am not."

Yes, you are. Everyone who knows you, feels sorry for you. Your friends, your mother—even old Joe E, your boss. You've no social life, whatsoever. In the five years since I died, you've done nothing for yourself.

"I've been busy. Working."

At a dead-end job. No pun intended. Meg, you have talent, energy, gumption. But you are putting it all to waste. You are young and beautiful. You should be living your life to the fullest.

"I am middle-aged. For God's sake, I'm thirty-five."

"That's young."

The newspaper rustled in agreement. "Very young."

Meg stared in disbelief at the two men eyeing her with concern. They had clearly given up all pretense of hiding their interest.

See, take it from the living, if you don't believe me. It's unhealthy, Meg. Going this long without—

"Don't say it."

Sex.

She pushed back her head against the chair and closed her eyes. "I can't believe you said it."

You're blushing, Meg.

"How the hell would you know? You keep telling me you're dead."

"Are you all right, miss? You're awfully flushed. Are you feverish?"

She opened her eyes and found herself looking into the face of another new arrival looking at her from the seat next to her.

"What are you, a doctor?"

"Uh, yes I am. I heard you talking to yourself and then..."

"She *likes* to talk to herself."

Meg turned and glared again across the way. The reading glasses were now off, and he was folding the paper in his lap.

"She's under some stress. She's had a fight with her husband."

"He's a jerk," the other passenger chirped. "You know. Screwing around."

"We think he's already left her," the newspaper cut in.

"Excuse me, I'm a lawyer and couldn't help but overhear the discussion." Meg turned and gaped dumbfounded at the man half-standing on the seat behind her. "Here is my business card. The fact that your husband has had multiple affairs..."

The conductor pushed open the door and stepped into the car. "Kingston, next stop. Kingston."

"Thanks," she said to him, hurriedly coming to her feet. "Not a moment too soon."

Climbing out of her seat and into the aisle, she tried to ignore the numerous heads that were turned at her direction. As she put her briefcase on the floor, a platinum-blond woman put a hand on her arm.

"I've been married three times, honey. After the first one dumped me, I said fool me once, but—"

"Sorry. Have to go," Meg blurted as cheerily as she could, reaching up to take down her traveling bag. Three men and a newspaper stood up to help her.

Forcing a smile that felt more like a grimace, she took the bag and started up the aisle. "Thanks, Robert. That was just great."

Sweetheart, this is only the beginning.

Just as the cab crunched to a stop in the gravel parking lot, the station's lone, outside speaker blared out.

"Arriving from Boston, Providence. Stopping at Westerly, New London..."

"We made it. Thanks for the ride."

"It's okay," Evan mumbled, climbing out of the car and moving around to open the trunk.

"So do you stick around and wait now?"

"No." He glared and dropped the kid's suitcase unceremoniously on the platform.

"I don't get back to Newport very much anymore. I was only supposed to come up for the weekend, this time. But I caught a bug or something, so I ended up staying longer. But maybe I'll see you around next time."

"I wouldn't count on it."

The whistle blast from the arriving train drowned out his words. Evan closed the trunk as he watched the kid turn and go stand in line with other passengers. He'd been short and impatient. But how could he be anything else, considering all he had on his mind?

He glanced again at young Matthew Rand. Dressed in his preppy clothes, his suitcase between his feet, he was already chatting with a couple of people and waiting for passengers to disembark. Caught a bug. He didn't have a care in the world. Everything was taken care of for him. So unlike Jada.

Shaking his head, he climbed into the cab. A half dozen arriving passengers were already trickling into the parking lot. Opening the dash, he checked the phone again. It was on. Jada wouldn't do anything stupid, like not calling him. No, one thing that girl had was a brain. What she lacked in experience, she was picking up too quick.

"Wakefield?"

"No," he barked without even turning to look.

Two businessmen huffed off.

Evan jammed the key into the ignition.

"How about Narragansett?"

"No." This time he turned and glared at the three college-age girls peering through the window. "Look at the side. N-E-W-P-O-R-T. Yellow cab. Do you want me to sound it out?"

"What a jerk," one of them crabbed, taking a step back.

"But *cute*," the other one whispered. "Did you see those eyelashes?"

Evan closed his eyes, shaking his head in disgust. Christ, they're getting dumber every year.

Just then the back door of the cab opened, and someone started to get in.

"Look, I'm not going to Wakefield. And I'm not going to Narragansett. And I'm not going to the goddamn North Pole."

Evan turned, prepared to continue, but the words stuck in his craw as he looked past a pair of wire-rimmed eyeglasses into the deepest, prettiest brown eyes he'd seen in a long time.

"Yes, I know. You're going to Newport." She smiled. "I can spell."

CHAPTER THREE

As the cab sped down the long incline of the new bridge, Meg gazed out the window at the remains of the ancient bridge that sat on the western end of it. The old Jamestown Bridge had been a decrepit, rusted, two-lane thing with gaping cracks in the cement pilings. Most of the structure had been taken down few years ago. The short stretch left was used as a fishing pier.

Meg looked ahead at the island in front of them. The hilly ridge that ran straight up the center of it was a patchwork of fields bordered with crumbling stone walls, dotted with old farmhouses and new developments. Beyond the island, through the bright afternoon haze, she could see the graceful tops of the Newport Bridge.

She craned her neck and took another look at what was left of the old bridge and the shimmering waters of the Narragansett Bay.

Aren't you glad that the old eyesore is gone?

She wasn't going to make another spectacle of herself, so she decided to ignore Robert's voice.

The old has to give way to the new. The dead to the living.

She turned her face out at the direction of other window and started counting the number of cars passing by.

You can't ignore it, Meg. I'm vapor, he is flesh. I am dead, he is alive.

"Who?" she asked irritably, looking around.

The taxi cab driver. Look at his name tag. Evan Knight. A good strong name.

Meg shook her head and peered out the front windshield as the two lanes of traffic suddenly slowed considerably.

A good-looking man. Strong jaw. Keen eyes. Needs a hair-cut, but—

"Go away," she snapped.

"Talking to me?" the driver asked adjusting his driver's mirror so he could see her face.

Hazel eyes. Meg, look at those eyelashes.

Meg pushed up her glasses on the bridge of her nose. "No. I mean yes. I said we aren't going...away. I mean, going a way I know very well."

Introduce yourself, Meg.

She ground her teeth and tried to keep calm.

A bit of small talk. It's not so difficult. Do it, Meg.

She pulled her briefcase onto her lap and pretended to rummage through it.

Do you want me to start something up?

"Leave it, Robert," she snapped under her breath.

"Something wrong?"

Meg peeked from behind her briefcase at the man behind the wheel. The traffic had come to a full stop, so it seemed there would be no escaping her meddling husband *or* the cool eyes of the driver.

"I was just talking to my..." She stopped herself. She was sick of people looking at her like she was some lunatic just out the bin for the day. "I just realized I left a book on the train."

"You said something else. Rob—"

"Robber," she added quickly. "I was wondering if a robber could have taken it."

"Robber. Interesting. A train robber."

When she saw the way he rolled his eyes, she had to fight back an urge to reach forward and smack him on the back of the head.

Very good, Meg. You're really off to a great start.

She closed her eyes for a moment, steeling herself against getting riled by her husband's antics. When she opened them, the driver's eyes flicked away from her face. He had *definitely* been staring at her. Slowly the traffic inched over the crest of the hill, and Meg could see the cars backed up all the way to the Newport Bridge.

"We don't seem to be moving, are we?"

Frowning into the rearview mirror at her, the driver pointed at the bridge. "Do you see the lights flashing just about halfway across? Accident."

"You mean we're stuck here?"

"This particular model cab isn't equipped with pontoons."

"Isn't there a short cut?"

The blue green eyes stared at her beneath furrowed brows. "Sure. We can cut across the median, drive all the way to Providence, fight through the traffic there, and come down the other side of the Bay. It should take about three hours at this time of day."

"I was being sarcastic."

"So was I," he said.

There was a moment of silence as the driver raked his hand through his hair and looked at his watch. "It shouldn't take them too long to clear the mess."

"Well, it's a pretty view. I guess I really don't mind waiting."

He rolled down his window, and the salt breeze swept through the cab.

"Do you come here often?" he asked.

She had to go back in her memory a few years, but that sounded like a pickup line.

"Once a year."

"Business? Or a little 'R and R'?"

"A bit of both." It wasn't exactly a lie, Meg quickly reminded herself. She had a briefcase full of manuscripts to read. She knew it would sound a little bit morbid to say she was here for a vacation with her dead husband. And there was no way she was going to give this guy the impression that she was here all alone.

"Well, it's a good time of the year to be here."

She just nodded and fell silent, sending thanks heavenward that Robert had decided to cut her a break. She placed the briefcase back on the floor next to her feet, double-checked the handle to her traveling bag, and—with great care—picked a speck of lint off her dress pants. Meg did anything and everything but look up and return the driver's gaze. She knew he was watching her, and that somehow flustered her.

"Well, looks like things are clearing up there."

She let out a breath of relief as the cab started moving again.

A moment later, as they left the toll booth Meg saw the driver answer his cell phone.

"Jada."

A Volvo cut in front of the cab, and Meg was thrown forward as the driver slammed on his brakes, simultaneously jamming his hand on the horn.

"What's wrong, Jada? I can't hear you."

Meg reached for the door grip as the cab swerved suddenly into the faster moving left lane. The driver gunned it, and the vehicle shot forward.

"You are in labor now? I'll be there in less than a half an hour."

She knew it was none of her business, but still she couldn't help but overhear.

"What do you mean, that'll be too late? What? You broke your water when?"

Meg put a hand on the back of the front seat, wedging herself in as the cab cut into the oncoming traffic lane for the length of a few cars and then swerved back into their own lane. She glanced on the seat in vain for a seatbelt.

"You're bleeding? Christ. Where's Mrs. Jeffers? What? Have you called the doctor? Call 911."

Meg sat forward in her seat, her eyes flitting back and forth from the road to the driver's profile.

"Don't cry, honey. Fine. Tell Mrs…Yeah, I'll be there. Yeah. I'm coming now. Right now."

Meg watched him throw the phone on the seat.

"I have an emergency."

"I understand," she said quickly.

He punched the button for his emergency flashers and pulled out again into the line of oncoming traffic. Meg's knuckles went white on the door handle.

"I don't have enough time to take you to the Inn. I won't even have enough time to drop you at the Visitor's Center. Get over, you sonovabitch."

"It's okay," she said, wincing as a van squeezed over just in time to avoid a head on collision. "Just…just do what you have to do. I'll call for a cab at the hospital."

"Right. But we've got one stop first."

"Fine," she said weakly, bouncing to one end of the seat as the cab cut across three lanes of traffic onto the exit ramp.

The Indy 500 had nothing on that quick trip through the narrow, back streets of Newport. Not the way this man drove. In the space of about a minute, Meg lost count of how many stop signs he'd run and decided it would be more in her interest to focus on keeping herself from getting thrown around like a sack of potatoes in the back seat. But nothing could prepare her for the final bank shot into a parking lot and the screeching stop. Her head practically came off its hinges before hitting the floor of the cab.

"You okay?"

With her butt in the air in the back seat, she rubbed her neck and looked into his face. "I think so."

"Good," he said, throwing open his door. Meg heard the trunk pop open. "Then throw your stuff in back. I'll get Jada. She'll be more comfortable sitting with you."

"Safer, anyway."

He grunted something unintelligible and hopped out of the cab.

It took Meg a moment to clear her head. Looking in the direction that the driver had sprinted, she saw him yank open a graffiti covered door of an apartment building. As the door swung wide, an elderly lady with a pair of toddlers hanging onto her skirts stepped out, holding the arm of a very pregnant young woman. Meg sprang into action.

She had all her stuff in the trunk and was standing holding open the door of the cab by the time they reached it.

"Do you want me to come with you, Jada?" the old woman asked anxiously, with a quick look at the two little ones now eyeing the action from the doorway.

"No. I'll be..."

Meg watched helplessly as the young woman grabbed at the door with one hand and her belly with the other. Her face drained of all color as she gasped for breath.

"What's wrong?" the driver asked.

Meg had seen enough movies to know what was happening. "She's having contractions."

"Do you know what to do?"

She looked into Jada's face and nodded quickly. "Yeah. Get her to the hospital. Now!"

Once the contraction passed and the young woman had been eased into the back seat, the cab took off like a bolt of lightning.

Meg held onto the pregnant woman's hand and looked at her with concern. Jada's head was now lying against Meg's shoulder, and a strange and precious feeling washed through her as the cab sped toward the hospital—the feeling that she was needed by this stranger. She stroked the soft hands and whispered words of comfort in her ear.

She was so young. Too young, Meg thought, glowering at the driver as he pulled another of his driving stunts, cutting around traffic stopped at a red light.

"I'm scared," Jada whispered quietly.

"I don't blame you, sweetheart, but you'll be just fine." Meg put her arm around her shoulder. "Everything will be just fine."

Meg looked up when she heard the driver on the phone with the hospital.

"It hurts. It hurts so much." Jada held her breath and twisted in obvious pain. "It's starting again."

Meg remembered something about timing the contractions and quickly glanced at her watch. The last one couldn't have been more than two minutes earlier. She frowned, wishing she knew if that was good or bad. "Breathe. Breathe."

The pain seemed to lessen in about a minute and Jada opened her eyes. "I'm bleeding," she whispered. "I think I'm going to lose the baby."

Meg wiped the young woman's tears. Looking down, she could see traces of a dark stain on the hem of her long blouse. If it was blood, there wasn't very much of it.

"Everything will be okay. Just try to relax, Jada. We'll be at the hospital soon."

"Don't leave me." She clutched tighter to Meg's hand. "I'm so scared. Please."

Meg looked up and found the driver's piercing eyes on her.

"We're almost there," he said quietly.

She nodded and looked again at Jada.

"It's coming again." This time she moaned out loud. "Oh, God. It hurts so much. It hurts!"

Two minutes between the contractions now. "Breathe."

"Please. Please don't leave me. I don't know what to do. I'm afraid."

Meg looked down at the contrast of Jada's pale face against her silky dark hair. There was a thin film of sweat appearing on the fair skin of her forehead. She looked young, fragile, and her eyes were wild with panic. The cab screeched up to the E.R. doors.

"I won't leave you, Jada." Meg promised quietly. "I promise."

CHAPTER FOUR

Evan grimaced at the terrible taste of the coffee. Holding the steaming paper cup in one hand, he headed back through the gray doors to the waiting area. Three hours of pacing were starting to take their toll on him, and he leaned wearily against a lime green wall.

When they'd arrived, Jada had been rushed into the delivery room after the briefest examination. And to his great relief, the woman—his passenger—had gone in there with her. Evan realized that he didn't even know her name.

He'd told himself this noon that he'd be ready. That he'd try to do better when the next time came. But faced with Jada's pain and her near hysteria, he'd proved to be an even bigger dope than he was last night. Struck speechless by the whole thing, all he'd been able to do was to drive like a maniac and get her here, but beyond that, he'd really offered no support at all. Some father stand-in he was turning out to be.

He shook his head. Someone up there must have been watching over this little girl to send someone like this woman to help out. Whoever she was, she seemed to know what she was doing; her confidence had really helped keep Jada calm. Funny, though, she'd looked kind of pale, too, before disappearing into the delivery room.

Evan's mind returned to Jada and how exhausted she must be by now. They had both been up for most of the night and all day today. He wasn't nine months pregnant, but he still felt like crap. Glancing over at a receptionist who was hurriedly typing away on a computer, he wondered if he could risk approaching her again. It had to be at least half an hour since he'd last checked with her.

Before he had taken two steps in the direction of the desk, he saw the double doors open and a rather pale ex-passenger step through.

He changed course and walked toward her, instead.

"Is she still in labor?"

"No," she said somewhat testily. "They're finishing up with Jada and the baby now, but she wanted you to know that it's a boy."

Even with her glasses on, he could see the dark circles under her eyes. She looked spent.

"That's great." he said excitedly. "Is she okay, then?"

"Is she okay?" She took a step closer to him. "Like *you* care if she is okay."

Evan frowned and then stared in disbelief as she suddenly erupted.

"How could you be such an insensitive ass? You just stand here and sip your coffee, Mr. Cool, and ask if she's okay?"

"What?" he asked uncomprehendingly, frowning in the direction of the receptionist who was eyeing them with amusement.

She shoved his hand and spilled the hot coffee down the front of his shirt.

"Damn it. What's the matter with you?"

"She's fifteen, for God's sake! But I have to hear it from one of the nurses. *Fifteen.*"

He pulled the shirt away from his skin and glared back at her.

Out of the corner of his eye, he saw the woman behind the desk pick up a phone.

"You are mad at me because I didn't tell you her age?"

"You're an idiot on top of being an ass!" She shoved him hard in the chest with both hands. "You should be taken out and shot."

He couldn't hold back a chuckle. "Now wait a minute. That seems like too severe a punishment, don't you think?"

"You think it's funny?" She let out a frustrated breath. She poked a finger threateningly into his chest. "I know there has to be a law in this state that will take care of you. See how funny you think this is from jail. You'll be—"

"Mr. Knight?"

Evan took hold of her wrist, forcing it away from his chest. He turned toward the woman who had just came in through the double doors.

"Dr. Patton," he acknowledged, remembering her name from this morning.

"I assume you've already heard that Jada had a baby boy."

Evan nodded, ignoring his accuser's covert struggle to free her hand. "How is she doing?"

"Jada's exhausted, but she'll be fine after a good night's rest. Over two hours of pushing is tough for anyone. But she was a champ. And the baby..."

"Something wrong?" he asked anxiously, not liking the doctor's pause.

"No. No. As we discussed this morning, Jada was three weeks early, so at four pounds eight ounces, the baby is a bit underweight. But other than that, his Apgar score was fine."

Evan looked at her blankly, and to his relief the doctor continued.

"The Apgar score is a number given to infants after the initial assessment of color, tone, activity, respiratory rate, and heart rate. And, considering the mother's age and the early delivery, the infant did fairly well."

His fiery passenger was still trying to wrest her hand out of Evan's grasp, but he didn't let go.

"So what's the problem?" he said to the doctor.

"I'd like to keep Jada and the baby here the full two days. We do release many of our mothers after twenty-four hours. But talking to our social workers and understanding that Jada would be home alone, I think it would be best for both of them to be here the extra day."

Evan nodded, agreeing wholeheartedly.

"As a friend of the family and in the absence of her father, you've been a great help. Jada tells me she's put you through a lot of trouble."

"She's been no trouble. There's a lot more that I'd like to do for her."

"Well, you'll have your chance," the doctor added. "Once she gets released, the weight of responsibility on her will affect every aspect of her life. The surge of hormones alone is enough to depress any new mother, but in her case, being so young and a single mother..." She shook her head. "When did you say her father will be back?"

"He's a fisherman. He's expected to be back by the middle of next week at the latest."

"Well, this is when you could be the most helpful."

The doctor looked at Evan and then turned to the silent woman at his side. Evan noticed that, for the first time, she wasn't struggling to free her hand. He released her.

"It's Meg, isn't it?" the doctor asked.

"Yes. Meg Murphy."

"You were a great help to her in there, Ms. Murphy." Dr. Patton smiled. "It was your first time, though, wasn't it?"

"Did it show?"

"No. You did great. She really responded to you. I hope, between you and Mr. Knight, that you can manage to be around

Jada and the baby a lot. For the first couple of weeks, anyway. At least until Jada's father gets back."

Before Evan could open his mouth, the doctor continued.

"Of course, the hospital will send a visiting nurse to her house during the first week to make sure everything is going well. But beyond the daytime visits, I don't think it would be wise for her to be left totally alone. I can't say enough how overwhelming life will seem to Jada over the next few weeks."

"I'll take care of it," Evan said decisively.

This morning, hanging around waiting, he'd had a chance to speak to some of the hospital social workers. He'd found out that a lot of these visiting nurses, for an additional charge, were willing to offer round the clock care to new mothers. The only thing was that he'd have to make Jada believe that the money for the extra care was coming out of her insurance, and not Evan's wallet.

He was still sorting through all that needed to be done when the doctor left them. He turned and found Meg Murphy sitting on a nearby chair with her face buried in her hands. He dumped what remained of his coffee in a trash can and took the seat next to her.

"Listen, I'm sorry you got dragged into all this." He patted her on the knee. "About all those things the doctor just said about you and me taking care of Jada. I want you to know that I've already started the ball rolling on that. You've been great, but that little girl's problems aren't yours to worry about. You've already done more than enough."

She turned her deep, brown eyes on him, and he found himself forgetting his words. She'd pushed up her glasses on top of her head, and it occurred to him that she looked so much younger without them. Her dark eyes and pale complexion, framed with the dark hair, made her look almost delicate. He took a moment and studied her face.

"I am *so* sorry."

He leaned down on his knees and stared into her eyes. "You should be, and it's about time you apologized."

She smacked his leg with the back of her hand before straightening up. "I'm serious."

"So am I," he scolded. "You accused me of impregnating a child."

"I did *not*." She brought down her glasses onto the bridge of her nose. "Not directly, anyway. And she's not a little girl. It was...it was just the circumstances."

"You were thinking the worst of me."

"I don't even know you." She pushed her hair behind one ear —a movement that he found quite attractive—and looked at him straight on. "In the cab, before we picked her up, I just thought she was your wife or your girlfriend. I mean, you were rushing like a madman to get to her. And then, your concern for her after. I just thought..." She stopped and after a long pause lowered her voice. "I'm sorry."

He let another moment go by before answering. "It's okay."

She nodded and gave him a half smile. "I'm going to call for a cab now. If you don't mind telling me where you're parked, I need to get my stuff."

"No need," he said, coming to his feet. "I'll take you myself. The doctor already said that Jada will need her rest. Just give me a minute to poke my head in and say hi to her, then we'll be on our way."

By the time Evan visited Jada and the baby, completed filling out another half a dozen forms, called old Mrs. Jeffers with the news, and finished making the necessary arrangements for her post-hospital care, the minute he'd asked for had stretched into the long side of an hour. But as he and Meg headed down to the parking lot, he felt better about the situation. At least, he knew Jada was comfortably ensconced in a room that she would be sharing with another new mother, and that she would be getting some much needed rest.

And even better, the brown-haired woman warrior walking beside him had never complained once. After reaching his cab, he was pleased to see she even took the seat next to him, rather than getting into the back seat.

They drove in silence to the Inn she was staying at out on Ocean Drive. But as he went up the long winding driveway of the place, he mentally kicked himself for not asking more questions of her.

The Inn at Castle Hill was glowing with the last orange rays of the sun as they rounded the last bend. But then, as he looked at the Mercedes, Jags, and BMW's in the parking lot, Evan was jarred with the thought that this Meg Murphy was exactly the type of woman that he'd been working so hard of late to avoid. The type with money and arrogance. The type that measured you by the size of your stock portfolio. He'd had his share of the type in years past, and he had no intention of going that route again. He stole a glance at her direction and found her gazing longingly at the rambling, old Inn.

"Your first time here?" he growled.

"No," she said quietly. "We...I always stay here."

Just as he'd figured. Evan swung sharply into the circular driveway. The most expensive place to stay in town. It would figure, he thought. She *would* be meeting up with someone here. His gaze dropped on reflex to the ring on her left hand. The cab screeched to a stop by the front door.

"Well, here we are," she said with an odd note in her voice that he couldn't decipher.

"Yeah. Better late than never, I guess," he muttered under his breath.

She extended her hand, looking at the hack license. "Mr. Knight."

"Ms. Murphy." He wrapped his fingers around hers. She had long delicate fingers. A strong grip.

"This certainly was an experience. One I'll never forget." She slowly withdrew her hand. "So, how much do I owe you?"

"Forget it."

"No, I insist."

"I said forget it."

"Well, thanks," she said pleasantly, opening the door. "Maybe I'll see you around town."

"Don't count on it."

CHAPTER FIVE

MEG STARED WEARILY into the face of the young man bent over the open book. She hadn't wanted to believe what she had just been told, so she'd asked, begged, and finally demanded that the desk clerk check the records again and hand her a key.

"I'm sorry, Ms. Murphy. But we show no record of you reserving this room."

"That's it," Meg whispered through clenched teeth. "Get me the manager."

"But she'll just tell you—"

"I *want* to see the manager," she snapped.

"Okay," he replied, shrugging his shoulders. "But the Inn's full, and—"

Meg slapped her palm smartly on the polished wood of the counter. "*Get* the manager." She couldn't remember the last time she'd felt so drained. The twitch of anger poked like needles at her scalp, and Meg felt her knees wobble beneath her weight.

She'd known longer days in her life, but never before had she had to face the emotional ups and downs of helping a fifteen-year-old give birth.

The desk clerk returned in a minute, trailing the manager, an attractive woman with long, brown hair. The woman looked at her, recognition lighting up her face.

"Oh, hi. Yes, Ms. Murphy. You were here last year and the year before, if I remember right."

"That's right," Meg said, feeling hopeful for the first time. "And the twelve years before that, too."

"George says there's some confusion about your reservation."

"There's no confusion. I made my reservation—the same reservation I make every year—and I want to check in."

"Hmm." the woman looked down at the book. "George, you checked everything? The cancellations?"

"There was no cancellation," Meg said, her tone testy enough to cause the manager to glance up at her.

"Yeah, I did," he answered. "No record of it, Mary. Anywhere."

"Here it is." She looked up with an embarrassed smile. "The reservation is for *next* Wednesday."

"*Next* Wednesday?" Meg murmured vaguely.

"Yes. Look for yourself. Murphy, the Tower Room, next Wednesday to the following Wednesday."

Meg stared in disbelief. Sure enough, the reservation was clearly marked in the book.

"But that's impossible. For fifteen years we...I have been coming here. It's *always* been this week."

"Sorry. We have a pretty good system."

Meg put her hand pleadingly on the woman's arm. "Don't you have any room. Mary, isn't it? Isn't there any room at the Inn?" Jeez, she thought, this was starting to sound like a Christmas play.

The manager slowly shook her head. "And I'm afraid you're going to have a tough time. With the Boat Show this week and the Heart Ball Sunday night, this is the one week in September when everything in town will be booked. I'm sorry."

She felt like crying. Staring at the politely indifferent expressions of the two standing behind the desk, Meg considered throwing a fit. But she knew it would do no good. They'd probably seen better tantrums than she could throw.

She picked up her briefcase and carrying bag. "Cancel my reservation for next week. And call me a cab, will you?"

"Perhaps the Visitor's Center can do something."

"Just call me a cab," Meg said, her shoulders sagging in defeat. "I'll wait outside."

She didn't know where she'd go or what she'd do, but she wasn't about to stand the humiliation of having those two look at her like she'd lost her mind. It didn't matter what they said, she *knew* she made the reservation for the right dates. It had to be *their* screwed-up system that had lost her week.

By the time she stepped outside the double entry doors, the golden sunset was only a purple memory in the western sky. A night breeze had sprung up, and she gazed out at mouth of the bay, at the black ocean beyond, and at the lights of a barge making its way slowly out the channel.

Meg took a deep breath and tried to fight back the gloom that was closing in on her soul. So what if there was no room for her in this place? She'd find a room elsewhere. In fact, her budget was tight enough without the added weight of the Inn's expense. She didn't need this kind of lavish self-pampering. When the cab arrived, she'd go right down to that Visitor's Center. There *had* to be someplace where she could find a roof over her head.

Out of the darkness, a young couple walked up from the paths that ran along the cliffs. She stepped aside to let them pass into the Inn. They looked like lovers. Just married, maybe. Or perhaps having a little fling, as her friend Rebekah the cynic would so aptly put it.

Meg, she'd say, you should have a little fling. Put aside the work, the worry, even the concern about if he's Mr. Right. What you need is a fall weekend for yourself.

You Meg, she'd continue, are the bookworm variety romantic. You like the idea, you dream up the scenarios, but then—when a real guy asks you out on a date—you turn tail and crawl back into the cocoon of those pages.

But that's not fair, Meg would correct. She's had her days. When Robert was alive, they'd had their days of romance, the getaways, the strolls in the sunset.

But that was back in the Dark Ages, Rebekah would argue.

Wrong. That was now, during their week together, Meg would always think. Robert always came back to her during this week.

"So where are you, Robert?" she murmured, watching as the lights of the barge disappeared from sight.

The slow, retching sound of an engine struggling to come to life drew her gaze toward the darkness of the drive. Out there, on the grass shoulder just beyond the curve of the circular driveway, the pale shape of a lonely cab was barely visible. As she looked, a tall figure emerged from behind the wheel and, clicking on a little pen light, moved to look under the open hood.

Him, she thought, not really surprised at the unexpected jolt of satisfaction at seeing him. Something had passed between them in the cab, and Meg was sure that they had both felt it. But then, in an instant, he had closed up like a fist, and she had left him. Now, wrestling to contain her excitement at seeing him here, she lifted the handle of her carrying bag onto one shoulder and dashed down the stone stairs.

Other than the rush of the tide and a bell buoy in the harbor, the only sound under the blue velvet sky was the crunch of gravel beneath the soles of her sensible shoes. She was still a dozen steps from the car when she heard him mutter something obscene and slam the hood shut.

Behind her, a faraway ship's horn echoed off the bluffs, and somewhere to her left, an owl hooted in response. Meg slowed her steps, hoping he would notice her approach. He did.

"What are you doing out here?" he asked, coming around the car.

"I was going to ask you the same thing." She built up her courage and stepped closer.

"The car—"

"My room—"

They both started and stopped at the same time.

"You first." He leaned against the car door.

"There was some confusion about my room." She dropped her bag and briefcase on the ground next to her feet. "Now, I *know* I made the reservation for this week, but they claim that they aren't expecting me until next week. And it doesn't seem to matter what I say or do, it's their word against mine. And too bad for me. So here I am, out of luck and out of a room."

She watched him cross his arms over his chest and give her a once over look that made her stomach flutter. Unconsciously, she returned the favor. For the first time she noticed the fit of the blue denim shirt over his broad chest. His sleeves were rolled up to reveal strong forearms. And a pair of snug jeans hugged narrow hips and strong legs that were crossed casually at the ankle. Realizing what she was doing, Meg caught herself and looked up into his amused face.

"So what did you have in mind?" he asked, a suggestive hint in his voice.

Her answer was quick. "They already called in to send a cab for me. The manager in there told me that the Visitor's Center has a service."

"They're closed," he cut in casually, pushing away from the car. "After Labor Day, they close that desk at six."

She swallowed an anxious lump that was rising in her throat and frowned back toward the double glass doors of the Inn, shining brightly in the darkness of the night.

"Perfect," she said. "Perhaps, if I call around—"

"It'll be tough to find a place this late," he interrupted. "There's a big charity banquet this weekend. The Heart Ball. Old money, politicians, the whole bit. And then there's the usual rat race of the weekend. You can count on most of the places downtown being booked all week."

Annoyed at his doomsaying, Meg frowned. He turned his back on her and hopped into his ailing cab. He acted as if he were totally disinterested in her dilemma and in her.

Pushing her stuff out of the driveway, Meg leaned against the cab and listened to him cursing under his breath as he fiddled beneath the dash.

"So what happened?" she asked after a moment had passed. "After you dropped me, did you try to take off so fast that the engine ejected into the bay?"

"It's not funny." He tried the ignition again, but only a continuous groaning sound rewarded his efforts. "I don't know what the hell happened. I dropped you off, came around the circle, and the damn thing just died on me."

"I can smell the gas. You flooded it."

"I didn't," he turned and growled at her through the open door.

"Have you checked the battery? It could be dead."

He flicked on the lights. "It's not dead."

She looked around and saw the twin shafts of light cutting into the woods beyond the winding driveway. "They look pretty dim to me. Before you flooded it, were you nearly out of gas?"

"No. And I didn't flood it."

"Check the spark plug wires?"

"Yes."

"Distributor cap? Sometimes they crack, and moisture gets in there."

In the dark, she wasn't sure if he was amused or annoyed, but she definitely had his attention.

"I even checked that. What are you, a mechanic or something?"

"No." Meg didn't really see the need to explain, but driving an old car and living on a tight budget had forced her long ago to learn the basics of auto care. Hey, listening to Click and Clack, the car guys, on the radio didn't hurt, either. "Did you jiggle the wheel?"

"No, that method completely slipped my mind." Evan chuckled, and she found the sound extremely pleasing. "And, you know, I haven't prayed to my voodoo doll yet, either."

"I wouldn't make light of it, if I were you. It always works for me."

"The doll or the jiggle?"

She put on the pretense of her best frown. "Of course the jiggle. You just have to give it three small—"

"Oh, please. Be my guest." He got out of the car and stood up. "I think I should just stand back and watch a master mechanic at work. Why don't *you* give it your magical touch and see how you make out?"

He was standing holding the driver's door open for her, and Meg felt a strong desire to wash the smirk off his handsome face.

"Fine, since you obviously can't handle it."

She ignored his condescending snort of amusement and hopped into the driver's seat. Without thinking, she reached back for the seatbelt. She grimaced at the sound of his snicker.

"You can never be too safe, especially in this car." She sat forward and took hold of the wheel. Giving it a quick tug to the right, then to the left, and then to the right again, she turned the key in the ignition.

The car roared to life.

Meg didn't have to turn to know that his jaw had hit the gravel, but she decided to save her tap dance for later. So, ever so dignified, she pressed the accelerator a couple of times to rev the engine, undid her seatbelt, and moved out from behind the wheel.

"Any questions?"

She thought his eyes had taken on a slightly murderous glint, but this only added to her amusement.

"Think you can handle it from here?"

"No," he said suddenly. "I *don't* think I can handle it from here."

Without another word, Evan yanked open the back door, threw her things in the back seat, and slammed the door. Then, handling her with no more gentleness, he took her by the elbow and pushed her toward the front seat.

She dug in her heels and looked at him challengingly. "What are you doing? You want me to drive you to town?"

"You live very dangerously," he stated, putting a hand on top of her head and guiding her into the car.

Grabbing hold of the wheel, she glared at him.

"Move over," he ordered.

She couldn't slide over to the passenger side fast enough as he started to climb in after her. She grabbed the door handle, though she really didn't think escape was necessary.

"What exactly do you mean, I live dangerously?"

He slammed the door shut and turned to her. "I mean, here you are in a strange town, flirting with a total stranger in the middle of a dark parking lot."

Her mouth fell open. "I was *not* flirting with you. I was only trying to help you with your silly car. I don't have to take this." She opened her door, but he reached over and took hold of her arm.

"Well, you should," he huffed. "Not all the cab drivers in town are as understanding and openminded as I am."

She gaped at him in disbelief.

"Shut the door."

Meg looked at him a moment longer, and then pulled the door shut.

"You are a foul tempered boor! I can't believe you have the brass to call yourself understanding and...and..."

"Openminded," he repeated, starting the car down the drive.

"Where are you taking me?"

"You said you needed a cab. So here I am."

"The Inn already called for one. A different one."

He picked up his radio mic, and she listened as he ordered someone named Roberta on the other end to cancel the call. Meg crossed her arms over her chest and stared up at the hack license, clipped to the overhead visor.

Oh, just as well, she thought. She needed to get to town, and at least she knew that Evan Knight, Lic. No. 26712, was not likely to cut her up and use her for fish bait. Nonetheless, she let a few minutes pass in silence while she double-checked the road he was taking. She recognized it as the direct route back to town, and soon they were crossing Thames Street. The Yachting Center was lit up with activity, and a fair number of people were strolling along the brick and cobblestone sidewalks, enjoying the warm September evening.

As they slowed for an elderly couple to cross, Meg turned to look at him. "So, what are my choices?"

He gave her a slow and meaningful side glance that made her toes curl.

"I mean as far as available rooms," she quickly added. "Inns, hotels, bed and breakfasts? Can you think of anyplace that might have a room available?"

She watched him ponder the question as he drove. Robert had been correct in calling him handsome. He didn't have classic, drop dead beauty like Robert, but his face had character—a hardness that spoke of experience. And a dangerous kind of charm, she added mentally, as he turned those eyes of his on her.

"Well, there's a place in Portsmouth, on the northern end of the island. Clean rooms, off the beaten track. The only bad thing is that it looks out over the sewage treatment plan. If you don't mind the smell."

"Charming. Anywhere else?"

"Hmm. One place I'm pretty sure has a room. A place in town. Right on the water. It's on Washington Street in the Point section. It looks out over the causeway and the bridge."

"I know that neighborhood. I've walked through there before. It's pretty."

"Well, I know this guy who rents out rooms."

"Now, wait a minute," she broke in. "You're not sending me to some flophouse, are you?"

He cocked a brow and gave her a critical once over. "Here in Newport, we gave up abducting women for Ottoman sultans a couple hundred years ago."

She faked a violent shudder. "So recent?"

He gave a low chuckle and turned his attention back to the road. "Do you want it or not? He has about half dozen rooms that he rents out, and as of last night, all but one was filled."

Meg felt a case of the jitters start to set in. "Do you know this guy? I mean, is he registered as a business?"

"Look, you'll be safe," he answered shortly. "Phil is listed with the Visitor's Center, and he has a hundred-ten-year-old Methuselah running the place. Believe me, she's even tougher than his Irish wolfhound."

She paused a minute and then decided. "Fine. I'll be adventurous. Take me there."

"Your wish is my command," he said, immediately swerving the cab into a parking spot on the tree lined street.

Meg looked up at the street sign by an antique gas lamp. Washington Street.

The overbearing rat, she thought. So much for making her own decisions. But then, with a quick glance at the well-kept colonial and Victorian homes lining the quiet street, she grudgingly gave in.

He was already out of the car and pulling her things from the back seat before she could say anything. So she got out the passenger side and waited on the slate sidewalk. A pretty little brownstone church at the next corner caught her eye, and she stopped to look at it, waiting for him to come around. Glancing over the cab, she saw him crossing the street with her things.

"Hey!"

"This is the place," he called over his shoulder, heading toward a very large old home on the water side.

She ran after him. "I think I should be able to handle it from here. I mean, I've already put you through enough trouble. I really appreciate all you've done."

"I like you better when you snap at me."

She couldn't help but smile. "Fine. Then just put my damn bags down and tell me how much I owe you."

Evan stopped before a set of double doors with ornately etched glass. "Let's call it even," he said. "You started my car; I brought you here."

She paused as he rang the bell and then nodded. "Fine. But to tell the truth, I think you got the better part of this deal."

"Don't push it," he snapped as one of the doors opened and a tall, seventyish woman looked out at them.

"Evan," she said brightly. "Have you forgotten your—?"

"I have a new guest for you, Nan," he interrupted. "They messed up her reservation at Castle Hill, and she's in dire need of a room."

"Well, we certainly can help you with that, dear," she said to Meg, stepping back into the foyer and gesturing toward an open parlor.

As she followed the woman toward a meticulously organized desk, Meg glanced around at the comfortable, Victorian furnishings, and at the open glass doors leading out onto a lit porch at the far end of the room.

"So you're all set?" Evan asked of the older woman, dropping the bags by Meg's feet.

"Yes, dear. And you'd better get some rest. You look like the walking dead."

"Thanks, Nan. You're looking pretty good yourself."

"Fresh thing," Nan scolded. Her eyes twinkled, though, as she shook her head amiably at Meg.

With that, Evan turned and headed up the wide stairs on the far side of the parlor. He did not even spare Meg a glance.

As she sat down across from the older woman at the desk, Meg leaned forward. "Where is he going?"

"Who? Evan?" Nan turned and gave her a sweet smile. "Why, my dear, didn't he tell you? Evan lives here."

CHAPTER SIX

MEG SMILED as she looked around the room. It was perfect.

From the outside of the huge old building, she hadn't been quite so sure, but she was now very happy with the way things were turning out.

Granted, it wasn't the Inn at Castle Hill. The room was a bit smaller, and the furnishings were not gleaming antiques like those she had come to know from her yearly trip there, but everything looked clean and comfortable. She let her eyes wander over the double bed with its cream-colored spread, the overstuffed chair with the wrought iron lamp beside it, the small wooden writing table with the Windsor chair.

Moving to the three huge windows that sat side by side between built in bookcases, she looked out at the black waters of the harbor. Kneeling on the cushioned window seat, she lifted the sash of the middle window and let the salty smell of the warm September evening drift into the room. She could see the lights of a few yachts reflecting off the still water. To her left, she spotted the causeway leading out to Goat Island and the big hotel there. To her right, the building jutted out in an L-shape, and beyond the windows of other rooms, the lights of the huge suspension bridge spanned the bay.

Suddenly, a thought of Robert struck her, and she sighed.

"And now for something completely different," she murmured, wondering where he was and what he was up to. She hadn't heard from him since the cab ride from the station. Remembering his comment back in the train—about being down here on other business—she wondered how much of what he'd said was the truth and how much of it had been said for the sake of saving her from herself, as he so often in the past had put it.

Too many people worried about her, Meg thought, looking down at her watch. Nine-thirty already. She took out her cell phone out of the bag and called Rebekah in Boston.

There were four rings and then the answering machine played back her friend's cheery voice. Meg decided to leave a quick message. "Hi. It's me. Change of plan. I am staying at a new place in Newport—"

"Wait. Wait a minute." Rebekah's laughing voice cut in through the line. "Meg. What did you say?"

"You were there all the time, you rat. What are you doing? Screening your calls?"

"Yeah. You might say that."

"You aren't alone, are you," Meg teased, hearing a whisper in the background.

"What did you say? I didn't hear you."

"Rat's ass, you didn't. Who is he?"

"Wait a minute."

Meg heard her friend put a hand over the receiver and had a mental image of Rebekah ordering the poor man around. It took a moment before she got back on the line. "Okay, the natives were restless. So what is this about staying in a new place? You're not *changing* on me now, are you Meg?"

"I don't know what you're talking about."

"Don't give me that. What's cooking with you?"

"Nothing, really. The Inn just screwed up my reservation and didn't have any room for me."

"You've got to be kidding? So, where are you?"

From where she sat, Meg could see the lights of Jamestown twinkling across the water. She didn't think Rebekah would think that was much of an answer.

"I'm at a little bed and breakfast...well, not so little, really. And not exactly a bed and breakfast, either. But it's right on the harbor..."

"Wait just a minute. Are you trying to tell me that Little Miss I'm-Not-Going-Anywhere-without-a-Published-Itinerary is staying in a 'maybe it is, maybe it isn't' B & B? Right. Tell me, does it rent rooms by the hour?"

"Very funny. No, it's really very nice," she said, running her fingers over the bedspread.

"And just how did you find this joint? Ask a sailor?"

"No. Evan suggested it."

"Evan?"

"Well, yeah. Evan Knight, the cab driver who brought me in from the station. He lives here, too."

There was a long pause at the other end of the phone, and Meg muffled her giggle. It felt good to be doing the ribbing for a change.

"Let me get this straight," Rebekah said finally. "You're staying in a flophouse with a total stranger who drives a cab?"

"No, he's not a stranger."

"Oh? He's an old friend."

"Well, no. But we practically had a baby together," Meg took the phone away from her face for a moment and washed the amusement out of her voice. "I mean, delivered a baby. Well, we would have if he hadn't gotten us to the hospital in time."

"Excuse me. Is this *my* Meg Murphy?"

"Yes, Bekah."

"Would you like to tell me what's going on?"

"Well, Evan is friends with Ted and Ted's daughter Jada."

"Wait a minute. Let me get this straight. Evan is the cabby you're living with."

"I'm not living with him. Excuse me, Rebekah." Meg muttered some gibberish to a non-existent visitor. "He has his own apartment in this house."

"You mean Ted and Jada's house."

"No. Ted and Jada don't live here."

"Wait a minute. Put this guy on the line," her friend ordered seriously from the other end. "I can't get a straight answer out of you."

"I can't. He...he isn't decent."

"You're shitting me. I know you are. You, Ms. Goody-Two-Shoes. With a man? I don't think so." There was a long pause on the other end. "Going away with your dead husband's ghost on your yearly virginal retreat and hitting on a man the first day? Taking him to bed? No way. Nice try, but I don't think so."

Meg let out a deep sigh. "Well, you can believe what you want, but I've got to go. It's going to be a *long* night."

"Meg. Meg."

She held on to the phone a few seconds longer and then spoke. "Yes, Bekah?"

"Meg, tell me you're a bald-faced liar. Tell me. *Please*? Otherwise, order in the universe is in jeopardy. Come on."

"Hmm. Okay, I'm a liar. Feel better? But now I really have to go."

"Wait. I don't believe you. Put him on line right now, Meg Murphy." She could hear a hint of mild panic in Rebekah's voice. "Listen, Meg, things are a lot different now than the last time you screwed a man. Have you ever even seen a condom? Meg?"

Meg ended the call and smiled.

Boy, that felt good.

He never messed around with married women.

Never, Evan reminded himself as he stepped out of the shower and into the large tiled bathroom. So what the hell was wrong with him now? Living and working, even under a pretense of a cab driver, in a resort town like this, he had his pick of the crop when it came to available women. So why was he getting so hung up over a pair of brown eyes and a mouth so soft looking that it cried out to be kissed?

He couldn't allow himself to be distracted, no matter how short a time it might be. Already, he could see she was a woman with time on her hands. And she wasn't the type that would be looking for a one-night stand. Hell, she was made for slow seduction and passionate lovemaking. A relationship with her would be the kind that could go for weeks before anyone even thought of surfacing for air.

Damn. He looked down at his hardening manhood and then at the pool of water his dripping frame had made on the floor.

"Start thinking with your brain, pal," he muttered to himself. Snatching a towel off the rack, he quickly dried himself.

He'd come to Newport six months ago with a purpose, and he had a job to do. A book to write. This was the way it had always been with him. He had to immerse himself, body and soul, into the book. Into the setting and into the characters. His stories had always "thrummed" with life. At least, that's what that reviewer from the *NY Times* had said a couple of books ago. But the feel of real life that he'd always tried to imbue his novels with did not come easy. All of it—or most of it, anyway—came from experience. This had been his ticket to success from that first day.

He smiled, thinking back. He was diving offshore rigs in Louisiana when his first break came. Eighteen years ago. It was like yesterday. He remembered coming off the rusty, old tub of a tender, bone tired after another twenty-eight-day stint in the muddy Gulf, with a hurricane blowing up the coast. And there it was, that letter, just waiting for him.

That letter. Cream-colored stationary. New York postmark. Forwarded from Dundee in Scotland to Morgan City, Louisiana. It was like an answer to a nearly forgotten prayer. After all those year-long contracts, diving everywhere from the Persian Gulf to the North Sea. All that time writing and hoping that, perhaps someday, someone would be interested in hearing the stories that he had to tell. And it was about to happen.

Henry, his agent, had come into his life right after that—and then a whole slew of books. He couldn't write them fast enough. There had been no stopping him, until this last year. Somehow, his creative juices seemed to have left him, but he wasn't giving up. So he'd worked it out with his friend Phil to come to Newport and live undercover. His plan had been to keep his ears open, watch the upper crust at play, and have at least half a book written in a couple of months. But here he was, six months later, still unable to step out of the fog.

Everyone had a different solution. His friend Phil, a guy he'd known since their days at State College, thought it was the lack of a steady life. What you need, Evan, he'd told him, was a life filled with routines and frequent, comfortable, 'no strings' relation-ships. No ups and downs.

On the other hand, Henry, his agent, thought Evan's problems were due to being too involved with everyday life. He accused him of taking in every stray person, animal, and thing, and making their problems his own. As a result, Henry argued Evan hadn't any time to focus on his writing.

Solid, practical, old Doug, his accountant, thought he should get professional help for his "Santa Claus complex." He would be more than happy, Doug had told him, to take care of the bill himself, if Evan's insurance wouldn't cover it. His publisher in New York, on the other hand, thought his problems were due to a lack of communication—the absence of bonding that they felt should exist between the writer and the editor.

That's just what he needed, Evan had thought. More quality

time with a smiley, fifteen-year-old Ivy Leaguer in suspenders and penny loafers. Somehow, he doubted that any of his former editors remembered him as Santa.

It had even occurred to him, more than once, that maybe he was finished as a writer. Hell, maybe he'd just been too successful. He'd worked hard to avoid the fame part of the business, and he had more money than he could ever spend, in spite of what his accountant said. Maybe he just didn't have the drive anymore. Maybe he had no more stories in him.

Evan wrapped the towel around his waist and stepped out of the bathroom. Glancing at the laptop on the kitchen table, he turned away and went to open the double French doors leading out onto the balcony.

The night was clear and warm, and he stepped out onto the smooth wood decking and breathed in the sea air. Tomorrow, he told himself. This was it, he needed to give himself an ultimatum and stick by it. Tomorrow. Tomorrow night, he'd start writing again. He leaned against the railing. No homeless winos, no runaway kids, no stray kittens would get in his way.

But before tomorrow night, he reminded himself, he would need to double-check on the arrangements for Jada and the baby. And couldn't put off calling Doug about Grady, the old trumpet player who rented the room in the Chittenden House down the street. Medicare wasn't going to cover all the costs for his upcoming heart surgery, and Doug could cut the check without Grady knowing. And then he had to check...

Evan stopped thinking.

Her middle window was open, and he could see her walking back and forth from the suitcase lying across her bed to the open drawers of the dresser across the room. He let his eyes take in all of her, from the loose towel wrapped like a turban around her head to the oversized T-shirt that ended just above her knees.

Nice legs, he thought, focusing on what he could see.

A moment later she tucked her empty carrying bag neatly

beneath the bed. Placing her glasses on the bedside table, she reached up, took the towel off her head, and shook her hair loose. He could tell that she was a creature of habit, as she ran the comb through her hair. Everything tidy and neat.

He didn't think to step back into the shadow when she walked toward the window and raised the sash of the two outer windows, as well. He was enjoying watching her and was planning to wave when she looked up. But to his great disappointment, she never did. Instead, she moved back to her bed and moved a stack of papers from her pillow to the side table, beneath her glasses.

"Work?" he asked aloud. "I sure can think of much better uses for that bed."

He swallowed hard. With her back to him, she pulled the T-shirt over her head with one swift motion.

"Damn," he whispered, admiring her naked back, buttocks, and slender legs. But then, when she reached for the light, he came to his senses and angrily cursed himself. "So that's it. You're a pervert, now."

Turning and storming back into his room, he continued to mutter to himself. Of everyone, he thought, maybe Doug's solution made the most sense.

He needed professional help, all right, but not the type his accountant had in mind.

CHAPTER SEVEN

THE SUN WAS warm on her shoulders as Meg stepped off the porch and turned to look at the half dozen gulls diving into the shimmering water of the harbor. Peeling off her windbreaker, she watched as the alabaster white birds hovered and dove. Over and over again, they skimmed across a patch of water that appeared to be teeming with activity. She could see little fish leaping into the air, and into the waiting beaks of the gulls.

Bluefish. Meg remembered the time she and Robert had watched the fishermen hauling in the dark, meaty creatures. Some were as long as a fisherman's arm. They had been told that in the fall the blues came into the bay, driving the schools of little fish to the surface in a feeding frenzy.

Meg squinted at a lobster boat that was just rounding the point of Goat Island, and wondered for a moment if Jada's father, Ted, could have been one of those men hauling in the bluefish.

When she had awakened this morning, she had not even put her feet on the floor before being struck with the idea of buying some kind of a gift for Jada and the baby. But now, as she turned her steps down Washington Street, she realized that it was probably too early for any of the stores to be open.

Well, she thought, maybe a walk down to that little waterfront park by the causeway would be nice, before she headed downtown.

By reflex, Meg tried to push up the glasses that usually sat on the bridge of her nose, but they weren't there. It was definitely going to take some time to get used to her new contact lenses. Well, it'd taken her six months, three visits, and four calls to the optometrist before she'd dared to pop the darn things into her eyes by herself. This morning, though, they went right in and, God willing, she'd be able to take them out just as smoothly. Heck, it had taken only forty-five minutes and half a box of tissue. Not too bad.

Moving briskly down the tree lined street, she reached into her tote bag, pulling out the pair of sunglasses she'd bought in Boston last week. Grudgingly, she had to admit that Rebekah had been right in talking her into switching to contacts. She felt light, happy. In a way, sophisticated. But most important, she could see. Thirty years behind the times, but what the heck.

Meg looked up at the plaque on the Hunter House, thinking how easy it was to read the information about the colonial "mansion" when the jogger coming out of the little park barreled into her.

As he tried to avoid her, he tripped and lost his balance. Jarred by the collision, she staggered as well, dropping her tote bag.

Out of the corner of her eye, Meg saw the jogger go down heavily, cushioned from the brick walk only by the nine dollar and ninety-nine cent sunglasses which Meg heard crunch threateningly beneath his butt. She cringed.

"I am so sorry," she said, quickly crouching down on her hands and knees, scooping her scattered things into her bag. "I was looking at the...well, I wasn't watching."

"No, I came around the corner too fast."

They both looked up sharply, and Meg's heart leaped in her chest. The sweating wall of muscle that she'd just bulldozed to the ground was her cab driver and new, albeit temporary, neighbor. Evan Knight.

"Hey, you. You look different."

Ignoring his comment, Meg tore her gaze away from piercing hazel eyes and glanced down to check the damage. Instantly, she wished she hadn't, since the sight of tan, muscular thighs beneath a pair of dark running shorts was clearly too much for her weak heart. She flushed and stared into her tote bag.

"Are these yours?" he asked casually, leaning to one side and retrieving a flattened pair of sunglasses, minus the lenses.

"They were." She nodded, taking the mangled wire from his hand.

"Expensive?"

"Priceless. A family heirloom, in fact. The women of my family have been wearing this particular pair of sunglasses for generations."

"Oh, good."

Meg looked up into his face.

"Then I can't possibly replace them." He took the broken frames out of her hands and made a hook shot at a nearby garbage can.

Gathering her tote bag hurriedly, Meg scurried to her feet and looked down at him. He was still sitting on his butt with his legs out in front of him. His thick brown hair fell in waves across his forehead. He looked younger than she remembered from the day before, but not that young. As Rebekah would put it, this was a man who oozed raw masculinity.

"You aren't hurt, are you?"

"I won't be able to tell until I stand up."

He stretched up one strong hand in her direction. She took it, and he sprang nimbly to his feet. He took a long moment before letting go.

"A couple of broken bones, a twisted ankle, and a severely lacerated behind. I'm okay."

Meg tried to think of something smart and witty, but nothing was coming to mind as she was uncomfortably too aware of him. She hadn't noticed yesterday how tall he was, or how broad his shoulders were?

"Well, I'd better get going," she said hurriedly.

"You know, you *do* look different," he said casually, stopping Meg in her tracks. "Cut your hair this morning?"

"No."

"Wearing make up?"

"No." She shook her head and flushed crimson under his close scrutiny.

"It must be the braces. You had a mouth full of them, yesterday, right?"

"No." She smiled. "You must be thinking of someone else. I've really got to get going."

"Hmm. Wait a minute. I'll get it."

He had to be one of the biggest flirts she'd met in her entire life. Not that she was used to hanging around that type. She looked up into eyes sparkling with amusement.

"It's the glasses. I'm not wearing my glasses."

"Oh. And to think I crushed them." He looked down at the shards of colored lenses on the paving. Leaning down, he picked them up and studied the dark plastic for a moment before throwing them in the trash can, as well. "Well, now that you can't see, how about letting me take you where you have to go today?"

"No. But thanks anyway," she said quickly, holding tighter to the handle of her tote bag on her shoulder. She just felt too flustered around him. "You've already lost one day of fares by not charging me. I can't let you lose another day."

"Why don't you let me worry about that?"

She shook her head. "All the same, thanks but no thanks."

Meg turned politely and took a step down the walkway before turning and facing him again. "By the way, have you heard anything from Jada this morning?"

"Yeah, I called her first thing. She and the baby both seem to be doing fine."

There was a hint of coldness in his voice that made Meg look up. "Well, if you could, tell her I said hi the next time you talk to her." Giving him a small smile, she turned again and started briskly down the sidewalk. As she turned the corner into the park, she threw a quick glance over her shoulder. The moment she did, Meg felt quite foolish, for she realized that she was hoping he'd still be there, looking at her. But that indeed was an absurd thought. Evan Knight was nowhere in sight.

Swallowing her disappointment, Meg walked to the waterfront pier. The sun was bright on the harbor water, and she reached without thinking into her bag for sunglasses. Remembering that they were no longer there, she jammed the bag onto her shoulder and plunked herself down on one of the stone benches.

"Robert, where are you?" she whispered, gazing out along the causeway to Goat Island and the big hotel directly across the water from her. Year after year she and her husband would come here for Sunday brunches. Afterward, they would catch the boat for the harbor tour and spend the next couple of hours cuddled next to each other on the top deck, peering at the mansions of the rich and famous from the bay side.

A couple of times they had gotten off with the crowd and walked through Hammersmith Farm, where Jackie Kennedy Onassis had grown up. But more often, the two of them had just sat and talked, enjoying the sun and the sea air.

In all that time, Meg thought, looking across the water at a huge yacht anchored in the harbor, they'd never dreamed of ever living in a mansion like those in Newport. They'd never spoken in terms like 'what if' and 'how about'. They were the observers of life, Robert used to say. The kind that could have fun just being bystanders, rather than participants.

Meg stood up and made her way onto the causeway and across the bridge toward the modern looking hotel. There had always been a real comfort and security in what the two of them had shared. They had so much in common. The same beliefs, the same interests. And between the two of them, they were able to draw a wall around that kept them safe. It was the same wall that, even five years after his death, Meg was fighting to keep from crumbling around her.

She didn't need Evan Knight, Meg reminded herself. Getting involved with a man like him would mean the destruction of the life that she and Robert had built. He was too alive, and she was happy with what she had. Meg reached the end of the bridge and looked about her, uncertain what direction she wanted to walk next. She was done grieving over Robert's death, and she was resigned to the little time they could share during this one week of the year. So what was wrong with that?

She turned and headed back across the bridge. As she went back, she was surprised to see a dozen people fishing over the railing of the bridge. They must have been there a moment ago, but she had walked by them without even noticing. Looking down into a white bucket, she saw it was half filled with flat white and gray fish.

"Wanna buy some flounder?" a little boy asked, turning from the railing where he stood, pole in hand, with his family. They turned and smiled.

"No. No thanks." Meg continued on, stepping around more white buckets.

As she reached the end of the bridge, she stopped and gazed at the park by the water. She looked at the Hunter House, and the sidewalk where she and Evan had collided.

"Robert," she called out aloud, suddenly frustrated. "Robert. Help me."

But there was no answer. No familiar, teasing, loving voice. Only the sounds of the gulls on the water. Only the far off voices of the people fishing on the bridge.

Only the whispers of the gentle sea breeze, conveying the hint of a changing season.

———

There was nothing like flat rejection to clear his mind.

Shoving the phone away from him on the table, Evan turned on the laptop, sitting rigidly as the flashing screens came one by one to life.

Damn his new editor. Damn the deadlines. Damn Henry and his four hours a day sitting in front of this machine.

And damn Meg Murphy.

Clicking open the file, Evan brought up the rough outline of his story on the screen. Glittery lifestyles. Extravagant parties. A rich wife. An unfaithful husband. Murder. Who done it?

A reader would have to be stupid not to be able to figure it out after the first chapter.

And how the hell was he going to write this story, anyway? Between giving rides to drunken sailors, pregnant teenagers, and snotty, married women on week-long screwing excursions, he couldn't be expected to produce anything readable, never mind marketable.

Sure, he'd decided to take on this guise of a taxi-cab driver. Everybody knew, after the bartenders and priests, they were the best source of dirt and gossip. Evan rubbed his chin. It sure seemed logical. He was sick of bars, and—God knows –he'd never make it impersonating a priest. But, hell, he'd written so little in the past few months. Obviously, he was hanging around the wrong crowd. Maybe it was time to shift gears a little.

Evan reached for the phone and dialed Phil's secretary downtown. Trying to limit the day-to-day hassles of his career, Evan had accepted his friend's offer of using Sarah for taking care of his correspondence while in Newport.

"And how is my gorgeous, red-headed sweetheart these days?"

"Hello, Evan." The pleasant voice brightened at the other end.

"Well, do you have anything to report?"

There was a soft laugh. "Emma is wonderful, and...yes, she is sending you bubbles right now."

"That's my girl." Emma was Sarah's nine-month-old daughter. From the first moment he had held the baby, it had been love at first sight. He knew he was a fool, but he just loved the way she slobbered all over him. "Anything else new?"

"Let's see. She's teething. And last night she left a permanent mark on David's chin."

"Good." He smiled. "That's what fathers are for."

There was a pause and the shuffle of some papers. "Before I forget, Henry called again yesterday and—"

"I talked to him this morning," he cut in. "And yes, I called Doug, as well. So if either of them calls you today for any reason, tell them I said to hang up on them. In fact, you're welcome to threaten them with harassment."

"Also, there was a voicemail left here from your publisher about the name of your new editor."

"I called him already, too."

"Aren't *we* efficient this morning? Well, that takes care of everything I had for you."

"Not everything," he said. "Remember the invitation I got for the Heart Ball?"

"Yes. This Sunday night. I responded for you about three months ago. I told them that you wouldn't be attending. I told you they were *very* disappointed that, as one of the leading donors to the charity—"

"Well, I've changed my mind," Evan announced. "Do you still have my tickets?"

"Sure. I've got them." He could hear her desk drawer open. "Yes, they're right here."

"Good. I'll need one of them."

"Evan?" The young woman cut in before he could hang up. "Are you planning to go alone?"

"Unless you want to dump your husband for the night. Or you decide to let me take that gorgeous daughter of yours to the ball."

"Hmm. I guess you'll be going alone, then."

"My lot in life, Sarah."

A moment later, as he sat back in his chair, Meg Murphy once again pushed into his mind. She'd probably be back with her husband by then, he reminded himself.

Evan got up from the chair and walked out onto the deck and stood by the railing. Glancing down at her half-opened window, his thoughts returned to their encounter in the park. To the way she had looked at him. She'd seemed interested, even inviting.

"Put her out of your mind," he whispered, annoyed. But then, in the gentle sea breeze, he thought he caught her scent.

Evan looked down at the brick courtyard, at the roses and the lawn leading to the little dock. There was no one that he could see, but still she seemed to be near.

He looked at the lighthouse way out in the bay. It didn't matter what he did, she was everywhere.

CHAPTER EIGHT

MEG KNOCKED GENTLY before stepping hesitantly into the hospital room. The woman lying in the bed closest to the door gave her a pleasant smile and pointed in the direction of the curtain that blocked off half of the room.

"Are you here to see her?"

"Jada?" Meg asked hopefully.

The new mother smiled and nodded encouragingly toward her roommate.

Meg whispered her thanks and smiled at the baby lying asleep in the mother's arms, before moving to the edge of curtain and peering beyond.

The blank look on the pretty, young woman lying back against the raised hospital bed caused a knot to form in Meg's throat.

She didn't even look up as Meg stepped in.

"Hi, Jada."

The young girl's dark eyes moved slowly from the window and rested on Meg's face. "Hi," she said glumly.

"Remember me? I'm Meg Murphy. I was here with you in the delivery room when your son was born."

There was a small glint of life in her dark eyes as Jada nodded silently.

"I was passing by the hospital and thought I'd stop by and say hi." She looked uncomfortably at the small vase of flowers and the two wrapped gifts which she held in her arms. "And these are something little for you and the baby."

"Thanks."

There was no joy in Jada's voice. No glow in the young woman's face. There wasn't even sadness. Just...nothing.

Meg suddenly wanted her hands free, so she turned around to find a place to put her packages down. It was then that she spotted a huge basket of wildflowers, an arrangement of crimson and white roses, and a number of colorful balloons tied to a portable table against the wall by the foot of her bed.

"These are beautiful," she said excitedly, smelling the roses. "From a devoted admirer?"

"Evan sent them," Jada said simply and turned her eyes away again.

Meg placed her packages on the same table and, dropping her tote bag on a nearby chair, turned and moved closer to the bed. "So how is the baby?"

"He sleeps all the time."

"Do you get to see him often?"

One of Jada's hands moved slightly in a half-hearted gesture toward something on the other side of the bed. Meg looked over and, with great delight, spotted the baby. He was sleeping in a small crib that looked like a glass-sided cart of some sort.

Meg reflected on the picture of maternal love she had been greeted with upon seeing the woman and her infant on the other side of dividing curtain. Her heart twisted in her chest at the absence of affection on this side.

"Well, he is a very handsome boy," she whispered softly, leaning over the baby to get a better look. "Have you picked a name?"

Jada shook her head and looked away at the flowers.

"May I hold him?" Meg asked hesitantly.

The young girl shrugged impassively, but then pointed to a hospital gown lying across a chair. "You'll have to wash your hands and put that thing on first."

"Okay." Meg nodded excitedly and hurried into the small bathroom that the two women shared. As she scrubbed her hands, she looked into the mirror and tried to put on some pretense of being a happy visitor. Jada was a child herself. She surely needed as much a shoulder to cry as her infant son.

Her mind suddenly became a stormy sea of emotions, and there was no voice of Robert to calm her. Meg turned off the faucet and reached for a towel to dry her hands. There were two fragile creatures on the other side of this door. Two very young people who needed some affection.

She opened the door and walked into the room. Picking up the simple, flowered gown off the chair, she pulled it over her shirt and slacks.

"Is there anything I can get for you before picking up the baby?"

Jada shook her head. Looking into her empty, black eyes, Meg knew that somehow, she had to draw the teenager out. Whatever pain this girl's young body had gone through yesterday to deliver this child, it was nothing in comparison with the struggles which faced her now.

"I wish I knew what to do," Meg said simply, moving to stand between the crib and window, but still facing her. "Is there a trick to this?"

"Trick to it? No, just pick him up like a baby."

"Under the arms? Just lift him up like this?" Meg wildly exaggerated the movement in the air, and to her delight saw a look of genuine concern cross Jada's face.

"Not under the arms. He's an infant. He has no neck muscles. You have to support his head at all times."

Meg knew she was making a fool of herself, but it was worth it. "So I put one hand behind the neck and one under his back and just lift him."

"Of course not. He's fragile." Jada sat up with alarm written all over her face. "Christmas, haven't you ever held a baby?"

"No," Meg lied. "But I always wanted to, and it's really nice of you to let me do it. A friend of mine at work had a baby a couple of years ago, but she was too scared to let me hold the infant. She said I'm a klutz, but I think I can handle it."

"You didn't seem that way yesterday in the delivery room," Jada said. "You were right there next to me. Even with all that stuff around us."

"But you had to see me when I came out. The first thing I did was spill Evan's coffee all over the front of his shirt. You should have seen his face. You couldn't tell if he wanted to laugh at hearing the good news or wring my neck for giving him a third-degree burn. But back to the baby. How do I lift him?"

"Wait," Jada said firmly. "Why don't you go and sit in that chair against the wall, and I'll bring him to you."

"You can't walk."

"The nurse has been telling me all morning that I should." Jada sat up and started swinging her legs over the edge. "I think it's time."

"Can't I help you? Can I get you anything?"

"Yeah. In that drawer, there should be a bathrobe of some sort. Could you get it for me?"

"Sure." Turning around, Meg intentionally knocked over a cup of water that was sitting with the flowers on the end of the portable table. Quickly running to the bathroom for a towel, she pretended to stumble, catching herself on the door jamb just short of going flat on her face.

"I'm all right," she chirped before going into the bathroom. *The Three Stooges have nothing on me*, she thought.

By the time her mess was cleaned up and she was back beside

Jada's bed with the cotton bathrobe in hand, the young girl's face had taken on a much healthier complexion.

"I still think," Meg argued, "that you should stay in bed and let *me* handle the baby."

"*No!*"

Meg controlled the urge to give Jada a big hug for rejecting her offer so absolutely.

"Now," the teenager ordered. "You go and sit in that chair and wait."

"Sit. Wait." Meg nodded. "Got it."

It was all so different, now. Whatever had been going on in Jada's brain when Meg arrived, had disappeared without a trace. The way the young mother reached over the crib and picked up her son, the tender way she nestled him against her chest, showed Meg the extent of the feelings she had for the baby. With her thick, black hair framing her pale face, she looked even younger than her fifteen years. And she took her time in bringing the newborn across the room.

Before Jada could reach the chair, Meg quickly got up and dragged another chair closer, putting it beside the other.

"He seems pretty comfortable," she said. "Why don't you sit and hold him awhile, until he can get used to me?"

Jada gave a small smile before nodding and sitting in the chair, all the while holding the sleeping infant securely in her arms. Meg silently watched the two for a moment before noticing the look of sadness that had crept into the young mother's quiet expression.

"Do you feed him yourself or is he on a bottle?"

Jada's fair skin turned a deep crimson as she looked down at her child.

"I...I really don't know what to do. They sent a nurse to me last night to show me everything, but it was a disaster. He kept going to sleep. He wouldn't accept me. They told me this morning that in the middle of night they gave him a supplement of formula."

Wouldn't accept me. She was getting rejected from all sides.

"You know," Meg said, glancing out the door into the hallway. "I saw some TV's on rolling carts when I came in. Do they have these things on a CD? The lessons, I mean."

"They said they do," Jada said quietly.

"Boy, am I in the mood for a movie." Meg jumped to her feet. "If I could only get us some popcorn, then we'd be all set."

"I think popcorn is supposed to give him gas," Jada called after her as Meg went out into the hall.

A few moments later, as Meg was tucking a pillow beneath the baby on Jada's lap, a young nurse rolled in their entertainment of the hour.

The next hour was not exactly sheer bliss, though Meg did her best to lighten the mood. They watched the tape twice. Once for its educational benefit, and a second time just for good measure. Then Jada tried again to breastfeed the sleeping baby, but he would have no part in it. After a couple of tries, Meg went after one of the nurses and came back with experienced help. That got the mother and child started on the right track, but Jada was still nervous about doing it right, and that continued to cast a shadow over the whole effort.

"It'll come," the nurse told her. "Try not to worry so much."

The woman went out, but while Jada was still in the chair, Meg decided to pamper her a bit. Picking up Jada's brush, she began running it through the young woman's long, silken blanket of hair. The simple act worked like magic. Jada relaxed. The baby woke up and started suckling on the offered breast, and Meg felt like a million bucks.

To be wanted. Meg had overlooked this simple human need. She'd just forgotten how wonderful the sensation really was.

Mrs. Jeffers, having found someone to watch the kids she normally sat for in the afternoons, was standing in the parking lot and waiting as Evan pulled in. All the way to the hospital, the older woman was as jittery as a first-time grandmothe, and never once stopped talking. After hearing all the weird, tragic, and unbelievable stories about childbirth that Mrs. Jeffers had to share, Evan was amazed that any woman could be coaxed, cajoled, or compelled into having a baby.

Evan liked the old woman, though. The way he understood it, from the ten years since Jada's mother died, the good-hearted neighbor had been the primary caregiver whenever Ted had to be away fishing.

A few minutes later Evan, feeling a bit like a pack horse, trailed Mrs. Jeffers down the hallway of the maternity ward. In one arm, he juggled a large grocery bag filled with the older woman's bran muffins and whatever else she'd thought to bring, and in the other the largest teddy bear he'd been able to find in the local toy store. The sales girl had sworn to him that this teddy was the 'hottest thing' for new infants. Of course, the damn thing had to be about four feet tall, and Evan couldn't quite shake the feeling that he'd been conned somewhere along the line.

Arriving at Jada's door, he followed Mrs. Jeffers into the room and ignored the repressed giggle of the woman occupying the first bed. Reaching the curtain, he paused to allow Jada and the old woman a moment to ooh and ahh over the baby before stepping in.

"Hi, Jada. I've brou..." Tripping over a pair of feet, size 15 at least, Evan twisted and tumbled in an awkward attempt to save the precious bag of food. Unable to retain his balance, he landed against the bed, moving the whole thing a good foot toward the window.

"What are you trying to do, break my neck?"

He looked up and found a pair of large brown eyes twinkling with laughter.

"I'm so sorry," she said, though her amused expression just didn't appear riddled with remorse. Not that Evan could see, anyway. "I was just trying to get out of the way of Gentle Ben. I didn't realize you were behind him."

He continued to frown into her pretty face and thrust the giant teddy bear in her direction, so he could right himself. She took it from him, smiling openly now, and turned to the chair against the wall where Jada sat with the baby in her arms.

"Grrr!"

"Oh no," Jada cried out, feigning terror. "Not Smokey the Bear."

"No, it's his cousin, Papa Bear, and he's rabid for porridge. Got any?"

Meg pretended to attack the mother and child, and Evan stared in amazement at hearing Jada's happy laugh. This was quite a transformation from yesterday.

"Mrs. Jeffers," Jada said, turning to the older woman. "This is my friend, Meg Murphy. She's from Boston and is going to be here in Newport for a week or so."

Evan placed the bag on the portable table beside the flowers and stepped back as the women exchanged pleasantries. Continuing to study Jada's bright face, he tried to imagine what could have brought about such a change. Was this what motherhood did to a woman? make her forget the pain? the loneliness? the rejection of her peers? His gaze descended to the tiny face of the sleeping infant in her lap. How peacefully he slept, totally clueless to the turmoil that surrounded his entry into this world.

"May I hold him?" He couldn't hold back any longer and took a step in the direction of the baby.

"Have you held a baby before?" Jada asked firmly, suspicion suddenly darkening her face.

"Of course."

"Are you accident prone? Have you stumbled, fallen, or dropped anything in the past three days?"

"No." He glanced questioningly in Meg's direction and found her shaking her head at Jada doubtfully. He would strangle her later.

"Now, tell the truth, Evan." Jada chided. "The three of us witnessed you almost fall only a minute ago."

"What is this, the inquisition? Listen, that was *her* fault. She tripped me, same as she tripped me this morning in the park."

"And yesterday, I suppose, she spilled your coffee on you."

"How do you know that?"

"Never mind," Jada said maternally. "You can just sit in the chair next to me and hold the baby. Now don't forget, his neck muscles are not—"

"I *know* how to hold him." He marched to the chair and sat. "I was holding babies before you were even a twinkle in your father's eyes. Mrs. Jeffers, you can be next in line. Okay, hand him over."

As Jada placed the little bundle in his arms, something thrilled within him, as it always did. He loved babies. He enjoyed holding them, rocking them, and even cleaning them off when they spit up. Not having children of his own was perhaps the only regret that he had about his life. But then, he'd never met a woman that he cared for enough to share the rest of his life with.

As much as he missed having children, he was a true believer in two people being in it together. He hadn't had two parents. His father, he had never known. His grandmother had been the one to raise him when his mother had died in a car crash. But he'd been lucky to turn out as he had. The product of two people who were not ready to commit to anything beyond their own immediate pleasures, he'd been left in this world to fend for himself. This was a risk he wouldn't be taking with his child.

"I think I'll name him Theodore. We could call him Ted, like Daddy."

Evan dragged his eyes away from the baby's round, sleeping face to Jada's earnest one. "That's a nice name," he said gruffly. "And it will also mean a lot to your father."

He looked up and caught Meg's eyes on him. She seemed a bit flushed.

"Do you have some of your own?" he asked bluntly. "Children, I mean?"

She shook her head, her lips pressed into a thin smile.

It didn't matter that Jada and Mrs. Jeffers were right here with them. At that moment, it was as if they were alone in the room, and Evan was suddenly compelled to ask some of the questions that had been on his mind since he'd picked her up at the station.

"Why? Don't you want them? Or do you and your husband think them a nuisance? Kids are a burden, is that it?"

Evan didn't release her from his piercing glare. She swallowed hard.

"No, my husband and I never thought of children as a burden."

"Then what is it? And where is your husband, anyway?" He was being rude, but he didn't care.

She had placed herself in his path continuously since yesterday. And he wasn't blind to the signals she was sending him. She was as attracted to him as he was to her. But she had no right to fool around like that. Not with *him*, anyway. She was a married woman.

"Let me guess, you have one of those modern marriages where each of you take your own separate vacations. Where each have your own friends." Your own lovers, he added silently. "Let's see. You've never had time to think of starting a family. Tell me I'm wrong."

"You're wrong," Meg answered sharply, her face drained of all color. She turned to Jada. "I have to go now, but if you don't mind, I'll stop by sometime this afternoon for another visit."

"I'd love that, Meg," Jada whispered softly. "Could you bring back some popcorn?"

Meg laughed. "You bet. Maybe we can catch a double feature, this time."

Without sparing him another glance, she nodded to Mrs. Jeffers and disappeared behind the curtain.

Evan listened to her footsteps click out the door...and felt like a dog. Turning his eyes back to the sleeping baby, he couldn't fathom what in hell had possessed his soul to make him speak to her so roughly.

A million things could be going on between Meg and her husband, none of which were any of his business.

"You owe her an apology."

Evan looked up and found Jada's disapproving face directed toward him.

"I was pretty bad, wasn't I?"

"Bad? Evan, I never knew you could be such a dork."

CHAPTER NINE

THEY HAD DREAMS. They had plans, too. But here she was five years after that terrible day, and what did she have to show for all that they had shared?

Meg swiped at her tears as she strode away from the hospital toward downtown Newport. Slinging her tote bag onto her shoulder, she quickened her steps along the busy sidewalk.

She and Robert had both wanted children from the moment they'd walked out of church on their wedding day. But she'd been a freshman in college, and Robert a young editor still establishing himself in the business. At that stage in their lives, it just had seemed too overwhelming to think of bringing a child into such an uphill financial struggle. So they'd waited. Then, the years had just slipped by. What Evan had said was partially true. Their careers had been demanding, Robert's career had taken off, and they'd had to steal their precious time for one another.

It had always seemed that there would be time. The future was a happy and colorful picture...no sunset in sight. But then reality had slammed home. What she'd thought impossible, unthinkable, occurred.

One morning Robert was there, and then he was dead.

They told her it was a heart attack, that he had a congenital disorder that had somehow gone undiagnosed for all those years. That it was simply bad luck that it should happen that way.

Meg suddenly cut across Broad Way, hardly aware of the cars slowing for her to cross. He could have lived, she thought. How could they miss it? How could they not have discovered the condition?

The people on the street all blurred together. Meg blinked back her tears. Damn you, Robert. Why did you have to go like that? Why did you have to leave me?

"You're a pretty fast walker."

She started at the familiar voice behind her, but then, thinking what a sorry condition her face must be, she nearly broke into a run.

"Did you know there are speed limits for pedestrians in this town?"

He was keeping pace, so she turned her face away. As she did, though, his hand shot out and roughly yanked her against him. Off balance, she stumbled, but he held her up. Meg gasped as a bicycle zoomed between them and the storefront they were passing. Evan had just saved her from being run down.

"Idiot," he yelled at the back of the rider. "This is a sidewalk, not the frigging Tour de France."

Feeling a bit dazed, she pushed herself away from his chest and tried to regain her footing.

"Are you okay?"

He turned her in his arms and held her by the shoulders. She found herself looking into his face.

"Are you hurt?" He paused. "What's wrong?"

Suddenly, all of her anguish and misery gathered like a volcano in her chest and spewed forth.

"Am I hurt? Do you actually have the gall to *ask* me what's wrong? You are an insufferable ass!" She stared through her tears at his stunned expression. "I don't want to talk to you. I don't want to see your face. Just let me go."

Meg tried to turn and leave, but his viselike grip allowed no escape.

"Whoa. Wait a minute. What's wrong?"

"I said let me go."

"Not until you tell me what the hell has brought all of this on."

She was a dish rag of emotions, and she knew it. So instead of opening her mouth and making more of a ruckus on a public street, Meg clamped her mouth shut. The heck with him, she thought. He didn't deserve an explanation.

"Are you upset because of what I asked you back in the hospital?"

She'd been fine, she thought. She'd been doing great until he'd wrapped his big hands around that little baby. It was too much. The gentleness he'd shown toward the infant. The affection that had shone in his eyes. It had all made her think of Robert. Of the way he *would* have been, had they ever had a child of their own.

Evan Knight had made her mourn what could have been, before he'd even asked his first stupid question.

"Okay. I was out of place to ask those things. It wasn't any of my business to probe into yours and your husband's life like that. I'm sorry."

She dug a tissue out of her bag and wiped her tears away. Glancing up into the deep bluish-green of his eyes, she saw the same hardness there that she'd seen back at the hospital when he'd asked her those questions.

"You're a liar. You aren't sorry at all."

"You're right. I'm not."

Meg was a bit taken aback by his open admission. He was still holding her by the shoulders, and she could hear the repressed anger in his words.

"What do you have against me?" she asked shortly.

The hard set of his mouth was the only response she got. It seemed that it was now his turn to play the silent one.

"Fine. If that's the way you want to be, I'm not going to waste my time standing here."

She tried to pull away, but he held her fast.

"You really want me to answer your question?" he growled.

"I wouldn't ask if I didn't."

"And what are you going to do when I tell you the truth? Collapse on the sidewalk? Throw a temper tantrum? Weep another flood?"

She shoved his hands away and faced him straight on. "I don't know what the heck your problem is, but I've done nothing—I repeat *nothing*—to deserve the way you're treating me now. So open your big mouth and say what's on your mind, or shut up and get out of my way."

"Okay. You asked for it." He first pulled her by the arm to the side until they were out of the direct line of passing pedestrians. For a moment Meg was overwhelmed by his angry glare and the way he towered over her, blocking her view of the busy street.

"Start," she snapped at him.

"I don't know what you think you're doing here, but I think you are easily the worst double-dealing piece of work that I've met in a long time."

"Double-dealing," she gasped incredulously.

"That's right. And I'm being mild."

"Why hold back?" she challenged. "Lay it on."

His eyes narrowed. "You're also a tease."

"A tease?" she repeated in shock.

"A tease. A flirt. There are other words for it. But trust me, honey, I've been around the block long enough to recognize a come on when I see one. From the first moment you got into my cab, you've done nothing but bat those big, brown eyes, and invite me in."

She gritted her teeth. "You're unbelievable! What kind of ego could possibly—?"

"I'm not done. You are also a liar. I don't know who the poor sap is that you're married to, but I sure hope he doesn't buy any of the fidelity shit you must sell at home. Not when you're running around for a week at a time without him, ready to screw the first man you cross paths with."

"Of all the arrogant, self-righteous, puritanical..." She couldn't believe it, but she'd reduced herself to his level. She knew she was rising to his bait, but he was going to be sorry he'd started this. "Let me tell you something. Who I screw, as you so delicately put it, is none of your business, because it will *never* be you. But who are *you* to judge *me*?"

"I'll tell you who. If you mess around with me, if you're going to come on to me, then that gives me the go ahead to judge as I please."

"You, Mr. Knight, can just clean the sap out of your ears, because I want you to hear this, loud and clear." Heck, why hold back? she thought angrily. "For your information, I've been around the block a few times myself."

"I thought so."

"Shut up and listen," she snapped. "In all my life, not once have I ever run into a more dirty minded creep than you. And as far as my husband goes—"

"The dolt."

"You have no right to talk of Robert like that. He was a man that on his *worst* day had a hundred times more character than you. You on the other hand—"

"What do you mean 'had'?"

"I said shut up and listen."

"Are you divorced? Where is this Robert?"

She felt her head beginning to pound from grinding her teeth so hard. "And you think you deserve an answer? After all the crap you've been handing to me, you think I should tell you about my life?"

"Yes, I do." Evan nodded, his anger evaporating into thin air.

"Well, that's too bad." She started to go around him, but he solidly blocked her. "Get the hell out of my way."

"Not until you hear me out."

"You mean there's more?" Meg snapped.

He nodded. "A bit more."

"Spare me the rest." She again tried to move around him, but he wrapped a firm hand around her wrist and forced her to look up. Her voice was like ice. "You'd better be very careful."

"Meg, I don't know what the hell it is about you, but whatever it is...well, you manage to bring out the worst in me."

"It's a mutual reaction. Maybe it would be safest for both of us just to go our separate ways." She again attempted to get away.

"Could you just hold your horse and listen?"

"No!"

"Well, like it or not, you are going to listen."

Meg watched him as he struggled to say what he had on his mind.

"And if you try one more time to get around me or move even a step, I swear I'll pull you into my arms right here and kiss that stubborn mouth of yours."

"Does the word 'consent' mean anything to you?" She gave him a killing stare. "What do you think this is, *Gone with the Wind?* You even try it, and I'll have your ass in court for assault so fast you'll think you're an extra on one of those cop shows."

"The people in this town are used to lovers' quarrels, sweetheart. You just call out, and we'll see who gets away with what."

She sharply looked about her at the busy street. There were cars and people milling about on both sides, but not one person even glanced in their direction, in spite of the ruckus they'd made. Her eyes snapped back up to him. "You wouldn't dare."

"Just try me."

"Jeez, you're a Neanderthal."

She was angry at the way he was holding her wrist, but not as angry as she should have been, she thought. And though she knew this was little more than a lot of hot air and a battle of wills, she couldn't help the shiver that coursed through her as Evan lowered his head. Her eyes fixed on his lips waiting just a breath away from hers. She swallowed and looked up into his eyes.

"So which is it?"

Meg paused, but only for a moment.

"Talk, Rhett."

"Are you married?"

"This isn't what you were going to say. You're changing the subject."

"Are you married, Meg?"

Why didn't he back off? She should just call his bluff and walk away. But then, she wasn't able to tear her gaze away from those piercing eyes. And, as much as it was killing her to admit it, she couldn't stop wondering what it would feel to be kissed by a man again. A man like him. All strength and passion.

"Why do you ask?" She choked out the words.

"Because...because you've got the wires in my head screwed up so bad that I can't think straight. How do you like that for an answer?" His voice was husky and still angry.

Meg stared at him. Suddenly, everything was different. She couldn't put her finger on it, but somehow she was no longer mad, and—in spite of his best efforts—he certainly didn't seem as outraged as he'd been earlier.

There was still heat between them. Heat so palpable that she felt it burning the skin of her face. In fact, she could feel a wild-fire spreading within her. She quickly lowered her gaze as his accusation of her being a flirt suddenly flashed across her brain.

"So, are you going to answer my question, or are we going to camp on this sidewalk till Christmas?"

"I...I was married," she blurted out. "I'm a widow."

His hand immediately released her wrist. She could have sworn that he took a step back. And he looked as if a bucket of cold water had been poured on top of his head.

"I'm sorry," he said after a long pause.

"You should be," she said, pulling her bag higher on her shoulder and gathering her wits. "Now, I know we got off to a bad start. But now that you have your sour mood under control, I want you to know that everything you said about me, about my character and my behavior, all the other foul things that you said to me..." She let out a long breath. "Well, I intend to hold all of that against you."

"But not because they aren't true."

"Of course, because they aren't true," she answered, rubbing at the imprints of his fingers on her wrist.

"You might not be a double-dealer or a liar, but I stand by my word that you're a flirt."

She scowled at him. It had certainly taken the man no time at all to recover.

"I would love to stand here and beat you to a pulp for what you just called me. But being the civilized woman that I am, I'll let you go this time."

"What are you? Chicken?"

She looked sharply up into his face and noticed the dimple was back.

"Look, I'm not a chicken. I'm not a pigeon. I'm not a duck. In fact I'm not a bird, at all. But what I am, is hungry, and a pig-roast —starring you—is not what I had in mind for lunch. So, if you'll forgive me, Mr. Knight, I'll be on my way."

Meg frowned at the pang of disappointment that lit up like a blowtorch in the pit of her stomach when he allowed her to go past him and down the street. She didn't dare turn and look over her shoulder at him. God only knew what other name he would call her if he ever caught her looking.

"So where are you going for lunch?"

She bit her lip to hide her smile at hearing his voice over her shoulder. She didn't slow down, and he fell in step with her as if nothing unpleasant had ever passed between them. This guy certainly had no self-esteem problems.

"Let me guess," he said, when she said nothing in response. "Where would a prig like you go for lunch?"

"From flirt to prig in thirty seconds." She paused by a side street as a car turned in front of them. "I'm amazing."

"If you say so," he growled. "But let's see, where would you go? The White Horse Tavern."

She shook her head, shooting him a scornful look.

"The Black Pearl?"

"No."

"La Petite Auberge?"

She turned and looked up into his face. "Actually, I was thinking of some place like the Newport Creamery. We normal folks obviously don't eat the same kind of lunches that you Newport cab drivers do."

He laughed. "Honey, save your hard luck story for someone else. Don't forget, I'm the one who drove you to the Inn at Castle Hill in the first place. If it wasn't that you screwed up your social calendar..."

"I didn't make the mistake. They did." She started crossing the street, leaving him behind.

"The same thing. So don't pull that."

"Don't you have somewhere to go?" She turned her best frown on him. "Don't you have someone else you can go and torment?"

"Well, not right this minute."

"Too bad."

He held her by the elbow, forcing her to stop as another crazy driver made a quick turn onto a side street. She looked both ways before starting again, but his hold on her stopped her advance.

"Meg, why don't you let me buy you lunch? I probably owe you that, at least."

She turned and looked at him over her shoulder. Jeez, he knew how to turn on the charm when he wanted to. With that killer smile and those incredible eyes, it was almost too easy to give in. Almost, she reminded herself.

"Wouldn't I be crazy to accept lunch from you, even if it were a peace offering? I mean, when you consider all the abuse you've been giving me."

"No. I think it would show good taste on your part. Not to mention, it would give you a great opportunity to use me for polishing up your flirting skills."

She gave an unladylike snort.

"Hey, you'll love it." Taking her silence for consent, he threw a friendly arm around her shoulder and steered her across the busy street between the oncoming cars.

She didn't stop him. As much as her sensible mind cried to put a halt to all of it, Meg couldn't. Jeez, maybe she was becoming a flirt after all, but he smelled wonderful. She glanced at him out of the corner of her eye. Dressed in his navy-blue polo shirt and khaki pants, he was also not like any of the cab drivers she was used to seeing in Boston.

When they reached the other side of Broad Way, she noticed that he didn't drop his hand. Resigned to the squadrons of butter-flies dogfighting in her stomach, she didn't complain.

They only went another hundred yards before he directed her toward the door of a small restaurant on the side of the street. From the outside, the faded half-curtains in the windows hid any hint of what the inside might be like, but with her stomach ready to devour her liver, Meg wasn't about to be picky, so long as they served edible food fast.

"Like clams?"

"Love them," Meg responded over the noise of the lunch crowd. "Necks, bellies, shells, the whole bit."

She peered into the dimly lit restaurant. It had to be about the homeliest dining room she'd ever seen, and that was saying something, considering some of the diners and hole in the wall places she'd eaten in over the years. Waitresses in gold, polyester uniforms hustled to and fro, exchanging insults with a burly, unshaven cook. Ugly, rusted metal stools with cracked, green leather seats sat screwed to the floor in front of a Formica-topped counter that had probably been old when Howard Johnson was a baby. But there wasn't an empty table in the joint, and the wonderful smell of a grill smoking steadily behind the crowded counter made Meg's stomach growl for food.

"Lobster?"

"Sure." Meg looked at a passing waitress. "Nobody seems to even see us here."

"They don't stand on ceremony around here. We'll just grab the first table that opens up."

She nodded and looked keenly at the heaping plates of food before the boisterous and somewhat rough-looking clientele. Before they'd stepped into this place and smell of food had reached her stomach, she hadn't even given much thought to her missed meals. But her hunger struck her now, and she realized it had been yesterday since she'd eaten, at the train station in Boston.

"Are you going to make it?"

She turned in Evan's direction and found him leaning casually against the wall close to the door and watching her. "I don't know. It's going to be close."

"You didn't eat today, did you?"

She moved to stand next to him. "Don't ask me about my last meal. In fact, let's not talk about food."

"Fine, we can talk about something else." He moved aside so that she too could lean against the wall. "So what is it that you do? I mean other than vacationing in expensive resort towns like this, and flirting with the cab drivers that give you rides."

She scowled at him and moved her bag from one shoulder to the other. "And I thought we'd established a truce."

"Sorry, I just can't help it. I enjoy teasing you."

"Sure, but I'm the tease, remember?"

"Oh, that's right. But you didn't tell me. What is it that you do?"

Meg tore her gaze away from his amused eyes and glanced at the direction of the bustling tables and old linoleum floors. She'd be damned if she'd give him a straight answer. Not after all the irritation he'd given her earlier. "I'm a janitor."

"Get out." His burst of laughter drew a few eyes in their direction. "And I suppose the Inn at Castle Hill is the hotel of choice among the janitorial set?"

"As a matter of fact, I was just checking it out for the annual conference."

"Conference?"

"Yes, for the National Organization of Maintenance Engineers. Good organization."

"Yeah, okay."

She put on her best insulted expression. "Mr. Knight, you're incredibly rude on top of being a jerk. Have I even once made fun of or criticized what you do for living? Why can't you do the same of me? A job is a job—you make what you will of it."

He reached down unexpectedly and took hold of her hand. Wordlessly, he brought it up. She followed his line of vision and stared at her short, no-nonsense, unmanicured nails.

"You don't pamper yourself," he announced with a bit of surprise in his voice. He ran his thumb over the skin. "But you have very soft hands."

She held her breath at the tingling sensation that was racing up her arm.

"No janitor has a hand like this."

"Have you heard of latex gloves? Our union frowns on us using strong chemicals without them. Not to mention OSHA regulations."

From the twinkle in his eyes, she knew he didn't believe a word of what she'd said.

"And no calluses," he continued, turning her hand over and running a slow finger down the middle of her palm.

She bit her bottom lip. "Work gloves," she managed to croak.

He brought her unresisting hand to his face. The roughness of the shave and then the mere touch of his lips against her skin made her shiver with excitement.

"Really. You know, I can't smell even a hint of Lysol."

"Well, I just changed the baby's diaper." He lifted his head an inch or two. "And I...I've been away...away from my job. You know, cleaning the bathrooms?"

Two people brushed past them on their way out the door, and Meg stole her hand out of his grasp. Peering into the dining room, she spotted the vacant table. A pile of dirty dishes sat on the glass-covered checkered table cloth. A heavyset waitress turned her back on the mess and continued chatting with the customer at the next table.

"Do we wait for her to clean it up, or should we jump for it?"

With a nod, he gently pushed her in the direction of the table, following close behind.

"If she thinks we're going to pocket her tip, she'll have that table cleared in no time."

As they approached the small table, Meg again found herself too aware of Evan. Quickly, he moved around her, holding her chair until she was settled, and then seating himself. He was a mass of contradictions, but there was something so graceful about certain things that he did. Meg eyed the few coins and the dollar bill sitting beside a plate.

She nodded at the money. "Looks like a fortune."

A meaty hand scooped up the tip.

"What can I get for you, honey?"

Meg looked up and found the waitress's eyes riveted on Evan. As far as the woman was concerned, Meg clearly didn't even exist.

"We'll have two lobster rolls." He gave their waitress one of his knockout smiles. "And I've heard you guys make the best clam chowder in town."

"We sure do, hon."

Meg couldn't believe her eyes, but the woman actually plunked a hand on his shoulder and leaned her large bosom toward his face. He glanced down with a devilish grin.

"Beautiful. Then bring us two cups of that, will you?"

"I'll have mine in a bowl...*hon*," Meg cut in brightly, addressing Evan and entwining her fingers in his. It took him only a moment to pick his jaw up off the table. "And I'll have iced tea to drink."

"Got it," the waitress remarked indifferently before cooing at Evan again. "And you, pumpkin?"

"Coke."

Meg watched through slitted eyes as the waitress took her time to clean the table. As the well-endowed woman bent over the table to brush off a non-existent crumb, Meg caught her again directing her deep cleavage in Evan's direction. And he had to be the oldest living adolescent, because he looked down and he looked deep.

When she was gone, Meg quickly tried to withdraw her hand, but he held on tight. "Jealous?"

"Not in this life."

"You could have fooled me."

"I was just too hungry," Meg stared at their entwined fingers. At the way his hand locked and unlocked around hers. She couldn't stop the steady flutter in her stomach—the strange sense of excitement that he brought out in her. She looked up and found his blue-green eyes studying her face. "So, you aren't a regular here."

"How can you tell?"

"Well, she didn't drag you to the back room for a quickie as soon as we walked in."

The low rumble of his laugh was hypnotic. "She usually does that after desert."

She gave him her best imitation of a frown, which he repaid with a killer smile in return. Pulling her hand out of his grasp, she hid it on her lap. She looked around, searching for something to say.

"So, have you lived in this town for all of your life?"

"No."

"Then what brought you here?"

She watched him as he took a long pause.

"Work. I've been here off and on before, but this time I came to Newport to work."

Before she could ask her next question, though, he turned the tables on her.

"And how about you? Have you always lived in Boston?"

"Pretty much."

"And as for being a janitor. Was cleaning toilets a dream since childhood, or something you picked up as a major in college?"

She sat up straight in her chair. "I don't just clean toilets. There are sinks...and floors...and windows..."

"Oh, you do windows?"

"Are you making fun of me again?"

"No, I'm not," he answered quickly, looking up and smiling at the waitress as she put their chowder and drinks on the table.

"Enjoy it, hon."

"Thanks, Grace."

Meg's eyes rounded in surprise as the woman swung her hips around and gave him a wink before moving off.

"You know her name?"

"What's so strange about that?"

"So you *do* come here often."

He didn't answer and instead started pouring oyster crackers into his chowder.

"And the joke about the back room?" she pressed.

"You don't have to worry about that. Not until desert, anyway."

He was pulling her leg, but feeling her stomach churn with hunger at the sight of the food, she turned her attention to the thick, creamy chowder.

"So back to your job," he asked again a few minutes later, when she'd had a chance to devour some. "Does your job pretty much fill up your life, or do you have hobbies?"

"Hobbies?"

"Yeah. Like watching professional wrestling or tying flies for fishing. Things like that."

"I guess..." Meg paused to consider her answer. "I guess when it comes to hobbies, you could call me a reader."

His eyes fixed on her face. "You mean books?"

"Of course I mean books. I didn't get all the way through first grade for nothing, you know. I can even sound out the big words."

His gaze flitted away, and he was trying to look casual, but Meg could see there was something going on.

"And what kind of stuff do you read?"

"Everything, pretty much." She shrugged her shoulders, thinking of all the manuscripts of aspiring authors sitting on the floor beside her bed. "I try not to focus on big names," she added. "I like to discover new voices."

"New voices?" he asked with raised eyebrows.

Wrong word for a janitor to use, she reminded herself.

"Well, I mean...I think that most bestselling authors tend to get themselves into a rut. The tell the same type of story again and again. That's fine for most readers, I guess." She stirred vacantly at the remnants of her chowder. "But for me, I want something different. I like to feel like I'm discovering new stuff. Something with bite to it. Not a rehash of so many other books that are out there. And I don't like snoozers. Once they hit the top lists, writers sometimes lose their quick starts. I think, very often they know they sell their books just based on their names.

So why rush into the story? On the other hand, you get a new author. Someone fresh and eager. I just love it when I get a chance to read a book when someone's new on the scene. Then I watch them grow big and famous."

"So you can dump them and find some other author to read."

She looked up into his eyes and smiled. "I guess you can say that. But at that point in their careers, the big guns don't need poor little me, anymore. They have the masses to drool after them."

Evan pushed his cup of chowder to the side and leaned forward on his elbows.

"Do you really think that's the way those writers are? The ones at the top? Grisham? Nora Roberts? You don't think that those types—no matter how big they are—that they're still vulnerable to the opinion of poor little you?"

She shook her head. "I might be prejudiced, but I don't think so. They've got all the numbers on their side. When you get to be as big a name as, say...Drew King, you don't even care what's in *your* heart. You have a certain style, maybe even a formula. One that you know sells millions of books. Put yourself in his position. Do you risk disappointing the masses who are comfortable with your work by stepping back and saying, 'I want to write my kind of story. Something different, perhaps with a little bit of heart,' or do you just crank out the next novel in the same old style for zillion dollars and lock up your creative drive in the attic?"

"I don't know," he said seriously. "What do *you* think Drew King would do?"

"Go for the gold. Jeez, his record speaks for itself."

Meg watched his long fingers as they organized and reorganized the place setting before him. She looked up at his eyes which were intense with concentration. Evan Knight was one of the most fascinating men she'd met in a long time. He was also one with more sides to his personality than she would have imagined.

"Have you read any of...of Drew King's work?" he asked suddenly, looking up.

Meg unconsciously bit at her lip as she felt a blush creep up her neck. Here we go again, she thought. Another Drew King fan. She'd have to spend the next hour defending herself. "I have a good friend who is probably the guy's biggest fan."

"Interesting," he said coolly. "But you still haven't answered my question."

She had an impulse to just throw in the towel, apologize, and end the discussion. But for heaven's sake, he hadn't even fed her lunch yet.

"My husband, while he was alive, was a fan, as well. So I've read a lot of his work."

"And you didn't like it?"

"Oh, no," she replied quickly. "I truly enjoyed his books...for a while. He had excitement, a freshness in his style that could leave a reader breathless for more. It's just his recent works that put me off." She took a sip of her iced tea. "You see, the same friend of mine that I was telling you is his biggest fan...well, anytime this guy has a new book out, Rebekah has it read within the first week. And then she spends the second week badgering me into reading it."

"And do you? Do you read them?"

"I used to," she answered honestly. "But he really lost me with a book that came out about two years ago. I'm not into ongoing self-abuse, you know. Since then, I've found I prefer to take my friend's harassment than open one of Drew King's books."

This time he had no smile for the waitress as she cleared away their soup dishes and replaced them with two plates with steak rolls overflowing with lobster salad. Her appetite only whetted by the chowder, Meg wasted no time diving in.

A moment later, though, with her mouth full, she looked up and found him still gazing thoughtfully at her.

"Something wrong?" she asked.

"No," he said casually, picking up his fork. "It's just that I've read all of Drew King's books, myself."

"That right?"

"And I was trying to think of the book that you're talking about. You said it came out about two years ago?"

She nodded. "I can't remember the name of it, but it had something to do with this journey of some refugees coming on some wreck of a freighter from China, and the terrible things that happened to them along the way."

"*The Long—*"

"*The Long Journey*," she finished quickly. "That's it."

"What didn't you like about that book?"

Meg put down her food. "Everything. There wasn't a thing that I liked about that book, including the title. In fact, after reading it I was tempted to write a letter to *The Boston Globe* and offer a free review of it. I could imagine how I'd word it." Posing dramatically, she waved her hand in the air. "The latest block-buster from Drew King, *The Long Journey*, is hardly more than a *Long, Boring Journey*. Don't spend the money on it. Save yourself the misery and donate the money to feed the needy."

She dropped her gaze to his face and found his eyes lit with anger.

"You see. You're having the same reaction that Rebekah had." She shook her head and looked down again at her food. "This is the story of my life. I've got to stop hanging out with Drew King's loyal legions. It's okay if you want to leave now and stick me with the bill. Really, I'm used to it."

She glanced up when he didn't answer and found him still looking at her through narrowed eyes.

"You go in big for dramatics. But you strike me as the type that wouldn't even read the damn book, and still form an opinion. The 'review,' as you put it, is only based on how cleverly you can twist the title." He leaned back and crossed his arms over his chest. "Also, I think you enjoy being ornery. Admit it, you love to play devil's advocate just for laughs."

"Wrong again." Meg leaned back and crossed her arms, mimicking him. "Let me tell you what I didn't like about that so-called novel. Drew King has a way of piling people together in his book like a herd of sheep. There is no distinction between individuals. No individual emotions. No *love*. Now, think back over that story. He describes a terrible journey. We go through scene after scene of stupid action to tell us in detail all the horrible things that these people go through."

"Come on."

"Seriously," she pressed. "We read about disease, violence, death. But other than a simple name, do we know who the hell these people are? Do we get any sense of what they are feeling? How are we supposed to feel for these folks when they are faceless pawns in the author's mind?" Meg pushed her own plate out of the way and leaned on her elbows facing him. "Here is another part of my review. Reading *The Long Journey* is like watching amateur bowling on a nine-inch black and white TV. Let's line the pins up...sorry, I meant people. Okay, bring in a disaster. Oh, no...bad roll...only three out of ten went down. You'll have a second chance. Better luck next chapter."

"Are you telling me that you never felt any compassion for them? You never felt their hardship, their suffering, their hope?"

"No," she said adamantly. "Drew King never showed us even a glimpse of their hearts. We were never inside them, at all. When I read, I want to get swept away by the people I meet on those pages. I want to know something of the lives they had to leave behind. I want to know what is driving them to risk so much. Even at the end, when some of them finally arrive on US soil, I could shed no tears of joy for these people. After four hundred pages of text, I would have gotten more satisfaction watching the eleven o'clock news."

His deep frown told her that he definitely didn't agree. She pushed her chair back and sat up straight. "I know. I sound too harsh. Fine. I'll admit that he is a good writer. A very good writer of *words*," she quickly added. "But he is no longer a story teller. Somewhere along the line, I'd say, he's lost his touch. There are no hearts beating in his books anymore."

He leaned back against his own chair and stared at her. She realized he hadn't touched his food.

"I'm sorry. I didn't mean to ruin your lunch."

He said nothing. Nor did he look her in the eye as he raised his soda to his lips.

Nice job, Meg thought, watching him for another moment before turning her attention back to her food. She'd forgotten all the rules. All those years out of the dating game didn't mean that things had really changed any. Men couldn't deal with opinionated women. Especially women whose opinions contradicted their own.

Somehow though, she thought as she ate, the lobster didn't seem to taste quite the same.

CHAPTER TEN

EVAN STEPPED BACK into the room from the balcony and started for the fridge. Where the hell was she anyway? he thought shortly. It was half-past eight, and they should have kicked her out of Jada's hospital room long before now.

Yanking the door of the fridge open, he surveyed the meager contents vacantly for a moment before pulling out a bottle of beer. He popped the top off before turning around and staring at his open laptop across the way.

Well, he'd held up his end of the bargain with Henry, anyway. He'd worked on that damn machine non-stop for the past four hours. But then, he'd be damned if he knew if any of what he'd written was good or not.

And it was all her fault. Sitting innocently across the table during lunch, she'd turned those big brown eyes of hers on him and had shred his very existence to pieces.

Still frustrated, he took a big swallow of beer.

"Shit," he muttered, looking at the copy of *The Long Journey* lying on the kitchen table.

She didn't know who he was. He was sure of that. Years ago, he'd demanded that his publishers stop putting his picture on the back of the books. He didn't want the hassles. He hated the notoriety.

Evan winced as he thought back over her words. Oh no, she definitely didn't know his true identity, or she wouldn't have dared to talk about his writing like that. In all of his years in this business, nobody had *ever*—to his face, anyway—torn up his work the way she had. Not even his very first editor.

He didn't know if he wanted to strangle her and use her body as an anchor for one of Phil's boats, or just handcuff her to his belt hook for a good luck charm.

Because the truth of it was that she'd been right. Despite all those glowingly bogus reviews that he'd gotten on that novel, she'd been right. He'd been so wrapped up in relating the events in that book that he'd lost the human story. Those refugees were no more than cardboard cutouts, background for an empty story. He thought he cared about those people. Hell, he *did* care about those people. But he'd sold them out. There *was* no heart beating in the story.

"Shit," he said again.

His two books after that had been no better. And he'd somewhere along the line decided that he was going to take out his frustrations on his editors. Hell, none of them had any guts. They were all too young or too afraid to put him in his place. To tell him that his stories sucked. But Meg sure as hell had spoken her mind.

He took the bottle with him outside and leaned against the balcony. Looking down at her window, he could still see no sign of her. He'd gotten the impression that she didn't know anybody in town, so then where was she? Damn, he was becoming a bigger fool than ever. She was a single woman, that he'd found out earlier. A beautiful and sharp-witted widow who most likely had come to this resort town with some thought of partying in mind.

He placed his bottle on the planking and looked across the harbor at the lighted pleasure boats. And what kind of a good time had *he* offered her? As she saw it, he was a taxi cab driver. A temperamental, ass hat of a taxi cab driver, he corrected, remembering the way she'd spoken to him. And why would she want to hang around someone like him?

"So where the hell are you?" he muttered again, picking up the half empty bottle and walking back inside. Unable to hold back any longer, he reached for the phone and called the number at the hospital. It took an operator and a few rings before he was able to get Jada on the phone. Before he'd even asked her directly, the young mother offered the information that Evan was after. Meg had left about an hour ago, and she'd told Jada that she was going to walk around and wind her way back to the place where she was staying. After asking about the baby, and about Jada, and trying not to sound ridiculously impatient, Evan hung up.

Well, damn her to hell, he thought as he reached for the key to the new SLK that he kept in Phil's driveway on the side. She wasn't the only one who could spend a night on the town.

Hell yeah. He could have fun too.

Maybe.

The flash of lamplight on the Mercedes convertible caught Meg's eye as it sped around the corner onto Poplar Street. It was a pretty car, but it wasn't the car that caught her eye. The gas lamps that lined the street hadn't afforded her a good look, but the way the man had turned his head, the wavy brown hair, made her think for a moment that it had been Evan driving.

Dismissing the idea with a shake of her head, she continued past the Hunter House. The moon was sinking behind the hills across the Narragansett Bay, and Meg turned to watch it for a moment. There was no breeze just then, and the night was warm and still. The sounds of the water lapping at the pilings just a few yards away lulled her, and then the sound of geese passing low overhead—calling to one another in the darkness—drew her attention.

Meg let out a long, deep sigh and turned up the street again.

She was just passing a big, restored colonial when the front door opened. A group of young women—all with the same long, straight blond hair and short, tight dresses—spilled noisily out onto the street and breezed past her in the direction of the downtown.

Meg smiled as she thought back over the ever-changing image of this town. When first she and Robert had started coming here, Newport had been a place where they could unwind. From visiting elaborate mansions along Bellevue Avenue and Ocean Drive to walking the endless sandy stretch of Second Beach, the two of them would be rested, totally renewed, by the time they headed back to Boston. But after seeing the hustle and bustle of downtown tonight, for the first time in her life Meg felt that she might be getting old.

There were people everywhere, packing the shops, the restaurants, the sidewalks. It was the same everywhere she went. And these were not just normal people. The women all seemed to be young and pretty, all trying for the same look as the ones who had just passed her with their long hair swept to the side. And the men. She shook her head. She *had* to be getting old, considering the fact that they all looked too young. Way, way, way too young.

But then, the interesting thing was that she had been coming here for five years since Robert's death, and she'd never been aware of any of this. She guessed that had to be mostly due to the fact that she'd continued to stay out at the Inn, so far removed from the activity downtown. And even when she'd ventured out, it had only been as far as the same places that she and Robert had gone every year.

The same places, she thought, slowing down and glancing to her left at the boats in the harbor. In all the years past, she'd never had a problem finding her way around, finding a way to relive the memories of their beautiful past. And Robert had always been with her. Every year. If only in spirit, he'd been here beside her. But this year, he was stubbornly staying away. No matter how lost and confused she felt, no matter how much she called him, he was not paying her any attention.

Meg squeezed her eyes shut and tried to hear his words. It's time, he'd said. You've got a life to be living, and I've got to be moving on.

But why now? she thought. Why did it have to be at the very time when she felt so vulnerable, so affected by someone else? By someone like Evan Knight. He was too much of a male even for a woman in her *right* mind.

Meg arrived at the door of the house where she was staying and slid the key that Nan had given her into the lock. Quietly, she stepped in and pushed the door shut.

"Get down, bitch."

The sharp voice of the man made Meg's blood run cold.

"Drop the keys."

Carefully, she laid the keys on the small table beside the door. The intruder's voice was coming from the large parlor directly behind her, but she didn't dare turn.

"Good girl." His tone was hardly gentle. "Now, sit."

Meg eyed the Windsor chair on the other side of the foyer, but she wasn't sure if she should risk walking to it, or just sit on the floor.

"Don't move. I said *sit.*"

She quickly sat cross-legged on the oriental rug covering the wooden floor.

"That's better." The man's voice softened a bit. "Now lie down."

She swallowed hard. She could just imagine the headlines. Tourist assaulted and murdered in historic bed and breakfast.

"*Lie down.*"

Meg cursed herself for not carrying the pepper spray she

always had with her in Boston. But she'd still put up a fight. If the bastard tried to lay one finger on her, she'd kick and bite him.

"*Down.*"

The sharp voice shook the hall. She obediently unfolded her legs and lay rigidly on her back with her eyes focused on the ceiling.

"Oh, you are the dumbest..." There was frustration and resignation in the man's voice that confused her.

Suddenly, as Meg stared upward, a huge, furry gray face appeared over her, its breath hot on her face.

And that Irish wolfhound just stood there, grinning down at her.

CHAPTER ELEVEN

Meg Murphy was nothing more than an inconsiderate snob, and she could go to hell as far as he was concerned.

Evan brought his car to a stop in the cobblestone driveway and turned off the headlights. For the past couple of hours, he'd driven every main and side street between here and the hospital looking for the damn woman. He'd even gone as far as parking his car downtown—something he hated to do—and poking his head into every bar and restaurant he knew. But she was nowhere.

Well, she could go screw herself, for all he cared. This type of distraction was something that he definitely didn't need in his life. Not now. Not ever.

As he hoisted himself out of the car, the deep laughter of his friend Phil came from behind the privet hedges. The big goon must have just arrived back in town, Evan thought. He hadn't seen Phil's sailboat anchored in the harbor earlier. Well, having a visit with him was as good an entertainment as any right now, he decided, considering his night was already ruined.

Closing the car door, Evan hesitated a moment as the softer voice of a woman also came from behind the privet. The devil! Back in town not two hours, and he already had company. But then, this was no surprise. Most women seemed to drop onto their backs instinctively when faced with Phil's dark looks and charming manners.

Again, there was the deep laughter of his friend, and Evan turned toward the brick walkway leading toward the house. His visit would have to wait until tomorrow.

But then the woman's voice again wafted in on the breeze, stopping him dead in his tracks. He listened. She was saying something but laughing softly at whatever Phil had just said.

"What the hell?"

He rounded the corner and stood in the arched gate to the private brick courtyard. The cozy sight that greeted him hit him like a punch in the gut.

With the view of the harbor before them, the two sat close together, facing the water and rocking in their wrought-iron chairs. They appeared to be involved in an intimate discussion. Evan's eyes riveted on Meg. With a drink in her hand and Phil's dog Swift stretched out right before her feet, she looked happy. No, she looked like a woman in absolute bliss, and very much charmed by the handsome devil sitting next to her.

The gentle sea breeze ruffled her hair, and Evan watched as she tucked a wayward curl behind an ear. She laughed softly again at something that Phil was whispering, and Evan frowned as his smooth-talking *ex*-friend casually placed a hand on the back of her chair.

"If it isn't Phil Campbell himself," Evan called out. "There is no end to the crap that washes up here." Then, without ceremony, he pushed open the gate and marched onto the brick patio and where the two sat. Their heads turned immediately. Evan focused on her face, ignoring Phil, who was rising from his chair. Even in the flickering light of the citronella candles around them, he could see the hint of a smile brightening those dark eyes.

Yeah, he thought, but was she glad to see him, or was this an amused response to his lack of manners in breaking in on their little tête-à-tête?

Well, there was only one way to find out, he thought. Hell, being a shocker was his stock in trade.

Without so much as a glance in Phil's direction, Evan moved to the side of her chair and leaned down. Her eyes widened in surprise, but they never left his as he dug one hand into the silky mass of hair at the nape of her neck.

"I've been looking all over for you," he whispered. Their lips were separated only by a breath. "You didn't mean to stand me up, did you?"

He heard the breath catch in her throat. But as he stared into the depth of her eyes, she never wavered in returning his gaze. Her eyes were dark, beautiful, and they shone with the brilliance of thousand stars. And then he lowered his gaze and saw her parted lips.

There was no turning back.

Meg's pulse jumped, but she couldn't move away even if her life depended on it. As she gazed up into his face, their surroundings —the tea roses still blooming along the walkway, the sound of the bay—all of it faded away into oblivion. Suddenly, nothing else existed. There was no one else in the world. There was only the two of them.

His lips parted and brushed over hers. At the same time, he dug his fingers deeper into her hair and brought her lips harder beneath his. And as his mouth firmly settled against hers, she experienced a moment of wonder. His lips were warm and gentle. Such a contrast to the rest of him.

She further parted her own lips because the craving for a taste of him was about to drive her mad. He drew at her bottom lip and touched the tip of her tongue with his own. The sensation sent her spiraling, and she brought her free hand up, wrapping it around his neck.

He drew back slightly.

"This is more like it," he whispered before taking possession of her mouth once more.

His tongue plunged inside, touching the deepest recesses of her being. She ignited, feeling within herself a molten river of passion that threatened to burst forth, consuming them both. A sense of wickedness swept through her as she rhythmically rubbed her tongue against his and answered his delving search. His low, approving groan only made her bolder in her actions. She tightened her hand on his neck and pressed herself harder against his demanding lips.

"Ahem." A man's voice interrupted from somewhere in the world beyond. "Good to see you too, Evan. Can I get you a drink or something?"

Meg jumped like a guilty adolescent, quickly breaking off the kiss. But in her attempt to salvage some of her lost dignity, she fumbled with her glass and managed to spill wine on her blouse.

She leaped to her feet.

"Oh, look what you've done," Evan noted in a teasing tone. "Can I be of assistance?"

She reached to accept a napkin from the outstretched hand of Phil, but then found herself fighting off Evan's attempts at brushing off her blouse.

"I think...Stop that. I think I'll be going," she stuttered to her host a minute later, once she had Evan's overly solicitous hands under control. "I had a lovely time. Thanks again."

She didn't dare try to stop and analyze the bewildered expression on Phil Campbell's face. Then, with a gentle pat to the dog's head—which had hardly bothered to lift her head in all the commotion—she mumbled another word of thanks and turned toward the porch doors leading into the house.

Evan's soft, husky voice stopped her dead in her tracks.

"Leave the light on. I'll be up in a minute."

She cringed. She cursed under her breath. And then she ran.

"You're not going in until you tell me what the hell that was all about."

Ignoring Phil, Evan pushed the large furry mass with one foot and moved between the wolfhound and the chair.

"Beautiful night, isn't it?" He sat himself comfortably in the rocking chair.

"You know Meg? Is she an old friend?"

"Yes and no. Get me a beer, will you?"

"Get your own. Hell, you know your way around my house better than I do."

"On second thought," Evan stretched tiredly in the chair. "I think I'll pass on the beer and just call it a night."

Before he could get to his feet, though, Phil was heading toward the porch. "Don't you dare move your ass out of that chair. Hear me? I want to hear about this woman."

Alone beneath the stars, Evan kicked off his sneakers and propped his feet up on the dog. Swift batted an eyebrow, took a deep breath, and closed her eyes again.

"Work, work, work. Eh, Swift?" Evan chuckled, craning his neck around to look at the house and the windows overlooking the harbor. As he watched, he saw her light turn on. A moment later, he saw her shadow flicker across a wall.

That woman sure as hell knew how to kiss, Evan thought. Even now, he was still conscious of the heat in his loins and the delicious taste of her mouth. He frowned in the darkness, wondering what had come over him to act so possessively.

Evan looked up again toward her window. Her T-shirted figure appeared, and the window opened. As he watched her disappear, he wondered what she would do if he actually *did* show up at her door tonight. He chuckled and leaned over to pet the 180 lb. furball at his feet. Oh, he *knew* what she would do. The hard slam of her door would most likely add a new, and flatter, dimension to his face.

At the sound of Phil's steps coming back from the house, Evan turned his gaze out at the view of the harbor. As much as he was captivated with Meg Murphy, Evan still didn't know how to explain her to his friend. Hell, he couldn't explain her to himself.

"Here you go, you lazy bastard."

Evan reached up and took the beer from Phil's hand. "Did you have to go to New Bedford for this beer?"

"No, I was looking for these in the kitchen." Phil held up a package of graham crackers. "I think Nan hid them on me."

"Damn, Phil. Graham crackers and beer?"

"Hey, I like it. You know I like it."

"Yeah, but the entire pretzel industry's been praying novenas that you'd grow out of it."

"Well, they can keep on praying."

Evan watched his friend settle into the chair beside him.

"So when the hell did you get back?"

"Tonight."

"And how was your trip?"

"Great sailing weather. Warm. Decent wind. We ran into..." Phil abruptly halted mid-sentence. "Wait a minute, you tricky sonovabitch. You're not slithering out of answering my questions like that."

Evan looked at his friend innocently. "What? I don't remember any questions."

"Meg Murphy? The woman you marched in here and kissed like a jealous newlywed. Who is she?"

"You two looked like you were pretty tight here. Don't tell me she didn't give you the scoop?"

Phil took a swig of his drink and smiled back at Evan. "No, to tell the truth, we didn't have much chance to talk about her...and your name definitely didn't come up."

"Then what the hell were you two so chatty about?"

"Things."

Phil's casual answer managed to irk Evan's temper. "What kind of things exactly?"

"You're such an asshole, Evan." Phil grinned and popped a piece of cracker in his mouth before casually bringing the drink to his lips for another swallow. "I don't know. Wolfhounds. Newport. Sailing. We were just about to get to sex."

"Oh, you were telling her your life story." Evan could see that Phil was entertained by the whole thing, but he couldn't help glaring at him.

"Just the highlights."

"Well, did you explain the rules? Did you give her the stats that she needs to beat?"

"The stats?"

"Yeah," Evan answered tersely. "Like the 'one-night stands only' rule. And the current land-speed record for putting her on her back."

Phil's dark eyes shone with mischief when they turned on him. "As a matter of fact, you might be interested to know that the Guinness Book people just left. Hell, she's already broken that record."

Evan felt his hackles go up. "Don't bullshit me, Phil."

Phil put his beer on the bricks and stretched his long, tanned legs out in front of him. He looked out at the boats on the harbor. "Hey, Evan, you know I never lie about these things."

He didn't know why, but suddenly Evan felt his stomach go sour. Taking another deep swallow of his beer, he tried to wash away the taste.

Feeling his anger rising like a storm inside of him, Evan turned and faced his friend. "So how was she in bed?"

"In bed?" Phil grinned. "You're such a stuffed shirt. We never got to bed."

"Then what the hell are you talking about?"

"I'm talking about the front entrance."

"The front entr...dammit to hell, Phil. You used to have some sense of decency."

"Hey, I didn't force her. I just asked, and she went down willingly."

Evan sat forward in his chair and glared threateningly at the other man. "Let me get this straight. You didn't know Meg before tonight. You never met her before."

"Right."

"And yet you managed to screw her in the front hall of your own damn house?"

Phil leaned back on his chair and fought down a smile. "I didn't say anything about screwing, Evan. I think it was you who said..."

He never had the opportunity to finish his words as Evan rose and upended him with one swift motion.

"Okay, you smart-assed sonovabitch," Evan said, standing over him with his hands on his hips. "Now let's just start all over again."

CHAPTER TWELVE

WITH A GENTLE TOUCH, Jada traced the delicate lines of the baby's ear and gazed in wonder at the little bundle tucked close to her breast.

It was so quiet. The only sound she could hear was the soft purring noise of the baby's breathing as he slept. He was done feeding and had dropped off, now awakening only occasionally to suckle contentedly and drift off again.

Jada lifted her head at the sound of a nurse's laugh out at the duty station. Sounded like she was on the phone. Take your time, the young mother thought, looking back down at her infant son. No hurry.

How different she felt tonight. So unlike last night, when she'd been relieved to have the nurse come at last and take the baby to the nursery. Tonight, she felt her chest tighten at the thought of parting with him, even for a moment.

She watched Ted's little mouth work in his sleep and smiled. Pushing his little cap aside, she ran her fingers across fine, black hair covering his head. His face wrinkled up and reddened as he prepared to cry.

"Shh," she cooed softly, stroking his cheek and watching as he quieted.

He definitely had her complexion, she thought happily. But his eyes. He'd opened them for her briefly tonight, and she thought they looked deep blue. She wondered if he'd end up with Matthew's eyes?

She didn't even notice the tears until one plopped on the baby's head. She smoothed the moist spot with her finger. Matthew. Matthew Rand. A name that, as long as she lived, she would never repeat aloud. Nobody could know. Nobody *would* know. She had vowed that long ago.

She leaned down and softly placed a kiss on her son's head. Despite the difficulties that she'd had to deal with, the most important thing to remember was that her baby had been conceived in love. Someday, she would tell him that.

And somehow, until that day, she would raise him in a world full of love.

Somehow, it would be a better world than the one she and Matthew had known. Confused, lost, deprived. Him— neglected by a family who thought writing a check was the way to buy affection. Her— raised without a parent for most of her life. Never having someone close enough to call a friend.

Matthew was a rich kid, and she was poor. His parents, wrapped up in their own lives, paid little attention to him. Jada's father sacrificed terribly to send her to the Priory School, but he would not listen to her fervent pleas to let her go to the public school, instead.

Although old enough to have his own license, Matthew had a driver take him to school. Jada preferred to miss the bus intentionally, so that she could hike the distance on foot. It was far better to be late than listen to the taunts of "Subsidy Kid!" on the bus.

But somehow, in spite of the huge difference between their

lives, they still found themselves drawn to each other like magnets from the first day he arrived.

Her life and his changed after that first day. Every moment they could spend together, they did. Outside of school, their time together was scarce, secret, stolen, precious.

Jada never dared to tell her father about Matthew. As much as she was certain of Ted's affection for her, she knew him to be a proud man and well aware of the social distinctions in this town. She never asked, but she knew that Matthew had never spoken of her to his family, either. But that was fine. What they shared, she thought was an innocent love. And it was based on a friendship, a kinship, that their families could never understand.

Matthew was two years older. He was more experienced. In his own way, he started teaching her that holding hands just wasn't enough to satisfy their young and curious bodies. He showed her heat, desire, passion...urges bubbling up from within that she couldn't understand. Urges she'd had no desire to control.

It had been the first time for Jada when they'd first crossed that line. She was scared and eager, but Matthew had been cautious enough to be prepared. Their young lives had become entwined as one. Because they had one another, the future seemed hopeful for the first time. But their dreams, their shared moments, their very existence, all suddenly disrupted by forces beyond their control. Matthew found himself in the middle of his parents' divorce. When his mother moved to their brownstone in New York City, he was forced to go with her, despite his pleas to remain in Newport.

Jada still remembered his anguish. He'd been given no choice.

And it had been during that last night together that they'd failed to take their usual precautions. In the middle of their tears of sorrow and their promises for the future, they failed to pay attention to their responsibilities for today.

Matthew was long gone when Jada first discovered her condition. But then, even in the midst of what everyone thought a disgrace, her choice was clear. She would keep their baby, and she would keep Matthew's name out of it. To her thinking, what good could come from him knowing the truth?

Jada ran a gentle finger down the baby's soft cheek.

"What choice did we have?" she whispered. There had been a moment, not long after she'd found out she was pregnant, that she considered aborting the child. But, when it came right down to it, she couldn't do it. And looking at the babe in her arms, she knew now that she had made the right decision.

The last months had been almost unbearable, and the childbirth more painful than anything she'd ever known. And then afterwards, she had felt so down, so tired, so empty. Like a zombie, she had not been able to wake herself up to this miracle in her arms. Until yesterday. Until Meg, with her goofy antics, had made her see the treasure that she'd brought into the world.

Yes, she could see.

Jada smiled again at her child. Everything would be fine now. Her father would come to love the baby. They'd be a family. Like that time so long ago, when her mother had been around. She stabbed at another runaway tear.

She'd be a good mother. A great mother. And they'd always be together.

Always.

***

Meg sat bolt upright at the sound of the sharp knock on her door.

Looking around in a moment of confusion, she quickly remembered where she was. After all, how could the room not be familiar? She'd spent most of the night tossing and turning, staring at the walls in the moonlight, comparing the symmetry of the flowered designs on the wallpaper of each wall in an effort to keep her mind off more alarming things. She hadn't been able to fall asleep until the first streaks of dawn had lightened the sky.

She rolled onto her side to glance at the clock-radio sitting on the bedside table, but then another louder knock on the door sent her scurrying out of the bed and reaching for the oversized T-shirt lying across the foot of the bed.

It was eight-thirty, way too early for any cleaning person to want to see to the room, but then, with one fluid motion she pulled the shirt over her head as yet another knock sounded at the door.

"Wait a minute. I'm coming," she called out, hurriedly reaching for her glasses and setting them on the bridge of her nose. Walking toward the door, she stole a quick glance in the mirror on the other side of the room and groaned at her disheveled condition. Combing one hand through her hair, she pressed her face against the door.

"Who is it?"

"'Tis your wayward and disobedient lover," a man's voice answered dramatically from other side. "Home after a night of drinking around town. But I promise to make it up to you. Let me in, my darling."

Meg felt her face heat up at the sound of Evan's teasing tone.

"You're such a goof," she answered, reaching for the latch and opening the door a crack. "Does somebody write this stuff for you?"

On the other side of the door he stood, again dressed in running shorts and a worn T-shirt which managed to enhance his build. He was leaning against the door jam and, as she opened the door, he casually pushed at it, opening it wider.

"You look pretty cute in that."

Flustered, Meg tore her eyes away from his face and looked down at her shapeless outfit and at the bare legs that stuck out beneath the knee length garment. There was absolutely nothing provocative about what she wore. He was just trying to rile her.

"Especially with the light from the window coming through your shirt."

She looked up and found his eyes traveling meaningfully down her curves as if he really could see everything beneath.

"Wrong door." She tried to close the door in his face, but he casually placed his size thirteen Nike in the doorway, stopping her from closing it completely.

"Oh, sorry. I should have known you weren't a morning person."

"I am *too* a morning person," she replied, giving his foot a kick before abandoning her thought of getting rid of him. "I'm very much a morning person, when it comes to normal routines."

"Then it's clear you're not accustomed to being told that you're irresistible in thin cotton shirts. Whoever it is you sleep with in Boston is a dope if he doesn't normally drag you back to bed when he sees you like this."

Meg swallowed hard and shook her head. "I don't think—"

"Hey, maybe you need a new routine."

She found herself entranced by the deep tone of his voice and the long lashed, hazel eyes that she swore could cast a spell. She watched helplessly as his hand reached toward her face and tucked a loose curl behind her ear. His finger lingered on the skin of her neck. Feeling her heart about to hammer its way out of her chest, she reached up and clumsily pushed his hand away.

"Jeez, don't you ever work?"

Evan stared at her a split second, and then grinned. "This is getting to be the world's most often asked question."

"Excuse me?"

"Look. It was a real good summer for cab drivers down here. Don't worry about it, okay?"

"Tell you what. I'll stop worrying if you'll stop practicing those corny pickup lines on me." She tried to put a note of reprimand in her voice. "Now, is there a reason why you're panting at my door so early?"

"Why, yes. There is. Four of them, in fact."

She looked at him critically. "Four?"

"Yup. There are four reasons for why I'm here. Which one do you want to hear first?"

"Is this like, good news/bad news? Or just bad, bad, bad, bad news?"

"Cute."

She crossed her arms over her chest and leaned against the door jam. "Give me number four and spare me the rest."

"Are you sure you don't want me start with number one?"

"Positive," she answered stubbornly.

"Okay. I'm here to pass on a message from Jada."

She straightened immediately. "Is she okay?"

"She sounded like it. They're releasing her and the baby from the hospital this morning. When I called her, she wanted to know if you wouldn't mind coming with me to take her home. She said something about needing a reminder of your clumsiness—or something like that—to make her feel more confident."

Meg smiled. "I'll be ready in a flash."

"You don't need to," he added right away. "They won't release them until around noon. That's after the doctors make their rounds. Anyway, I'm going for a run, and after that I still need to shower and shave. Have you eaten anything yet?"

Meg shook her head.

"Why don't you clean up and come up to my place in about an hour. I'm known for my killer Cheerios. We could take off from there."

"I'd love some Cheerios."

"Good. Top of the stairs. You can't miss it. It's the only door. See you in an hour."

Meg wistfully watched him turn and move quickly down the steps. She walked back inside the room and closed the door behind her. She had to get her act straight. Rebekah was right to scold her for not having pursued even the most innocent relationships with men. She had managed to become totally inept in dealing with them. Last night, after just a simple kiss, she had succeeded in losing a full night of sleep. Lying in bed, she had found herself tossing and turning, thoughts of Evan Knight invading her brain. Naturally, that had been followed by a longing for Robert, and by feelings of betrayal for thinking about another man. But despite her tears, despite her call for him, the spirit of her husband had stayed away.

Meg brought her hands to her cheeks as she remembered the rest of her night. Finally falling asleep, she'd had the most erotic dreams imaginable. And in all of them, Evan Knight managed to have the starring role.

CHAPTER THIRTEEN

MEG HAD DONE her darnedest to take her time getting ready. But, not too accustomed to the luxury of time, she was showered, dressed, and ready in twenty minutes. So trying to pass time, she called and checked her voicemail at work. She was relieved to find out that there was no doomsday message from her boss, Joe E.

The ninety-seven-year-old publishing house was closing its doors sometime this year. There were many pink slips handed out already. She was resigned to be out of a job sometime soon, but she'd still not started looking at other places yet. She had a good degree and over ten years of experience—this all should count for something, she thought. And then, there had been calls from other publishers over the years. And the ongoing word of mouth that so and so was looking for someone with just her qualifications. But those other jobs, with their better pay and seemingly brighter futures, had mostly been in New York. Somehow, she had never quite envisioned herself leaving the place where she and Robert had lived so happily.

Meg moved about the room, tidying everything she could put her hands on. She was a creature of habit. One who despised big changes. She loathed surprises. This was all part of what had drawn her and Robert together. He'd been ten years older than she was, but that hadn't mattered a bit.

From the first moment they'd met, it had been magic. They were so much the same in their personalities and wants. Early in his career, Robert had given up the hustle and bustle of big publishing in New York to move to Boston and work with a small publisher. She remembered him always saying that he much preferred to be the big fish in the small pond than the reverse. And that was exactly what he had been. He'd started working for Joe E. while she'd still been at school. Later, by the time she started there as a junior editor, Robert had moved into the position of managing editor.

As much as she didn't want to admit it to herself, Meg knew that was the real reason Joe E. hadn't let her go yet. Out of his loyalty to Robert. The years her husband ran the small publishing company had been the most profitable ones that anyone could remember.

Meg picked up a manuscript and sat in the window. She looked out at a lobster boat working a line of traps in the harbor. Publishing was an entirely different business today than it had been ten or twenty years ago. Perhaps it was best for her to be where she was, at present. An exhausted senior editor whose job was hanging by a thread. Heck, she could always move into the janitorial business.

Meg looked down at her watch. Close enough to an hour. She could risk going upstairs. And for once in her life, she wasn't going to think or worry about all the misgivings that always managed to hinder her enjoyment of life. They were going to Newport Hospital to take Jada and baby Ted home. That was it. Simple, with no complications.

Stealing a glance at her image in the wall mirror, she frowned. Simple, with lots of complications.

She climbed the flight of stairs to Evan's apartment and quickly lifted a hand and knocked at the closed door. Getting no immediate response, she glanced down at her watch. She was still five minutes early.

From her vantage point on top of the stairs, she had a view of the entrance foyer four stories beneath her. Looking down at the Oriental rug and the small table beside the door, she couldn't help but smile at her strange run-in with Phil Campbell last night. Considering what a fool she'd made out of herself, her landlord had been most gracious, even managing to ease her embarrassment over a drink and a few stories about his dog, Swift.

"Ah, you *are* out here. I was just getting out of the shower when I thought I heard a knock."

Meg forced herself to look up from his muscled chest, still spattered with drops of water. His hair was still wet, as well, and lay in attractive disarray around his face.

"You're wearing your glasses again. What happened, did I step on your contacts or something?"

She shook her head. "I wish I could blame you for that, too. But somehow this morning I couldn't get my eyes open wide enough to pop them in."

He gave her a dimpled half smile. "Late night partying?"

"Late night of something," she offered noncommittally, looking past him inside the bright apartment.

"Well, I guess I better let you in." He stepped back and held the door open for her. "I still have to shave, but the coffee is ready. There's some orange juice in the fridge."

She just nodded and stepped past him, breathing in his clean smell. At least he was wearing his jeans, she thought, watching him head toward a door that she assumed must be the bathroom.

"I thought we could eat outside on the balcony. It's a pretty nice day out."

His voice was a mere muffle over the water running in the sink. Sliding her hands up and down her arms, she looked around at the large room she was standing in and smiled. Decorated in roughly the same style as her room, this one had the added charm of built-in bookcases covering one wall. Outside double French doors opened to a rooftop balcony and Meg could see the harbor and the sparkling Narragansett Bay beyond it.

Out of the corner of her eye, she caught him sticking his foam-covered face out of the bathroom door.

"Very attractive look," she quipped.

"Oh, thanks," he replied, pointing a razor at the kitchen. "If you don't like coffee, you can put water on for tea. But I don't think I have any fancy, herbal tea stuff."

"Coffee would be great."

"Good. Then pour me a cup, too."

She placed her tote bag on a nearby chair and followed the smell of the brewing coffee to the kitchenette, where a steaming pot sat waiting.

It was matter of habit to pick up the phone on the first ring. But then, as soon as she did it, she looked at the receiver in her hand in embarrassment. Cursing herself, she glanced in the direction of the bathroom, but once again she could hear the water in the sink running. Well, the heck with it, she decided finally, bringing the phone to her ear.

"Hello."

There was a short silence on the other side before a man's voice boomed out. "Excuse me, but I must have the wrong number. This is not Evan Knight's residence, is it?"

"Yes, it is," she admitted, looking hopefully toward the bathroom.

There was a short laugh. "Sorry. I'm just trying to recover from having the phone answered on the first ring." There was a pause. "Let me see, is this Jada?"

"No, it isn't," she said with a smile. "This is Meg Murphy. And you, you're not Ted, are you?"

"No, this is Henry."

"Hold on, please."

She tore the phone away from her ear and pressed it to her chest. Evan was glaring at her from the bathroom door.

"Sorry. The phone rang and…" Meg decided it was not worth explaining and instead stretched the receiver in his direction. "Someone named Henry. I didn't get the last name."

With a hand towel thrown over one shoulder, she watched him close the distance between them and take the phone.

He looked genuinely aggravated, and Meg quickly decided that it would be best to give him as much privacy as possible, so she quietly moved out onto the rooftop balcony.

She would never in the world describe herself as a person driven by curiosity, but Meg was finding Evan Knight more and more interesting every day. She couldn't remember ever *knowing* a cab driver before, but he just didn't fit the mold of what she would have imagined.

From where she stood with her back to the balcony railing, she stared at full bookcases lining the wall. The books must be Phil's, she reasoned. Like the furniture in the apartment, and the house itself.

What was Evan doing living here? This place was certainly not as expensive as the Inn, but it still wasn't cheap, either. And an apartment like this—she turned and glanced at the view of the harbor—had to cost some money. Well, maybe he was some kind of house sitter or something. A handy man, she thought. Phil had mentioned to her last night that he spent a lot of his time sailing and traveling to buy and sell boats. Maybe that was it. Evan Knight, in addition to being a cab driver, was a handy man.

He sure as heck didn't look like one, though. She swallowed, watching as he balanced two cups of coffee and two glasses of orange juice, and tried to open the screen door, as well. He looked more like a cover model for *GQ*. She quickly moved forward and opened the door.

"Thanks," he said, moving toward the porch furniture.

"Can I give you a hand?"

"Sure." He turned as he headed past her. "Come in and fix your cereal."

She did as she was told, following him into the kitchen. It wouldn't have bothered her at all, she realized, if he hadn't put on a shirt. She noticed that he was still barefoot.

After a couple more trips, Meg found herself seated on the balcony beneath a broad umbrella, with a spread of cold cereal, English muffins, coffee, and juice before her. Certainly a better spread than what she was used to back in Boston.

To Meg's relief, Evan didn't mix any mention of the previous evening with their cereal. Instead, like the merry maidens of Penzance, they talked about the weather, and then lapsed into a comfortable silence as they sat back with their coffee.

"I went back last night and read a couple of chapters of *The Long Journey* again."

Meg winced openly. "Before you start, I have to apologize for the way I acted."

"Oh?"

She looked up and met his piercing gaze.

"People, I mean fans, have a right to admire and to believe in their heroes. To follow them to the end of the earth if they want. I mean that's true not just with writers. Just look at team sports. I mean, I'm a rabid Red Sox fan." She smiled hesitantly. "Well, the more I thought about our talk yesterday, the more I was convinced that it was wrong of me to be so snappish about the work of someone whom you obviously enjoy. Someone you respect."

"So does that mean you've changed your mind about reading Drew King's books again?"

"What are you, his agent?"

"Not the last time I looked."

"Perhaps. Sometime. There are a lot more writers out there that I like to read first." She paused. "But I know I need to work on not being so opinionated. There's no need for me to force my beliefs down anyone else's throat."

She watched him looking at her over the array of dirty dishes. She had no idea what he was thinking, and his silent scrutiny was a bit unnerving.

"So..." She reached forward and picked up her coffee cup again. "You mentioned that you picked up *The Long Journey* again. What do you think?"

He looked out across the harbor before shaking his head and looking back at her.

"It was lacking some things."

"*Yes!*"

He scowled at her. "No gloating."

"I never gloat." She hid her grin in her cup. "But I *am* used to being always right."

"You're joking." He arched one eyebrow as he leaned forward and plunked an elbow on the table. "Or are you?"

"Good coffee," Meg said brightly. "Are you a big reader?"

"Reader and a writer."

She looked up and met his eyes. "Really? What kind of writing?"

"I do a little bit of everything. Right now, I'm working on a cab driver's manual. But I'm thinking about a book on my life dealing with ornery but cute tourists."

"You're joking," She leaned forward in her chair and leaned on one elbow, mimicking him. "Or are you?"

He gave her an amused smile and then frowned, raking one hand through his hair.

"I'm also trying my hand at a book. Fiction."

"*Really?*" This Evan Knight was a surprise a minute. "That's wonderful. How far along are you?"

A wince crossed his face, and Meg immediately backed up.

"I'm sorry." She started again. "I didn't mean to be pushy. It takes…I'm sure it takes a lot of work to finish a book. I was just wondering…"

Evan's look told her he was sorry he'd started this conversation. Well, no sense letting him off the hook.

"I was wondering, do you have an outline, or do you just dive in?" She gazed encouragingly at him. "And how many chapters have you finished so far? But most important, what the heck are you doing chatting over breakfast with an ornery tourist when you should be writing the next blockbuster of a novel?"

He looked at her askance. "What did you say you do for a living?"

She blushed. "Sorry, that was my personal greediness talking. I'm just too desperate to find a good book to read."

"And what makes you believe I'm capable of writing a *good* book."

She paused and gave him a scrutinizing once over. "Let's see. Well, you definitely have a warped sense of humor, and that helps. And as much as you like to act tough, you're clearly thoughtful and well spoken. You've also admitted to me that you are a reader. Now, as far as actually writing the book, did you ever take any courses in creative writing?"

"Once. When I was in college," he answered casually. "I didn't get much out of it, though."

"No?"

"Nah, they were mostly poets and capital 'L' literary types."

"And you didn't fit in with them."

"I never looked good in a beret."

"Okay, so you have one style point we have to detract from your score." She continued to study him. "Oh, I forgot to mention that you hate your present job."

"How the hell do you figure that?"

"Easy. You never do it. If I were your boss, I'd have tossed your you know what out on the street long ago."

"You mean my ass?"

She paused, and then waved a hand in the air. "Back to the writing. I still don't know a thing about your ability as a story teller."

He gave a snort. "What's there to know?"

"Well, you tell me. Give me a plot. A twist. Some characters. A snapshot of what you're writing about. And then I'll tell you if it's worth—"

"Shit?"

"There's no need to be vulgar. But yes, I'll tell you if it's worth shit."

"You know, this could just be a line I'm throwing you."

"Could be. Guess that depends on what you say next, doesn't it?"

"Well, wait a minute, now." He pushed his chair back a bit from the table and stretched his legs out. "Before I start telling you any of this, what are your qualifications for recognizing shit from Shinola?" He grinned at her.

She picked up an English muffin, carefully spread some straw-berry jam on it, and handed it to him. He took a bite out of it and gave it back to her.

"I'm waiting."

Meg racked her brain to think of a good answer that wouldn't give away her profession. The idea of not telling him what she did for a living had all started as a joke, but now—knowing that he was really an aspiring writer—the thought of throwing 'expert' cold water on a dream held her back.

Meg knew he would be a lot more comfortable talking about this if he never knew what she did for living. But on the other hand, no matter how excellent she thought his story was, she was in no position to buy any manuscripts for their soon to be closed publishing company. In fact, the only reason why she had taken it on herself to bring all those manuscripts with her was so she could write a personal rejection and maybe some positive remarks to the writers.

"I don't know." He leaned forward and brought her hand with the English muffin to his mouth and took another bite. "When you were trying to figure my qualifications, you were pretty quick to list the good and the bad. So what's wrong? How come you're tongue-tied when it comes to yourself?"

"Maybe I was hoping for you to figure *me* out in that department?"

"Fine," he smiled, reaching over again and taking the last of the muffin out of her hand. "I'm game."

"Let's see. You're obviously an avid reader."

"You're cheating," she responded, looking at him crossly. "You jumped to that conclusion based on what I have told you."

"No. That conclusion was based on a first-hand, eyewitness experience."

"What do you mean, eyewitness?"

He pointed to the ledge of the balcony, just beyond where they sat. "I can see you at night. The first night, I think you were too tired, so I just saw you go to bed. But last night...you had that midnight oil burning late."

In her futile attempt to keep him out of her mind last night, she'd resorted to reading some of her manuscripts. But what did he mean about seeing her getting into bed? She looked down at the three windows.

"I'm pulling my shades down from now on."

"Don't do it on my account," he replied, his dimple mischievously reappearing.

Meg thought back, trying to remember if she'd taken her shirt off before or after she'd turned off the light.

"Fine," she sighed. "I'm a reader. Is there anything else about me that makes me qualified to hear your story?"

"You're brutally honest," he added, growing serious. "And you're no wimp."

"Thanks, but what does not being a wimp have to do with all of this?"

"In case if you don't like my story and I have to beat you up."

"Okay," she nodded, satisfied. "Sounds to me like I'm quali-fied. Does that mean that I get to hear it now?"

He scowled at her. "Only after you promise to accept my conditions."

"Oh no." She sighed. "Let me guess. This doesn't have anything to do with sex, violence, or slavery in Newport, does it?"

"No. But if you'd like, I could add those in as perks of employment."

"I was just joking. Now start. I want to hear this before we have to go and pick up Jada and Little Ted."

They both looked down at their wrist watches the same time. Ten o'clock.

"And my conditions?" he pressed.

"Jeez, you're a pain. Tell me what they are."

He gave her a pleased look, and Meg almost laughed out loud.

"I have just one condition," he said finally. "Be gentle. I'm very sensitive when it comes to this stuff. I'm just starting to like you, so watch it."

She rolled her eyes. "Yeah. Fine. I'll behave. As long as you stop acting the part of your idol, Drew King, and just be yourself."

He paused a second and looked at her curiously. "'You think he's sensitive?"

"Sure, he has to be. You know he changes editors every five minutes. Why else would he do that? He's got to have some serious insecurities about his work."

"How do you know all of that stuff? About his editors and all?"

"*The Boston Globe*. They had an article about him Wednesday." She pushed all the dishes to one side and leaned on her elbows, facing him. "Now I'm sick of talking about him. Let's start on you."

"Me?" he repeated.

"Tell me the story."

"Okay."

Meg saw the muscles in his jaw flicker once. Then, taking a deep breath, Evan lunged into his story.

She sat attentively and listened. He explained the story of a murder that takes place amid the high society of Newport. The victim, a popular and valued member of the upper crust, is found dead on the rocks beneath the Cliff Walk that borders the sumptuous mansions of the moneyed elite. In the wake of the murder, a husband and an estranged half-sister face a pressured police force and a frenzied news media.

Meg nodded as Evan talked about the importance of this work not being a standard mystery novel, but a psychological thriller in a real-life setting.

He talked a bit about the details—the fillers, the snapshots of the glamorous life, the sex and the violence—and about the final resolution of the novel where he reveals that the victim's half-sister, rather than the husband, has skillfully engineered the cold-blooded murder.

When he finished, she sat back and studied him for a moment.

"Well, tell me," he asked impatiently. "What do you think?"

"It's good. Very good."

"For an amateur."

"No." She shook her head. "On the contrary. This is an excellent book for someone who is already established, but not for someone trying to get published for the first time. To set yourself apart from all the other murder suspense out there—to attract the reader to a name they're not familiar with—you'll need more complications in your characters and in your plot. You need a twist that sucks the reader in."

Upon seeing his face cloud over, she quickly leaned across the table and caught his hand in hers.

"Look, I know I sound harsh, but listen to me first, before you get bent out of shape and decide to throw me over this railing."

"I am bent out of shape," he snapped. "And I don't see the difference. A good book should stand on its own. No matter who wrote the damn thing."

"True," she snapped back. "Then what do you want me to tell you? You asked me to be gentle. I'm trying to be."

He took his hand out of her grasp. "Forget what the hell I told you. I want to hear all of this. And let me have it straight."

"Look, I was trying to do just that before you lost your temper." She waited a moment to make sure he could handle it.

"Go ahead."

"Evan, the story is great. You have it mapped out really clean. But there isn't much depth in the relationships, based on what you've told me."

"How the hell am I going to tell you the whole thing in five minutes? Those are things I'll invent as I go along."

"Okay," she conceded. "How about the murder?"

"What do you mean?"

"Is the focus on her death or the struggles of the husband who is being accused of her murder? Or is the focus on the dead woman's sister, who you say is the real murderer."

He put a hand on top of his head and stared at her for a long moment. "What are you getting at?"

"Well, I'm thinking motives," she continued. "You hinted something about the surviving sister having been in love with the husband. Since *forever*, if I got that right. And also, that her life-long jealousy was the reason for the murder. How about the husband's feelings? Perhaps he could have been in love with the sister, as well."

"Sure, but they were too young back then. Just teenagers. He definitely had a thing for her, but it was puppy love. They weren't old enough to be held responsible for their promises or their actions."

"How old were they then? Fifteen, sixteen? What about this?"

She leaned forward and stared at him. "Maybe they had a child. Maybe she'd had to have the baby all alone."

"You're talking about Jada."

"I'm talking about your book," she corrected. "Could it be that the killing was not a ruthless crime? Could it be that it was one of revenge, justified at least in the killer's mind?Revenge for a much more hideous crime committed by the dead sister long ago?"

"You're trying to force a twist into the plot."

"No. I'm trying to introduce you to your characters. The secret of who we are now always lies in the past, doesn't it? Your characters are all there, waiting to tell you more about themselves, and their pasts." She leaned back against her chair and met his eyes. "Our lives aren't simple, so don't force theirs to be any different."

Evan stared thoughtfully at her for a moment.

"You have a great story, Evan. But I think you should spend a little more time and get to know your characters. And when *you* feel comfortable, you're there."

CHAPTER FOURTEEN

JADA TIDILY PILED her belongings on the bed. Looking at the care packages that the hospital was sending her home with, she knew her backpack would never hold all of it.

At least when Evan and Meg came, they'd have plenty of hands to carry the stuff down. She glanced at the little clock radio on the night stand, wondering if she should call Evan and remind him about the infant car seat. But she shook her head. He'd remember.

She'd planned to leave most of the flowers, but the balloons were coming home. She smiled at the big teddy bear, sitting like some scowling person on the chair.

"You're definitely coming along," she said out loud.

Jada looked up and smiled as the nurse brought in another package of diapers for her to take home.

"I saw the staff pediatrician going in to check on your son now. It should be no time at all before you'll be ready to go."

The young woman nodded and wrapped her arms around her still bulging middle. Her own doctor had been in to see her earlier, and everything was fine. She just couldn't wait to get home. Her father might get back by the end of the weekend, and she so desperately wanted to have the apartment ready for him. When he came through that door, she wanted to present him with a happy picture of life with his new grandson.

And she knew, despite all his gruffness, he was happy that she'd kept the baby rather than give it up for adoption.

Jada heard the dividing curtain move, and she turned, her eyes focusing on the grave-faced doctor who'd just stepped in. Her heart dropped into the pit of her stomach.

"Hello. Ms. Serra?"

Tensely, Jada stepped forward and shook hands with the man.

"One of the hospital's social workers is on her way in, but why don't you sit down. We've got some things to talk about."

His mind suddenly elsewhere, Evan closed the dishwasher and ran the towel vacantly over the countertop.

A minute or two earlier, Meg had disappeared into the bathroom, and Evan now leaned against the kitchen counter. Through the door into the sitting room, he could see the laptop on the table by the couch.

For several minutes, not a muscle moved in his body, but his mind was racing. Standing there, he found himself organizing all the new ideas and thoughts flooding through his mind.

There was a lot of truth in what she'd said about his grasp of the characters. When *he* felt comfortable, when *he* knew them, he'd be ready. No, he'd be there, she said.

Since *The Long Journey*, he hadn't been there. But now, suddenly, a roaring excitement was building within him, racing in his blood, and he felt the itch at his fingertips. Ideas were beginning to explode in his head. And every one of them was crying out to be written down, tested, heard.

Heard. He glanced in the direction of the closed bathroom door. Never before today had he ever asked for someone else's input on an idea or on a proposal for a book. He worked alone, wrote alone, and he alone told Henry where to sell them. Simple as that.

But today, with Meg, he'd felt different. Something else had been going on. He'd been looking for, hoping for, her approval. But why? He ran a hand through his hair. Was it because he'd heard her rip his alter ego, Drew King, to shreds?

He watched her appear in the doorway. Any other woman, he thought, would have been fixing her makeup or some such nonsense. But not her. She didn't even look like she wore makeup. She looked fresh and scrubbed and as beautiful as he remembered.

She smiled at him as she came into the kitchen. She looked around at the empty counters.

"Hey, perfect timing," she quipped. She took the towel out of his hand and hung it up on the little hook by the sink.

In the small space of the kitchen, he was all too aware of her sweet scent, of the brush of a hand, of the curve of her buttock as she leaned forward over the sink.

He couldn't stop himself from touching her. In a sudden rush, Evan felt his creative juices mixing in with a strong and lustful urge to hold her and to kiss her and to run his hand beneath the sensible white shirt that she had so neatly tucked inside her khakis.

As she turned around, he moved until he stood right before her. Evan watched her look up and meet his gaze. A rosy hue crept into her cheeks, but she didn't back up and that gave him all the permission he was after.

He removed her glasses and laid them on the counter. As he did, she placed her hands against his chest.

"What's this all about?"

"How about if we just consider it part of the breakfast menu." He encircled her waist. "Call it dessert."

"Oh." She smiled. "I've never had dessert with breakfast."

As she lifted her parted lips to his, Evan felt the fires of desire flare up in his loins.

It was madness. It was pure lust. It was the most carnal mating of tongues and mouths that he'd ever experienced. Withdrawing and plunging, searching and delving. Over and over again, he found himself making love to her mouth. The heat blazed between them, engulfing them both in a scorching and passionate madness.

She shivered in his arms as he pulled her body tight against his. He groaned into her mouth when she rubbed her hips seductively against him.

He hungrily tugged the shirt from her pants and reached beneath it to feel her skin. She was silky soft, and when he ran his hand upward, cupping her breast over her bra, she moaned deep in her throat.

There was no holding back. They turned until her back was against the fridge door. He shifted her into his arms, and she lifted one knee as he pressed against her inner thighs. Meg leaned her head against the fridge door as he hurriedly stripped the shirt over her head and tossed it onto the counter.

He gazed into her half-closed eyes before delving his tongue once again into her mouth. Then, drawing back slightly, he slid his hands along her spine until he reached the clasp of her bra. That, too, joined the shirt on the counter.

"You are so beautiful."

He looked at the nipples hardening under his circling thumbs. Her breasts were round and full. Perfect, he thought appreciatively. She gasped when he lowered his head and suckled the waiting prize. As her fingers raked through his hair, he continued his play, kneading and caressing one breast while his mouth and tongue paid homage to the other.

But it wasn't enough. Her hips ground against his thigh and her half gasps of breath told him how close she was to release. He reached down quickly for her belt and zipper and undid them. She turned slightly, and his fingers slid over the downy mound and slipped into her, drawing from her a moan of pure pleasure.

Damn, she was sweet, he thought, continuing to stroke her and feeling her rock intimately against his hand.

She clutched his hair and lifted his mouth to hers as their tempo increased. He plunged into her mouth again and again, his tongue and lips playing out what his body craved to be doing. Suddenly, she cried out—her body rigid with ecstasy—then moaned and wrapped herself tightly around him. And he held her, gentling his strokes as she continued to shudder.

A moment later though, she pulled back and tucked her face into the crook of his neck. He still could feel the tremors of pleasure running through her, the aftermath of her climax traveling in waves through her limbs. He placed gentle kisses against her hair, the soft skin of her neck, and drawing his hand from the juncture of her thighs, he cupped her firm buttocks.

She straightened her head. Her face was flushed, her lips swollen, her eyes still glazed with rapture.

"I...I'm..." she breathed.

"Shh." He silenced her words with a brush of his lips. She was perfect. Beautiful and sexy and so much ready for more.

Hesitantly, she slid her hand down over his chest, continuing lower to his jeans until she found his aching manhood. He was so aroused that he figured he'd burst through the denim any second now.

And then he couldn't think anymore.

"When you came down to my room this morning..." Meg placed a soft kiss on his chin. "I remember you mentioning something about four reasons for coming to my door?"

"What?" Evan frowned, trying to focus on what she was saying. Then he smiled, moving them both until his back leaned against the counter. She stepped in between his legs, and he looked down appreciatively at her perfectly shaped breasts pressing against his chest. "But I thought you didn't want to hear those reasons."

Meg's hands worked themselves beneath his shirt. With one fluid motion he peeled the thing over his head. Her skin was cool and smooth against his.

"How about if I say I do now."

"Well, I told you the fourth reason." He pushed her khakis over her hips, giving her just enough freedom to step out of them. "But the first one. Let's see. Oh yeah. I couldn't sleep last night. In fact, I think I wore a path between my bedroom and the balcony. Kept watching you, sitting curled up in the window for a while and then moving to your bed. To be truthful, I was looking forward to seeing you take that T-shirt off again."

Although she was standing practically naked in his arms, Meg turned a pretty shade of pink. "So reason number one is that you're a voyeur."

"Only under certain conditions."

"I suppose that's all right, then. And I guess you saw me take my shirt off."

"Only the first night." He took her chin and lifted it to look into her face. "But I have to tell you, I like this view much better."

She nodded mischievously, then reached down and started undoing his belt. "And the second reason?"

Hooking his thumbs into her panties, he pushed them down her legs.

"The kiss." He brought her tightly against his chest and bent his head. Slowly, seductively, he took possession of her mouth once again. "But you know, even *this* is better than I remember."

She reached between their bodies and started lowering his zipper. "And the third reason?"

He paused, holding his breath, as her soft hand reached in and encircled his throbbing member. "You just discovered the third reason all on your own."

As she pushed his pants over his buttocks, he realized that they were not going to wait until they could get to his bedroom. Not even the sofa, he thought, growing wild at the feel of her fingers fondling and massaging the length of him.

Hell, the counter will do just fine, he thought, turning her as he quickly lifted her onto the edge. It'll do for this first time, anyway.

Suddenly he stopped. Reaching over, he opened a drawer next to them and rooted blindly through the contents. She left off kissing and biting his neck and looked into his face.

"What are you doing?" she asked innocently.

"Protection. Condoms."

She smiled with amusement even as she reddened. "You keep them here in your kitchen?"

"In the catch-all drawer." He pulled one out and tore the wrapping with his teeth before handing it to her. But she simply studied it as if she were looking at one for the first time. He took it gently out of her hand. "I'll take care of it."

But before Evan could do anything more, Meg reached over and answered the phone on the first ring.

───────

She didn't have enough time even to fasten her seatbelt before the Range Rover took off like a shot.

"Are you sure Phil won't mind you just taking his car?"

"I don't give a shit what Phil minds," Evan growled, running the stop sign and cutting across America's Cup Avenue. Meg turned her head and stared as two cars veered and slammed on their brakes, avoiding a collision.

"So was there anything else that Jada said?"

"No."

Meg placed a hand on the dash as the vehicle sped up a narrow street.

"Just that they're not releasing the baby," he said, concern evident in his voice. "She was too hysterical to make any sense beyond that."

Seeing the approaching stop sign and intersection, Meg decided it would be best if she didn't look. She played back in her mind the short telephone conversation that had launched them out of that apartment.

Though she'd handed the phone to him directly, she could hear Jada's tears, the broken phrases, and the plea for them to come right away.

They'd both dressed in a flash and raced downstairs. He hadn't been able to start the cab and had dashed back into the house. In about five seconds, he'd burst out the door again, waving toward the Range Rover.

Meg pressed her foot hard on the floor mat, trying to brake for him as a car suddenly pulled out of parking space and into their path, but Evan jerked the vehicle onto the empty sidewalk and around the unsuspecting slowpoke. She didn't even want to think what would have happened had anyone been stupid enough to be walking there.

They screeched to a halt in front of the hospital in record time. Stepping out of the car, he clutched her hand, and Meg had to run to keep up with Evan's long strides.

Jada was slouched against the wall in the hall of maternity ward. Her puffy, red eyes spoke clearly of how shaken she was. When Evan opened his arms, she walked straight into them and began to sob. He stared grimly at Meg over the young mother's head.

"They aren't giving my baby to me, Evan. I can't take him home." She cried softly into the tissue that Meg offered her and tried unsuccessfully to dry her face. "They're saying that he has a heart murmur or something, and because he is underweight, they want to keep him here a few more days."

"Where's the doctor?" Evan pulled back and looked into the young woman's face. "Do you mind if we talk to him again?"

"No." Jada shook her head, and then flashed a look of anger. "But I'm not a fool, Evan. I heard everything that he had to say. He's not letting my baby go, but I am not leaving here without him."

Meg watched, feeling completely useless as the raw emotions of the young mother burst to the surface. Standing there, she remembered that horrible day five years ago, when she had stood her ground and angrily demanded the doctors and nurses release her husband. She simply couldn't understand that Robert was dead.

No. They were lying to her. He couldn't have gone like that. Without a warning. Without a word of good-bye.

Evan's calm words penetrated her thoughts. She reached up and dashed away at a tear from her own cheek.

"You stay here with Meg. Let me go and talk to him. I'm the fool. And I'll ask the same questions again and again until he gives us the answer that we want to hear." He leaned down and looked directly in Jada's eyes. "You don't want to do anything that would hurt little Ted by taking him out of here before he's ready."

Jada choked out a soft cry and shook her head. "I love him, Evan. I love him more than anything else in my whole life. But I won't live through this if they take him away from me. I couldn't put him up for adoption—these social workers talked to me again about that. But I couldn't. I can't. Now I am afraid I'm going to lose him anyway."

"You're not going to lose him. Nobody is going to even try to do that. Do you hear me? *Nobody* will take Ted away from you."

Meg moved close and put an arm around the young mother's shoulders. "How about if we wait in your room, sweetheart. Just give him a chance to go and find out whatever he can."

As Jada nodded, Meg looked up at Evan and for an instant

their gazes locked. She knew he would do whatever needed to be done. Whatever was humanly possible.

Meg didn't think her legs were much steadier than Jada's as the two of them moved back into her room. Seeing her bags and the baby's belongings already folded and ready to go on the bed brought another pang of sadness to Meg's heart. She sat the young woman in the chair in the corner, and then pulled up the straight chair beside her.

The next half an hour, though, had to be one of the longest she'd ever experienced. There was no point trying to cheer her up. Meg offered her a cup of juice and a pillow, but Jada just withdrew into her shell. Holding the young mother's hand in her own, listening to the hospital sounds, Meg felt totally helpless.

When Evan walked into the room, they both straightened at once. But rather than spilling out all he knew, he pulled a chair from the other side and sat before them.

Meg listened silently as he went through and started explaining why the doctors had decided to keep the baby in the hospital for another day or so. He also added that Jada was encouraged to spend as much time as she liked with the baby, keeping him company. And then he started talking about the heart murmur and despite the fact that a large number of children are born with them and have no further complications, because of Ted's size the doctors just wanted to be on the safe side. They simply wanted to run some tests. Just in case.

He went on and explained exactly the sequence of tests that they would perform—electrocardiogram, echocardiogram, and a few others—but Meg's mind was already drifting back to Robert. His condition could have started just as simply as Ted's. Maybe if they'd found his problems when he'd been younger. She forced herself to focus on the discussion.

"I'll take you home," Evan was saying. "You can drop your things off at the apartment, and I'll drive you back here as soon as you're ready. We need to be sure that—"

"I can't jerk you around like a chauffeur." Jada seemed calmer, more composed. But somehow Meg knew this was all a pretense, perhaps for Evan's sake. "You've already done so much."

"Listen to me, young woman. I've already told this to you before. Until your father returns from his trip, you are—"

"I know. I'm your responsibility."

Jada came to her feet and moved to the bed. She absentmindedly began to jam everything into the small backpack.

"This is no trouble for me." Evan came to his feet and ran a hand through his hair. "You have that baby to think of. Why don't you leave everything else to me?"

"It's not that simple," Jada whispered, never turning.

"You're the one making more of this than there is. From what I just heard, these kinds of procedures are quite common these days. So there is no reason for you to act like it's the end of the world."

There was no response from Jada.

"I know, it's not fair to drag a kid like you through this whole business like this. But if you weren't so stubborn about protecting the scum-bag that...well...then you wouldn't be feeling this miserable and alone. It takes two to make a child, and it takes two to take care of it."

As Meg saw Jada's chin drop to her chest, she came to her feet and stared sharply at him.

She whispered quietly to the young mother. "How about if we have him drop us off at your place. We can find a way back here, ourselves. He's just trying to be helpful, but he's upset too. I think he needs to cool his jets. What do you say?"

Jada considered for a moment and then turned her dark eyes toward her appreciatively.

"I'd love to have you hang with me, but this can't be the way you imagined spending your vacation. Babysitting a rotten teenager? I don't think so."

Meg put her arm around Jada and squeezed her, placing a kiss on her cheek. "Sweetheart, I wouldn't have missed this for the world. Meeting you has been one of the highlights of my life."

When she pulled back, she saw the tears again gathering in her eyes. Without warning, the young woman put her arms around her and hugged Meg tight.

Holding her protectively in her arms, Meg ran a hand down the young girl's hair and thought of how Jada was nearly the same age of any daughter she and Robert would have had, if they'd had children of their own. Biting her lip, she blinked back her own tears.

But she was no child. She was a woman. A young mother. One who was being forced to face the problems of adulthood and motherhood all in a same roll of the die. And she needed to be treated as an adult.

She saw him move into her line of vision. Evan Knight. The man who no doubt had the best of intentions, but who had not a clue of the turmoil in this young woman's mind. Jada simply didn't need fathering right now. She didn't need someone to make her decisions for her.

"I'll take few days off," he started.

"You don't need to, Evan." Meg was the one this time who cut him short. "We can call you when we need you."

His darkening glare told her that he was clearly not happy with her intruding into what he considered his responsibility. She'd explain it to him later. She had no intention of interfering with a supportive relationship that was essential to Jada and the baby. She didn't want to replace Evan. She only wanted to complement him.

"I'm here with nothing to do and nowhere to go. So I thought, rather than you losing some pay and missing work, I can hang around and spend time with Jada. This sure beats doing the same touristy things I have been doing every other time I've been down here."

"She's right, Evan," Jada added, turning and facing him. "I

would just as soon have Meg with me than have you get in trouble with your boss."

To Meg's thinking, most men would have been relieved to hear what they were saying to him, but instead, Evan looked genuinely ticked off.

Picking up the giant teddy bear from the chair and stuffing it under his arm, he started toward the door.

"I have some things to take care of. I'll meet you by the car."

Jada was first one to speak after Evan disappeared through the door. "I think I hurt his feelings."

"No, I made him mad. But he'll get over it."

Jada sank against the bed. "I'm the one that made a mistake. I can't allow other people's lives to be ruined trying to help me. If I'm stupid enough to have unprotected sex—if I am old enough to have a child—then I'd better be old enough to walk or take a cab back and forth from our house to this hospital."

Meg couldn't help but smile. "I don't know. Walking is one thing but taking a cab—especially with a maniac driver like Evan —I don't think anyone is ever old enough for that."

As the trace of a smile brightened Jada's face, more than ever before Meg thought that everything would work out. The teenager had intelligence, good sense, and she was well aware of her responsibilities and the rough road that lay ahead of her.

Meg glanced at the open door. And that was much more than she could say about herself.

CHAPTER FIFTEEN

EVAN CURSED OUT ALOUD. The first thing he was doing tomorrow was to buy Jada a new goddamn cell phone. She'd lost hers last week and wasn't answering her home number.

He shouldn't have let those two get away with what they did.

Still brooding this morning, he'd driven Jada and Meg back to the apartment in the project off Memorial Boulevard. They'd specifically told her they'd call when they needed him.

And did they call? he steamed. No, dammit!

For chrissakes, he should have known they wouldn't call. They'd never called. He'd been home all day, sitting at his computer, patient as a time bomb.

What was he supposed to be doing? Ignoring his responsibility?

Plunking himself down at the table again, he stared angrily at the computer screen and the jumbled mass of gibberish he'd written. He'd worked the whole goddamn day and hadn't even been able to write a decent murder scene. He'd thought it would come easy to him today. Hell, all he had to do was imagine Meg as the victim and himself as the murderer. But somehow, he couldn't do it. In his warped mind, he was more inclined to feature her as a lover than as a corpse. As an opinionated, big-mouthed, interfering mistress.

And aggravating. And kindhearted. And sexy, with a body that—

"Don't start," Evan muttered sharply, disgusted with himself.

They had gone back to the hospital, that much he knew, since he'd called there himself this afternoon and talked to one of the nurses. But it was past nine o'clock now, and they should have arrived back home already.

Friday night in Newport. Evan just hoped that between the two of them, they had enough brains to catch a cab or something back to Jada's house. He didn't even want to think of the trouble they might run into if they'd decided to walk.

For the first time in a millennium, he leaped out of the chair and picked up the phone on the first ring. Jada couldn't even get two words out before Evan let her have a piece of his mind. But that was nothing, compared to what he was saving for Meg, who got the phone as soon as Jada could pass it to her.

"I heard you shouting from the other side of the apartment, and I wasn't even trying to listen." She never gave him a chance to cut in. "For a man your age, you are the biggest baby. We had every intention of calling you, but when visiting hours were over, Jada just wanted to get some fresh air."

"Please don't tell me you two walked home."

"Jeez, Evan. Of course not. Jada only delivered two days ago. We took a cab up to the corner of Bellevue and Memorial Boulevard and walked from there. It wasn't far."

"I can't believe you could be so irresponsible."

"Really, I don't see why you're so bent out of shape."

"For a woman who lives in a city, how could you be so completely clueless to dangers."

"This is Newport, Evan. Not New York."

"And where do you think the well-to-do New York rapist hangs out on the weekends?"

"You're ridiculous," she scolded. "If you could only hear yourself. Listen, Mrs. Jeffers is here, and Jada is going to bed. So if you're done chewing us up…"

"What are you doing? Staying over?"

"No, I'm walking home."

"You step out of that place and I swear I'll wring your neck with my own two hands." He let out a frustrated breath. "They have riots in that neighborhood at night, Meg. Between there and here, there are drug pushers and weirdoes lurking in every dark alley."

Her voice lowered to a whisper. "Sounds like a lovely spot to raise a child."

"Jada knows how to live in those streets, and Little Ted will be safe, because most of those kids are scared shitless of her father. But you, on the other hand, are fair game."

There was a pause on the other end. "Fine. I'll call for a cab, even though I know you're only saying these things to scare me for nothing."

"Just wait there," he ordered, his voice becoming calmer. "I'll come and pick you up."

"Why? Not done chewing me up for today?"

"As a matter of fact, I'm not." Evan paused for effect. "But that's not the only unfinished business we have…if you recall."

From the long silence Evan could tell that she had picked up his hint. Even through the phone, he could tell she was smiling. It was that cute, almost shy, little half-smile. Dammit, he thought, for the past couple of hours, in between trying to murder her, all he'd been able to think of was how much he wanted to crawl into bed with her tonight.

"I don't know, Evan."

"I'll pick you up in fifteen minutes."

"I'll be waiting outside."

"No. Inside," he ordered. "Hear me, Meg? You wait inside."

"I'll be here."

She hung up on him, and he gave the place a quick and cursory look. Hell, everything looked okay, he thought as he pulled on a clean shirt and headed out. Pausing at the door, he stopped and crossed the room to the kitchen. Pulling two bottles of wine out of the cupboard, he looked at them. White or pink, he mused, a frown creasing his forehead.

"Hell," he muttered, stuffing them both into the fridge. "She probably likes red."

Outside, the cab would not start again. Evan sat for a moment, and then banged the wheel with his hand. He'd bought the damn thing used six months ago, but not even once had it given him any trouble...until this week. And the strange thing was that he couldn't figure what was wrong with it. He was pretty good with cars. In his younger days, before he had a Porsche to piss in, he'd kept his own junks running. But come Monday morning, he knew he'd be dropping this lemon-yellow clunker at the garage.

Before giving up completely, Evan looked around and made sure no one was watching. Feeling stupid even as he tried, he jiggled the wheel three times, the way Meg had done it. No luck. Obviously, there was no magic in his touch.

As he crossed the threshold into the house, he contemplated taking one of Phil's cars, but something inside him made him climb the stairs three at a time to his own apartment. Going to the kitchen, he picked up the keys to his Mercedes.

Despite all his warnings, she was waiting by the curb when he pulled into the lot in front of Jada's building. When he brought the car to a stop, Evan watched her study the expensive sports car carefully before hesitantly climbing in.

He watched her every movement keenly. But all of the reprimand he'd saved up sailed right out the open roof as soon as he looked into her serious face. She ran a shy hand over the leather seats before sitting back.

Evan found himself putting both hands on the wheel to stop from reaching over and pulling her against him. The urge to devour that sexy mouth was nearly overpowering, but the sudden click of her seatbelt drew an amused smile to his lips.

"Nobody bothered you, I take it."

"Actually, a gang of kids came by, so I shot them and dragged their bodies into the shrubs over there."

"Oh, that's a good spot." Evan backed the convertible out of the space.

"I'm amazed Phil allows you to drive his expensive cars around dangerous old Newport at this hour of the night."

He knew she intended it as a joke, but somehow, the fact that she automatically assumed the car belonged to Phil rankled his male ego.

"Is Jada already asleep?"

She studied the gadgets on the dash. "You were driving this thing around the Point section last night. Weren't you?"

"Yeah, I was." Evan felt his gasket ready to blow. "It was me all right. As you've already guessed, I'm nothing more than an errand boy for the great master. I house-sit Phil's bed and breakfast. I drive his cars around and fill up his stinking gas tanks when he commands. I even pick up and drop off his girlfriends whenever the lord of the manor wishes it."

He slammed on the brakes at the corner, and then screeched into the traffic racing along Memorial Boulevard.

"Sensitive subject, I see."

Evan growled and jerked the car into the left lane. As he stopped for a light, he glanced over at her. She was staring straight ahead. He wanted to strangle her and kiss her at the same time. There was something in this woman that just managed to melt him from the inside. He needed help.

He turned and gave her a half glance as the traffic started

again. Crouched against the door, rubbing her arms with her hands, she looked tired and a bit fragile.

"Are you cold? I know there's a sweatshirt in the back."

"No. Thanks, I'm fine."

Ignoring her, he reached behind them and handed her the gray sweatshirt.

"Have you had anything solid to eat today?"

There was a trace of a smile on her face when he looked over.

"Do you always feel that you have to take care of everybody?"

"What?" He didn't answer, but then, following an impulse, he veered to the left and turned onto Lower Thames rather than heading back toward the house.

"Where are you going?"

"It's a beautiful night. I thought before returning dear old Phil's car back to him, we could take a ride out on Ocean Drive. How about it?"

"Sounds wonderful," she whispered quietly, watching the people on the sidewalks as they passed.

They drove in silence for a few moments until the boutiques, museums, restaurants, and bars gave way to neighborhoods and then farms. As they passed the manicured fairways of the country club, the fresh, salt air felt even cooler as it washed over them. Again glancing at her direction, he felt a surge of raw desire ignite within him as he watched her tuck the sweatshirt around her, close her eyes, and lose herself to the feel of wind on her face and in her hair.

"What did you mean by saying what you did back there? About me feeling that I have to take care of everybody?"

"You asked me if I'd eaten today." She pushed her glasses up on top of her head and turned those magical eyes of hers on him. "You were worried about me. As you worry about Jada and Baby Ted and their future. And about Mrs. Smith and her hip replacement. And about Grady and his bypass surgery. And about—"

"Hold it there. Where are you getting all this stuff?"

"Jada and I had plenty of opportunity to talk today. But that's not even half of it. There seems to be this mysterious source of funds that happens to appear whenever anyone you know is in a need. This afternoon Jada called their insurance company, and then talked to accounting folks at the hospital. You know what? She found out that *somehow* all the deductibles and even some more costs had been taken care of. Isn't that amazing?"

"Her father must have taken care of everything before he left on his trip."

"Nice try. Like Ted, Sr. would pay for Mrs. Smith's private nurse when she got home with the new hip."

"What's the point of all this?"

"You." She gave him one of her enchanting smiles. "Seeing the way you help all these people and knowing how little time you actually spend at your job, I'm convinced that you must be embezzling money somewhere and just haven't been caught yet. Actually, the only thing missing in this picture is a band of merry men to help you steal from the rich before you give it to the poor. Now do I have it right, or do I have it right?"

"Stealing from the rich." He furrowed his brow. "Like *Robin Hood* or *To Catch a Thief*?"

"Hmm. Definitely Robin Hood. Besides, you look more like Errol Flynn than Cary Grant." She nodded with certainty. "No, this is no Sherwood Forest. This is absolutely *To Catch a Thief* with a plot twist. You're certainly into helping others. Much more than Cary Grant, if I remember the movie correctly."

He couldn't hold back his own smile.

"Ha! I'm close." She straightened and leaned at his direction. "So let's go back and correct the misperceptions. This is not Phil's car, but yours. The house, as well, is yours, and you use him as a front to hide your operation. Now, the cab thing is a perfect ruse for you to get in past the high voltage fences and security gates around these mansions. I see you're still smiling. I think I'm getting hot."

"You are really hot."

"Yeah? Well, I'm not Grace Kelly hot, in case you haven't noticed."

"As a matter of fact, I *have* noticed," he corrected, making a sharp turn into Brenton Point Park.

Evan loved this part of Newport. Down here, with the long concrete seawall and the wide grassy stretch running beside it, a person could feel truly alive with the ocean crashing onto the rocks, and the wind buffeting one with the salty sprays. Coming here always brought him back to memories of his past. To the days of diving. To the nights of going ashore. To his love of the sea.

His eyes spanned the open stretch of rocky shore. There were always people out here, day and night. Summer and winter. Never too many, but always a few. Fishermen, kite flyers, sunbathers, scuba divers...lovers. Pulling the car into a parking space over-looking the ocean, he shut off the engine and turned off the lights.

"How beautiful."

He turned in his seat and looked at her awed expression. "Yes, you are."

Reaching over, he took her glasses off and placed them on the dash.

Suddenly struck silent, she sat looking at him.

"And you were saying?" he growled, running one hand through her wind-blown hair. "About illicit activities?"

"Are you armed?"

He nodded. "And dangerous."

Evan watched her throat pulse as she tried to swallow.

"What do you plan to do with me?" She quickly glanced at the direction of the waves rolling onto the dark rocks straight ahead. He could see her hiding the beginning of a smile. "I mean, now that I've discovered your deep dark secret."

"I think I'll just have my way with you, and then get rid of the body." He dug his fingers into the thick hair at the nape of her neck, holding her in place as he softly began to massage the tenseness from the muscles there. "Let me see. I'll start with a kiss first, to catch you off guard."

Using his other hand, he traced her lips with the tips of his fingers, smiling as she parted them at his touch.

"And after I'm done with the mouth, I'll just strip off this very pretty shirt of yours." With deliberate slowness, he pulled away the sweatshirt she'd draped over her. Then, with equally deliberate slowness, Evan ran the backs of his fingers down her throat, lingering over the little hollow at the base. He heard her breath catch as he brushed his hand against her breast. "How are you holding up so far?"

Meg nodded vaguely.

"I'm sorry to hear that, because you should really be suffering by now. Well, after I've disposed of your shirt, I'm tearing off the bra and throwing it away. They're stupid things, anyway. And right after that, I'm going to work you out of these pants."

Running his thumb along the waistband of her pants, he smiled as she shuddered and closed her eyes. Gently, he slid his hand down into the juncture of her legs. With a low moan, she opened them ever so slightly.

"Ah, this is good," he whispered, massaging her through her pants. "But somehow I have to get myself over to your side of the car, without you escaping, so that I can force you to sit on my lap."

He hadn't even kissed her yet, but her parted lips were full, ripe with desire. Her eyes had that dreamy, glazed look, and he knew he had the power to take her to a blissful release. He moved closer, his face hovering over hers, his fingers increasing the tempo as she began to move with him.

"And then, when you think you can't take any more, I'll make you take me out of my pants and fit me inside of you. I'll make you ride me, Meg. With the sea breeze blowing in your hair. With the damp sea air on your face. With my lips on your breasts, I'll be sucking at your nipples. You'll force me to fill you up until we're both ready to explode."

"You're a devil, Evan," she panted, reaching out and gripping his arm. She moaned again. "Oh, my God. I can't."

"Then don't." Quickly, he unfastened her pants and slid his fingers into the wet, pulsing folds of her womanhood. "Ride me, Meg. Ride me hard and let me see you fly."

Twisting and convulsing in his arms, Meg cried out in an explosion of ecstasy, and Evan smiled as she sank onto his shoulder, the aftershocks of rapture still racking her trembling body.

Lifting her gently, he dragged her across the center console and fitted her in the snug space on his lap. As she lay her head against his shoulder, he just held her tight. He could find no words to describe the feeling that suddenly filled his heart at having her curled up in his arms.

"I must be the easiest woman you've ever met."

"No. But you may be the sexiest."

"I fall apart as soon as you touch me."

"You're passionate. Beautiful. Full of life." He lifted her chin until he could look into her dark eyes. "I can't help myself, Meg. I just can't seem to get enough of you."

He lowered his head and kissed her mouth. She was a dream, just as he remembered her to be. All willing and soft and giving. For a second the thought came to his mind that if ever there was a woman that he could spend never-ending days with, it was this one.

Evan put a quick end to their kiss as the lights of another car pulling into the park drew his attention. As Meg hurriedly scurried to her side, straightening her pants and grabbing for her glasses, he laughed out loud. She had the look of a teenager who had gotten caught in the back seat with the preacher's son.

He reached over and tucked a loose curl behind her ear. "I'm not done with you," he growled. "And I still need to dispose of the body."

She gave him a shy and hesitant smile, but then sighed contentedly.

The newcomers pulled into a space too close for Evan's comfort, and he turned to glare at them.

"They have the whole damn lot."

Starting the car, he pulled out, and in a minute the Mercedes was snaking along the dark curves of Ocean Drive.

"You never did tell me if you had any dinner."

"No, I haven't."

"How about if we pick up some food and go back to my place and have a midnight picnic on the roof?" He knew from her smile that he didn't have to be any more enticing than that.

As they rode along, he realized it hurt to think how much he wanted her.

"How about if you let *me* buy *you* dinner, this time?"

He frowned at her.

"Come on. It's only fair."

She seemed determined.

"Okay, as long as it's 'take out'."

"No way."

"Why not? I have chairs in my apartment. I'll let you sit."

She shook her head. "Dinner, wine, candlelight, something a little bit formal."

"I can do that in the apartment. I'll even be the waiter. White gloves and the whole bit, if you want."

Meg smiled mischievously. "Knowing you, you'll probably wear white gloves and nothing else."

"Yeah, but I'll wear them formally." He placed his hand on her thigh. "We'll set a new standard for formal dining. You undress me, and I'll undress you...except for the gloves, of course. Then, instead of utensils, we'll use our fingers and feed each other."

Shyly, she reached over and ran her fingers along his leg until they reached the pronounced bulge in his jeans. The engine roared as he nearly ran right into the car in front of them.

"I don't know, Evan." She gave a soft giggle. "Do you think you can last that long?"

"Just try me. I dare you."

Her laugh thrilled him, and he grinned.

"Do you want to skip the dinner part?"

"Love to," he replied with a meaningful look. "But you haven't eaten, and La Forge is just ahead. We can order take out from the bar. Sound okay?"

Hearing no immediate response, he turned and glanced at her again. Suddenly she looked deep in thought.

"What's the matter? If you don't like La Forge, we could go someplace else."

She shook her head. "No. I'm just being silly. I used to go there all the time. I think I've been there every year since I started coming to Newport. It has great food."

"Good. But I'm not letting you buy this dinner. That place is too expensive. This is on me."

"No, it's not," she replied. "A deal is a deal. You provide the place and the white glove service and I provide the food."

He slapped the wheel with both hands. "Boy, I love pushy women."

It took Evan a couple times around the parking lot across the street before he found a parking space.

Crossing Bellevue Avenue to the restaurant, Evan noticed Meg looking up at the Casino, the Tudor-style building that housed La Forge, a dozen little shops, and the Tennis Hall of Fame.

"Interesting building. It was built by Stanford White, I think."

"They like to preserve the old here in Newport, don't they?"

"Only what's worth saving," he said, wrapping an arm around her as they reached the sidewalk. As a passerby approached, giving Meg the once over, Evan glared at the over aged preppy in his penny-loafers and blue blazer. "And anything that'll draw a tourist."

Inside, the place was crowded with people, most of them still waiting for a table in the restaurant, and the ancient teak bar was three-deep with customers. Pushing through the throng, they made their way to the hostess and ordered dinners.

"Do you want a drink?" he asked once their orders were in.

"No, thanks."

"Good." He said, keeping his face serious. "I want you sober, at least until we get to the apartment."

"Maybe I'd better get a double of something," she replied with a smile.

Pulling her back toward the door, Evan tucked Meg next to him, noticing that her smile quickly faded into a thoughtful, almost troubled, look.

"Are you sure this place is okay? We can wait outside if you want."

She shook her head.

He ran his knuckle on her soft cheek, and she looked up and met his gaze.

"What's wrong?"

She paused a moment before answering. "I guess I just have too many memories from this place."

"What kind of memories?"

She looked back into the crowd. "My husband and I..." She stopped and cleared her throat. "When Robert was alive, we used to come to Newport every year, and this was one of the places we used to go out and eat. We always took out a table overlooking the grass tennis court."

"Well, this was a great choice on my part, wasn't it?"

"It's a good choice. I told you I was just being silly. That was all in the past." She reached out and took his hand in hers. "Come on, let's talk about now."

"Okay. Let's see."

"Did you get a chance to write today?"

"What are you, my agent?"

"No." She smiled. "Do you need one?"

Damn. It would be so easy to give himself away. Maybe he should, Evan considered for a moment. But then he knew she would be angry for the way he let her rip Drew King apart to his face. And embarrassed. No, he decided, it would be much better to wait. For now, anyway.

"Hell, no."

"Well, did you get anything done?"

"I did. But I don't think it's any good." He crossed his arms over his chest and glared at her. "In fact, I think it's all your fault. I used to be able to sit and write for hours without ever doubting anything I wrote."

"Really?" she replied, amazement in her voice.

"Yes, I did. But now, after talking to you, I'm not sure anymore. I keep questioning myself. Doubting my judgment."

"I'm sorry," she said thoughtfully, brightening immediately. "But the things you used to write before, where they any good? Are you still happy with how they came out?"

"Not all of it. A lot of it was shit."

"Well, that's good then." She smiled warmly at him. "I guess, in a selfish way, I'm glad. See, now you're the one who's reaching for something more. A story that is perhaps better. Doesn't that make you a better writer?"

He leaned one shoulder against the wall. "I guess so. But what about all these newfound insecurities? What about all of the sudden feeling like I need a second opinion on what I write?"

She paused a moment. "You need a critique partner. I've heard that a lot of writers have somebody they can talk to about their work."

"No way in hell."

"Okay. Maybe that's not for everybody. But how about having someone who could just stay on your butt?"

"Hey, I like the sound of that, as long as it's you."

"I'm serious. I'm talking about somebody who could keep you to a daily routine, who can sometimes be a sounding board for you to bounce your ideas off of. You must know somebody."

"And this 'somebody.' You think I'd let them read my unfinished stuff and give me an honest opinion of whether they think it's a pile of shit or not?"

"Exactly."

He couldn't stop a grin from creeping onto his face. "So, will you take the job?"

Meg stared at him for a moment. "Sure. I'll read your work if you want me to. But don't get too used to it. Don't forget, I'm heading back to Boston next week."

Evan had a vague sensation of that pubescent, teenage demon again taking possession of his soul. "I didn't mean just for this week. I meant do you want this on a more permanent basis?"

She looked at him in awe for an instant and then, as the meaning of his words sank in, he saw her become visibly flustered. But how could he blame her? Just what in hell was he saying, anyhow?

"I wasn't suggesting all those things because I was fishing for work."

"I know," he answered. "Look, I value your insight. I just asked you a simple question. What do you think?"

She frowned and glanced up at him. "You know, you're one of the most puzzling people I've ever met in my life. I don't know what's going on with you. I never know if you're serious or not."

He continued to look at her in an unwavering expression. "Do you want it or not?"

He could hear the coldness creeping into his tone and her look told him that she heard it too.

"And just give up my present job? I don't think you can afford me."

"No?" he replied, forcing himself to lighten his tone. "Hey, I thought you were the one who had me all figured. I can afford you the same way that I can afford to help Jada and Little Ted and Mrs. Smith *and* Grady. Being a cab driver in Newport is a profitable business. Hell, especially for someone like me, who also gets to work as errand boy for Phil Campbell, the all-powerful Oz."

She gave him a grim smile before turning her gaze back to the crowded bar. He could have sworn that she seemed disappointed. And what the hell did he mean by all that? For an instant, he'd even fooled himself. But his offer had been genuine. He'd wanted her to say yes and stick around. For some reason, he needed to know that she wouldn't be walking out of his life next week.

"*Evan*! My God! Lucy, look over there. Evan Knight!"

"Shit." He never even had a chance to turn his back before the taller of two identically blonde women literally threw herself at him, plastering her body against his chest and looping her tanned arms around his neck. "Ah, Cornelia."

"I've been trying to get hold of you for weeks."

"Evan?" Lucy unceremoniously yanked Cornelia's arms away and took possession of his neck, herself. "This is a fabulous surprise. Except for you, there's not a man left in this town."

A wave of disgust washed over Evan at the thought that as lately as six months ago, he'd tolerated rich bimbos like these two in his bed. He tried unsuccessfully to pull Lucy from his neck as Cornelia pushed up against him.

"So, handsome, here for the weekend?"

Lucy never gave him a chance to answer her friend's question before she started jabbering in his ear. "Evan, we have my Uncle Willie's place out on Ocean Drive all to ourselves for the weekend. For old time's sake, how about if we pick up some food and head out there. Just the three of us. We won't have to surface until Sunday for the Ball. Ooh! This is so exciting. A hot and steamy weekend with Evan Knight. Hey, maybe you can use us in one of your books."

Cornelia laughed inanely. "He's done that already. Don't you remember the—"

"Look," he barked, desperate to shut them up. "It's great seeing you two, but I have other—"

"Come on, Evan," Lucy whined, her face falling into a well-practiced pout. "There's nothing to do down here if you won't come out and play."

"Look, I..." He physically pushed the two away and turned to look at Meg. Suddenly, though, everyone in the place seemed to be crowding around him, except Meg.

"I had new implants done this summer. You've got to see them."

He dragged his hand out of Cornelia's grasp before she could pull it to her breast. Where was she? he thought shortly, looking around the two in search of her.

"Meg?" he shouted over the noise of the crowd.

"Who's Meg?"

The one woman's question was answered by the other. "I think she was that geeky looking little thing he was talking to before we came over."

"Come on, Evan."

"Meg?" He shoved past the two, looking for her. But she was nowhere to be found. Thinking that perhaps she had gone to the ladies room, he ducked through into the little hallway by the restroom doors. Evan waited for a few minutes, but after watching a league of women go in and out with still no sign of her, he gave up on that idea.

Shoving his way through the bar and ignoring the pleas of his two former playmates, he took a peek outside, hoping that she'd just stepped out to get some fresh air. But he could find no sign of her. Worry started to mix with irritation as he searched out the hostess who had taken their order.

"Yes," she told him in response to his question. "The woman

you came in with paid for your food and left. Uh, will you be needing a cab?"

Angrily, he charged out of the place. Where the hell could she have disappeared to, anyway? Storming back to his car, he realized that already, in their short acquaintance, he'd spent more time driving around looking for her than he had done for all the other women he'd ever known. Driving the streets at five miles an hour, checking every alleyway and deadend street between the restaurant and the apartment, Evan was beside himself by the time he reached the B&B.

He took the steps three at the time until he reached her room. But before he could wake up the house hammering down the door with his fist, he spotted the neatly handwritten note taped to her door.

Hi Evan. I've got a terrible headache, so I'm hitting the sack early. Left the dinner by your door. Enjoy, Meg

"Enjoy, Meg," he repeated sarcastically. He stood there for a long moment as he contemplated knocking on her door and letting her have a piece of his mind for taking off like that. But in the end, he decided against it. They had been having a good time until those two "Debbie Does Debutantes" had cut in on them.

Then a devilish gleam came into his eyes. She was jealous.

Well, first thing in the morning, he would clear the slate with Meg about Lucy and Cornelia. Those two women meant nothing to him, other than to remind him of the immaturity of some of his past, uh, relationships. He wouldn't give either of them a second look. On the other hand, he was growing really fond of Meg. Perhaps it was time that he should let her know that, too.

Maybe it was time to start revealing some of the truth.

CHAPTER SIXTEEN

COME ON, Robert, Meg pleaded. *Please, talk to me.*

She stared out at the harbor tour boat bringing in a group of tourists from a huge luxury liner anchored in the harbor. As the white boat swung noisily around the huge yachts, she turned and strode along the water, her sneakers scuffing at the wooden walkway.

I know you're around. I know you are just doing all this to spite me.

Only the cries of some gulls hovering over the sparkling water came back in response.

I mean, isn't there something we can do together? Can't you at least help me through this insanity?

She was miserable. Even this morning, her mind continued to torment her with the images of those two young women draping themselves across the same shoulders she had so trustingly leaned against only moments before, down by the ocean.

She sighed and tried to push Evan Knight out of her mind, forcing herself to think of the discussion she'd had with Jada this morning. When Meg had spoken with her first thing, the young mother had said that the hospital had called saying that Little Ted was doing great, and that when Jada arrived, they'd take him in for the first of the tests.

But Jada had refused Meg's offer of accompanying her this morning. She insisted on doing this alone—at least for the morning. She'd call Meg and leave a message if she wanted company later on.

After hanging up, Meg thought that Jada had sounded quite confident and self-assured. Definitely more confident than she was feeling right now.

"How can you be such a dip?" she muttered, unable to stop her thoughts from returning again to the events of last night. She watched a pair of sparrows skittering along the walkway and onto the grass, wrestling over a bit of stale bread that one of them had.

Evan Knight was a playboy and obviously had a different woman for every week of the year. Rich women, she corrected, remembering the comment one of them had made about her uncle's place along Ocean Drive. There were only mansions along that winding stretch of road.

Meg knew what Rebekah would say in a situation like this. Have a good time. Who cares if he's slept with every available female in town? Life's a fling and then you die.

Good old Rebekah.

Jeez, maybe she's right, Meg thought with a sigh. He's a man and she's a woman. He was certainly interested. That was clear enough. And she had definitely been living the life of a nun for the past five years. Meg felt a quiver in her belly at the thought of their few moments down by the ocean.

After all, it was ridiculous to expect that the first guy she got intimate with after Robert's death would be Mister Right. Rebekah had a line for that, too. In the absence of the other, go for Mister Right Now. 'Lasting Relationship' was clearly not Evan Knight's motto, so far as Meg could see. He was sexy, passionate, and knew exactly what to do to charm her out of her pants. In fact, he'd put her fulfillment ahead of his own from the very start.

What did she have to complain about? Why, for once, couldn't she accept Rebekah's advice and just think of this as a fling?

Meg closed her eyes for an instant and breathed in a lung full of the sea air. Unfortunately, she knew the answer. Because she was not Rebekah. She was Meg Murphy, the same unchanging person who was terrified of the thought of stepping out of her little world. She was a bird who had never lived outside of the comfortable cage she had constructed. She had never tried to fly on an ocean breeze.

This morning, she'd needed to escape the house. She'd needed to disappear and avoid any chance of running into Evan. Through the long hours of yet another sleepless night, Meg had decided that after all these years, she was far too fragile to be able to handle a man like him.

Meg slowed her steps and looked around. She needed to find Robert. To get back to where she would be safe, to where she knew she would be protected and loved for eternity.

"Did you know brooding is bad for your complexion?"

Startled, Meg whirled and then smiled as Phil Campbell fell in step beside her. She eyed with curiosity the large duffel bag that he shifted from one shoulder to the other.

"I wasn't brooding."

"If you say so. Then what's eating at you?"

"Nothing. Really. I was just taking a walk."

"Well, I don't buy it." He placed a friendly hand on her shoulder. "I spotted you when I came out of the marina office. You were lost to the world."

"So you took it on yourself to come and rescue me."

"Something like that." He turned her around until she faced the docks and pointed to a large, hunter green sailboat tied by the gas tanks. Swift was grinning at them from the boat, her long tail thumping on the teak deck. "Actually, I was going for a sail around the bay, and I just hoped that you'd come along."

She was actually pleased with the invitation but quickly shook her head. "That's really nice of you to ask. But I just don't think—"

"You don't think Evan would like it?"

She found herself rising to the bait. "He has nothing to do with it."

"Great, because it's a perfect day." Phil grabbed her by the arm and started toward the boat. "I've got everything aboard that we'll need. Nan packed a lunch big enough to feed half of Newport."

She planted her feet and looked up into his handsome face. "I'm not really sure about this."

"Come on, Meg. It'll be fun. Besides, we've got Swift to chaperone us. I'll call Nan and tell her you're with me."

"I don't think that's really necessary."

She hesitated for another moment to think it over. There was something about Phil Campbell that was so easygoing. And knowing that, romantically speaking, he had no effect on her made the whole thing very innocent.

Oh, the heck with it, she thought. It *was* a beautiful day. What did she have to lose?

A cheery faced nurse asked Jada to stay in the waiting area as an orderly wheeled the sedated infant in for a second echocardiogram. With a thudding heart, the young mother watched Little Ted disappear through the swinging doors.

He'll make it through all this. He will, she kept reminding herself. Trying to swallow the large knot that had risen in her throat and was threatening to choke her, Jada plunked herself down in the closest chair and absentmindedly dragged a copy of the local paper onto her lap.

She'd wanted to go through this alone this morning. She'd wanted to prove to herself that she was capable of dealing with the problems of life. But now, sitting all alone in this waiting room, her baby in the hands of doctors and nurses, all she could think of was the sense of helplessness that was making her feel so hollow inside. Yes, she was almost sixteen, but at her age—with no education and no job—how was she to support herself and Little Ted?

She loved her father, and it wasn't fair to expect him to do everything for them. Jada gnawed at her lip, thinking of the man who had suffered so much, financially and emotionally, during and after the long years of her mother's struggle with cancer. With a pang of uncertainty, she wondered how he would deal with the fact that his new grandson had an ailment. How would he deal with the possibility of more medical bills and more hospital stays?

She brushed away the tears that had dropped onto her cheeks. Reaching inside her backpack and taking out a tissue, she blew her nose.

"Sad story?"

She looked up in surprise as Evan sat down beside her.

He took the paper off her lap.

"The baby in there?" He nodded toward the door to the testing facility.

"Uh huh."

He frowned and gave the open page a cursory glance. From the scowl on his face she could see that he was in a terrible mood.

"What are you doing here?"

"Since when do I need a reason to come and check on you?"

"Since I'm no longer the helpless, pregnant teenager. Since I can take a cab across town myself."

He looked at her, and Jada could see the wheels turning in his head. But before he could start the lecture she was sure he was about to deliver, she leaned her head affectionately against his shoulder.

"I know. I know. You're the grown up, and I'm the kid. And until my father comes home, you feel totally responsible for taking care of me. Did I get it right?"

He grunted with a short nod and looked back at the paper.

Despite her struggle to prove she could do this on her own, she had a very special place in her heart for Evan. From the first time he had walked through their front door with her father six months ago or so, he'd continued to prove himself a great friend to them.

Looking up into his face again, though, she knew something was eating away at him. There weren't too many times that you could find Evan Knight in public with a day-old shave and such a beat look on his face.

"Are you still mad at me for not calling you sooner yesterday?"

"No."

"Are you mad at me for not asking you to drive me to the hospital this morning?"

"No."

"Did you lose your job?"

"No." He turned and eyed her suspiciously. "All right, enough with the questions, Miss Marple."

"Miss Who?"

"Never mind."

"Did you and Meg get into a fight?"

He turned his attention back to the paper, but she saw the hard clench of his jaws.

"You and Meg had a fight," she announced with certainty.

"Don't you have something to do? Something to read?"

She placed a hand on his bare arm. "Evan, aren't I your friend?"

It took him a long moment before he turned his hazel eyes on her face. She didn't even realize it until then, that she was holding her breath. Having Evan think of her as a grown up and not a kid, as a friend and not a responsibility, suddenly meant the world to her.

"Yes, I *do* consider you a friend."

She smiled. Hooking her arm through his, she sat silently for a moment as he continued to glance at the paper.

"I like Meg," she whispered a moment later. "I don't know, there's something about her that is so real, so caring. She's very cool, in her own way."

He didn't say anything.

"And I think you like her, too. She is different from most of the women who hang around this town, isn't she? For someone who is so, you know, desperate in her own life, she is so giving."

"What do you mean desperate?"

Jada bit her lips, forcing back a smile while she pretended to take her time to answer. She sure had his attention, now. All Evan Knight needed to know was that Meg needed help in some way, and he would rise to the bait. This might be her first attempt at matchmaking.

"Well, you know she's on the verge of losing her job." Jada pulled another tissue out of her bag. "And I think she's still bothered by her dead husband. Did you know she hasn't been able to go out with anyone since his death? And that was five years ago. She's getting older, too. She's already thirty-five. She said a friend told her she had a better chance of getting hit by an asteroid than finding a marriageable bachelor at her age. But she told me she's sorry that she and her husband never had a child of their own, in spite of what some dork we both know said the other day. What else do you want to know?"

He looked at her in silence for a long moment. Whatever he and Meg were fighting about, Jada knew that Evan was trying to push it all aside and focus on what she'd just told him.

"How do you know all this?"

"Women talk, you know. And Meg and I have spent a lot of time together the past couple of days." Jada paused a moment and then turned and looked into Evan's face. Suddenly, he didn't look so beat. "Now that I think of it, though, some of that might have been meant in confidence. Don't say anything. In fact, forget everything I just told you."

He regarded her in silence for another moment.

"You know," she continued, "I talked to her this morning. She sounded pretty bummed out when I told her I wouldn't need her here with me today."

"Not too bummed out," he put in shortly. "She's out sailing with Phil."

Well, at least now she understood what his problem was.

"Great day to be on the water. Did you talk to her before she left?"

"No." He started staring at the paper again. "I heard about it from Nan."

The cloud descended over Evan so quickly that Jada could only look on in wonder. In some ways, Evan reminded her of Matthew.

How many times had the two of them escaped down the Cliff Walk, him brooding silently, her trying to drag out of him whatever it was that was bothering him that day? How many times had they climbed to the bottom of the beat-up old Forty Steps, just to sit by the water and talk until they were both feeling better?

"She hasn't had much of a vacation so far, do you think?"

A muffled grunt came through the dark cloud. With a hard shake of the paper, Evan refolded the thing and focused on some article.

"Evan, she told me about how she met Phil. She doesn't care a thing about him, you know."

He moved a bit in his chair but continued the pretense of ignoring her.

"I really think she likes you. I mean, anytime I'd bring up your name, she'd get this pretty blush on her face, and her eyes would get all wide and dreamy."

He tapped the newspaper on his lap. "You know, I gave this kid a ride to the train station a couple of days ago."

He was being such a goof, she thought, trying to change the topic. "Evan, I'm talking about Meg."

"Well, I'm not," he said shortly, dropping the paper in her lap. "Did you ever see him when you went to the Priory School? Must be a pretty smart kid. He was just named a National Merit Scholar."

Jada looked down at the picture and felt the floor give way beneath her. Matthew Rand stared unsmilingly up at her from beneath the caption.

"As much as I detest the whole lot of them, he seemed like a pretty normal kid."

He'd been in town. He'd come back to Newport. But he had never called her. The picture dissolved before her eyes as Jada struggled with her emotions. What a fool she'd been to think that perhaps he would. What a fool! Unaware of everything else, she bit at her lip and struggled to breathe.

"So, did you know him?"

She shook her head numbly and got quickly to her feet. "Could you hold the fort? I have to use the bathroom."

Jada walked quickly from the waiting room with the paper clutched to her chest. She no longer had any control over her emotions. The hurt she felt was tearing her apart.

She had been such a fool. *Such a fool!* Here he was free to travel all over. His future was bright. National Merit Scholar. Matthew was all set.

And what about her? What about Little Ted?

She burst through the door into the bathroom. She'd be here. Right here. Ruined.

A total screw-up.

CHAPTER SEVENTEEN

It was time to learn a bit more about Meg Murphy.

Time to find out the reason behind all the secrecy about her job. And what the hell she was doing here in Newport. And it was definitely time to find out the truth behind what she had told Jada about herself.

He liked to help people. Everyone knew that he liked to help people. But he wasn't about to let anybody play him for a sap. Particularly, not her. He'd find out what was going on with her before going through with his plan...whether she wanted to confide in him or not. He didn't care if there were ghosts in Meg's closets, but he sure as hell wanted to know what they were.

Checking his watch, he reached for the phone and dialed the private number of his lawyer's office in Manhattan. It was almost noon on Saturday, but there was no doubt in his mind that John Peck would be in his office.

As the lawyer picked up the phone, Evan leaned against the door of the kitchen and stared out at the harbor.

"I'm glad you have no life, John."

"Evan. Here to serve, big guy. Are you in New York?"

"No." Evan was in no mood to chitchat, so he got right to the point. "I need you to find all you can about a woman named Meg Murphy. Here's her address and phone number."

On the way up to his apartment, Evan had taken the liberty of looking through Nan's books.

"Okay. Got it. Boston, eh? What is she, another charity case?"

"Not exactly."

"Okay. Well, what is it exactly that you want to know?"

"I want to know everything. Where she works. How much money she's got in her bank account. I want the names of any husbands or boyfriends. What she does with her spare time. Whatever else you think of."

"Bra size? Kinky habits?"

"You really do need a life, John."

"So true. And let me guess how quickly you want all this."

"I wanted it yesterday."

"I knew that. Well, Evan, I'm glad you called. You've just paid my salary for the day."

"If I know you, John, this call is probably paying your *week's* salary."

"Hey, it *is* Saturday. And besides, we just finished hammering out the movie deal on that classic of modern fiction Henry says you're hard at work on, so I know you can afford it."

"Well, you're on my time now, so get to work." Evan frowned and looked again at his watch. "Call me back with whatever you can get in a couple of hours. The rest, I guess, can wait until Monday morning."

"What, are you giving me Sunday off for good behavior?"

"Hey, I don't want to cut into your church time or anything. And John, when we talk on Monday, remind me to give you the details on a trust I want you to draw up for a young woman and a baby."

"Paternity suit potential, Evan?"

"Wishful thinking, pal." He paused for a moment as the sunlight flashed off the windshield of a yacht in the harbor. "One more thing. Send one of your people out to Tiffany's to buy a diamond necklace."

"What?"

"It's got to be today. And it's got to be like the one Grace Kelly wore in *To Catch a Thief*."

There was a noticeable pause on the other side. "A diamond necklace? From a...what, thirty-year-old movie?"

"Doesn't have to be exactly a duplicate. But yes, genuine diamonds. I want it in my hand by tomorrow noon."

"Tomorrow noon?"

"Hey, you said you're 'here to serve.'"

"I did say that, didn't I. Okay, Evan. We'll do what we can, but it's going to cost you."

"It always does, John."

Hanging up the phone, Evan grinned. If Meg Murphy was all he thought her to be, then he couldn't wait to see the look on her face when he gives her this little bauble.

As he stood at the counter, though, his grin was quickly replaced by a frown, and he headed outside to his balcony to look for any sign of Phil's damned sailboat.

He had been irritated as hell when he heard Meg had gone off so easily with his scumbag of a best friend, but Evan was much too stubborn to let that alone get in the way of his plans.

Hell, he was no fool. She'd done this to teach him a lesson, and he didn't really blame her. Trying to put himself in her place, Evan knew he wouldn't have been too happy if two studs had come up to them in a bar and felt her up in front of him.

After getting back to his room last night, he'd spent most of the night thinking of the offer he'd made to her in the bar at La Forge. He really botched that completely. But this morning, hearing Jada say that Meg was almost out of a job, everything had jelled for Evan. Now he had a plan.

Hell, call it an assistant, an editorial assistant. Just the way she herself had described it. Someone he could use to help him with his work. He already knew she'd be perfect for the job. Her honesty alone made her perfect.

The hunter green sailboat cruised around the northern point of Goat Island, and Evan watched the son of a bitch guide it skillfully toward its mooring.

Of course, Evan thought with a frown, there was still a bit of a complication in all this that he didn't really know how to handle.

After all, he'd never fallen head over heels for a potential employee before.

Meg, wearing her Red Sox hat, pulled the tote bag high on one shoulder and picked up the picnic basket off the wooden dock. Swift hopped out, nearly knocking Meg over as she passed, and loped away into the grass.

Hauling the dingy up onto the dock, Phil picked his other gear and stepped up beside her.

"I really want to thank you, Phil. It was a very nice morning."

"We'll do it again." He leaned over and took the basket out of her hand. "But next time, we'll go out for more than just a morning. We could take off for one of the islands? Maybe Block Island or Cuttyhunk or someplace like that."

Meg smiled as they started walking back toward the house. She truly did have a pleasant time sailing on the bay, but despite all of Phil's charm, her thoughts had never strayed too far from Evan Knight.

She just couldn't get herself adjusted to being so darned attracted to him. With the sun on her face and the rugged shoreline speeding by, her mind had wrestled over and over again with how confused he made her. She knew so little about him. Last night was proof of that. But during their morning together, Phil had spoken a couple of times about different things that Evan had involved himself in. Things like working with the fisherman's coop and helping families who needed it. Everything he said supported what Jada had told her.

She just couldn't figure him out. And short of just coming out and drilling Phil with all sorts of questions about the man, Meg could think of no other way to find the whole truth. But as soon as she'd started to ask, she had seen an almost protective look come into Phil's face. So she'd stopped. It was all *very* confusing.

Meg stopped and smelled a late blooming rose bud beside the path. Straightening up, she looked at the rosebushes leading toward the house.

Suddenly, she froze inwardly at the picture of perfect harmony before her eyes. At the top of the long stretch of the lawn Evan sat with a beautiful red-haired woman on the grass. And in Evan's grip, Meg noticed the baby. A babbling, happy baby who looked too much at home.

Meg couldn't force her legs to take the next step. She watched the woman lean toward Evan and whisper something into his ear. He gave a hearty laugh before lying back on the grass with the baby on top of his chest.

So this was it, she thought. This was the hidden truth about Evan Knight. Now she was going to be told that the redhead and the baby were Evan's. Finding Phil waiting for her to catch up, Meg pushed herself forward. The redhead lifted a hand and waved at them.

"Hi, Phil."

Meg watched the woman come to her feet. Figures. Drop dead gorgeous with flowing red hair that hung below her shoulders and a sun dress that did very little to block the view of a perfectly toned body beneath.

"Hi, Sarah."

"Just got here about fifteen minutes ago. I hope it's okay I brought Emma. She's been homesick at not seeing Evan much lately."

Meg looked down at the smiling baby jumping up and down on Evan's lap.

"Hi, Emma." Phil leaned down and tried to touch the baby, but Evan pulled her affectionately against his chest. "Hands off, Svengali. This one, at least, is mine."

Mine, Meg repeated silently. Suddenly, her anger drove inward like a spike, piercing her heart with an unbearable pain. She had to get away from here. Phil's words, though, stopped her in her tracks.

"Meg, I want you to meet my secretary, Sarah Owens, and her daughter Emma." The baby gave a loud shriek of laughter. "Emma has a way with men. Everyone, including her father Dave, who is all of two hundred twenty pounds, an ex-New England Patriots linebacker. She has all of us eating out of her chubby, little hands."

"They're not chubby," Evan protested.

"Thanks, Evan," Sarah responded with a smile.

Meg, struck speechless as the stupidity of her earlier assumption sank in, smiled weakly at the baby. She glanced down at the outstretched hand of Phil's secretary and grasped it like a life line.

"You have a beautiful daughter."

"Thanks, but she's really just a big flirt." The young woman leaned down to take the baby. "I don't mean to spoil your fun, Evan, but I have some papers for Phil to sign right away. And then we have to be on the road. You know Dave. He's a bear if he gets home for lunch and we're not there."

Meg watched as Evan reluctantly handed up the kicking child. For an instant, their eyes met, and she knew she had to get away. But with a quickness of a cat, he reached up and took her hand, using it to pull himself to his feet.

For a moment, the question ran through her mind of what she would do if he decided to kiss her in front of these two—to put his brand on her lips just as he'd done that the other night, when he'd found her and Phil alone here. But that was no more than wishful thinking, she realized. He let go of her hand and turned abruptly to Phil.

"We need to talk as soon as you are done with Sarah."

It was clear to Meg that Evan's words were not a request, but a curt demand. And like everything else, it only added to the confusion in her mind.

She decided this was the best time to flee. She needed to put as much distance as she could between herself and Evan, right now. So, with a few courteous words to Phil and Sarah, Meg headed quickly toward the house.

He caught up with her on the stairs.

"Have a nice time sailing?"

Meg paused, searching for the right answer.

"Fabulous."

She increased her speed up the steps. With Evan taking the steps two at a time, though, that didn't do much good.

"So what did you two do? I mean, other than sailing."

She stopped on the landing and shot a saucy glare in his direction. "Nothing more than what you and dear Cornelia and Lucy might do in a situation like that." She exaggerated Lucy's drawl. "I don't have to tell you, though. After all, other than Phil, there's not a man left in this town."

Meg had hoped for a show of anger, a little embarrassment, anything along those lines. But instead, he let out a hoot of laughter. She gave him her most venomous look.

"Oh, that's good. *Real* good."

She just about had it with him. Turning on her heel, she started toward her room, but before she could put the key in her lock, he moved in next to her, leaning against the door frame.

"You look very cute with that hat on, by the way. And no glasses. Giving the contact lenses another try?"

She tried to ignore the effect of his deep voice on her, but she missed her first try at jamming the key into the lock.

"Got some sunburn on your face. And on your arms."

She didn't want to turn and look at him, but her whole body warmed as she felt his eyes go over her.

"Never seen you in shorts before, but I sure remember what's underneath. Do you want me to spread some cream on you?"

"No thanks." Meg turned her head and stared as indifferently as she could into his hazel eyes. They were as deep as the sea. Ignore it, she told herself. Go inside. Close the door.

She couldn't.

"Phil did that for me. When we were on the boat."

As much as he tried to hide with a casual smile the quick flash of temper, she saw the color that crept into his face. This was the reaction she was after.

"He is just fabulous. He does everything just right."

The trace of smile was quickly disappearing.

"In fact, he invited me to go sailing with him to Block Island." She drove the key successfully into the lock and turned it this time. "Ooh! A hot and steamy weekend with Phil Campbell and Swift. Just the three of us."

"Well, that's pretty kinky."

"Only a shade kinkier than some other people I know."

She quickly opened her door and tried to close it behind her, but she had no chance as Evan shoved his way in, slamming the door behind him. Before she even had a chance to demand that he leave, he started on her.

"I can't believe you are behaving so immaturely."

"I'm immature?" she exploded, throwing her tote bag to the side. "Look who's talking? Casanova himself. Taking not one, but *two* bimbos to bed at a time. And you call *me* immature?"

"So you were threatened by those two, last night?"

"Threatened? Ha! But there sure as heck wasn't much left to the imagination, hearing them planning your hot and steamy weekend rendezvous."

He glared at her for a moment. "I am not going to stand here and apologize for my past. What's past is past, and that's all you need to know."

"Fine, you've said your piece. Now get out."

"I won't. I'm not done with you."

"That's what *you* think." She stormed past him and started yanking open the door, but he slammed it shut again.

"Look at yourself. You're acting like a jealous wife."

She whirled around. "And how about you? If you're so cool and indifferent, then why the heck were you ready to chop Phil's head off as soon we got back? And why did you follow me up the stairs? And why does it matter what Phil and I did on that boat. Or who I decide to screw in this town?"

It took him a moment to answer, during which his hot gaze burned a path down her face to her lips. "I don't know, but I'm sure as hell planning to find out."

As he took a step toward her in an attempt to trap her against the door, she quickly sidestepped and moved to the middle of the room.

"Now, just hold your horse right there. You aren't getting out of this argument that easy."

"Easy?" He gave a sarcastic snort. "You call chasing you, easy? You've got more evasive moves than an All-Pro wide receiver."

She gritted her teeth. "And *you've* got more tricks up your sleeve than a Vegas—."

"What do you mean, 'tricks'?" he growled. "Unlike you, what you see is what you get. When I say, let's have sex, I mean it. But you? You bat your lashes, you pucker your lips, and then, when I try to give you a peck on the cheek, you scream and hide under the bed."

She placed her hands on her hips and let him have it. "Peck on the cheek? You call tricking me into your apartment and then standing me stark naked in the middle of your kitchen a peck on the cheek?"

"But I didn't tear your clothes off now, did I?"

"I'm not finished," she growled back. "Talking about saying what you mean. You invited me for breakfast and not...not..."

"Sex. Say the damn word."

"I won't. Why do you have to be such an ass?"

"Look, I *didn't* invite you to have sex. What happened, it just happened. I don't plan out my life from here for eternity. I like spontaneity. Whatever happens, it happens."

"You're full of shit, you know that?"

"For someone who doesn't like vulgarity, you still manage to emphasize your points."

She lifted a finger and jabbed him in the chest. "Don't interrupt me again. I wasn't done throwing your lies back in your face."

"What lies?"

"The one about spontaneity, about not planning ahead." She knew she was shouting now. "Do you call putting a condom in a catch-all drawer, not planning ahead."

"I like having sex in the kitchen. Don't tell me you only keep your screwdriver and a tape measure in yours?"

"It's none of your business what I keep in mine."

She saw a devilish look come into his eyes. "You know, you are the one who is full of shit. You act like the Virgin Mary, but when it comes right down to it, you are as lusty and eager as they come."

"I am not."

"Now don't forget who you are talking to, sweetheart. Do I have to remind you of our first night?"

She raised a brow. "Nothing happened that night."

"Hey, I don't call a woman taking her shirt off and parading naked across a room nothing. Flaunting all that delicious skin, knowing all the while I'm standing on my balcony watching...suffering."

She couldn't hold in the burst of laughter. "You're a pervert. You just admitted to it. A peeping pervert who keeps condoms in his catch-all drawer and—"

"Can't get enough of his neighbor?" His voice dropped in decibels to an intimate growl. "Admit it, Meg. You're passionate, beautiful, sexy, full of life. And despite the pretense you like to put up for the world to see, you yearn to experience life. You long to be swept away on the lust that flows through you."

She *did* feel the blood racing in her veins. He was too close to the truth, to that inner truth which she had kept so carefully hidden for so long.

"I want you out of this room."

"You and I both know that you don't." He advanced on her, a sense of purpose lighting his eyes. "We've started something between us and until the time comes when we both understand what the hell it is that's drawing us together like this, neither of us is about to let go."

She shook her head. Suddenly everything had taken a too serious a turn. She knew she didn't have the inner strength to stop him. Lust wasn't the only thing driving her...but how could she tell him the truth when she was no longer even sure who she was?

"I think this is a mistake." Her words didn't sound convincing even to her own ears. "I'm not like your other women. I can't pretend to be here today and gone tomorrow."

Suddenly she couldn't go on. Backed up to her bed, he was so close. And the desire to be wrapped in his arms was blotting out all rational thought. She wanted to kiss him. She lifted her fists and banged them on his chest in frustration.

"I'm so confused."

He encircled her wrists with his hands. "Then let me help you get one thing straight."

He leaned forward, bringing her hands behind her back. She felt trapped but at the same time cherished, even protected. Most of all, she felt wanted and desired as a woman.

As he gazed down, her heart kicked hard at the walls of her chest. "This time, we take it easy. This time, we take it very slow."

His head dipped, and his mouth brushed across hers. His lips were full, soft, and warm.

"You tell me, Meg. Tell me when you want to stop. Tell me when you want me to leave. See, I know something about consent."

She still could feel his gentle fingers holding her tight beside the bed, but she had no desire to free herself from his grip.

"Did you go with those women back to their house."

He brushed her lips again with his own. "You have to ask? I followed you home like a lost puppy. To my thinking, there could be no offer more attractive than the shrimp scampi and the beautiful woman whom I hoped would be waiting for me here." He looked mischievously into her eyes. "Not in that order, of course."

She frowned, but he kissed away the look. Her eyes shut as he continued to graze over her face with his lips.

"But...but it was two of them, and there's only one of me."

He drew back and gave her a melting look. "One perfect you. One sexy you. One who turns me on even when we fight."

"Is that so?" She couldn't stand it any longer, and she stretched on her tiptoes. He took full possession of her lips. With his hands holding hers, he used only his mouth, filling her with his tongue and leaning into her until she could feel his passion merging with her own.

She pressed her body against his and lost herself in the kiss, in this mating that was more erotic than any sex that she could recall. She moved her body against him, rubbing against him with her breasts and belly, hips and thighs. Her body burned with the thrill of anticipation of what it would be like. When at last they came together. The two bodies as one.

She heard him moan. It was urgent, hoarse, muffled. Her hands were suddenly free as he reached down, cupping her buttocks and pulling her hard against him. They tumbled onto the bed.

She laughed softly as he rolled them both until she lay

sprawled on top of him. Then, reaching up, he took her baseball cap and threw it across the room.

"I hate the Red Sox."

"You'd better get used to it."

She smiled as he dug his fingers into her hair and brought her mouth down, kissing her deeply and leaving her dizzy with its power.

"Let's do it," he said hoarsely, nipping at her neck, running his hands over her shirt, tracing the sides of her breasts. "Let's really do it."

She sat up and straddled him. She could feel him, hard and erect and pressing intimately against her through his tight jeans.

"Only if you let me get you naked first." She started undoing the buttons on his shirt. "And after you are down to bare skin, you have to march back and forth across the room, *flaunting* yourself in front of the window."

"You get me naked, baby, and there won't be any leaving this bed."

"Good thing I don't have a kitchen."

He grabbed her by the waist and pulled them both higher on the bed. Meg laughed as he struggled to pull her shirt over her head. She sat there on top of him, her shear bra the only thing blocking his scorching gaze. But she wasn't about to let him advance any further, not until she'd given him some of his own medicine. She grabbed his busy hands and pushed them in mock bondage above his head.

"Now, stay. Don't move."

"And if I do?"

"I'll have Phil put plywood over my windows."

"I won't move."

She smiled down at his handsome face. His eyes turned a deep, dangerous blue as she leaned down and started using her mouth to caress his chest. Pulling his shirt apart, she moved down his hard stomach, biting and then licking his skin. She ran a hand down over the bulge on his jeans and listened with satisfaction to his loud groan.

"Before we get too far into this," he warned, lifting his head and looking at her with smoldering eyes. "Do you have a catch-all drawer in this room?"

It took her a split second to understand, but then she giggled and shook her head.

"Well, how about a sugar bowl?"

Her brow shot up. "A sugar bowl?"

"A shoe box?"

Meg moved up his body and wrapped her fingers around his neck, throttling him gently. "A shoe box? Don't tell me you've done it in the closet?"

Instead of answering her question, he grabbed her by the waist and rolled her in bed until she laid pinned beneath him. "How about a cigar humidor?"

"A what?"

"A cigar humidor. I have one on my desk."

She laughed and tucked her face in the crook of his neck. "Sorry, I don't smoke."

"Neither do I." He scowled at her, half in jest. "Please, at least tell me that you're using some kind of protection yourself."

She slowly lifted her eyes to his and shook her head in embarrassment. "I'm sorry. But I don't...I haven't...I never thought..."

The loud ring of the phone next to the bed made Meg's heart leap in her chest. Before she could reach for it though, he pinned her arms and hands in between their bodies.

"You answer that, and I'll strangle you."

"Deal." She placed a kiss on the corner of his mouth. "You answer it."

"No way in hell."

"It could be Jada."

"I was with her this morning."

"She told me she'd call me this afternoon."

"You can call her back in a few minutes."

She raised a brow and gave him a challenging glare. "Do you really think it's going to be that quick?"

Evan reached immediately for the phone and, lifting the receiver from its cradle, tucked it against his ear.

Meg cringed at the sound of Rebekah's surprised voice at the other end.

CHAPTER EIGHTEEN

"I'M NOT sure if I have the right number."

"Let's hope you don't," Evan said shortly, ignoring Meg's mouthed demands to hand over the phone.

"Is there a Meg Murphy there?"

"Maybe there is. Maybe there isn't." He jammed the phone against the mattress for a moment and leaned down to crush Meg's stubborn lips beneath his own. She struggled for a second but then gave in and kissed him back.

"Hello? Hello?" The woman's persistent voice cut into their play.

"I'm going to hang up on her."

"Don't," Meg pleaded. "That's my friend Rebekah."

He reluctantly brought the phone to his ear, again. "Hi, Rebekah. Meg wants to know what the hell you want?"

He groaned dramatically as Meg pinched him beneath the ribs. He shifted his weight, giving her a playful glare. There was only silence at the other end of the phone.

"Are you still there, Rebekah?"

"I am. And I want to know what you have done with my friend?"

"Sorry, can't tell you. The FCC frowns on obscene phone calls."

It was getting tougher to take Meg's physical blows.

"Were you two in the middle of something?"

"We were. Ouch! We are. Is there anything else you want to know? I really need to hang up. She's really getting restless, if you know what I mean."

"Yeah. I know very well what you mean. Just have her call me, will you? Also, I don't care who the heck you think you are, but you make sure you take care of...of *things*. Do you get my meaning?"

He smiled at Meg's closed eyes and the red flush that had quickly crept into her face. "I sure do."

He leaned over and hung up the phone. It took her a long moment before she overcame her shyness and met his eyes.

"I'm sorry. I'm just so embarrassed."

He shifted his weight, and she laughed a bit nervously.

"This must be a first, even for you. Having a woman call from a hundred miles away to remind you to use a condom on her thirty-five-year-old friend."

As Evan rolled off and settled beside her, he smiled at the feeling of warmth that suddenly filled his heart. He was used to women who were bold and pushy, who knew their way around a man's bed, women who were proficient when it came to this kind of thing.

But here was Meg, so soft and beautiful—a hundred times more desirable than the whole lot of them—and yet so unsure of her own power. So innocent of the havoc that she was wreaking in his heart, never mind in his life.

"How long has it been, Meg?" he asked, running his knuckles down the soft skin of her face.

She laughed again and struggled to edge away from him, but he wrapped one hand around her waist. He wasn't about to let her get away.

"How long has it been since you've had a relationship with a man?"

She turned slightly and faced him. "Five years."

"Since your husband died."

She nodded and stared at his chin. Evan could see that she didn't want to say any more. And he accepted and respected her for it.

Somehow, somewhere in the back of his mind, he'd come to realize that she would be like that. A one-man woman. A very lucky man's woman.

He watched the way she shyly wrapped her arms over her breasts, blocking his view of them. She was drifting off someplace, deep in her own thoughts.

He wanted to lean over and kiss that little frown off of her forehead. She was made for passion, but after so many years of celibacy, she deserved to be wooed, courted, charmed. Meg deserved to be brought slowly to the heights of true passion.

"How about a date?"

Her eyes lifted to his. "A date?"

He nodded framing her face. "Knowing our luck, Jada will be calling in the next couple of minutes. And after that, Phil is probably going to check here when he finds I'm not upstairs."

"And knowing my friend," Meg added, "Rebekah will probably call in twenty minutes to find out how it was."

"How what was?" he growled suggestively.

"It," she added quietly. "To Rebekah, making love is *it*."

"Is that right? She sounds like a soul mate for Phil." He stopped. "So how about it? We'll go on a real date. And while we're gone, I'll have the phone disconnected and have a bullet-proof, soundproof door installed on my apartment." He ran a finger down the naked curve of her neck. "But I don't mean to distract you with what might come after. I'll trick you into coming up there later. How about if you just think about the date."

She gave him a tantalizing smile. "A sit-down dinner by candlelight?"

"And more." He took her hand and brought it to his lips. "How about if we go all the way. We'll have cocktails before, and do some dancing after dinner? We could really get dressed up and go out and have some fun."

He could tell she liked the idea as her eyes began to sparkle like diamonds in the sun. "That really sounds like a lot of fun, Evan, but—"

"No buts," he interrupted, knowing exactly what she was about to say. "And no, you can't pay for dinner. Or even chip in for half of it. Tomorrow night is on me. Understand?"

He could almost see the wheels turning in her pretty head.

"That's too much," she said finally. "I can't let you."

"Yes, you can, Meg. For once, just let me have my way." He pulled himself up and sat against the headboard. "I want to do this."

"Then give me something to do," she argued.

"Like what? Wash the cab so it's clean when we go out?"

"No." She sat up cross-legged in front of him, but to his great disappointment she pulled a pillow from beneath the spread and hugged it against her chest. "But give me something. Anything. If you aren't letting me pay for this, I want to do something for you."

Evan looked at her seriously. This was his chance to broach the subject and to find out if she was even interested.

"How about reading my work?"

"What?"

"The stuff I've been writing. You said you want to do something for me, so how about if you read what I've done so far and tell me your thoughts."

Her reaction delighted him. "Do you really mean it?"

"I wouldn't ask if I didn't want you to. But—"

"I know. I have to be gentle. I have to be kind. Or you'll drop me like an anchor into the harbor."

"You've got it."

"So when do I start?"

"Today, .if Jada is okay with Little Ted. How about this after-noon?" He'd been right to think her perfect for the job. Her excite-ment about reading his work was an incredible relief. "I just need a couple of hours to read it over myself and run a spell check."

"That's cheating," she scolded. "I want to start now."

"Hey, you just be a good girl and give me all high marks on these first couple of chapters, and I'll give you a special treat tomorrow night."

"It's a deal."

<hr>

She no longer had a job.

Meg hung up the phone and looked with mixed feelings at the pile of manuscripts sitting on the floor beside the bed.

She'd always thought that when the time came, when the ax finally fell, she'd go through a moment or two of hysteria over the loss of her livelihood, of the job that she had grown so fond of over the years. Rebekah had just given her the bad news, but to her surprise and relief Meg had felt no sense of mourning.

When Meg had called back, she'd been surprised that her friend hadn't launched right in, teasing her about Evan. Instead, Rebekah had simply given her the bad news.

The creditors had at last taken charge. And just like *that*, the business was finished. The Elgin Publishing Company was no more. Thank you for your efforts. Have a nice day. Have a nice life.

Rebekah said that Joe E. looked pale as he'd given the last of them the news. He'd even looked around for Meg, having somehow forgotten that she was on vacation. Rebekah told her they'd all been given an hour to clean out their personal belongings, so she'd boxed Meg's things and taken them home with her.

There were even guys putting a padlock on the front door when the last of the employees had filed out. The end.

Meg sat down on the floor next to the pile of loose manuscripts. The top one belonged to Mrs. Wilson. Meg felt like she really knew this woman. A nice old lady who wrote one book a year about her cats' adventures. She knew she'd miss talking to gentle hearted folks like her. Mrs. Wilson had never been published and would probably never be published, but the retired school teacher was a lesson in perseverance. She loved her cats, loved writing, and loved sharing her stories with her friends. No matter how many rejection letters she might get from heaven knows how many different publishing houses, Meg knew that every August, she could count on a new cat manuscript hitting her desk.

She shuffled through the pile and pulled out another manuscript, laying it on top. This one was from a veteran, a handicapped soldier back from Iraq who'd written a good story, but one that was just too close to a book that had hit the stands less than a month ago.

She picked up a thinner manuscript. She had started reading this one the other night when she couldn't push Evan out of her mind. This one was about a woman who had suffered multiple miscarriages and was now finding her marriage on the rocks.

She put the manuscript down and stared across the room toward the open window.

She would still answer these people. Even though she was now out of a job, she promised herself she'd take the time and tell each one the truth about their work...as she saw it. These people had finished a book. Two books. Many books. They deserved to get an answer, and she'd give it to them, padlock on the door or not.

There were parts of her job that she knew she'd miss, and

looking for good, new writers was one of them. Despite working for a small publishing house that had had no budget to speak of for the past two or three years, Meg still considered herself a good judge of talent.

Robert had always told her that, while he'd been around. But even after his death, she'd seen a good number of her writers, people that she'd gotten started, go on to become big names.

She continued going through the rest of manuscripts in the pile. She truly loved this. The feel of the paper against the tips of her fingers. The enticing dance of the words on the page. To look at a passage and know exactly where the author should add a word, revise a phrase. To watch the novel become a master work, a story with the power to ensnare a reader with its magic.

She leaned her head back against the bed and gave out a quiet laugh. In truth, work had been changing dramatically since Robert's death. For so long now, everyone in the place had been more worried about how to charm and pacify their dwindling number of steady writers, so that they wouldn't abandon ship and go after the fame and fortune that they deserved.

But all through these last years, she still had continued to dream. She'd never once given up hope or cast aside the talent that she knew she possessed. More than once, she'd offered editorial input to some author's work, only to see him or her go and sign with some other house. For Meg, the work itself held the gratification that she needed. That, and knowing she'd been able to help someone else achieve their dream.

She looked down at her watch and then piled up the manuscripts again. By letting her read his work, Evan was giving her the chance of perhaps doing the same for him. And that gave her a deep and heartfelt sense of satisfaction.

Sure, she was out of job. Sure, she was left with only enough money in her checking account to pay her rent for a maximum of two months. Maybe she *was* hanging out with a cab driver-slash-philanthropist-slash-philanderer that she didn't really know a thing about.

But what the heck. She was happy.

Getting to her feet, Meg took a cotton sundress out of the closet and headed for the bathroom. She kept repeating Robert's words in her head. *The old has to give away to the new. The dead to the living.*

Evan hammered away on the keyboard at about a hundred miles an hour. He was in a frenzy. It wasn't as if he didn't have enough of a story drafted for Meg to read, but knowing that she'd be up here shortly, and reading, and more than likely tearing apart his work, pumped him with adrenaline and creative energy. Sure, he was a glutton for punishment. He wanted it bad. The truth was, he couldn't wait to sit across from her and argue against whatever she said.

This was the best work he'd done in a long time. He could tell the difference, himself. Since their talk yesterday, he'd looked hard at his characters and their motives. Hell, he really felt like he was getting to know these people. Really understanding what made them tick.

He continued to attack the computer with a vengeance. But his fingers couldn't keep up with his brain. The words and ideas were washing over him, flooding around him. He was trying to stay above water while at the same time forcing himself to push ahead. To cover as much distance as he could.

"Bastard," he cursed his computer as a pop-up appeared.

"What the hell's the matter now?"

Evan whirled in his chair.

"Oh. I didn't hear you come in." Looking at his friend, he figured Phil must have been watching him for a while, since he'd already helped himself to a beer and was leaning against the divider to the kitchen, dipping his graham crackers in Evan's favorite pilsner glass.

"Hey, it's so rare these days to see you so fired up, I hated to interrupt."

Evan started to respond but decided against it. Of all people, Phil was one friend who had been through it all with him—good and bad—and there was no denying his struggle to write over the past few months.

Evan closed the file before coming to his feet.

"What took you so long? I told you that wanted to talk to you."

"I figured I'd give you enough time to cool your jets."

Evan chuckled. "Yeah. Since when are you afraid of my temper."

"I'm not. The truth of it is, I wanted to give you enough time to get yourself kicked out of Meg's room first."

Evan moved around the counter and got himself a beer out of the fridge as well. "And how the hell did you know I was there? By the way, don't worry yourself, I can drink *my* beer out of a juice glass."

"Hey, everybody in Newport heard you two yelling. I called the Daily News and gave them the exclusive on the story. I even gave them the headline." Phil dipped another cracker into the beer and popped it into his mouth. "Bestselling author gets ass kicked by gorgeous tourist."

"You've got a real future writing headlines, let me tell you." Evan snatched the package of graham crackers out of Phil's hand and marched back across the room to the sofa. "But it really was shitty of you to take Meg sailing this morning. You had me genuinely ticked off."

"Good." Phil followed behind. "It's about time you got it where it hurts, after all the stupid jokes you've been making about me."

"She is different, Phil." He didn't like it a bit, but even to himself, he was suddenly sounding too serious. "She's not like the usual suspects you and I seem to attract."

"I know." Phil nodded. "That's why I intend to ask her out again."

"Forget it, asshole. She's mine."

Phil put on one of his innocent smiles, but Evan knew it was solely because his friend knew how much that irritated him.

"I don't know what you mean. Are you telling me that you two have already achieved something deep, something meaningful, something...etc., etc., bullshit, bullshit, etc.?"

"Yes, that's exactly what I'm saying. Minus the bullshit, etc."

"Then why the hell haven't you told her who you are? You are a piece of work. Don't you think she has a right to know? What if she happens to be the one in the million who just hates Drew King and his arrogant public persona?"

Evan laughed scoffingly and then subsided with a thoughtful frown. He glanced at his friend. "She *does* hate my books."

Phil chortled with amusement. "Ha! At last. There is justice. And how did you get her to admit that?"

"*That* is none of your business." Evan started to prop his legs on the table, but the ring of the phone sent him bolting across the apartment for it.

"I can't believe this," Phil muttered incredulously. "Since when do you actually answer the phone?"

"Shut up. This is important."

Just as Evan had suspected, John Peck was on the line.

"What did you find out?" he demanded, grabbing for a pencil and a pad.

"Let's see," Evan heard the rustle of papers on the other end. "Meg Murphy is thirty-five and a widow."

"Tell me what I don't know."

"Okay. She's been living in the same apartment building for the past fifteen years. A very good tenant. Quiet. Always pays the rent on time. The lease still has her dead husband's name listed on it."

"Any boyfriends?"

"Not that she takes back to her apartment. She's got some friends, but from all accounts, she is pretty much a loner."

"What does she do for a living?"

"You mean, *did* for a living. She has been officially out of a job since yesterday. From what I was able to gather, the creditors closed the door of the place she used to work."

"What did she do?"

There was a long pause before John said, "You're not going to like it."

"No." Evan ran an angry hand through his hair. "Just don't tell me she's a goddamn editor."

"She's a senior editor." There was another pause. "But not like the ones that you're used to. The company she worked for was pretty small. Unknown authors. Nothing too fancy."

"I can't frigging believe this."

"Before you jump to any conclusions, there's something else you should know."

Throwing down his pencil and pad, Evan started pacing back and forth. "Let me guess, she's really a frigging Drew King fan and has a history of violent mental disorders."

"No. Nothing like that."

"What is it?" Evan snapped shortly.

"She was married to Robert Luckenbrager."

Suddenly, Evan was at a loss for words. Moving to the closest chair and sitting down, he stared blankly ahead. There had been no one in his life—*no one*—whom he'd ever felt indebted to.

No one but Robert. He was the editor who discovered him first. He was the only one with enough patience and insight to give him a chance. Robert Luckenbrager had believed in his work and had laid out a path for him to succeed.

Evan had been hurt when Robert decided to leave the Big

Apple and take his chances with a small publishing house in Boston. He'd felt lost. He'd been ready to change publishers and go with him, but Robert wouldn't have it. He'd told him that the place he was going to work for was hardly ready to handle someone as big as he was getting to be.

So they'd lost touch over the years, and Evan had started going through a parade of editors who could never match up to Robert Luckenbrager. No one had his talent. His honesty. His courage. No one, except his wife.

"Are you still there?"

Evan stared at his laptop sitting across the room. "Yeah. I'm still here."

"Evan, I don't believe...I mean, there is nothing about this Meg Murphy that I've learned so far that gives me any reason to believe that she cares a bit about Drew King. I remember even when her husband died five years ago or so, you weren't in the country. So it couldn't be that she saw you at his funeral."

"I know," Evan said simply.

"She's pretty straightforward," John continued. "Clean living. Lives for her work. No personal life, but very well-liked and respected by everyone that I spoke to. But as far as her financial situation and all that, I can't get any of those things until Monday, but—"

"That's fine," he said quietly. "You've given me a lot to think about."

Evan hung up the phone and continued to stare numbly across the room. All of a sudden everything was becoming quite clear. Meg's talent in dissecting his work, her style of attack, even her attempts to compromise reminded him so much of Robert. Without knowing the truth, he'd been very excited to have her read his work and now he knew why. In the back of his mind, all along he'd been comparing her to Robert, to the way he would have acted reading some of the shit he'd written for the past couple of years. And it was scary to think how close to the truth he'd been.

"Hey, if you've lost interest, I don't happen to have anything against editors."

Evan glared at his friend.

"She's different, Evan. You told me so, yourself."

"And in more ways than you think." He ran a hand down his face and stalked back to the sofa. "She's Robert Luckenbrager's widow."

"Your first editor? The guy you went to Rome to have canonized?"

"Don't joke about him. He was a good man."

Phil paused thoughtfully. "You know, it's strange, but I really don't think she knows who you are."

"I believe you're right about that."

Phil looked at him questioningly. "But with all the time you two have been spending together, how come you never learned the truth about who she was, or even what she did for a living?"

Evan shook his head. "I guess that was partly my fault. I was so wrapped up in not letting her know I'm Drew King, that when she started kidding about her job, I let her get away with it."

Evan started pacing the room.

"So what are you going to do with her?"

"Nothing different than what I originally planned."

"Bullshit," Phil snorted. "You can't fool me. I know you and I know the sense of loyalty you felt toward the husband."

"He's been dead for five years. And I got to know Meg as herself first."

"I still don't believe you."

"What the hell do you want from me?" Even felt his temper slipping out of control. "Do you think I should just pretend we never met? Do you think I should just stop seeing her just because of who she was married to years ago?"

"No, but I do think you should put an end to this stupid game and tell her who the hell you are. I think you should put the decision of whether she wants to go out with you or not, in her hands."

"It has always been in her hands."

"Yes, but she thinks you're Evan Knight."

"I *am* Evan Knight."

"She thinks you're penniless, devil-may-care, cab driver with endless charm and bottomless generosity."

Evan turned on his friend. "I still don't know what the hell you are getting at with all this?"

"Just think this through. I know you, Evan. You are like a bouncing ball. One minute, you are going to feel like a million bucks being with her. The next thing you know, you're going to be so bummed out, because of who she is, that you are going to ask her to marry you out of some ridiculous sense of duty." Phil's deep frown showed the depth of his concern. "Think this through, Evan. Don't let something like this mess up your life."

This was no messing, as far as Evan could tell. And what was wrong if things did work out that way. Meg had told him herself that she hadn't gone out with anybody since Robert's death. Maybe this was just meant to be. For the two of them to pick up where he and Robert had left off professionally and she and Robert had left off personally.

There was nothing wrong with any of that, though putting it in those terms didn't sound all that normal. Ah, what the hell was normal in his life, anyway?

"I already told Sarah to get me another ticket. I'm taking Meg to the Heart Ball tomorrow night."

"After you tell her the truth," Phil stressed. "There is going to be more than one person at that ball who knows your true identity."

"But you're still planning to come. Right?"

"No, I hate those things."

"Well. You'll love this one. I need you there, Phil."

"Why? To play the chaperone for the two of you?"

"No. To act as my bodyguard."

Phil gave a snort of laughter. "Since when…"

"Look, I just want you to be your charming, handsome self and attract the attention of every available female in the place."

"I assume that's so long as I don't come close to Meg."

"Right. And so long as you keep every other woman we know away from me."

"Oh, great. I get to be the blocking dummy."

"Right."

"I don't know. That's a tall order."

"Well, you'll have to try."

"And will you tell her? The whole bit? Your identity? Your working relationship with Robert?"

"I will. When the time is right, I will."

CHAPTER NINETEEN

"ARE you sure you don't need me?"

"I'm sure, Meg." Jada seemed quite determined. "They're already done with all the tests, but I won't get results until Monday. The baby is not due to wake up for a while, and even my doctor's already gone for the weekend. There's nothing happening here."

Meg felt something tearing inside her. As much as she wanted to start reading Evan's work, she was still worried about Jada.

"How about if I just come over just for couple of hours? Just to keep you company."

"Thanks, Meg. But not today. Maybe tomorrow. I'm just kind of really beat. As soon as the baby wakes up, I'm going to feed him. When he goes back to sleep, I'm heading back to the apartment and catch some z's myself. How about if I call you tomorrow?"

Resigning herself to Jada's wishes, Meg reluctantly told her young friend good night.

She couldn't put her finger on it, but there was something in the tone of her voice that felt wrong. It wasn't the denial and melancholy that she'd witnessed when Ted had just been born. This seemed a lot more refined. It seemed to be the hint of a deeper pain, of something that the young mother was trying to hide behind the voice of a mature woman.

Evan was very busy.

He made a pot of coffee. Called Mrs. Jeffers about Jada. Walked around the apartment. Made a printout of the first four chapters. Called Sarah to make sure everything was on schedule for tomorrow night. Walked around the apartment. Straightened things out in the apartment. Called Doug, his accountant, about looking into the financial difficulties of Elgin Publishing Company. Went around and strategically messed up what he'd just straightened in the apartment. Answered the phone on the first ring. Read the riot act to some poor woman who wanted to have him do a phone survey. Walked around the apartment. Cursed out aloud for not getting herbal tea. Walked. Sat. Jumped at the soft knock on his door.

Charging the door like a bear, Evan practically yanked the thing off its hinges. Meg stood outside, one eyebrow registering her surprise at the suddenness with which the door opened.

"You're not nervous or anything, are you?"

Evan cursed. Dressed in a soft, shape molding sundress, she looked breathtakingly beautiful. Eyeing the ringlets of hair that framed her pretty face and exquisite neck, he tried to imagine her as Robert's wife.

He couldn't. This was Meg. The woman whom he had gone crazy over from the first moment they'd met. And he could remember very clearly how good her body had felt sprawled on top of his only couple of hours ago.

Dammit, he just had to push the fact that she was a widow

right out of his mind. Evan was certain that Robert would give him his blessing if he knew what he was planning for his lonely, unemployed wife. Well, pretty certain.

"So, do I stay out here, or do I come in?"

He frowned at the pretty smile. "Come in, before I change my mind."

She breezed past him. He couldn't help but admire the silky-smooth skin showing above the low dip in the back of the dress.

"I thought you were coming to work, and here you are trying to seduce me."

She turned around and gave him a heart-melting smile. "I am here to work, and I don't know what you mean."

Evan struggled to keep from reaching out and taking her into his arms, fought to keep from showing her exactly how dangerous it was to come to his apartment dressed like that.

"Just don't come too close to me." He started walking toward the kitchen. "And *don't* stand in front of the window."

"Whatever you say."

"Want some coffee?"

She sat on a high stool and looked at him across the divider into the kitchen. "Do you think I need it?"

"How the hell do I know what you need?"

She was an editor, for chrissakes, Evan reminded himself. He should be tougher, more ruthless, just plain mean, the way he always behaved toward the whole bunch of them. But he just couldn't bring himself to do it. This was a whole new deal.

"I'd just like to start, if you don't mind."

He poured himself a cup and came around the divider. "I printed out fifty pages or so. They're on that table. I also have it on the laptop. I didn't know which way you'd prefer to read."

"What are you going to do while I am reading?"

"Sit back on the sofa and sulk."

She smiled. "That'd be kind of distracting, don't you think?

How about if you work too? You can write on the laptop, and I'll read the printed pages. Then we could talk and just keep going like that."

Sounded reasonable, Evan thought. Too reasonable, he chided himself. "That sounds like work."

"It is." Meg got up and took him by the arm, pushing him toward the computer. "Let's put in a good solid evening of work. Come on, you can do it. It'd be exciting. Fun."

Evan let her lead him across the room, but with every step he continued to grumble, enjoying her amused reaction.

"Saturday night. Everybody in this town is partying, and here I am stuck in front of a goddamn computer."

"Save your energy." She pushed him down in his chair. "Save it, since whatever you don't use writing, you'll need fighting me later on."

He sat down at his desk, and Meg curled up in a corner of the sofa not too far away with his manuscript on her lap and a pad of paper beside her.

Trying to stare at his computer and pick up where he'd left off, Evan's eyes kept drifting to Meg. He wished he could read her mind. He wanted her to tell him after each paragraph how she felt. But she went on reading, ignoring him, so he finally gave up and started to write.

Amazingly, he was somehow able to pick up where he'd left off before. The story engulfed him, its action surging forward like a runaway train. Sometime later, he heard her laugh, and he lifted his head for a moment to see her smiling down at the page in her hand. She, too, seemed lost to everything around her. He went back to work.

The long, golden beams of the sun moved across the room and up the far wall, the light gradually giving way to dusk and then to night. Somehow, his coffee cup refilled. And the words kept rushing onto the page. When he finally found himself at a sticking point in the chapter he was writing, he lifted his head again, only to find the corner of the sofa empty.

Turning sharply around, he found Meg leaning against the divider to the kitchen. There was something haunting in her expression. Something magical.

She'd liked it.

"So? What do you think?"

"What do I think?" she repeated, lifting her head for an instant, obviously searching for the right words. "I think you're wasting your time driving that cab around this town. I think you have incredible talent. A very expressive voice. And you have a story with a lot of heart." She looked at him directly. "I think you are on your way to stardom, to bestseller land, to the world of fame and fortune and publishers who will extend a red carpet for you to spit on. If that's what you want."

He had millions of adoring fans. He'd had a whole slew of editors willing to dance to his every whim. The critics loved him in spite of his ability to sell a lot of books. But none of the praises had ever affected him like these words.

"But I also think there is arrogance in the way you write. You know you have talent, so you sometimes get lazy. You take short-cuts. You bring the reader within one step of the moon, but then leave them there."

He found the muscles in his face tightening. She had praised him, so she could dump on him. He started stalking across the room toward her.

"But this is minor stuff, Evan. Little things," she added quickly, scurrying into the kitchen and putting the divider between them. "Little details that you fail to put in. Most readers won't even notice it, but the smart ones will. And the final effect will blow them away."

"This is a first draft."

"It's not a first draft. I've never read any first draft that was this good."

"And with your job as a janitor, cleaning engineer, or whatever the hell you called it, how many first drafts of unpublished novels do you get to read?"

He saw her face redden. "That's beside the point. Do you want to hear my comments or not?"

He considered it for a moment. This was the same way Robert had started with him years ago. Praising him to the sky and then cutting his legs from under him. But then, in the process, Robert had taught Evan how to walk. And how to write a damn good book.

"I do want to hear your comments."

"Then stop acting like such an immature jerk and go and sit at that table. I've marked some of my comments on the margins, but we'd better go through it together."

And that they did. He argued vehemently against some of her observations, but reluctantly gave in to others. She was a master negotiator, much more difficult and brutal than any he'd ever faced. But he had something over her. He was Drew King, and she didn't know it. He knew damn well how to write. And he knew his first drafts were better than the finished work of most of the other authors she was used to.

She didn't want to show it, but he knew he'd impressed her. A few times she would try to drive a point home and then he would twist it, give it back to her, argue it; and he would see the spark ignite in her dark eyes. A lightning flash of challenge, intelligence, excitement. She was made for this type of work. He could tell. It was in her blood.

When they finished with her comments, she forced him to go and make the changes. And then she sat next to him, and together they read the work through again.

To his absolute and utter dismay, it was better. In fact, it was damn good.

But then she wouldn't let him call it a night. She wanted to read more. Demanded it. Dared him to let her. So, realizing it was already half past ten, he turned the laptop over to her, and called out for pizza.

This time she didn't let him get too far away from her. In fact, she forced him to sit beside her. He watched her, gauging her response from the animated expressions that were flickering across her face. At times, he read along with her as she paged downed the screen.

She was almost caught up with everything he'd written thus far when the pizza arrived at the door. Going to the kitchen to get plates and drinks for them, Evan realized that he was actually disappointed that he didn't have any more of the novel to share with her. Despite all their bickering and all the heavy-handed attacks on one another, these past few hours had been the most exciting and productive he could recall.

"Have you thought about shopping what you have so far, to some agents or publishers?"

He placed the pizza in the middle of the table, watching her fold some paper napkins before putting them beside the plates. He was tempted to tell her who he was, but then he found himself thinking of the evening that they'd shared. Being a bestselling author had one troubling disadvantage. Loneliness. The self-imposed need to produce something readable without the kind of collaboration that had taken place between the two of them tonight.

"Yeah." He finally met her gaze. "I could see doing that."

He went to the kitchen and returned with their drinks, but she hesitated a moment before sitting down. "And do you know how to go about the whole thing. About finding an agent and contacting publishers?"

"Do you?"

Evan helped himself to a slice of the pizza and took a bite out of it, his eyes all the while continuously studying her troubled face. He knew she was trying to help him, but at the same time he wondered how long she would keep up trying to hide the truth of her profession. Probably as long as he kept hiding his identity.

"I'm an editor, Evan. I mean, I was until yesterday, before I lost my job."

Evan almost choked on the food in his mouth. Dammit. She had him making one wrong assumption after the other about her.

"I know," she continued. "And you have every right to be mad at me for not telling you earlier. But then, I've learned from experience not to talk about my job." Her fingers nervously played with the napkin as her gaze slowly lifted to his. "By the time I thought I could tell you what I did for living, you'd already told me about your writing. And so...so I didn't want to intimidate you. I figured it'd be best if I just shut my mouth. I really did hope you'd let me read your work."

"I..." Evan searched for the words as she placed her elbows on the table and leaned toward him.

"When I said you're *really* good, I meant it. That wasn't just a general observation, but a professional opinion. It's always a risky business, but if you let me, I can put you in contact with some savvy agents. And even some big publishers who will start you on your way."

Feeling like the town idiot, he just continued to stare.

"I know. You must be asking yourself, what the heck does she want? Why is she telling me all this? Why now?"

This was frigging unbelievable. But she was doing great, carrying both sides of the conversation.

"You just have to accept what I'm telling you, because there's no way I can explain how I feel." She let out a long, shaky breath. "I want to help you. Just *help* you. I think you are a great writer, and someday I will love standing and admiring a bookstore window filled with your books, and thinking, I knew you when. And I *can* help. Even if a writer has a world of talent and lifelong habit of hard work, there is still a lot of luck involved in getting your work read by the right people."

Meg was really rolling now, and Evan knew he couldn't have gotten in a word if he wanted to.

"And I know some of those people. I've been in the business for a while now. I can put you in contact with the editors at Morgan Publishing in New York. I've had a few of my authors sign with them. So I could pull some strings. They'd be a perfect publishing house for someone with your talent. They'll push you, and they'll promote you. They can take you where you *should* be headed."

Evan couldn't believe it. She was going to introduce him to his own publisher.

She looked up into his face. "So what do you think?"

Shit. And what could he say to that offer? Thanks, but no thanks, honey? You see, I'm already there. I'm Drew King.

"I'm speechless," he said, starting to feel miserable.

He watched her look at him for another long moment. She reached over for a piece of pizza.

"Are you mad at me for not telling you sooner?"

Yes, he was mad at her, for telling him sooner than *he* had told the truth about himself. "No, I'm not mad."

"And you won't treat me any differently?"

"Of course not."

She paused before taking another bite. "Will you still let me read your work?"

"Yes, I'm counting on you to continue looking at my work."

Finally. It felt good to be able to speak the truth for a change. And he nearly smiled, seeing the happy expression his last words brought to her face.

As they continued to eat, Evan's mind kept working through a tactful approach to bring up the truth. But for the first time in his life, he felt helpless—inept even— at something as simple as speaking his own mind.

Hi, I'm Drew King. Meg, please...please, you have got to understand.

Having you read my work and give me your input was not a joke. I really needed help. I still do. Would you consider working for me? Staying with me? Meg I have an offer...

"For someone who kept whining for the past couple of hours about being so starved, you sure haven't made much of a dent in this pizza."

He looked at the half-eaten slice on his plate. Damn it. His appetite had sure managed to disappear in a hurry.

Meg, I have something to tell you. I want you to know that you've already made a difference in my writing. In my life. Don't get upset at this, but I'm really Drew King. All those stories...

"I was afraid of that," she said softly, pushing her own plate to the side. "Perhaps it would have been much better if I'd just shut my mouth and not said all that about my job. I told you myself, didn't I? People who write somehow get intimidated when they're faced with an editor for the first time. You see them clam up. It's as if they suddenly feel like they have to run a grammar-check on everything they say."

"Now, that's a crock of shit, if I ever heard one."

She beamed a smile. "Yes. This is more like it. For a moment I was afraid you were going to turn polite on me."

"I thought you don't like vulgarity."

"That was before I met you. I want you to be you." She leaned her chin on her palm and looked into his eyes.

He felt the fire igniting in his loins. "Are you flirting with me?"

"I'm sorry, I didn't know I was so obvious."

He wanted her. But first, he had to tell the truth and be done with it. "Meg, there is something—"

"How about if I make us a fresh pot of coffee."

He watched her quickly come to her feet, taking their plates into the kitchen. He picked up the rest of the dinner and followed her.

"Meg, let me get this out while I can."

"No." She put everything in the sink and turned toward him. "I know what you're going to say."

"You do?" he said, suddenly dumbfounded.

"Yes, I do. So don't say it."

He reached out, grabbed her by the shoulders, and looked straight into her eyes. "And what is it exactly that you don't want me to say."

"That you won't need my help. That your ego is bruised. That your feelings are hurt. That it's *you* who is always the giver. That you can manage perfectly well all by yourself."

"I do need your help," he interrupted. "And I have tried, but somehow I can't seem to manage any longer by myself. Meg, I—"

Pushing herself onto her toes, she kissed him hard on the mouth, and suddenly Evan lost his desire to be talking. He kissed her back with all the stormy passions that were raging within him.

"Make love to me, Evan," she said softly against his ear when he buried his lips in her neck. "Now."

He felt his heart leap. "But what about our date?"

"We can still have our date." She ran her hands down his chest, over his stomach. "We can just think of this as something to hold us over until then."

Before he could answer, she was again ravaging his mouth, her arms around his neck.

The hell with it, he thought. The hell with reason. The hell with telling her the truth first. The hell with knowing that he was falling in love for the first time in his life.

He swept her up in his arms and started toward the bedroom. He felt her smile into the crook of his neck.

"Should I grab the sugar bowl as we go by?"

"No need. I have a brand new, five-hundred package, economy size box tucked right under the bed. Just for you."

"I knew you'd be economy size."

As they burst into the bedroom, she worked herself out of his arms. Pushing his hands away, she started undressing him. Evan reached for her, but again she stopped him, smiling. With her lips and mouth scorching every newly exposed inch of hard flesh, Meg stripped him out of every stitch of clothing he had on. Then, just as he thought he'd burst if he didn't put his hands on her soon, Meg pushed herself back and, with a warning hand up, lay back on the bed.

"Okay," she said with a mischievous smile. "I want you to march naked around the bed."

"I'll kill you," he threatened, watching her move back and perch higher in his bed. Her soft sundress still on.

"So this is how it's done," she teased, pulling out a pillow and tucking it behind her. "A little flaunting now. Turn a little to the right...right. Just like that. Now to the left. Oh, nice profile."

He scowled and dived after her on the bed, but she was too quick and rolled to the floor. With the agility of a cat, he tackled her there.

She opened her mouth to protest, but then sighed with pleasure as he pulled down the straps of her sundress, one at a time, before slowly pushing the bodice down to her waist. He slid his hands along her thighs and made short work of her underwear. Tossing them aside, he leaned forward and took her nipple between his lips.

She writhed restlessly beneath him as he suckled. Then, he raised his head when she reached her hand blindly under the bed.

"Where are they?"

Evan paused for a moment and then smiled devilishly.

"And this is the new game that we'll be playing now." He lifted his weight off of her and freed her body of the dress. She was a stunning picture of curves and sheer beauty. His breath caught in his throat. "You...you look for the condoms up that way."

He waved his hand vaguely in the direction of the bed, and Meg giggled softly and pushed herself up on the rug. Lifting up the edge of the spread, she peeked under the bed.

Evan felt the rush of desire racing through him at the sight of her long, naked limbs stretched so gracefully before him. He lowered his head and ran his tongue along her thigh.

"And I'll look down here."

CHAPTER TWENTY

MEG'S EYES took in the dark wood of the pews and the gold and marble of the altar of St. Mary's. In the morning light, the church was still quiet and somber. One of the acolytes moved about the altar, preparing for the Sunday Mass.

Behind the pew where she and Jada sat, the door opened and more church-goers entered. The place had been empty when the two of them arrived, but that was quickly changing. A small group sat down a few pews back and began to talk about the church's history. The voices were hushed, but she could hear them mentioning the wedding that took place here so long ago.

Meg thought briefly how high the energy level in St. Mary's must have been that day when a young war hero named John F. Kennedy took Jacqueline Bouvier to be his bride. She wondered if those two people had any idea how much the world would change because of the vows they took that day.

Changes. She turned to Jada.

"I didn't tell you, but I got a call from my friend in Boston. I'm officially unemployed."

"Oh, no," Jada said, concern etched on her pretty face. "What will you do?"

"I don't know. Get another job, I suppose."

"Jobs are kind of tight these days, aren't they?"

"I'll find something."

Jada turned, and Meg watched her stare at a statue by the altar.

"What's the matter?"

"It must be nice to have your confidence."

The young woman was wrong. If anything, except during some very special moments in bed with Evan, she had no confidence at all these days. Evan. Just the simple thought of him was enough to spread warmth through her. She quickly tried to clear her mind of the night they'd shared and turned to her friend.

"You'll be okay."

"I wish I could believe that. But how can I do it all? I've got a tenth-grade education, a sick baby, and no...and no one else. What kind of job am I going to get?"

"It will be very difficult for a while, but you'll make it. You're smart. You'll get your education." She laid a hand on Jada's arm. "And everything will work out with Little Ted. You'll see."

Together, they sat in silence for a few minutes as the church began to fill.

"Do you pray, Meg?"

"I used to. But I think it's been about five years since I've been to a church. I think I forced myself to give up my belief in the power of prayer. You know...all the stuff that you get drilled into you when you're a kid."

"Me, too. I kind of stopped believing in it after my mother died."

Jada had asked her to come with her this morning and now Meg was glad that she had.

"You were pretty young then, weren't you?"

"I guess. But while she was dying, I could see everyone around us praying. People would stop us and say that they were praying for her. They even prayed for her from that altar right there." Jada nodded grimly at the front of the church. "We all knew she was going to die. She told me that herself. Then, one day, just a couple of days before she died, I realized that my father wasn't praying anymore. I looked around, and all of a sudden, I realized that nobody was praying. They were just sitting and waiting. I guess everyone just got to a point where they thought, what's the use? After she died, that idea just kind of stuck with me."

Meg took Jada's hand in her own.

"That must have been a pretty tough time."

Jada nodded slightly, and Meg saw the tear run down her cheek. Somehow, she felt she had to share a piece of herself.

"When my husband died, I didn't believe it. It just didn't seem possible that he could be gone. I got so angry then. It was the doctor's fault. It was the ambulance driver's. It was his parent's fault. The hospital's. It was the stress from his job. I blamed everything and anything." She looked at Jada. "I stopped praying then. I suppose it was because I didn't see any purpose in it. I suppose that was the time when I decided that his death was really my fault."

"But you said it was a genetic heart condition."

"I know. But that didn't stop me. You can find a thousand ways to blame yourself if you want to." Meg stopped, thinking of that awful first year after Robert's death.

"So what did you do?"

"I don't know. I suppose I just kept getting up in the morning and doing what I had to do. And then, almost a year later, I found myself coming back to Newport, to the same place he and I had always stayed. Doing the same things we had always done. It probably sounds crazy, but I found him here."

Jada nodded uncertainly, and Meg decided not to linger over that. But just then, Mass started, and they both sat silently through the opening prayers.

Surrounded by the group of worshipers, vacantly absorbing the humming voices around her, Meg's mind drifted to Robert.

Leaving Evan's apartment early this morning, she'd felt the gnawing edges of guilt pushing her down the steps. As she stepped into her own room, she'd self-consciously paused and scanned the contents of the place. Something was different—that was true enough. But even as she looked, she knew it wasn't the room. It was she herself who was different, and Meg didn't feel entirely comfortable with the change.

Later on, dressing to go meet Jada, she thought she'd heard a voice. She was expecting it. She truly thought Robert would appear to her, upbraiding her for her infidelity.

The truth of the matter was that she'd have been a lot happier if he had. At least that way she could have washed the guilt out of her system. At least she would have had the opportunity to say out loud what he had said to her. That he had indeed moved on. That she had been left behind with no option but to live.

But Robert had not appeared or made himself heard. He had left her to deal with her rollercoaster of emotions herself.

Looking up at the stained-glass windows of the church—at the depiction of the angels reflected there—Meg for the first time questioned her own beliefs.

Was it truly the ghost of Robert whom she had caught up with here in Newport, year after year? Or was it her own desperate need to cling to remnants of a happier time? Perhaps it was all just a dream-wish of her own invention to believe her husband was still around.

All those years, all the self-help books, all the hours of trying to puzzle out the meaning of her life. And here, everything changed with one passionate night in the embrace of Evan Knight. Now, all of the sudden, a different window which she could look upon life.

Meg turned her attention back to the Mass and to the young woman seated beside her. Whatever problems she had in her own life, they were nothing in comparison with what lay ahead for her. And being with Jada—trying to be of some help to her—struck

Meg as being the most important thing she could be doing right now.

After all, perhaps it wasn't Evan alone that had made her awaken and want to live. Perhaps it was Jada, as well. Jada and her struggles. Jada and her inner strength.

Evan waited across the street and watched the people spilling out of the church. He truly hoped that Mrs. Jeffers had been right in thinking that Jada and Meg had come to the Mass at St. Mary's this morning. He wanted to find them.

He wanted to see Meg.

Waking up this morning to find her already gone, Evan had been stunned by the oppressively empty feeling suddenly pervading the apartment. Moving about, he'd lingered by the places where she stood, and sat. And slept. What they'd shared last night had been a lot more than great sex. He'd been touched, redefined. He felt whole and fulfilled as he'd never felt before. She'd somehow worked her way into his heart, into his soul, and now the void caused by her absence filled him with incredible longing.

And that scared the shit out of him.

Evan knew he just had to find her and make sure she was feeling as half-witted as he was this morning. He had to find out if she had the same stars sparkling in her eyes as she had last night.

They were among the last of the people to exit the church. Evan's heart tightened in his chest at seeing her. She was smiling and talking softly into Jada's ear, and the young girl seemed captivated by whatever it was Meg was telling her.

Evan let his eyes take her in fully. Even in a conservative navy-blue dress, she still was the sexiest woman alive. He smiled, thinking that she could wear a nun's habit and still knock him dead. His gaze traveled down her slender frame, and he recalled the way those long, elegant limbs had hugged his hips. The taste of her skin beneath his lips. He groaned inwardly and shifted his weight from one foot to the other.

"Evan."

Jada was the first of the two to notice him waiting. In the five days since she'd given birth to Ted, the young woman had lost a considerable amount of weight. The only sign that she had undergone a pregnancy at all was the slight bulge at her waist.

Looking up into Jada's face, he noticed also the dark lines under her eyes. As little as he knew about the childbirth, none of this looked normal to him.

"Evan," Jada called out again. "What happened? Too afraid to come in?"

He turned and met Meg's sparkly eyes. "I just didn't want anything to happen to you two when the bolt of lightning hit. If you know what I mean."

Without a warning, he reached down and placed a kiss on Meg's lips.

"Good morning."

She immediately blushed, and that made him smile.

"How about some breakfast?"

"It's almost noon." Jada put in with amusement, studying Meg's reaction.

"Then how about some brunch."

"I have to get back to the hospital."

"Only after you eat," he scolded. "You are getting as thin as a rail."

"We'd love to have brunch with you, Evan. Wouldn't we, Jada?"

Meg's interruption brought an amused look into Jada's face.

"Yeah. Sure," the young mother said. "Anything to keep from hearing another sermon."

"Good. That settles it." He tucked a hand into each woman's elbow and started them down the street and toward his car. "I am absolutely starving."

"I think food is the only thing Evan ever thinks of."

"Not the only thing," he whispered suggestively in Meg's direction. "But you can correct her on that score, can't you, sweetheart?"

She never looked at him, but he saw the trace of a smile and the lingering blush in her cheeks.

When they reached his convertible, Jada climbed into the cramped back seat without a word, but Meg gave him a questioning glance.

"Out of gas again?" she asked suspiciously.

"No. This time I'm taking it for an oil change."

"On Sunday?"

"Phil doesn't know Sunday from New Year's Day, unless there's a sailing regatta scheduled."

She shot him a disbelieving glance but got in without further comment.

The brunch at the big hotel on Goat Island was crowded, but they were soon seated. During their meal, it was all too apparent to Evan that Meg was trying to divert the conversation away from herself and toward the young mother.

In no time, Meg had engaged Jada's attention with some old school stories and soon had the teenager talking about her own experiences. Evan listened with amazement, asking questions and joking, as she blossomed talking about her favorite classes. She grew quite animated sharing descriptions of the rowdies, townies, heads, and preps that attended her school. And they laughed at her story about a geeky history teacher who—with his tongue dragging on the floor—was continually dogging the girls' gym teacher. As their meal wore on, the two of them successfully drew Jada into a discussion that focused on the good things the future could hold.

Meg suddenly shifted direction. "Jada, are there any clothing stores open in this town on a Sunday afternoon?"

"Sure," she said brightly, going on to list a dozen places.

"How about if you and I do some shopping this afternoon? I need a few things, and I'd also like to buy you a little present. How about a new dress?"

Jada shook her head and smiled gratefully. "Thanks, Meg. But I have all the jeans I'll ever need. And besides, I have to be back at the hospital soon. When I was there this morning, Baby Ted actually grabbed my finger. I think he fusses less and eats better when I'm holding him."

"Of course he does."

"Listen, you two. How about if I take both of you to the hospital, and after Jada's spent some time with the baby, I'll take you both shopping."

They turned and looked at him as if he'd grown an extra head.

"What's wrong with that?" He glowered from one astounded face to the other. "Men do occasionally go shopping. And besides, Meg, you need a dress."

She gave him an incredulous look. "What's wrong with what I have on now?"

"Nothing." Except that covers too much, he finished silently. "I told you tonight is a dress-up affair."

"Meg told me that you two are going on a date."

"How dress-up?"

He looked at one woman then to the next. "I'm wearing a tux."

"A tux?" they exclaimed in chorus.

He glared at them. "Yes, a tux."

"Evan, when I asked for a sit-down dinner—"

"Too late," he interrupted Meg's explanation. "Like it or not, I'm dragging both of you out shopping this afternoon, and you are both going to buy a dress."

"Oh good. So that means you're taking me out tonight, too."

"Fat chance," he scowled at Jada's teasing. "Tonight, I want her all to myself, if you know what I mean."

"Sure. And I like it, too." Jada brightened. "Hey, I know a

perfect place where we can take her. They have, you know, those hot cocktail dresses."

"The hotter the better."

"And you know those high pumps."

"Do they have garter belts, too?"

"I think they do. Oh, and black stockings."

"Now you are talking, baby."

"Would you two stop talking about me like I'm not even here."

Evan and Jada turned and looked innocently into Meg's face.

"Oh, you're still here?"

"I thought you went to the ladies room."

"That's it," Meg scolded. "Let's get this show on the road before you really get me p.o.'d."

"'Pissed off' is the expression," Evan corrected, grabbing Meg's darting hand and picking up the check himself. "Remember, honey? Today is on me."

"I thought that was supposed to be tonight."

"It was supposed to be." He gave her a meaningful smile. "But someone just got things started a bit earlier than planned. And who are we to complain? Ready?"

<hr>

At the hospital, while Jada was busy with the baby, Evan and Meg spent the time torturing one another with lurid suggestions about games they might play later on.

Shopping, however, did not prove to be Evan's forte. As he yawned and paced about making unflattering comments about the latest styles, Meg managed to find a fall outfit for Jada. Evan sneaked his credit card to the sales clerk before Meg and Jada had a chance to reach the register.

With Jada taken care of, he hoped that Meg might now be more open to focusing on herself.

Open. Another laugh, Evan thought as he and Jada literally dragged her into a clothing store specializing in women's evening wear. Unfortunately, they all agreed that the selection went from the very ugly to the absolutely ugly.

Excusing himself, Evan called Sarah. And just as he thought, Phil's secretary knew the place to go. The small boutique, though outrageously expensive, had the best selection of designer evening clothes one could hope to find on the island. And the best part of it, as far as Evan was concerned, was that they catered to their customer's needs. Saying it plainly, Sarah told him, money talked.

Instructing Sarah to call to the boutique while they were en route ensured the kind of welcome and service Evan was hoping for. Prices were 'miraculously' slashed, and while Meg was in the dressing room with Jada, Evan worked out the payment details with the manager. Suddenly, a phenomenal new selection of 'sale' dresses appeared—lacking price tags. From those, Jada excitedly relayed to Evan, Meg found the dress she was looking for. A dress that she was determined to not show him. Not until tonight.

Sometime later, quite satisfied with himself and the way things were turning out, Evan handed Meg the keys to the car, leaving the two of them to what they called 'accessory shopping' and hoofed it back to the house.

He still had a great deal to do before tonight. And the most important thing, he thought, would be telling her the truth before she found it out from someone else.

But that was something he now knew exactly how to do.

CHAPTER TWENTY-ONE

STILL EXUBERANT FROM the day she'd spent with Meg and Evan, Jada stopped in the corridor of the maternity ward and crouched to tie her sneaker. With the exception of the three mothers that had given birth over the last few days, she knew that the ward was empty. The floor certainly was quiet, and if it weren't for a janitor working at one end of the corridor and the two nurses talking at the duty station just beyond her, the place would have seemed completely deserted. But then, what else one would expect on a Sunday evening.

As she stood up, Jada stopped dead as she thought she heard her name. Listening, she realized the two nurses were talking about her.

"She should have given him up," one was saying. "How is she going to handle the expense and the effort it's going to take to care for him?"

"It's hard enough to take care of an infant. These kids aren't prepared for motherhood. They think it's like playing with a doll."

"You're right. And then the neglect starts, and then they end up with a boyfriend who can't deal with a baby any more than they can."

"It's bad. You can see it on the news every night. Teenage pregnancy…"

Jada clenched her fists at her side. She might not be perfect. She might not even be all that prepared. But she was going to make sure that Ted was cared for. And loved.

"Well, they say she's got a father, out fishing or something."

"At least that's something."

"If it's true."

"Jazelle from Social says that it might not make a difference."

"What do you mean? I thought that guy who was signing all the papers was vouching for everything."

"He's not family. He's got no real connection. Jazelle says with the girl's father out on a boat so much, the state's more than likely going to step in anyway."

"She doesn't know any of this. When is Social planning to tell her?"

"Hey, don't ask me. I think they're just hoping her father comes in before the baby's ready to go home."

"You think they're afraid she won't be able to handle the news?"

"What do you think? She's already attached to the infant, but she's not even sixteen. That spells unstable under the best of conditions. You think they're going to release a sick infant to her? I don't think so."

The lights in the corridor suddenly began to flash, growing so bright that Jada had to close her eyes. Reaching out for the railing, she realized the flashing lights were in her head. Her lungs were unable to take in air.

"Well, I'm glad I don't have to tell her she's not getting her baby, even if there is no way she can cope with it all." There was some shuffling of papers. "Is the door to the nursery locked?"

"Of course."

She had to get air. She stumbled back down the hall. She had to get out of here.

Jamming a fist into her mouth to silence her sobs, she ran solidly into the janitor mopping the floors. She didn't hear her own words. Jada was only conscious of numbness setting in where her heart had been.

Stumbling, but then finding her footing, she started to run again.

They were taking away her baby. *Her baby*!

They might as well tear her lungs out, she thought frantically. Without him, she couldn't see how her life could go on.

Evan finished inserting his cufflinks and walked toward the large bookcase covering one of the bedroom walls. Finding the hardcover book he wanted on the fourth shelf, he pulled it out. Turning it, he glanced at the picture of a very young Drew King staring at him from the back cover.

"Arrogant bastard."

Damn, he was glad he stopped letting his publishers put pictures of him on the dust jackets. This one was embarrassment enough. Opening the book, he paged through until he found the dedication. Reading the caption, a grim smile came to his face. It was so ironic to think that this had to be the very same book.

Walking into the living room, he placed the book on the divider to the kitchen. Beside the book lay an elegant box with the words "Tiffany and Co." embossed on it. Picking the box up, Evan tried to straighten out the bow on the ribbon he'd tied himself.

His lawyer had followed his instructions to the letter. It was precisely the piece of jewelry he'd asked for. Heading back to his room to pick up his jacket, he gave a final look of approval around his bedroom.

There was an excitement in this that Evan had never experienced before. To charm her, to court her, to woo Meg Murphy filled him with incredible happiness. She was worth all this. And more.

Pulling on his tuxedo jacket and straightening his tie in the mirror, he tucked the gift box in his pocket. So much for the ribbon, he thought wryly.

He was prepared. She'd learn the truth tonight. If it wasn't Evan himself spilling the beans, the clues he'd left around his apartment would serve the same purpose. But one way or another, Meg would know before the night was over.

Evan's face grew grim as he considered how important it was that he be around during this. He'd need to talk fast and work quickly to keep any feelings of anger or betrayal from forming. And he'd have to make her understand that even his original thoughts of hiring her as an assistant were no longer enough.

He'd get her to listen to him, because he knew with a certainty that resonated in every bone in his body, he could not let her walk out of his life.

He had to let Meg know that he loved her.

Looking at his watch, Evan decided that it was time. Taking one last look around, he closed the apartment door behind him and started down the stairs.

He only tapped once lightly before the sound of footsteps could be heard on the other side. Patting the box in his pocket, he anxiously waited as the door swung open.

But then he forgot to breathe.

She looked like something out of a dream. An incredibly beautiful, fairy tale dream.

Wearing a strapless, white chiffon dress that hugged her breasts and flared out softly beneath a tight bodice, Meg was the picture of style and elegance.

"Damn," he breathed. The dress was so much like the one Grace Kelly wore in *To Catch a Thief* that, as his eyes swept over her, Evan began to wonder exactly which celestial being was directing this romance. He couldn't help but smile appreciatively at her hair, pulled back and knotted in the same fashionable style. His eyes traveled slowly down her bare neck and arms, and up again until he found her eyes, shining and expectant.

"You are absolutely stunning."

"But I'm no Grace Kelly."

"No. You are more beautiful, more real, more—"

"You don't have to say it, Evan." She stepped closer and wrapped a hand behind his neck. Raising herself slowly, she brushed his lips with her own. "I saw it in your eyes."

But like a starved man, he couldn't let her go. Not until he had feasted on her mouth. It was utter torture when at last he broke off the kiss, and he continued to hold both her hands as she took a step back.

"And you clean up pretty well, yourself."

"Thanks," he said, holding his breath as her eyes traveled appraisingly down his body. "You keep that up and there won't be any dinner tonight."

Meg smiled. "Maybe that's not so terrible."

He shook his head. "No, we'll save it. The pumpkin carriage is waiting downstairs, and we'd better get going."

She picked up a small white purse, and Evan closed the door behind them.

"Yes, we can't forget about midnight."

"And what happens then?"

"You know, pumpkin carriage?" She gave him a seductive glance. "That's when everything disappears, remember? All these clothes. Everything."

"Ah. Well." He raised one eyebrow as he gazed at her dress. "I, for one, can't wait for midnight."

Meg did her best to hide her surprise at the sight of the stretch limo awaiting them outside.

"Don't tell me this is another of Phil's toys that we're taking for a ride?"

"No, this one I arranged all by myself." He gave her a wry wink. "We're all in the same union, you know. Cab drivers, limo drivers, bus drivers, writers. We're all hacks."

She smiled at him, and then nodded to the big man who came around to open the door for them. Despite what Evan had said, she noticed a much more formal style of addressing him than Meg would have assumed from a fellow worker.

Once they were seated inside the roomy vehicle, she was again dumbfounded by the bottle of champagne and glasses that were chilled and ready.

"You robbed a bank, didn't you?"

"I did. And I have until tomorrow morning to turn myself in."

"I'll turn myself over, too. I'll say I was your accomplice."

"It won't be a pretty picture. The sentencing, the confinement, the prison."

She leaned back against the seat and smiled at him. "As long as it's both of us, I don't think I'd mind a bit. Wouldn't be wonderful if they let us share a cell?"

"Even if it's a life sentence?"

"All the better."

She saw his expression suddenly turn serious. "Tuck that thought away for now, since I may just be holding you to it."

Something in her stomach fluttered. Her lips parted, and her mouth went dry.

His face, so full of expression, changed once again as he chuckled to himself.

"I can't believe I almost forgot."

She looked at the box that suddenly seemed to appear from nowhere. Taking her hand, he turned it face up and set the box in her open palm.

"What is this for?"

"Just open it and see."

She looked at the box more closely. "Tiffany's?"

"Oh. I happened to be looking for a box, and Phil happened to have one."

She didn't know why, but suddenly she felt her hands begin to tremble. All the teasing aside, she knew she was being swept away by this man. And it wasn't this pretense of grandeur and wealth that was impressing her, but the real person behind it all.

Sure, Evan had good looks and charm. He had genuine talent. But most important of all, he was one of the only men she'd ever met so filled with compassion and understanding. And something else, too, that so much resembled love.

"Open it."

She slowly undid the ribbon and picked up the lid to the box. The sight of the diamond necklace left her gasping for breath. The stones, set in platinum, sparkled and glittered on the velvet lining of the case.

She gazed into his eyes, they looked so intense and blue tonight, and then she glanced down again at the necklace that suddenly struck her as familiar.

"I...how...I..." She felt like an idiot, but she couldn't even summon the words to express her shock. Evan didn't help matters any, either. With a satisfied smile, he simply lifted the necklace from the case and placed it around her neck.

"Amazingly enough, it's a replica of what Grace Kelly wore in *To Catch a Thief*." His voice deepened, and he whispered seductively into her ear as he clasped the glittering gems around her neck. "We must have read each other's mind. You picking out this dress."

She felt his fingers trailing along the necklace until they reached the sensitive spot beneath her ear.

She let her eyes roam his body. She gazed at the starched whiteness of his shirt and the black satin tie. His jacket, so eternally stylish, hugged his magnificent shoulders. Looking up at his face, she even noticed that he must have stopped for a haircut after leaving her and Jada this afternoon.

"You know, all dressed up like this, you are at least ten times more gorgeous than Cary Grant."

"Considering he is long dead and buried, I suppose that's a safe enough compliment."

"I didn't mean..." She stopped as the dimple deepened in his cheek. "I meant that you are simply so breathtaking."

The feel of his fingertips on her skin made her forget her words, as she found herself melting under his touch. With a sigh, she reached up and touched the delicate stones at her neck.

"Please tell me these are not real, Evan."

He didn't answer, but his eyes bore into hers, mesmerizing her with their power, with the mystery that lurked in their depths. This *was* like the movie. She even remembered the lines the two spoke. The only thing missing was the fireworks display in the distant sky above Monte Carlo.

"Please say it. Please tell me this is an imitation."

"Forget the necklace."

He pushed away her hand and cradled her face in his palm. She couldn't resist him. She wouldn't resist him.

"*You* are real, Meg. That's all that matters."

When he kissed her, the world ceased to spin. When his tongue swept past her parted lips, he touched the very core of her. Nothing else existed. Time no longer mattered. They could have been in a limousine, on the French Riviera, or on the far side of the moon. She was lost to all but the senses he had once again awakened in her.

All that mattered was the two of them. Touching. Holding one another. Their lips, their hearts, their souls joined in a sacred dance that knows no beginning and acknowledges no end.

Only when he drew away, breaking off their kiss, did she

suddenly become aware of the torn fabric of time. It was like magic, and she felt it hovering over them. Surrounding them with an aura of golden light.

The limousine stopped in front of a white, brilliantly lit terra-cotta palace that could easily have fit in at Versailles.

She looked incredulously out the window at the line of limousines, Rolls Royces, Bentleys, and other luxury cars. Valets were scurrying about, directing drivers and parking cars, as formally dressed men and women were entering Rosecliff.

"We're having dinner at one of the mansions?"

He tucked a loose strand of hair behind her ear and nodded toward the place. She glanced again at the front of Rosecliff, which she had visited only once as a wide-eyed tourist.

"Just a little charity affair. Couldn't pass up the opportunity to show you off."

And to her utter disbelief, that was exactly what he did, leading her into a sumptuously appointed hall. The sounds of laughter and music filled the air, and Evan snatched two glasses of champagne from the tray of a passing waiter.

As they made their way through the crowds, heads nodded and more than a few stopped them, making small talk and even thanking Evan for his continued generosity. As each person approached, Evan graciously introduced Meg and then courte-ously excused the two of them, moving her toward the tall arched windows that looked out over acres of lawn and the Atlantic Ocean.

She repeated Evan's name over and over again in her mind. Could it be that he was one of descendants of the very rich who had built their summer 'cottages' here in during America's gilded age? Perhaps he was like so many of the younger generations of the wealthy whom she'd heard of so often, working at common jobs under the pretext of being normal. Hadn't she read some-place that some of the Aster and Van Pelt descendants had openly rejected the way of life of their ancestors? Was this what Evan Knight was all about?

She spotted Phil approaching them.

Suddenly everything started making sense. Evan's incredible generosity. His lack of concern over losing his job. Even his close friendship with Phil Campbell. That had to be it. Finally, the pieces were starting to fall into place. At last, she understood.

"Senator." Phil nodded to the distinguished looking man who had just taken Evan by the elbow. "Ms. Murphy."

Evan ignored him and proceeded to introduce Meg to the elder statesman. It was difficult for Meg to ignore Phil, however, aware as she was of his open and thorough scrutiny of her appearance. The Senator, whom she knew to be a friend to the Kennedys and to nearly every liberal cause for the past forty years or so, begged her pardon before launching into a discussion with Evan about some valuable project that was in the offing. The truth of Evan's background was becoming more certain with every passing moment.

"Man, Meg. You're a knockout."

Meg gave a polite nod to Phil's whispered compliment. "And you're looking quite dashing yourself, Mr. Campbell. Is the plaid in your cummerbund and tie a Campbell plaid?"

"As a matter of fact, it is. But never mind about that. How about if you dump the guy you came here with, and you and I take a stroll through the gardens. There is a phenomenal rose garden, which is still in bloom, and there is a tent with tables set up out there as well. What do you say?"

Evan must have had been using both ears, since his attention was immediately drawn to Meg and Phil. "I'm with you, Senator. But did you know this reprobate Phil Campbell voted against you during the last election? I'm telling you, I honestly believe he is one Republican who could easily be won over. He only needs to hear about all the wonderful things you've been involved with lately, but be sure to avoid any discussion of yacht taxes."

As the politician turned smilingly to Phil, Evan slipped his arm around Meg and ushered her quickly away.

"Sorry, sweetheart. I promise it won't be like this all night. Once they start to serve dinner, everyone settles down at a table. And after that, most everybody is too drunk to talk politics." He had a passing waitress refill their glasses with champagne.

"Where I grew up, most people were never too drunk to talk politics." She looked back at the Senator and Phil. "He seems like a nice man. Know him well?"

Evan cast a quick glance over his shoulder. "Who? The Senator? Not too well. He's a pretty good guy, though, from what I know. Are you having a good time?"

"I am having a great time," Meg said earnestly. "A very unusual group."

He rolled his eyes. "Well, you haven't seen the worst of it yet. Let me tell you something, though. I learned long ago that the secret of dealing with these people is to just go with the flow. Don't ask any questions. Avoid engaging the enemy and take no prisoners. Just smile and nod and go with the flow."

Meg considered for a moment that maybe this was a good time to probe into his past a little. But just as she made up her mind, a rather convivial husband and wife approached them, and without even thinking to introduce themselves, the woman asked Evan if she could have an autograph.

"Didn't I tell you?" he whispered against her ear after scribbling something on a cocktail napkin and watching them walk away.

"Right. Just go with the flow."

"I think it's time that *I* gave you that tour of the gardens. How about it? Just the two of us?"

She nodded with a smile. She could tell that the champagne was already going to her head, a sensation not entirely unpleasant. The ballroom shone in the magic of the huge twin chandeliers of crystal and gold. As she gazed up at the center of the ceiling, painted to look as if it opened to a summer sky, Meg felt as though she could take flight and soar like a bird amid those clouds. Only the sounds of the orchestra's music and the festive chatter of people gathered in groups around them kept her earthbound.

As a waitress passed, offering more champagne, Evan set both of their glasses on her tray, replacing them with two full ones.

Meg shivered with excitement the way he wrapped his other hand around hers and led her toward one of the tall, arched doors leading to the gardens and the lawn. As he pushed his broad shoulders through the throng, the suave confidence that he exuded, and the glances he continually drew as he went by, thrilled her and filled her with an unprecedented sense of pride that she was the woman with him. That *she* was his choice.

Like a vision from some dream or a passage from a romance, Evan Knight was taking her to the gardens. For time immemorial, lovers had been escaping to gardens. A thousand stories told of some beautiful garden of love. Some bower of bliss. Here, in the gardens of Rosecliff, in the light of the rising moon, beneath the glimmering eyes of a million stars, she hoped he would kiss her and make love to her as no one else could.

"Evan. Evan Knight."

Meg groaned inwardly as the two blonde women who had practically attacked him two nights ago appeared in their path. This time, to her shock, Evan wrapped a protective hand around her waist and pulled her snugly against his side.

"Oh, this is fabulous."

"Cornelia, Lucy. I didn't get a chance the other night to introduce you to my fiancée, Meg Murphy."

Meg felt her knees nearly buckle with the shock of his statement, but he continued to hold her steady at his side.

"Fiancée?"

"When?"

"You can't be."

She held her breath as Evan turned to her. With a slow, sensual movement he brushed his lips against hers.

"I'm sorry, love," he said in a low growl. "Just hold on a minute longer?"

Meg nodded as he turned back to the two, gawking women.

"I know Phil Campbell came tonight only because he knows you two are in town. He's probably circulating looking for you right now. Let's see, where could he be?"

Meg bit back a smile. Evan Knight might be the devil himself, she thought, but his diversion worked as the two perennial debutantes tripped off in search of poor Phil.

"Fiancée?" she scolded under her breath as Evan again started toward the doors.

"I know. Not too convincing." He stepped back to allow her through first. "I should have said my wife," he whispered.

Meg swallowed her retort as they passed through the French doors and into the comfortably warm September night. But to her disappointment, quite a few other people already preceded them, ambling along on the stone walkways and sitting in pairs and small groups on the benches leading down through the garden toward the ocean cliff.

"This way, Grace." Evan smiled, taking her hand again and directing her away from all of them.

Walking away from the huge yellow and white striped tent, past the lights, and onto the immense stretch of lawn, they casually made their way down to a fence that separated the grounds of the mansions from the Cliff Walk. Meg remembered walking many times along the narrow path on the other side of the fence, looking in at the ornate and gilded grandeur of these 'cottages.'

Out beyond the Cliff Walk, a round, golden moon had pushed her way up from the shimmering waters into a sky so deep and blue that it hurt Meg to look at it. A night so clear and yet so filled with the mysteries of life. Mysteries that had been evading Meg for a long, long time.

Evan handed her a glass of wine. She accepted it and touched it against his.

"If you think, Mr. Knight, that you are going to get me so drunk that I won't be able to ask any questions…"

"I was hoping to get you just drunk enough to take advantage of you."

"Talk to me, Evan."

"All right. But first tell me what it is that you want to know?"

She took a sip of her wine and watched him move in beside her. She looked up into his eyes, so dark now, reflecting only the light of the moon. The smooth fabric of his jacket brushed against her bare arm, and she shivered, forgetting for an instant what she'd wanted to ask.

"Are you cold? They should have given you a wrap to go with this dress."

She felt his arm encircle around her, bringing her to him. She felt so right, nestled against him.

"Not cold, Evan. A little afraid, maybe."

"Afraid? Not of me, I hope."

"Yes, of you," she whispered. "I don't know you."

He lifted her chin until she was looking into his eyes. "The truth is that you are one of very few people in the world who *does* know me. What you don't know is the peculiar façade that the rest of the world sees. The other…the other Evan Knight."

"And this other Evan Knight, this stranger." She swallowed. "Is he so bad? Is he someone you need to keep from me?"

"I wouldn't have brought you here tonight if that were true."

She reached up and smoothed the furrowed lines on his forehead. She'd been right. Whatever that other Evan might be, the real man standing before her was not ready to unleash that demon on her. And who the heck was she to force him to speak his mind before it was time?

"You talked about fear." He gazed into her eyes. "Meg, I can't come up with any explanation for it. I can't put my finger on what specific thing triggered it. But somehow, from the first moment I met you, you have been under my skin. Somehow, my...my heart opened and wrapped itself around you. That's never happened to me before, and it's an amazing thing. But the down side of it is that it has filled me with this fear...or maybe anxiety...or whatever else you want to call it. Whatever it is, it has made me hold back from telling you everything."

"Evan, you don't have to tell me anything."

"But I want to. I mean, it's not something really terrible that I've hidden from you. It's not like I'm going to turn into a were-wolf or anything. It's just...well, I guess I'm afraid that you won't like what you see." He gave a nervous chuckle. "For the first time in my life, Meg, I'm afraid that I won't measure up."

She dropped her glass lightly into the grass and put her arms around him. "Measure up to whom?"

"To myself." He peered down at her. She could see in his face the discomfort he was feeling, hear the edge that had crept into his voice. "Usually people meet...well, that other me, and I don't give a damn what they like or don't like. I never *want* them to know me beyond that. But with you it's the other way around. With you I've been myself from the beginning."

Suddenly, Meg hated herself for doing this to him. He was upset, and she was the cause. Did it matter to her really if she didn't know everything from his date of birth to his social security number to his favorite dessert? Of course not. She wanted him. No matter what. She loved the man she was holding in her arms.

"Hey, we're on a date." She pressed her face against his chest to hide her own distress. She loved Evan Knight. That was all she needed to know. "Let's not talk about this anymore."

She heard his glass drop onto the lawn, and then she felt his warm embrace. "All right," he whispered. "But sooner or later, you have to know."

"Let it be later." Meg raised herself and placed a kiss against his throat. "Not now."

Before he could voice another objection, she brushed her lips against his.

Breaking away, Evan pulled her across the grass to a rose arbor near the corner of the property. As she entered it, Meg glanced back up the acres of lawn and garden to the mansion. No one had ventured as far down as they, and the music and laughter from the ball rose and fell in the drifting currents of a soft sea breeze.

He drew her to a marble bench inside of the arbor, where they sat in shadows made from moon and vine.

"How much time do you think we have before dinner," she whispered mischievously, moving herself onto his lap.

"What dinner?" he said hoarsely before taking possession of her willing mouth.

A moment later, she moaned deep in her throat as she felt his hand move along the chiffon covering her belly to her breast. She was certain he must feel the hammering of her heart as he dipped his finger inside the low neckline, teasing her nipple.

"I've been wanting to do this since you answered your door tonight."

Her head rolled back languorously as he tugged on the front of her dress until one of her breasts sprang free. When he lowered his mouth to her nipple, she arched her back at the shock of the sensation.

Electricity raced through her veins. Like an inferno her insides erupted in a blaze of heat and passion. Meg threaded her fingers into his hair, holding herself steady against the dizzying waves of desire that were washing over her.

"Evan," she whispered huskily. "Let's forget about the dinner. Let's go."

"Oh, no you don't. You're not getting away that easily." He pulled her higher on his lap, until even through their layers of clothing, she could feel him, hot and hard beneath her.

"I had to do a lot of planning for tonight, and until we've enjoyed each and every step, you're not getting me alone in that bed."

"That borders on sadism, you know," she rasped, smiling at him.

"Why not just consider it extended foreplay." He reached down and slowly pulled up the hem of her skirts.

"What kind of forepl..." She couldn't finish. His fingers were gliding up her leg. They paused for a moment when he touched the bare skin above her stocking.

"A garter belt." He gave a devilish grin. "And no underwear."

She gasped as he delved gently inside her.

"Evan," she cried against his lips. "What happens if someone comes?"

"Someone *will* come." He stroked the moist folds. "And I hope she enjoys it."

Meg gasped and reached between their bodies, feeling for him through his pants.

"Oh, no." He pushed her hand away. "That will have to wait."

"It's not fair." She gasped again as he increased the tempo of his touch. "You...you're trying to distract me. I want to do this to you."

The pulsing in her body was beginning to consume Meg moved, rocking to the rhythm of his fingers, her body lifting higher and higher in a quickening spiral of heat and desire. Something wild and primeval—something deep inside her—was rising to the surface, screaming for release.

"I want you, Evan. I want to taste you...and do the things...you do to me. I..."

Unable to hold back any longer, she cried out, her last shred of control obliterated in a crescendo of white heat.

She was only half conscious of him gathering her tightly to his chest as her wind borne spirit floated gently back to her shuddering body. It took a long moment before she was able to find her voice once again.

"Will the limo take us back home?"

He looked down at her with a curious smile. "Sure, but we still have dinner, don't forget."

"Okay, Mr. Marquis de Sade. But we're *not* staying for desert."

CHAPTER TWENTY-TWO

Evan never liked cherry flambé, anyway.

As they stood waiting for the limo to be brought around, he gazed proudly at Meg, still in discussion with a woman who had joined them at dinner. The other woman, a high-profile business executive from New York, had happened to be one of the people they'd shared their table, and she and Meg had immediately found a mutual point of concern regarding the dismal future our society offered unmarried, teen mothers. Evan enjoyed the way Meg, with the support of her newfound ally, had presented the plight of these young women in a way the rest of the old money sitting at the table could understand. Indeed, they had not been so amiable at first. But that had quickly changed.

Leave it to Meg, Evan thought, playing rabble rouser with a bunch of fourth-generation millionaires. These were people for whom trusts had been set up ensuring the wealth of their grand-children before they themselves had even been born.

He could almost read her mind. He certainly could appreciate her line of thinking. This was a charity function for terminally ill children, and the people attending had the means and the interest in making a difference in the lives of the patients. It was their money that was going into the research and to help find the cure for these horrible diseases.

So why not use the opportunity to raise the consciousness of a few on a topic close to Meg's heart.

Evan watched the other woman hand Meg one of her business cards as a valet brought her sports car around. He only heard the tail end of the invitation.

"I'm in Boston at least three or four days a month. Please call me. I'd love to get together for lunch and discuss this some more."

"I'll be heading home in a couple of days. Perhaps we could do that."

Another couple of days, he repeated silently. Well, not if *he* had anything to say about it.

As the other car took off, Meg beamed at him. He felt a twisting sensation in his gut even as his heart began to race.

"I think we started something tonight."

"You sure did."

He didn't wait for the driver to come around but opened the door of the limo for her himself as the long, black vehicle pulled to the curb. She climbed in first and turned to him excitedly.

"Could we take a drive around?"

"Sure. Where to?"

"How about along Ocean Drive?"

Evan gave directions to the driver and closed the privacy screen. Meg slipped her arm around his neck and kissed him hard on the lips.

"Thanks, Evan. I really had a great time."

He couldn't help but smile. To think for how many years he'd dreaded going to functions like this, and here in one night she'd changed his view of them completely. Meg had shown him the usefulness of getting together a tableful of the East Coast elite.

He ran a finger across her lower lip, thinking how much he wanted to kiss her, how much he wanted to tell her that he loved her and how proud of her he'd been tonight.

"I guess I had a good time too," he said instead, trying his best to sound pouty. "That is, considering...one, I never got to dance with you, and...two, from the time we went back up to the mansion, I hardly even got a word in edgewise without two other people elbowing me out and vying for your attention."

"You poor baby," she cooed, cradling his face in her hands. "Did your feelings get hurt? Were you upset?"

Meg started placing soft, tender kisses on his cheek, then his chin, then his other cheek. By the time she was finished with his face and started on his neck, he knew he was looking placated, but forced back his smile.

"Yes, I was very upset. In fact, I was devastated. Probably scarred for life."

"That's sounds pretty bad. And this was to be such a special night."

He let out an exaggerated yelp as she bit on his earlobe.

"I'll just have to see if there is something I can do to mend your wounds. I did take a course in first aid once...when I was a scout."

She helped him to take off his jacket, and then tossed it along with his tie onto the seat facing them across the way. He reached behind her, running his hand over her bottom, but she quickly placed his hand firmly on the leather seat.

"Now you can't do that. You just have to lay back and relax and let me take care of you. These first few minutes are critical in such a sensitive situation."

"Are they?"

"Very."

Meg moved closer and started kissing a path down his neck and throat, following the line of buttons her fingers were busily undoing on his chest.

"Just sit back," she coed, pushing his shirt open and running her lips over his exposed chest. "Just leave yourself in my capable hands."

"I hope you got a merit badge for this," he rasped through clenched jaws.

He saw her grin mischievously and decided he must have died and gone to heaven. Growling deep in his throat as she moved down along the tautened muscles of his stomach, he held his breath as she reached around him and unclipped his cummerbund.

When he reached over and pulled at her skirts, she slapped his hands away again. "You're my patient, and this is my turn to take care of you."

Slowly, she unzipped his trousers.

"Remember me asking about the limo ride home?"

"Yeah?" he managed to whisper.

"Well, get ready for the ride of your life."

Evan groaned out loud as she freed his aroused manhood from his pants and lowered her mouth, taking him in. But a few short moments of that sweet torture was all he could take.

He lifted her bodily, pulling her skirts up to her waist and kneeling her astride him on the seat.

She hesitated momentarily, and he eyed the downy mound and the ivory skin above her stockings as she started searching in his pockets.

"Okay, where is it?" she asked breathlessly.

"Where's what?" He pulled down the neckline of her dress until her breasts were free.

"You know. The economy package?"

"And do you think I would go to a ball with something like that in my pockets?"

He leaned down and took her nipple into his mouth. She ceased breathing, moaned, then rubbed her moist folds against his long, hard shaft.

"I want you," she whispered. "I want to feel you inside of me."

She didn't have to ask again. He was just about ready to

explode. Reaching down, he took a silver case out of his trouser pocket and handed it to her.

She looked at it curiously, and then opened it as a soft giggle slipped out of her.

He looked down, too, at the two condoms tucked snugly inside the silver clasp. "What's so funny?"

"A cigarette case?"

"Well, I don't smoke."

"And *two* of them."

"You don't think it'll be enough?"

Her open smile warmed his heart. She leaned her head against his and looked into his eyes.

"What am I going to do with you, Evan Knight?"

He reached between their bodies and began to stroke the sensitive spot. Her dark eyes quickly clouded over with passion.

"To start with, why don't you open one of those packages and wrap me. Then we'll *both* have the ride of our lives."

He didn't have to say anything more, and that was exactly what she did. And after she'd lowered herself onto him and ridden him so hard that they both gasped for breath, the two rose together in one harmonious explosion of ecstasy.

Then, as the limousine rolled on past a moonlit sea, he whispered in her ear the words that came straight from his heart.

"I love you."

Jada stumbled along the Cliff Walk and cast a blurred eye up at the stone-cold moon.

She stopped, wiping her eyes. She didn't think there could be a tear left in her body. As she looked down through the wild vegetation clinging to the bluffs and the rock, she knew she could find her way to the Forty Steps blindfolded.

She worked her way down past the warning sign intended to

keep tourists off the decrepit stairway. The Forty Steps lay before her, steep and broken, the ancient pipe railing rusted with long sections missing entirely.

So many times she and Matthew had sneaked down after dark to sit in their special place halfway down. From there, they could see the rock platform at the bottom and at times, depending on the tide, the stony beach beneath. Like a picture out of the album of memories past, she could see the two of them, Matthew's arm around her shoulder. Huddled together against the sharp sea air and a winter wind that bit at their hands and faces. There was no other world besides them then.

What a lie. What a stupid lie! What a fool she'd been to think that they were living in the same world. That they would turn over the next page of lives together, side by side.

Matthew had money, a family name. He was young. He had the smarts to excel, to make it. He alone.

So he had just moved on. She should have known all along that he would leave her behind. Never looking back. Just tearing out the page in his life where she had written her name and moving on.

Jada sobbed and sat on the steps, her arms wrapping around her middle.

And what about her?

It was her own fault. Her own foolishness. Her own naiveté to think that two hundred years of class difference in a town like this would not suck the very lifeblood out of their friendship. Out of their love.

So she was left here. And, of course, she had to be punished for her stupidity.

But her banishment from school and the shame that she had brought on her father, meant nothing in comparison with the pain she'd endured tonight, hearing that they were taking her baby.

A laugh rose in her throat, sad and almost bitter. Sometime

during this last week, she had started hoping again. Somewhere, holding Ted in her arms, she'd begun to dream of a future again.

Why couldn't she start to live again? Why couldn't everything work out? She'd work hard. She'd learn to be a good mother. She could learn to take care of her baby.

But then she'd heard the truth. They were taking away her baby. She was an unfit mother.

It figured. Unfit as a mother. Unfit as a student. Unfit as a daughter. Unfit as a friend and lover to someone like Matthew Rand. Unfit as stinking human being.

Whatever her faults, however great her sins, there was only one thing that she had prayed for again and again. And that had been for the welfare of her son. But then the bitter realization struck her that maybe those prayers had been answered. Little Ted would be cared for...but she was not going to be in the picture.

Of course. He was too young to carry the burden of her mistakes. He was too innocent to face the shame of her sin.

She looked up into the endless emptiness of space. At the zillion stars connected by nothing. At the hard, white, lunar disk.

She gazed back down at the ocean beneath her. She could step off, throw herself down these steps, and end it all right here. One step and she'd find release in death. Why continue to mess things up for her child? He'd be so much better off without her. He would never even know.

Jada stared at the waves breaking in over the rocks and took a deep breath.

"He would never even know."

She didn't feel the breeze pick up, curling around her and embracing her with its life force. She didn't see the sea rising, the waves reaching out to touch and bathe her with a love that was maternal, universal, unending.

Like an automaton, Jada rose mechanically to her feet. She had to do it. If she were to take her life tonight, if she were to step off here and crush her skull, then Ted would have a future. A clean, open path.

Sit down, Jada.

Startled, she whirled around with such force that she nearly lost her footing and plunged down the steps into the dark waters churning below. Clinging to the railing, she searched wildly about her in the darkness.

"Who...? Where are you?"

The breeze pushed her hair into her face, and she swept it back. There was no answer to her questions but the sounds of the surging tide. There was no sign of any living creature anywhere near her.

"I've totally lost my mind." She straightened herself and started to climb the steps.

Don't go, Jada.

She stopped abruptly and fixed her gaze on the empty stairs before her. The voice had come not from a distance, but from someplace quite close. Too close. She hesitantly felt the air around her, looking for something that she knew had to be lurking right beside her. Nothing.

I'm here.

Her heart was thudding uncontrollably in her chest. "Where? I can't see you."

You're not supposed to. I don't exist.

"But I hear you." She placed both hands over her ears, trying to block the sound of the man's voice.

I'm still here, Jada. You can't shut me out.

She shook her head. "Look, you can't stop me. I know what I have to do. It's the only way."

She started climbing the steps.

You're wrong, Jada. It's not the only way. You are only doing this because you think you've been deserted. Because you're alone.

"But I *am* alone. Alone to screw up everything for me and my baby."

No, Jada. I know you're down now, but you have to trust me. Things have a way of working out.

She shook her head and started running up the steps. "I don't need this. I don't need empty talk. I don't need some stupid Casper the Ghost telling me..."

Something tripped her, but when she reached out for the step, Jada felt nothing but air. And then she was falling.

It was the strangest of sensations. A weightlessness. Like a flying dream. No smashing of her skull. No broken limbs from the fall. No watery grave at the bottom. Just floating. She felt herself floating, a puff on goose down on the sea breeze, never touching a stair until she reached the bottom.

She landed on the bottom step. Reality seized her, and she stood frozen there, the tide coming in just beneath her feet.

Sit down, Jada.

Feeling her head about to burst from the fear that was gripping her, Jada obediently, solemnly, sat down.

Much better. Now we can talk.

The voice was beside her on the step and she stared uncomfortably into the empty space.

First things first. My name is not Casper.

She nodded obediently.

Call me Robert.

CHAPTER TWENTY-THREE

HE LOVED HER. He said so himself. He really loved her.

Lazing dreamily in the big bed as the morning light played on the books along the far wall, Meg smiled happily. Evan stirred in his sleep and gathered her tightly to his naked body. One leg stretched across her thighs, an arm draped over her breasts.

She turned her head and looked at his handsome, sleeping face. With his hair mussed and the night's growth of whiskers shadowing his lean, chiseled features, he looked like the picture-perfect rogue. A very sexy and delicious rogue, she corrected, recalling with an impish smile every detail of the night they'd had together.

Meg grimaced. She just hoped that she'd never run into that limo driver again. As much as she'd tried to straighten herself out before being dropped at the house, she knew the man couldn't have had any illusions what they'd been doing in the back seat.

It had been quite a night. Meg couldn't stop a smile from breaking across her lips. Leading her up the stairs, Evan had been the perfect gentleman, but then the rogue had quickly emerged.

After a kind of surreal hunt in which she'd raced around his apartment in search of condoms, all hidden in the strangest of places, Meg had found herself pinned to the sofa. Stripping her clothes off, Evan had proceeded to drag her naked to the rooftop balcony.

Making love to him under a blanket of stars, the breeze cool on their skin, was like a dream. Of course, going in to take a shower and finding another package in the soap dish—and Evan climbing in behind her—had also turned out to be a fantasy come true. And then, when she'd been just about ready to collapse from exhaustion, she'd found herself being tenderly patted dry and carried to bed where another package—tied up with a pretty green bow—had been waiting for her on top of the pillow.

Well, she wasn't about to look a gift horse in the mouth.

Meg sighed, relishing the feel of her cheek against his arm. Before meeting Evan, even through her ten years of marriage, she'd never considered herself to be overly consumed by sex. But now her boldness surprised her. She just loved the way Evan's touch stirred something deep and primal within her. Never had she experienced such flights of incredible passion.

She turned and placed a soft kiss on his chin. And there was something they had between them that was much more than sex. Evan Knight knew how to make her feel smart. He knew how to make her feel desired, needed even. He made her feel complete.

And last night, in the car, he had told her that he loved her.

It could have been the champagne talking, she supposed, the edges of doubt immediately scratching at her happiness. It could also have been that, consumed by their newfound passion, Evan had felt that she needed to hear something more.

But if that's what it was, Meg thought with a frown creasing her brow, she wouldn't hold him to it. For what it was worth, his words had made her feel incredibly wonderful.

"That's some heavy thinking you're doing there."

She looked up and found his eyes open and studying her. Next to the navy-blue sheets of the bed, his eyes were as blue as a dawn sky.

"Actually, I was trying to devise a plan of escape." She glanced down at the well-muscled arm and leg trapping her beneath their weight.

"Well, you can forget it." Evan rolled nimbly on top of her, and she smiled at the feel of his arousal against her legs. "The jailer is now awake and ready to hand out more punishment."

She arched her back and wrapped her arms around his neck. "Oh good. You know, this is one position you haven't used in punishing me yet."

"You're right. But on second thought, this way would be much too quick!" He threw the sheets off the two of them. "How about taking another shower with me?"

Meg smiled shyly. "So long as washing each other's back is not the only thing you have in mind."

It wasn't. And afterwards, as she was drying herself in the spacious bathroom and he was still finishing in the shower, they planned out their day.

They both agreed that the first thing on the agenda was to call Jada and go up to the hospital to spend some time with her and the baby. After that, Evan said he wanted to take Meg horseback riding on Second Beach. From there, they could go on a hike and picnic along the trails of the Bird Sanctuary.

"But there's something else that needs to be done before we even start the day." She pulled a large T-shirt of Evan's over her head and looked down at the logo. "Oh, no. You expect me to wear a *Yankees* shirt?"

"What were you saying needs to be done?" She could see him grinning through the frosted glass of the shower door.

"I think you should put in a couple of hours of writing."

As he turned off the water and opened the door to complain, she threw him his towel.

"I know I don't know much about the other you and your real jobs, but one thing I'm certain of is that you have a great talent for writing. So please don't shake that image for me."

With the towel held to his chest, he stared at her earnestly. A knot formed in her gut as he paused a moment. There was no remnant of jocularity in his face.

"Meg, I think it's time you learned everything there is to know about me."

She nervously folded her towel and hung it on the rack. "Seriously, Evan. I don't want you to feel that you owe me anything."

"It's time, Meg."

She was suddenly afraid of what he had to say. "Why don't I go and make us some coffee." She took a step back out of the bathroom through the living room door.

"Just give me a second to shave. I'll be right there."

Meg nodded and started toward the kitchen. But on her way, she picked up her discarded dress and laid it on a chair. The pants and jacket to his tux had been tossed aside, as well, so she picked them up and carried them back into his bedroom. The neat line of tailor made sports jackets and pants in the closet again caused a knot to tighten in her stomach. Everything about Evan spoke of money, she thought soberly. A lot of money.

And what the heck was an unemployed, middle-aged woman like her going to do with a guy like that.

Quickly hanging the tux in the closet, she closed the door and headed for the kitchen. Looking around at his things, she tried to muster her courage. After all, she knew him pretty well. It was just foolishness to be so pessimistic. There was no reason whatsoever to think that what Evan had to say would be in the least bit damaging to what they had.

She was being too hot-headed. Too stubborn. Too proud. It was just the matter of his money, she decided. She picked up the necklace that was sitting on the kitchen divider and let it drape over her hand. In the daylight the diamonds seemed even larger than they appeared last night. They were real; she knew that now. The trouble he must have gone through to get it. Never mind that the little trinket was probably a year's salary for most people.

She carefully placed the necklace back on the countertop beside a hardcover book that she hadn't seen there yesterday.

It took just a minute to get the coffee started, and after laying out the mugs, she reached over and picked the book up from the divider.

The phone rang and, without thinking, she answered it on the first ring. Well, Meg thought, realizing that she'd done it again, some habits never die.

She smiled weakly and waved as Evan stuck his head out of the bathroom but brightened as soon as she heard Jada's voice on the other end. "Oh. Hi, Jada."

"I called your room, and when I didn't get any answer I thought, I hoped maybe you'd be with Evan."

Meg looked down at her watch. It was eight thirty already. She blushed at the thought that Jada could figure out so easily where she'd spent the night.

"Have you gotten any results on the baby's tests."

"Yeah. I'm at the hospital now. I got a chance to talk to the doctor right before he started his rounds."

Evan came across the living room. Meg covered the mouthpiece and whispered that Jada had gotten some results. But as he made his way into the kitchen, she didn't miss the way his eyes dropped to the book in her other hand.

"Ted needs to have surgery."

Meg closed her eyes and tried to fight back the sudden tightness in her throat.

"The doctor called it closed heart surgery."

"I...I'm so sorry, honey."

Meg watched as Evan crossed the room and picked up the phone in the living room.

"Hi, Jada. It's Evan."

"Hey, pretty good deal. I have both of you on at the same time."

Their eyes met and there was a silent communication that passed between them.

"So what's this news?"

Jada repeated what she'd told Meg and continued on. To Meg's amazement, the young mother's voice seemed to get stronger as they talked.

"But everything is under control. When I talked to Ted's doctor, he said that, from what they can tell, the tests indicate that my baby has a congenital heart condition they call a coarctation of the aorta. Still, to be a hundred percent certain, he wants Ted to go up to the Children's Hospital in Boston. If their findings turn out to be the same as what they figured down here, then they can do the surgery right there."

"What's the prognosis for recovery after the surgery?"

Meg felt a jolt of pride, looking at Evan. He was treating Jada just the way she needed to be treated. As an intelligent adult. As a capable and caring mother.

"The prognosis is good. Very good."

"That's wonderful," Meg chirped in. "For a doctor to make that kind of statement."

"My information doesn't only come from the doctor but..." There was a pause at the other end of the line. "Evan, would you mind letting me talk to Meg for a few moments? In private?"

"No, of course not," he said quickly. "I'll hang up right now."

"Wait," Jada added. "Before you hang up, I want you to know that Little Ted and I both need you. I need you more than ever, as a friend and also as an acting guardian until my father gets back. Okay?"

"You know that I'm always here for you, sweetheart."

"So don't get mad at me for wanting to talk to Meg first. This is just woman to woman talk."

"I understand."

"And Evan, maybe later this afternoon, if you have couple of minutes, I'd love you to come here to the hospital and help me yank some chains."

"Is anyone giving you a hard time?"

"Not openly. Not yet, anyway. But it always helps to be prepared."

"Got it, kid."

"I love you, Evan. Thanks for being such a good friend."

"I love you too."

Blinking back a tear, Meg smiled as Evan hung up the phone and stood up. Grabbing his laptop from the end table, he moved out onto the rooftop balcony. From the way he avoided looking at her, she could tell that he was touched by Jada's words.

"I'm here," Meg said softly a moment later, unconsciously hugging the book she'd picked up earlier to her chest.

"Did I hurt his feelings?"

"I don't think so."

"What I had to talk to you about...you know, I just felt the two of us might be the only ones who could understand it."

Meg felt honored and touched that the young mother would feel this way about her. "Sure, Jada. Do you want me to come now? We could meet—"

"No, I'm not letting this baby out of my sight."

Meg waited as she sensed Jada was gathering her thoughts.

"I think I met someone last night. Someone you know."

Meg turned and leaned her back against the counter, rubbing her chin against the edges of the book.

"Someone *I* know?" Her mind raced with the possibilities of whom she might have met. Maybe one of her co-workers over the years? There was no one she knew in Newport.

"He told me his name was Robert."

She suddenly felt her heart start to pound in her chest. She opened her mouth to say a word, but her voice caught in her throat.

"Meg?"

"Yeah. I...I'm here."

"Remember yesterday in church when you were telling me the story of your husband and his death?"

Even from outside the balcony doors, Meg could feel Evan's eyes on her. She turned around, gripping the book tightly. "Yes, Jada. What about it?"

"You told me that you were able to find him here in Newport. You said that's why you've kept coming back here."

"I remember."

There was a long pause on the other end. "Meg, were you just talking philosophically? I guess I need to know if you meant that you *really* would see your husband here."

"Jada, why are you asking these questions?" No, it couldn't be possible that Robert had contacted her. Meg tried to keep her voice sounding normal. "I was...I was speaking figuratively. You know, as in catching up with memories of my past."

The silence on the line told Meg that she hadn't been too convincing.

"Meg," Jada said finally. "I need you to tell me the truth. If you don't, I may just as well go and get myself committed."

"What do you mean 'committed'? You said this person, this Robert..." She took a deep breath. "There are a lot of people named Robert."

"He wasn't 'a lot of people.' In fact, he wasn't a person at all." She lowered her voice. "Meg, these past few days have been bad. I can't let anybody think I am nuts. This Robert. He was a ghost."

Meg closed her eyes and rested the book against her forehead. What was he doing to her now?

"Meg?"

"I'm here, sweetheart." Meg's mind kept flooding with Robert's last words. About him being here for someone else.

"Have I lost it?"

"No, you haven't lost it." Meg let out a weary breath. "Did you actually see him?"

"No. He was just this voice. I couldn't get away from him, and then I just found myself accepting that he was there. He *was* there, Meg, right next to me."

"That's the way he's come to me too. Just a voice."

"It was kind of scary at first. I was really spooked. I tried to run away, but then I found myself plunked right back where I'd started. He was determined not to leave me alone. It was pretty weird. Though he was pretty cool."

"Yeah, he's cool, all right." Meg pressed the phone tighter to her shoulder. She had been calling him for days. "Did he tell you...I mean, do you know why he decided to come to you?"

"He didn't have to tell me. I knew why."

"Tell me, Jada."

"Promise you won't get mad at me."

Meg smiled. There was still a bit of the little girl in Jada.

"I promise."

"Promise me you won't ever tell Evan about this."

Meg paused and glanced over her shoulder at Evan's profile out on the balcony. "I promise."

"I was pretty bummed about some stuff I heard."

"What do you mean 'bummed'? What did you hear?"

"I mean, I wasn't *actually* borderline suicidal, but I was...well, pretty close."

As Meg brought a hand to her mouth, the book dropped to the floor with a bang.

"Oh, Jada."

"Don't get hysterical on me, Meg. I'm fine now."

"You weren't really trying to take your own—"

"I don't think I could have. But after he showed up, I definitely couldn't go through with it."

Meg raked a hand through her hair, trying to quell the pounding in her head.

"Jada, there is nothing in this world more important than your life. And you should allow nothing—no bad news, no turn of bad luck, no disaster, *nothing*—convince you that ending it will accomplish anything."

"I know, Meg. I've got the whole thing pretty straight now. Meeting Robert—I mean talking to him—it was like being in a concrete box and then having a wall just blow out in front of you. Suddenly, there was sunshine and fresh air. Suddenly, I could breathe again." Jada let out a shaky sigh. "I don't think I've felt this high about the future in a long, long time."

Meg squeezed her eyes shut for a moment and then opened them. Thanks, Robert, she thought. You really came through this time.

"I'm glad, Jada."

The book she'd dropped at her feet caught her eye. Leaning down to pick it up, she froze halfway, seeing the photograph of the author staring back at her from the jacket cover.

"You know, Meg, things have been so down in my life for so long that at every turn, I think I expect the worst. I've just been trained to go from one disaster to the next. Pretty gruesome, huh?"

"I don't..." Meg picked up the book and stared at the picture of a younger Evan Knight. Her hands were shaking as she turned it over.

"But after talking to Robert, I just know that he's right. Things *will* improve for our family."

Jada continued to talk, but Meg hardly heard her as she gazed helplessly at the novel's title. The author's name. She looked at them again and again.

Drew King.

A phenomenal debut!

Death on a Reef.

Drew King.

Meg turned the book over again and stared.

"...I mean, look what he did for you and Evan. To work it out so you two would meet like that."

Meg felt the tears welling up in her eyes. She scanned the spine for the publisher's name.

"Maybe I shouldn't tell you this. But last night, he even talked a little bit about you. About the importance of moving on. About the importance of living."

Morgan Publishing. The same place that Robert had worked before coming to Boston.

There was a slip of paper marking a page at the very beginning of the book. Meg knew what it marked before she even opened the book.

"Robert said that he knew Evan. That he..."

Her hands shook as she thumbed through the first couple of pages. She looked at the copyright and the date. Copyright by Evan Knight. The book was published long before Drew King, Inc. had come into being.

"He's a funny guy. He seemed pretty pleased with himself about you two. About..."

Meg opened to the page with the slip of paper and stared at the dedication. Again and again she let her eyes travel across the single line.

To Robert Luckenbrager with deepest gratitude for your belief in me. I owe you.

"...and how he arranged for you two to meet..."

She couldn't stop the flood of tears that were suddenly coursing down her cheeks. Oh, Robert! she cried out silently. How could you do this to me?

"Thanks, Meg, for telling me the truth. If I thought all that came out of my head..." Jada paused. "Christmas, I don't know how I'd handle it. I mean, it's so weird, you know?"

Meg didn't know what she said in response, but whatever it was, it must have sounded fairly coherent. At any rate, Jada seemed satisfied and hung up a moment or two later.

Standing there with the receiver in one hand and the book in the other, Meg turned in time to see Evan walking toward the kitchen. He stopped. She saw his gaze drop to the open page of the book and then travel up to her face. She hung up the telephone.

"Meg, I thought this might be the best way for you to find out. I tried, but I could never find the right moment to tell you the truth. So I thought if you saw the book. My old picture."

She halfheartedly waved the open book in his direction. It was like a terrible dream, as if she were standing outside herself, watching the action. She could even hear her own voice. It was flat and lifeless.

"You knew Robert."

"I knew him. He was my editor. My first one. The one who discovered me." He took a step toward her. "Meg, listen to me. When I first met you, I didn't know anything about Robert. I didn't make the connection between the two of you."

Her tears had turned into quiet sobs and her breaths began to come with difficulty.

"You wouldn't," she whispered brokenly. "But he knew."

"What do you mean? Who knew?"

"*He* knew. He set this whole thing up."

She saw the confusion cloud his face, but he shook his head and moved toward her again.

"I don't know what you're talking about. But Meg, listen to me. I know you're probably angry, knowing who I am. I know you probably hate me for not telling you the truth right off the bat. But I want you to understand that I really fell for you. I didn't start this whole thing to hurt or deceive you. I was just down here doing my own thing. This is my way of finding material for my work. I've been in a slump, of sorts. That was what the whole business about working as a cab driver was about. And then, you came on the scene. You just showed up in my life and everything changed. Whatever I did, there was no way I could keep away."

He had his hands on her shoulders, drawing her toward him.

"Don't."

She stepped back, shaking her head, fighting the flood of emotions that was taking her under, drowning her.

"Don't, Evan. You don't understand. So please, just don't say any more."

Her heart wrenched to think how he'd been used. How Robert had just manipulated him, making him fall in love with her.

"Please, Meg." His blue-green eyes were dark and troubled. She put the book on the counter and looked away. "I know, seeing that dedication, you probably think—"

"How did you find out about Robert and me?"

"My lawyer," he said quietly. "I had to know more about you. I needed to know that you were for real."

"When was that?"

"Yesterday. No. Saturday. It wasn't until Saturday that I made the connection." He reached out a hand and took hold of her wrist. "Look at me, Meg. Don't shut me out. What I told you last night, about being afraid that you might not like the other me, that was the truth. You told me so yourself. You hated Drew King. I had to find a way to—"

"Don't," she pleaded, batting her tears away. Evan was falling apart right in front of her, and it was all her fault. Her fault for allowing Robert to run her life. For actually waiting while he did something about her future. "Please don't make this more difficult than it is."

"Meg, I love you. Can't you see, I never felt this way about anyone else in my entire life. I've never said that to anyone."

"But you don't love me, Evan." From the look on his face, she might as well have shot him with a gun. She bit her lip and pushed past him. She had to put as much distance as she could between them. "Trust me on this. You don't love me. You've just been had. You were set up."

"Dammit. Don't talk to me like that. Just because you're angry

—and you've got every right to be—don't just throw what I said away. I know my own feelings."

"No. You don't." She raised a hand, motioning for him to keep his distance. He stopped dead in his tracks. "Robert set this whole thing up."

"Robert?"

"Yes, Robert. He caused our paths to cross. From the first moment that I got into your cab—probably even long before that—he was matchmaking. He knew who you were. He knew your true identity. But he never told me the truth."

"Meg, I don't understand you. Robert is dead. He has nothing to do with any of this."

"But he does." Damn her weakness, she cursed, trying to stop her tears. But she might as well try to stop the tide, because she damn well couldn't stop the tearing sensation in her heart. "Remember your car not starting at Castle Hill? That was Robert. About my reservation? The week being pushed back? About you tripping over me in the park? That was Robert."

"Come on. It's been five years, Meg. He's been dead for five years."

"But he's *here*." Her voice broke and she stopped for a moment, wrapping her hands around her middle. "It was my fault. Completely. I kept him here. He couldn't leave while he was worried about me."

"I don't think it works that way."

"Well, it does, Evan. You see, he's never moved on."

"Meg."

"So he took it on himself to plan my future. To interfere with my life."

She stared at him through a curtain of tears.

"You're upset, sweetheart. None of this makes any sense."

"To you, it wouldn't make sense." She shook her head and started backing up. "Look, just forget me, Evan. Forget you ever met me. Think of it as a bad dream. Like a prank that went sour. Just put this whole week behind you. It never happened."

She turned and glanced around wildly for her purse. She needed her key. She needed to run fast and get as far away as she could from this man.

He caught up to her as she picked up the purse on the sofa. Taking her roughly by the shoulders, he spun her around. She looked up into eyes on fire with anger. The timbre of his voice betrayed a fury barely held in check.

"I'm trying to be reasonable. I'm telling myself that I was an idiot to wait. I should have told you right off who I am. I should have told you about knowing Robert when I found out. I take the blame for all that. I'm at fault. But Meg, don't walk away like this."

All she could do was just shake her head and try to swallow the knot that was choking her.

"Dammit, Meg. I just can't make any sense out of this stuff about Robert." As she opened her mouth to speak, he rolled on. "But I don't care. You and I met and something special happened between us. Now, I don't care if it was Robert, Cupid, or the devil himself who arranged this affair. I walked into it with my eyes completely open. And I'm glad I did."

"But you didn't come into it with your eyes open. You were fooled. He knew if we were to step enough times on each other's toes, then we'd connect. And he also knew that once you learned the truth about me, about who my dead husband was, then you feel obligated to stick around."

"That's ridiculous."

"Is it? He's been around, Evan. He knows about your sense of duty, about your generosity, about the streak in you that makes you feel responsible for everyone who needs help and happens to cross paths with you. And I read that dedication; Robert meant a lot to you. The sick part of the whole business is that Robert was trying to collect on what you think you owe him."

As he flushed crimson Meg had the gut-wrenching feeling that she'd hit too close to home. She twisted her arm out of his hands, and he let her go.

"Trust me, Evan. This was a match made in heaven, and it can never work."

"Meg..."

She couldn't stand there any longer. She couldn't contain the pain that was shredding her insides. Reaching out, she gently ran her fingers over the back of his extended hand. Then, without another word, Meg turned and fled the room.

This was the end. She was certain of it. The end of a newfound love that should have worked. And the end of an old love that she should have buried long ago.

CHAPTER TWENTY-FOUR

Denial is a wonderful thing.

It's comforting, in its own way, and Evan spent the morning assuring himself that Meg would come to her senses without any prodding from him.

Shortly after she left his apartment, he took off for the hospital. There had been something that the two of them had talked about on the phone, something that had bothered Meg a lot more than discovering the truth about who he was. But questioning Jada did nothing to clarify matters, since all she did was clam up when he asked about their 'woman to woman' chat.

So he let it drop without pushing her. Considering all she had to worry about, Evan certainly didn't have the heart to tell her about the little disagreement between Meg and him.

Before leaving the hospital, he and Jada sat down for a long chat with the staff social worker. And it was amazing how much better she looked and clearly felt after the woman told them that no decisions regarding the baby's future would be made in haste. The top priority for all involved was to get the child the medical attention he needed. There would be plenty of time to discuss anything else that needed to be done when Jada's father returned.

Back at the house, Evan made up his mind to stop at Meg's room. Dammit, he cursed climbing the stairs, enough was enough. She'd had all morning to straighten out in her head any confusion she had over what their relationship was all about. He sure as hell couldn't make any sense out of her talk of Robert.

Her door was ajar when he arrived at the top of the steps. Knocking softly and calling her name, he was shocked to find out that the room was empty, and the cleaning woman was already at work.

"So what the hell happened?"

Evan whipped around at the sound of Phil's voice. His friend was standing with one foot on the top step.

"Where is she?" Evan snapped.

"Looks to me like she's gone."

"Don't screw around, Phil."

"I don't know where she went. I just got back from the marina, and Nan told me Meg had checked out."

Evan fought against the urge to slam the door shut. To pound his fist into the wall.

"Dammit!" He swore with a cold fierceness violent enough to make his friend move back a step.

She ran. Just like that, she got scared and ran.

"You told her the truth, didn't you?"

He ignored Phil's words and stormed up the stairs.

"You did. Didn't you, Evan? She didn't find it out by herself, did she?"

Arriving at his own door, he kicked the thing open and charged through.

"What difference does it make?" he muttered. "She didn't like what she saw. So she just tucked her tail between her legs and took off for parts unknown."

He stalked into his kitchen and opened the fridge for a beer. The bottles of wine, the ones that they'd never gotten to last night, greeted him first. He slammed the door shut, ignoring the rattling and the sounds of breaking glass, and turned back to the counter to make coffee instead. The diamond necklace he'd bought her lay partially hidden beneath *Death on a Reef*. With a growl, he picked up the book and flung it across the room.

Dammit. He couldn't breathe. Yanking at the collar of his shirt, he marched out of the kitchen and headed for the balcony. Her dress lay neatly arranged across the back of a chair. Picking up both chair and the dress, he threw them both out of his path.

"Why don't you go after her?"

"Why the hell should I?" He slammed the French door open and stared at the blanket lying on the plank decking of the balcony. He squeezed his eyes shut, trying to blot out the image of the two of them making love.

"Well, for one thing, it'll save me on furniture replacement costs."

He swung around toward Phil, who was leaning with a shoulder against the doorjamb.

"She dumped me. Plain and simple. She dumped me. You and I both should understand that pretty well. She just gave me a taste of my own medicine."

Phil continued to stand silently.

"But you know, the thing that really ticks me off about the whole thing is that she didn't have the guts to tell me the truth. She couldn't just stand there and say, 'Hey, we had pretty good sex, and I got what I came on this vacation for.' No, she had to make up this bizarre story about her...about her..." Frustrated, he raked a hand through his hair. "Ah, Christ! I don't know why the hell I'm even worrying about it. The hell with her. She can just disappear from the face of the earth as far as I'm concerned. They're a dime a dozen, women like her."

He stomped to his computer and turned on the damn machine. Even the buzzers and beeps sounded judgmental.

"I'm gonna work, so you can just drag your ass out of here."

Plunking himself down in front of the flashing screen, Evan

felt the anger roiling in his veins. His head was pounding, but that pain was nothing to the knife twisting in his gut.

He never should have let down his guard. He never should have gotten attached. Damn her for making him feel this miserable.

Damn her to hell!

Order might be heaven's first rule, but it didn't apply to Meg's bedroom at the moment.

Clothes, torn from their hangers, lay in a huge pile where they'd been thrown in the middle of the floor. Books were mounded to one side. Photo albums and framed photographs sat beside the books. On the queen size bed two suitcases lay open, but neither of them held much.

Meg stood in the nearly empty closet, working quickly and almost methodically. There was a kind of cool detachment in the way she yanked a shirt from its hanger, and as she moved toward the pile, she was no more aware of the garment in her hand than she was of the state of the Tasmanian economy. There was an empty look in Meg's face as she added the shirt to the others, a look that spoke very clearly of a heart that had been all too recently broken.

Finishing up with the closet, Meg moved on the large chest of drawers beneath the antique, oak mirror. Opening the top drawer, she pulled out the neatly folded polo shirts that had once belonged to Robert.

Everything was as he'd left it. The shirts, the socks, the underwear, the handkerchiefs. Nothing had been moved. Nothing disturbed. Not for five years.

She must have been out of her mind, she thought with disgust, to hold on to Robert's things so many years after his death. When a chapter of a book is done, you turn the page and it's over. When you finish a book, you write, 'The End" and that's it.

That was all part of it. That was where she'd gone wrong from the start. If she had done any of this, if she'd been brave enough to turn the page in her life, then perhaps she wouldn't be hurting so much right now. Then perhaps she wouldn't be mourning not one but two men whom she loved and had now lost.

The sound of the door buzzer roused Meg from her reverie. Wiping the remnants of tears from beneath her eyes, she moved to open the door. Just as she'd hoped, Rebekah stood amid a pile of empty cardboard crates in the hallway.

"Are you getting evicted already?"

Meg held the door open as her friend pushed the boxes into the apartment. She had called Rebekah as soon as she'd gotten in from the train station.

"No, I'm not getting evicted. But I did give notice on my lease." Meg closed the door and started heading back for the bedroom, but Rebekah's hand on her arm stopped her short.

"Meg, what's wrong?"

"Nothing."

"Really, you look like shit."

"Well, I can't help that."

"Meg—"

"Look, I'm just doing what I should have done five years ago. I'm sorting through and getting rid of Robert's things. Don't you think it's about time?"

Rebekah gave a suspicious nod and followed Meg to the bedroom. But at the sight of the huge mess, her shocked gasp made Meg's ears burn with embarrassment.

Robert had been a creature of habit, and so had Meg. Orderliness and neatness had been a part of their day to 'day life. For all the years the two women had known each other, Meg knew Rebekah had never seen her bedroom in such a condition.

"As you can see," Meg mumbled in explanation, "I've already started."

"Uh, yeah. But what are you going to do with all of this stuff?"

"Give it to charity. There are plenty of homeless men out there."

"I know. I've dated most of them."

"They could have used some of these things years ago." Meg bent over the open drawer and started pulling out the neat stacks of T-shirts. "That's where I'll send all of these. To a homeless shelter."

There was a pause, and Meg heard her friend rummaging through the piles.

"Oh. and I'm sure these photos of you and Robert will really keep them warm this winter. And these books. Who cares if they're starving to death? At least they'll have some serious literary shit to read for entertainment. Impressive."

"I don't need your criticism. But I could use a little help." She knew she sounded short, but she didn't care. She motioned toward the boxes Rebekah had brought with her. "Why don't you start putting the books and those things in that pile into those. I have some trash bags underneath the sink that we can use for the bulkier clothes."

Without waiting for an answer, Meg pulled out the next drawer, gazing at the contents. Polo shirts.

"Meg, what are the suitcases for?"

"For me. I'm packing."

There was a pause, but Meg didn't look up as she placed the shirts on the floor.

"Have you decided where you're going?"

"I don't know. I thought to start with I thought maybe New York."

"You have an interview? Any prospects?"

"I wish." Pulling open the next drawer, Meg shook her head at yet another stack of polo shirts. How come she didn't remember him having so many stupid shirts? "That does it."

Her patience gone, she pulled the drawer sharply out of its track and dumped the shirts unceremoniously on top of the pile.

"No, I don't have an interview. I don't have any prospects. I'm just going to get a one-way ticket to New York. And when I get there, I'm going to knock on some doors. Maybe even beg for a job. Whatever it takes."

The handle on the drawer came off in her hand. With an angry cry, she added the drawer, as well, to the top of the pile.

"They can't wear that."

"What?"

Rebekah pointed sheepishly at the broken drawer. "The homeless. They can't wear that."

"They can burn it for heat, for all I care." Meg stopped short and turned her back to her friend.

She could hear Rebekah quietly putting things into boxes behind her. Meg crouched down and opened the bottom drawer. Cardigan sweaters.

"Evan. That was his name, wasn't it?"

Meg ran her fingers lightly over the cashmere. All of the sudden, she couldn't hold back the pooling of tears in her eyes. She wiped away a drop that fell on the soft wool.

"He was a really good influence," Rebekah continued in an ironic tone of voice. I don't think I ever heard you come close to saying the 'f' word before."

"Don't start on me, Rebekah. I'm really in no mood right now."

"I can see that."

Meg tried to pull the bottom drawer out of the dresser, but it stuck.

"Dammit!"

"That's another new one."

"Rebekah."

"Okay. Well, how was Newport, anyway?"

"I don't want to talk about it."

Meg tried to blink back her tears, and probably would have succeeded, but when she felt her friend's hand on her shoulder, a sob rose in her chest that would not be ignored.

"Okay," Rebekah said softly, crouching beside her. "Then let's talk about Evan."

CHAPTER TWENTY-FIVE

JADA'S FATHER Ted navigated back into Newport harbor on Monday with the best catch of fish he'd taken in ten years.

No longer having to worry about Jada and the day to day needs of a new mother and her baby, Evan finally had all the time he wanted to sulk. It takes practice to be a good sulker, though, and he was only in moderately good form by Monday night, when Phil tried to drag him out on a double date with two socialites just in from Aspen. Evan begged off, complaining of a sudden attack of flu.

On Tuesday, miraculously recovered from the flu, he'd stared at his computer for most of the morning. By noon, he'd deleted nearly everything that he'd written the preceding day. By three in the afternoon, Evan decided to get drunk. Very drunk. The boys down at the pub were more than happy to keep him company as long as he was picking up the tab.

At exactly 1:07 a.m., an entirely inebriated mob of singers exited the Thames Street Pub and began their parade through the center of Newport toward the Point section of town. Most of these wayward troubadours would never see the inside of Carnegie Hall based on their vocal talent. Nonetheless, as the entourage continued its early morning tour through a lightly falling drizzle, the town was treated to an incredibly loud and off-key version of the old Rod Stewart song "Maggie."

Damn, Evan thought, trying to focus on one of the gas lamps along Washington Street. For the life of him he couldn't remember telling them about Meg. Later, though, after dismissing his escort with a ceremony no less solemn than General Washington's dismissal of his troops, it occurred to him that, quite possibly, Maggie...er, Meg had been the only thing he'd talked about all night.

Wednesday morning—at least the minute or two that Evan saw of it—was gray and dismal. Sometime in the early afternoon, he woke up again with a jackhammer in his head and a phone ringing off the hook. Jerking the receiver off its cradle, Evan growled menacingly into the thing. Unfortunately, it was his lawyer John, whining that he'd been trying to get hold of Evan since Monday with the additional information about Meg Murphy.

Evan told John to go and fly a kite, and that he didn't know any Meg Murphy.

Thursday, he gave the cab to a young Haitian mechanic working at the cab company.

Friday night, Jada called to tell him the results of the day's travels. She and her father had taken the baby to Boston that day for more tests and to meet with the heart surgeon. Meg had showed up in the hospital and eaten lunch with them.

Evan immediately changed the topic and asked about the baby.

"He's fine. I mean, he still needs surgery, but they think that should wait another six months or so, until he is a little bit older and stronger. But he's in no danger right now. And Evan, we can take him home now."

"That's great, sweetheart. About time, don't you think?"

"I'll say. I am so excited. And dad's thrilled too. He is so funny.

He just sits there, smiling and holding Little Ted in those big, rough hands of his." Jada gave a little sigh. "You know, after seeing how attached they've gotten in just these past few days, I've begun to see things a little different."

"What do you mean?"

"I mean, like questioning the past. Daddy's been so great, and we've talked a lot. I've decided that it doesn't make any sense to beat yourself up over stuff that's over and done with. I'm going to accept what's done, learn from it, and look ahead."

If only he could do the same, Evan thought. Drunk or sober, he could still feel Meg around him. It didn't matter if he were sitting in front of his computer or going out and running until his legs were ready to fold, he could still hear her soft laugh. He could smell her in the autumn breeze. He could feel her breath on his ear as she whispered words of passion. She was everywhere. In his mind. In his heart. In his soul.

"I think she's lost some weight she didn't need to lose."

"Who?" he asked as casually as he could.

"Come off it, Evan. You can't fool me with that stuff."

"I don't want to talk about her."

There was a pause on the line. "Okay. If we don't talk about her, then I won't have to ask you what happened between you."

"That's true."

"And I won't have to ask why two people who are so perfectly matched, all of the sudden have to act like a pair of immature teenagers."

"Watch what you say, sweetheart. I think you might still be considered one yourself."

"Exactly my point. It takes one to know one...or two."

Evan walked over to the counter and refilled his coffee cup. "I'd love to stand around and chat, Jada, but I have a hot date."

"A date?"

"Uh, yeah, Mom. Can I have the keys to the car?"

"Is she as beautiful as Meg?"

He glanced across the room at the laptop computer sitting on the sofa. "Well, she is pretty well built."

"Is she as funny?"

"As a matter of fact, she's got a great memory for jokes."

"Better in bed?"

The cup hit the counter with a bang. "Do you want *all* the gory details? Don't you think you're a bit young to be asking these questions?"

"Look," she replied, her voice rising a dozen decibels or so. "You're my friend. But so is Meg, and I think it's incredibly low—in fact, bordering on despicable—for you to go out on a date with another woman so soon after breaking up with Meg. Evan?"

"Yes."

"You're a miserable old, no good—"

"Don't say it."

"Sonovabitch."

Evan couldn't stop the smile that tugged at the corner of his mouth. "Okay. You said it. Feel better?"

"No."

"There is no other woman, Jada. And no, I'm not going on a date tonight. Are you happy?"

There was an audible sigh of relief on the other end. "Really?"

"Really."

"What about the bimbo with the good memory?"

"I was talking about the computer."

"Very funny."

"If Your Highness is done with me, I should be getting back to work."

"Okay. Oh, Evan, I hope you don't mind, but Dad told me the truth about you being that writer guy. I mean, I think it's pretty awesome how you've been faking it as a cab driver and all that."

He leaned against the counter, and his eye fixed on the necklace that had been lying untouched for so many days now.

"Yeah, well. I won't be driving the cab anymore."

"I just want you to know that I think it's pretty cool. Dad said that you two met when you went along on one of the boats as a fisherman a few years ago. He said..."

Jada continued to talk, but Evan was hearing something else. The sound of Meg's soft laughter rippled through his mind. It was the same laugh that he'd heard when he unclasped the necklace from her neck before taking her to the sofa. He looked across the room and saw in his mind's eye the two of them stretched naked on it. For a moment he could almost feel the softness of her skin beneath his lips, under the tips of his fingers.

"Are you still there?"

"I'm here." He shook his head. "But I've got to go."

"She's moving, Evan. In case if you wanted to know."

"No, I don't want to know."

"Her old phone number is no good anymore."

"I'm not calling her."

"And she's living out of a suitcase at a friend's house."

"Jada, I'm hanging up."

"She is looking for a job too."

"Jada."

"I think she is hurting, Evan. She gave me the new number."

"Bye, Jada."

For a few minutes, Evan continued to gaze at the phone on the wall. Today, for the first time since Meg had walked out of his life, he'd thought he was getting better. He had actually been able to tolerate a couple of hours of staring at the computer. Not that he'd done much, but it was a start. Now, though, his insides again felt like a school of barracudas had used him for a buffet.

Why the hell did Jada have to tell him that Meg looked thin? And why was *she* hurting? It had been her choice to walk out of his life.

Evan banged his palms on the counter and stared with unseeing eyes at the fading streaks of orange in the western sky.

He couldn't count the number of times that he'd gone over all that she'd said. Robert. Why the hell even bring up Robert? A dead man.

Well, if she thought she could just shift the blame to a long dead husband, a guy that Evan truly respected, she could just forget it. If she thought for a minute that he would forgive her for what she'd said and done because Robert was still supposedly hanging around, then she was totally full of shit. Evan had been around her long enough to know that she had her head on straight. She was no crazier than he was.

No. What she'd done was a planned break. A denial of his love. A flat rejection.

"How the hell could you do that? I know people who would kill for an opportunity like that. We're talking Morgan Publishing here." Rebekah stared at her across an open box of mortally wounded pizza. "Do you know who they publish? Meg, I'd murder my own cat to get an interview at Morgan Publishing."

Meg threw her half-eaten slice of pizza back in the box and patted her lap. Rebekah's little, white dustmop of a dog jumped up happily.

"You don't have a cat. You have a Dudley."

"Doesn't make a difference. Morgan Publishing, Meg. One of the biggest publishing houses in New York and certainly one of the best paying."

"I couldn't do it." Meg shrugged indifferently. "First of all, I never sent them a resume. They just came after me. Which tells me that Robert—"

"No, Meg," Rebekah snapped. "Robert is dead. Dead. Gone. Expired."

The dog rolled onto his back, his little paws in the air, as Meg continued to pet his chest and belly. Since making the decision not to sleep in the apartment that she and Robert lived in for her entire married life, his death had become more real than it had ever been. No longer surrounded with daily remembrances of him, she had begun to feel more detached from those years, and from that relationship she had striven to keep alive.

"Despite what you think of yourself, Meg, and in spite of having worked your entire life for Elgin Publishing Company, that Goliath of the industry, you have somehow succeeded in making a name for yourself. Look at all the authors that you helped to get started. I can name a half dozen right off the bat who went on to make the lists after changing houses." Rebekah slammed the box of pizza closed. Frowning at her friend, she stood up and carried it to the kitchen counter. "Can't you understand that those people in New York would naturally *want* to talk to you? And I'm talking about wanting you because of your own reputation, not because they remember some guy who used to work there fifteen years ago."

"Robert wasn't just some guy, Rebekah."

"Wake up, Meg. You know that there is no loyalty in this business. Nobody in New York is going to take you on out of pity."

Meg petted Dudley absently and then shrugged her shoulders.

"I still couldn't do it."

"Why? Because of Drew King?"

Meg didn't look up. Even knowing that her friend was going in this direction, she could not help the knot that was forming in her chest.

Rebekah knew almost everything that there was to know about Evan. Meg had told her who he was and how he'd been working undercover, sort of, as a cab driver when Meg had met him. But Meg had not been able to reveal to her friend the depth of feelings—the love—that had developed within her. Neither had she felt competent, even, to explain how he'd been duped into thinking he was attracted to her.

No. As far as Rebekah knew, Meg had simply had her first

fling since Robert's death, and that, by an odd twist of fate, it had happened to be with Rebekah's idol, Drew King.

"Meg, people move on after little encounters like that. It's suicidal to jeopardize your future, or even throw away an opportunity for a good job, just because of the one day a year when he might step into the same building. I mean, following that line of reasoning, you can't even work in a Dairy Queen for fear of him stopping at your window for a cone."

"I know. You've already told me. And in a week, he probably won't even remember my face. But still, I just couldn't bring myself to jump in like that." She put the dog on the floor and got up to put on the kettle for tea. "Maybe my problem is that I just feel like I have to ease into this change."

"So you buy a train ticket to New York and then leave it pinned to the wall?"

"Yeah. I guess I just want to feel like I'll be ready when the time is right."

Rebekah took two cups from the cupboard next to the sink and put tea bags in them. "You know it's not because you're staying here that I'm saying these things."

"Of course I know." Meg and Rebekah had been friends for years, and it was almost laughable that Bekah's questions and advice could come from any source other than her concern for Meg. "Are you working tomorrow?"

Since getting laid off, Rebekah had increased her hours waiting tables. She'd picked up the second job at a classy French restaurant in Cambridge about two years ago as a way to supplement her income at Elgin Publishing. Actually, according to Rebekah, the restaurant job paid her rent and expenses, and the editing job provided play money.

"I'm doing a lunch shift tomorrow." Rebekah's eyes were fixed on Meg's face. "So, what are you going to do short-term?"

The kettle came to the boil, and Meg filled both of their cups with hot water, sliding one along the counter to her friend.

"I'm looking for freelance work." Rebekah's response was immediate and her scowl a clear indication of her skepticism. Meg continued on, ignoring the look. "Not as a permanent thing, of course. I know that I have to get my face out there among living people. But I thought if I could line up a couple of clients just to carry me through a month or two, then I'd have a better chance of finding the perfect job."

"Oh, there's a perfect job out there?"

"Of course," she said stubbornly, busily squeezing out the tea bag. Her mind flickered back to her time spent with Evan. How exciting—and how satisfying, too—to read his work. How productive it had been, focusing her complete attention on just one author. That was an indulgence that she'd never had at Elgin Publishing. But working with Evan had been the thing that had given her the idea of freelancing.

"So are you calling some of your old authors? Is that the way you're going about it?"

"What?" Meg met Rebekah's probing eyes. "No, I'd like to work with new names. You know as well as I do how many unpublished writers there are out there. I placed a couple of ads in different papers. I hope you don't mind, but I gave your phone number as a backup."

"Hey, whatever works. So long as you don't quote prices to any of my male friends when they call here." Rebekah brightened. "On second thought, maybe we could get into that business. You know, you almost look miserable enough to pass as a pimp."

"Oh, thanks. Then you can play the part of the slut."

Rebekah let out a snort of laughter. "You know, Meg? I think Drew King somehow screwed the beginnings of a sense of humor into you. Remind me to send him a thank you note, will you?"

CHAPTER TWENTY-SIX

PHIL DROPPED the Sunday Book Review section of the *New York Times* on top of the round table. Looking around the room, he stared at the mess of dirty dishes and empty beer bottles and picked up one of the open reference books lying on the floor by an overturned chair.

"Don't eat anything more than a day old, you dope," he told Swift, who was nosing through a bag of take-out from the Imperial Garden.

He glanced at the partially open bathroom door. The shower was running. At least he's mobile this morning, he thought somewhat thankfully, picking up trash and straightening furniture.

Moving into the kitchen, Phil emptied the day-old coffee grounds out of the pot and washed the thing. For all the years they'd known each other, Phil had never seen his friend so affected by a relationship with a woman. He'd never gotten down in the dumps the way he did this past week.

He was really hooked on Meg. That was clear. She had affected him in a much deeper way than Phil could ever have imagined. But then, he himself was no expert when it came to loving a woman. For all the many relationships he'd gotten himself in and out of over the years, not once had he become as disoriented as Evan was right now.

But then, he'd never been in love.

Phil measured the water and poured it into the coffee maker. That was exactly what Evan's problem was. He was indeed in love.

As the smell of coffee began to waft through the kitchen, Phil opened the dishwasher and started piling the dirty dishes onto the racks. Wiping off the counter, Phil took two cups out of the cabinet and set them by the brewing coffee. There had to be something that he could do. There had to be a way that he could help Evan get over this.

The sound of Evan's curses brought a smile to Phil's lips. Knowing his dog Swift's predilection for licking wet bodies fresh out of the shower gave him a clear picture of the scene in the bathroom.

"Phil! You call this pervert she-devil of a dog of yours right now, or I'll swear to reupholster my sofa with her."

"Come here, girl." Phil poured the two cups of coffee. "Come on, good girl. He is mean old man, and he really means it."

The Irish wolfhound poked her head out of Evan's bedroom, gave Phil a disbelieving smirk, and trotted back into the bathroom through the bedroom. But a couple of minutes later, as Phil was gathering dirty dishes and bringing them back into the kitchen, he saw Evan emerge alone from the bedroom. He paused and gave his friend a once over. Even cleaned up, he still looked pretty ragged with an almost week-old beard covering his face.

"What did you do with Swift?"

"Shut her in the shower." Evan moved to the dividing counter and helped himself to one of the cups of coffee. After he'd taken a sip, he glanced disapprovingly at the results of Phil's efforts. "I don't need a frigging maid."

"Really? What do you want for breakfast?"

Evan took a large sip of the hot coffee. "You just made my breakfast, so stop playing house and get the hell out of here."

"Well, I'm not ready to go yet. Like it or not, if it was me instead of you feeling like shit, I know you'd be dragging my butt out of here and knocking some sense into me."

"Wrong." Looking away, Evan took the cup of coffee and headed for the round table in the dining area. "Look, I'm fine. Really. Last night I even started writing again."

Phil glanced at the books piled around the apartment, but he still was not convinced.

"How about taking a couple of days off and going sailing? We could head for Nantucket. Or the Vineyard."

Evan sat down at the table and stared blankly at the Book Review section that Phil had brought along. "Not yet. Maybe...what's today?"

"Sunday."

"Maybe next weekend. What, you couldn't afford the rest of the paper?"

"Nan's looking at it." Phil took the dishes that he'd picked up to the sink. "By the way, she said if you keep out the cleaning woman out of this place for one more day, she's calling the health department on you."

"She can start again tomorrow."

Phil glanced back at Evan. He didn't seem to have gotten beyond the first page of the paper.

"I'm going to head out to New York for a few days. I think I need a change of scenery."

"Good. I think that's a great idea."

"Both Henry and John have been bugging me to get down there to see to some business."

"You don't need an excuse, Evan. Why don't you just get up and go, the way you used to."

"The way I used to. Christ." He ran a hand through his hair and came to his feet. "I can't do anything the way I used to. I feel like I've had a goddamn lobotomy. I can't think. I can't move. I can't work without..." He started for his bedroom. "I'm going for a run."

Phil just nodded as he saw his friend disappear into the bedroom. Well, this was the first sign of life he'd seen in a week. A change of scenery was exactly what Evan needed.

"Hey," he yelled after Evan. "Send my dog out, or we'll have the ASPCA as well as the health department in after you."

She got two calls the same day the ad was posted.

The first call came from an engineering grad student in Texas who wanted a proof reader rather than an editor, and the second came from an elderly gentleman in Maine who was interested in having someone write his World War II memoir for him. Although neither were exactly what Meg was after, they still gave her hope that the money she'd put up for the advertising was not going to be a total loss.

Having Rebekah at work on Sunday also gave Meg the chance to sneak one of Drew King's earlier books out of her friend's bookcase. For fear of being reprimanded by her friend for not letting go, reading one of his books was something she could never do in the open. So all day, curled up on the sofa with the book, Meg jumped like a sneak thief every time the phone rang or someone's footsteps could be heard in the hall outside.

But all the same, she found herself getting lost in the pages—in the story and in his seemingly artless style of writing. To think that she had criticized him. To imagine that she'd thought he would even be interested in her input.

Every writer had books that just don't work. And that one book, *The Long Journey*, must have been the one for Drew King. But to think that he'd just sat there and taken all the caviling, carping criticism without so much as a word in defense of his own work, made her feel all that much worse.

Perhaps, though, she thought, she would have been better off if he'd done just that. Reading his words, hearing his voice in her head—their days together came back to Meg with a vividness that shredded her insides into an unholy mess.

Sitting there on that sofa, his book on her lap, she found herself reliving in her mind everything that they'd shared. Every moment. Every caress.

And burning a hole in her chest was every word of love that she'd kept locked in her heart.

After changing into his running clothes and returning to the living room, Evan was somewhat relieved to find that Phil was gone. He picked up his coffee cup from the open Book Review section of the paper.

As he drained the cup, his eyes briefly scanned the page. A review of some movie star's biography. His gaze was drawn to the "Specialists—Services" heading where his coffee cup had left a ring around an advertisement.

"'Experienced Editor...'" Evan read, frowning and heading for the door. "Yeah, right."

The day was windless and sunny, and Evan pushed himself to run farther than he normally ran. Every turn, though, brought back another memory of her. By the ocean at Brenton Point, passing the mansions and Rosecliff, crossing Bellevue by La Forge restaurant, Evan thought of her.

Upon returning to his apartment, Evan climbed the stairs and stopped at the landing outside his door. Spotting a piece of newspaper stuck to the bottom of his sneaker, he pulled the piece away.

As he started to crumple the scrap up something odd about it struck him, and he stopped dead. On the torn paper, the ring from a coffee mug circled an ad.

Experienced Editor...

Evan stared at the paper for a moment until his curiosity propelled him through the door. Carrying the scrap of paper to the table, he laid it down on the open newspaper. It was a perfect match, circular coffee stain and the ad, as well. He read the advertisement again. An editor looking for freelance work.

He stood over the table for a long minute, trying to make sense of what lay before him.

"No," he muttered finally, stubbornly denying what he was seeing. "It can't be."

Evan closed the paper and folded it, dumping it in the garbage pail beneath the kitchen sink.

Fifteen minutes later, showered and changed, he headed downstairs and found Phil stretched out on a porch sofa reading the rest of the paper.

"Come on, pal. I think I owe you a lunch. How about fish and chips at the Pub?"

"Great," Phil replied, standing and stretching. "I was just thinking about grabbing a bite."

The Pub always served their fish and chips the same way, on top of a piece of newspaper in a wicker basket. Today was no different. Nonetheless, halfway through his meal, Evan sat and stared with disbelief into his food.

"What's the matter?" Phil asked. "Find a deep-fried cockroach or something?"

Evan didn't answer. There, at the bottom, inside of a coffee colored ring, that same ad peeked up at him.

Pulling out the paper, Evan stared at the advertisement. Damn. What were the chances of him running across the same section of a paper three times like this?

Without warning, Evan reached over and dumped Phil's unfinished portion of food on the table and yanked out the newspaper in his basket. He looked at one side and then the other. No sign of any circle and no ad. He looked again at the piece of paper in front of him.

Experienced Editor...

Evan had always considered himself rational if not wise. He'd always considered himself a perceptive man. But never, *never* had he considered himself superstitious.

"And would you care to tell me what the hell this is all about?"

Evan glanced over at the mess he'd made of Phil's food. "What's wrong? You don't like your food served *a la carte*?"

"I think your French is a little rusty." Phil snatched the paper out of Evan's hand and scanned it, front and back. "What're you looking for?"

"For all the years you've been having fish and chips in this place, have you ever seen them serve it on top of the Sunday *New York Times*?"

"How the hell would I know? I come here in for the food, not for any intellectual enrichment."

"Just look at this." Evan snatched back the paper. "Yours is served on the birth announcements of the *Newport Daily News* and mine is on the Book Review section of the *New York Times*."

"So what? Is that supposed to be some kind of a sign? Oh, I get it. I'm to be cursed with faulty condoms, and you're to get yet another glowing review in that paper. Is that it?" Phil sat back in his chair. "Evan, it means one of two things. Either Ray the short order cook is starting his own fortune cookie-horoscope routine,or you're in the market for a Prozac dealing shrink."

"Look, I don't know what the hell is going on." Evan again glanced down at the paper. "All I know is that three times today, I've seen the same ad from the same paper with the same goddamn ring around it."

"Maybe it's a national brand or something. What's the advertisement for?"

Evan took a slug of his beer and looked again at the already familiar phone number. "An editor, looking for freelance work."

"In the book section. Gee, that's pretty strange."

"You're such an asshole. See this ring?" Evan pointed to the stain on the paper. "There are advertisements above and below it. People advertising the same thing. But the ring keeps showing up around this one ad."

"Maybe something went wrong during the printing. Maybe, every one of the papers they printed has that mark on that ad."

"Maybe," Evan said absently.

Or maybe, he thought, he wanted to believe that there was some magic left in his life. Maybe he even hoped that the ad had some connection with Meg. He knew from giving it to his lawyer that the phone number wasn't hers, but it was a Boston number. And Jada had said something about Meg changing her number.

He took another swig of his drink. No, there had to be dozens of would-be or ex- editors in Boston. Maybe he should just pick up a phone and call the number. That might be one way to figure out what the hell this thing was all about.

"I'll be right back."

Evan looked up to find Phil pushing his chair back and standing up. "Where are you going?"

"Order me another beer. I'll be right back."

Evan watched as his friend walked out of the bar. Throwing the paper aside, he decided that maybe he was getting too weird for his own good. First, it was all his sulking over Meg, and now it was hallucinations with extraterrestrials and an evil plan to brainwash him with coffee stained tabloids.

He would leave for New York tomorrow. That would certainly put an end to all this nonsense. Over the past year, his housekeeper had spent more hours in his apartment there than he had himself. It was time to get back to normal routines.

Hell, he had a deadline to meet and a book to push out. Maybe it wouldn't turn out to his liking. There was no way to know that beforehand. But at least he still knew how the hell to finish a book.

Phil walked back in with a newspaper tucked under his arm. "Here, take a look at this one. I'm betting you'll find the same circular stain."

"I can't believe you went and got another paper."

"Hey, it was worth it to prove my point." He sat down and began to rummage through the sections. "Here it is. You want to do the honors?"

His curiosity getting the best of him, Evan reached for the book section and opened it to the appropriate page. The advertisement was there.

No sign of any ring.

"Nice try, Sherlock. No stain on this one."

"Could be a different edition."

"Forget it. I have." Evan folded the paper and pushed it away from him. "I didn't order you another beer. I'd just as soon be getting back to the house."

"So you are definitely leaving for New York."

"Yep. But I want to take care of the business stuff in the first couple of days. Then I focus on nothing but writing."

"Hey, don't stay away too long."

Evan nodded appreciatively. In his gruff way, Phil was the most loyal friend he'd ever had.

"I'll be back."

As they left the pub, Evan tucked the folded book section from the paper under his arm. Back in his apartment, he dropped it on the table without giving it another glance until a few hours later when he was talking on the phone to his agent in New York. Absently, he started thumbing through the section until he reached the page. He froze mid-sentence.

There, on the page where there had been no stain, a coffee colored ring circled an ad offering the services of a certain *Experienced Editor...*

"I'll have to call you back, Henry."

"Evan? Evan, are you alri—?"

The receiver dropped into its cradle, and Evan ran his fingers over the page.

It wasn't possible. Since coming back from the pub that paper had not been touched, and unless somebody was playing a very elaborate prank on him, Evan couldn't imagine how the hell that same ring could appear where it hadn't been before.

Thinking over the whole thing again, there was no doubt in his mind what he had to do. He picked up the phone and dialed the number in the ad.

He frowned, feeling his own heart hammering away as he waited for the phone to ring. On the first ring she answered, and there was no question in Evan's mind who was on the other end.

He hung up without speaking, and a pall quickly descended on his soul. But what, he thought, could he have said? How could he explain that his subconscious was in overdrive? How could he tell her that silent vibes were coming to him long distance?

It took Evan only a couple of minutes to go downstairs and rifle Nan's drawer of room keys. The registration book showed that someone had stayed for three days in the same room that Meg had occupied, but that the room was empty now. Grabbing one of the keys, Evan climbed the stairs and unlocked her door.

He leaned his back against the door and gazed into the tidy room. It was the strangest sensation to see in his mind's eye the two of them arguing in the middle of the room. To remember the way they'd kissed. To see himself backing her toward the bed. To recall how they'd tumbled on that mattress.

He crossed the room and ran his hand over the wooden bedpost and then walked to the windows. Pulling one open, he stepped back as a rush of autumn air suddenly filled the room. But as he breathed in the air, he frowned. She was still here. He could sense her presence.

He turned around and again let his eyes roam the room. No, it was his imagination. The room was clean and empty. There was nothing for him here.

The puff of breeze blew in, lifting the bed skirt, and Evan spotted a little triangle of white peeking from beneath it. He bent over and pulled out a piece of paper that had somehow wedged itself up between the bed skirt and the box spring.

It was a handwritten draft of a note to someone named Mrs. Wilson. A response to a submitted manuscript. It was from Meg.

Evan poured over the letter, devouring it like someone who had been isolated from any contact with humankind for half a lifetime.

Firmly, but with a lot more tact than she'd ever used with him, Meg was rejecting the manuscript, and not simply because of Elgin Publishing's demise. She commended the author for her talent and her persistence in the subject but told her that the material lacked an audience. Evan read on. Considering the fact that for so many years Mrs. Wilson had tried to sell her work unsuccessfully for a mainstream market, perhaps it was time, Meg argued, to switch genres. Evan continued to read, smiling at the convincing way that Meg tried to talk the author into writing children's stories using the same material. She even referred to story lines that she'd obviously seen in Mrs. Wilson's past submissions.

He looked away, trying to put himself in this Mrs. Wilson's place. The encouraging tone of the note and the extremely viable suggestions Meg made were enough to make anyone feel good about their work. And Meg had finished the letter with the names of potential editors at houses which might very well be interested in this type of work.

Evan folded the letter and put it in his pocket.

"One in a million," he murmured, turning to go.

Reaching the door, he turned, remembering the open window. As he walked back, he looked over the room once more. And this time his eyes were caught by something on the dresser. He stopped dead. Even from this distance, he could see it was a business card. He worked his way around the bed and picked up the white card.

Meg Murphy
  Senior Editor

He looked up and stared in the mirror above the dresser. Someone else had stayed in this room. The room had been cleaned. More to the point, this card hadn't been here when he looked around only minutes before.

The incoming breeze swirled around Evan, and a movement in the mirror drew his eye to the windows.

He wasn't alone. There was someone else here. Something present.

And it wasn't Meg.

He wasn't mad. He could feel it. A presence. A force that was making itself known. And suddenly, Evan knew who it was.

His question was a mere whisper. "So what else are you planning to pull out of your sleeve?"

This time the wind gusted about the room.

Angrily, Evan stalked to the other two windows and threw each of them open wide as well.

"If you *are* real—if you're not just a figment of my overly active imagination—then show me something. Prove to me that you're really here. Or go to hell!"

The full blast of the wind came with a suddenness that took him by surprise, pushing him back a step with its power. It had been a fairly calm day when he and Phil had walked back to the house, but now a veritable hurricane seemed to be taking place in the room where Meg had slept.

The pictures on the wall rattled and the mirror on the far wall banged ominously under the rushing wind. Evan pushed toward the windows, intending to close them. But when he reached for the first one, a scrap of paper rocketed in and smacked him squarely in the face. He knew what it was before he even looked at it.

Page 10 of the *Times* Book Review section. Meg's ad in a coffee-colored ring.

"Is this the best you can do?" Evan shouted. "Is this the extent of your tricks?"

The gusting wind encircled him, pushing him toward the bedside table with the phone sitting on top.

"No, I won't do it, Robert. Not until we've had it out. You and me."

Nearly yanked from his feet, Evan found himself sliding across the floor. Fighting with all his strength, he still ended up beside the bed, fingerprints from some unseen hand suddenly visible on his wrist as his clenched fist was dragged toward the phone.

"Not yet, dammit! You can't force me do *your* will. I fell in love with her all on my own. You had nothing to do with it. You hear me, Robert? Nothing."

The next powerful surge had his hand on the receiver. With one swift move, Evan yanked the phone cord out of the wall and threw the entire thing across the room.

"Now cut the shit and start listening, pal. I've had just about enough of your second-rate special effects." He stalked toward the window and slammed the middle one shut. "You've already made me a believer. Fine, I admit you exist. But I also know now that you're a coward. A pitiful, indecisive spirit who can't let go."

The breeze gentled a bit but still swirled about the room.

"It's time, Robert, that you and I had a talk."

CHAPTER TWENTY-SEVEN

THE 10:45 train from Boston's South Station was twenty minutes late arriving in New York.

Shifting her briefcase from one hand to the other, Meg ran practically all the way through Penn Station to the 32nd Street exit. She must have been crazy to think that she could jam three interviews into half a day. At least, she thought with chagrin, she could have listened to Rebekah and come into the city last night.

There was a line of cabs waiting when she burst out of the building, and Meg leaped into the first one. As soon as she gave the address for Morgan Publishing Company, though, the car coughed and stalled.

"Oh, no. Not again," she murmured, with a quick look at the driver. But before she could decide whether stay or find another taxi, the cabby cranked the engine back to life and took off like a shot into the surging traffic.

As they pushed uptown, Meg kept reminding herself that everything would be just fine. This was only an interview, and they would understand her reason for being late.

But then again, she knew that wasn't the only reason why she was so wound up. What would happen if they actually offered her the job? She shook her head. More than likely, it wouldn't happen, and even if they did offer her something, she was by no means obligated to take it.

The second call from Morgan Publishing Co. had come in the wake of two other phone calls requesting interviews. All in New York. She had even been able to schedule them back to back. So when one of the managing editors at Morgan had called her again, Meg couldn't bring herself to say no right away. With the sudden departure of one of their top editors, he'd told her, they were in dire need of someone with her background.

Meg glanced at her watch. Her interview with the publishing house was scheduled for 11:30. She was going to make it. Then, at two, she was supposed to meet up with the lawyer with an itch to turn author, at his office on Madison Avenue. From there, she was to meet Mrs. Stenerud at her apartment on Fifth Avenue at five o'clock. Pretty hectic day, she thought, noticing that was 11:20 already. But in seven minutes, Meg walked up to the receptionist at Morgan Publishing.

Personnel had forms to read and sign. And then, after declining the offer for lunch to the shock of the human resources director, she spoke for twenty minutes with one of the senior editors and then spent another half hour chatting with the managing editor who'd called her.

During both interviews she was at first amazed and then delighted that she wasn't being interviewed, but instead openly courted. The ultimate shock, however, came when she was taken to a spacious corner office overlooking Rockefeller Center, to be interviewed by the publisher, Fred Shaw. There, Meg was told straight out that she had the job if she wanted it, and all they needed to agree on would be her salary and benefits package.

Meg sat, straight backed and dumbfounded, listening to the older gentleman speak of all the years that the company had been a leader in the publishing. He reminded her of the outstanding line of authors that they continued to nourish and support. Authors like...Drew King, for instance.

She tried to keep her face expressionless. There was no way these people could have any idea about her brief affair with their gold mine of author.

"In fact, this is part of our new strategy, Ms. Murphy. May I call you Meg? Established authors like Drew don't feel comfortable working with the new generation of young editors. They want stability. They demand to work with people who have considerable experience."

He was calling her old and hackneyed to her face, but Meg still didn't even flinch. In fact, to hide her discomfort, she brought the cup of coffee to her mouth.

"So how would you feel about working with Drew King?"

It was a miracle that she didn't splutter the entire mouthful down the front of her white shirt.

"I...hmm..." She carefully put the cup back on the side table. "I was...I thought I heard someplace that he already had a new editor. Wasn't that just a couple of weeks ago?"

"It was. It is. But that's just the point." The seasoned publisher took a book from the crowded bookshelf and handed to her. Meg looked down at Drew King's oversized name on the cover. This book, ready for release, hadn't hit the bookstores yet.

"We went through five editors on this one alone. And to tell the truth, I don't think Bill Maxwell, his present editor, has what it takes to see Drew through the book he's working on right now. I mean, the word is that he's already too intimidated even to call and see how he's making out. Bill's a good man though, don't get me wrong, and we really don't want to lose him."

Meg began to say something in support of the editor but then quickly closed her mouth again. She wasn't supposed to know the man. She was supposed to be clueless of Evan's temper tantrums and his distaste for talking on the phone.

"Anyway, we've decided on a new approach this time." Fred

Shaw started pacing the room. "We've already invested a lot of money, and there is a great deal of potential for the novel that Drew is working on right now. So, to get to the point, we're not waiting until we get to the crisis point. We're not going to wait until Drew's complaints—and he's certain to make them—about another competent editor begin. No, we've decided to take a more proactive role. We're determined to find the right match for Evan and get an editor who will not be bullied."

All Meg could do was just nod.

"But to do all of this right, we've been searching for the ideal editor, someone competent and seasoned. One with great deal of talent and...ahem, a lot of patience. But also one who is not afraid to face a big-name author like Drew King and tell it the way it is."

"And you think I have what it takes?"

"I do."

"And may I ask what evidence you have that makes you think so highly of my qualifications and abilities?"

"Fair question. As a matter of fact, we have a total of eight of your previous authors under contract with us right now. I think you know who they are. And I have to tell you that every one of those people still worships the ground you walk on and wants you in this organization. Every one of them, Meg, speaks of you as an excellent and gutsy editor." A slow smile broke out on the man's tanned and wrinkled face. "Hiring you would be a great investment for Morgan Publishing. We could even use you as a bargaining chip when it comes to negotiating some pretty hefty contracts."

She'd been never one to accept complements easily, especially when they were based purely on rumor.

"So what do you think, Ms. Murphy?"

She couldn't. The answer was no. Evan would have nothing to do with her, considering everything they'd been through. It didn't matter how much she enjoyed reading his new work. It didn't matter that the most exciting times of her life were the moments and days she'd spent with him. Evan would throw the whole thing back in Fred Shaw's face.

Hers would be the shortest and most humiliating career in New York publishing history.

But looking up into Mr. Shaw's benign and grandfatherly face, she just couldn't bring herself to give a definite answer now. In this man's mind, in the collective mind of the entire publishing industry, it would be madness to refuse an offer such as this with no sound reason. It was a small world, and there were ears everywhere. She had to have an excuse for turning him down. A reason good enough to keep the door open for other houses that might consider giving her a job.

"I'm afraid that I have another interview scheduled in less than half an hour." This was the only excuse she could think of. But at least, it was better than nothing. "So if you don't mind, I'd prefer to call you tomorrow with my answer."

"I understand perfectly. And tomorrow will be just fine. By then, I'll even have a nice financial package laid out. And I promise, you won't be disappointed."

She could see from his face that he was assuming she'd take the job. But he was wrong. Evan wouldn't have her. He was not about to be duped twice.

Glancing again at her watch and making appropriate excuses, Meg left Morgan Publishing with twenty-two minutes to make it to her next appointment.

It was faster to walk to the address on Madison Avenue than trying to hassle the traffic. So that's what she did. But all along the way, her mind battered around with thoughts of Evan. She tried to imagine what his reaction would be if she were stupid enough, or gutsy enough, to actually take the job.

There was no question in her mind what he would do. He would get even. Perhaps having her get fired right off wouldn't be his style. But he'd rub her nose in what they no longer had.

Meg sped up her steps. She wouldn't be able to take it. She

couldn't pretend that she was just his editor and there was no past.

No. She couldn't allow her heart to break. Not again.

Arriving at the address she was given, Meg stepped into the elegant lobby. Perhaps this was her chance. If she were able to finalize an arrangement here, then she would have the temporary relief she was after. Feeling more determined than before to make a positive impression in this interview, she marched into the elevator like a woman with purpose.

Stepping out on the fourteenth floor, Meg was immediately taken by the large, attractive front entrance and the personable receptionist.

A secretary immediately came out to greet her and she was led down a long hallway flanked with offices. At the very end, Meg was introduced into a bright and spacious office with wonderful view of St. Patrick's Cathedral.

Talking at length on the phone Monday, Meg and her potential employer had decided that it would be best for them to meet in person first, rather than mailing manuscripts back and forth and trying to make sense out of the direction they needed to be heading. But finally having the chance to meet the man, Meg quickly realized that John Peck was not at all what she had expected him to be.

For one thing, he was much younger than the seasoned lawyer, ready to follow a lifelong dream of writing that she had envisioned. On the phone, John had mentioned to Meg that being a principal in his own firm left him with little time to pursue his true interests. In meeting with her, he'd said, he was hoping to take a positive step toward his goal.

Gesturing to a comfortable sitting area at one end of the cavernous office, the lawyer led Meg to a brown, leather chair and sat down in one just like it, facing her across a mahogany coffee table. Declining coffee or tea, she sat and waited for him to begin, and she did not have long to wait.

Unlike her last interview, in which she'd been more of an observer than anything else, John Peck drilled her with questions about her past and her work experience and about the different authors that she'd worked with. His questions were pointed, and he listened attentively to her responses, making notes occasionally in a folder that she noticed had her name typed on the tab.

And actually, when she was done saying all that she cared to say, Meg felt very good about the whole thing. This was what she needed, she realized. Someone who would look at her credentials from a purely objective standpoint.

In return, Meg noticed that John said more about himself than his writing, though even those details were minimal. But before they were finished talking, he had identified how much he was ready to commit to this freelance, co-authoring venture financially, and that amount nearly took Meg's breath away.

Who was she to argue? This was a great job, more suited to her present needs than she could have hoped for. In addition, she could use this offer as an excuse to decline the job at Morgan Publishing. But still, to be fair to him, she did tell the lawyer that she had another interview and that she didn't want to make up her mind until she had completed the three interviews she'd come to New York for.

John Peck agreed and chatted amiably with her as he walked her past the front receptionist to the elevator, himself. But as they waited for the elevator door to open, he paused and frowned.

"There is just one final thing, Ms. Murphy. And I hope you'll understand my reasoning for waiting until this last minute to mention it."

Meg's heart dropped. She should have known that this whole thing was too good to be true.

"The work that I'd like your assistance with...well, the actual writing is not my own."

Puzzled, she waited for the man to continue.

"As you can imagine, we have a number of clients who are

quite circumspect with regard to their privacy and their private matters. So, when it comes to their various needs, we try to offer them services that are sometimes a bit beyond the normal realm of legal advice."

"Are you telling me that you were interviewing me, not for yourself, but for a client of yours?"

He brightened. "Exactly. As you have guessed, my firm has taken it on itself to assist one of our top clients in this journey of writing, publishing, struggling, whatever you want to call it. Therefore, we thought if we were to interview and hire someone of your obvious caliber, then..."

Meg could actually feel the man's discomfort.

"I just thought you should know this before we go any further." He leaned over and pressed the down button on the elevator again.

"And may I ask the name of your client?"

"No, I'm afraid that I can't divulge that. Not yet. At least, not until you call me back and agree to take the position."

The elevator door opened. Quickly stepping inside and putting her briefcase down, Meg pressed her finger on the 'Open Door' button.

"I'm sorry, Mr. Peck. It would be totally impossible for me to accept the position without knowing my true client."

Their eyes locked for a long, awkward moment.

"I'm sorry, Mr. Peck," she said finally, letting go of the button.

"Drew King."

Meg watched the door slide shut.

"The name of my client is Drew Ki..."

CHAPTER TWENTY-EIGHT

THE WOMAN ACTUALLY HUGGED HER.

Dressed in a hunter green jogging suit and Nikes, Mrs. Evelyn Stenerud was perhaps the sweetest and loveliest old woman Meg had ever met.

Arriving at the Fifth Avenue address a few minutes earlier than she'd planned, Meg was directed by the uniformed doorman to an elderly, white haired woman just crossing the street from Central Park. Though she had to be in her eighties, she was as vibrant as a sixteen-year-old.

Still a bit rattled by the two sets of interviews, each of which had directed her straight at Drew King, Meg hadn't even been sure she wanted to sit through another one. But now, climbing into the elevator with the talkative and affectionate creature at her side, Meg thought perhaps that this was exactly what she needed.

"You will, of course, be staying for dinner."

Meg looked down at her watch. Quarter to five. She tried to remember when the last train was leaving for Boston.

"Actually," she said, stepping out onto the tenth floor behind her fast walking companion, "I was planning to—"

"Nonsense." Mrs. Stenerud dismissed the thought with a wave of one hand as she fished with the other into a waist pouch for her keys. "We have to have a night on the town. I have a friend too, whom we can call. He can always get tickets to a show."

"Really, Mrs. Stenerud—"

"Call me Eve, dear."

"Fine, Eve." Meg watched her pull a huge key chain with countless keys from the pouch. "I just thought we could spend a couple of hours chatting about your work."

"My work? But that's so boring. I want to hear about you, dear."

"Well, you know most of my background from our telephone conversation yesterday."

"No, no, no. I want to know about the *real* you."

Meg didn't know what to say as they came to a stop before the door of an apartment. She watched Eve try one key after the next in the keyhole. But from the look of pain in the older woman's face, Meg could see that Eve was suffering from arthritis, or some similar ailment.

"Can I help you with that?"

"I'd be grateful if you would, dear. You see, my problem is that I hate to get rid of things."

Meg glanced up at her.

"Are you like that, too?"

"To be honest, I'm trying to change."

"Oh, I've tried a dozen times. But I'm still a packrat. I have a key to every place I ever lived on that chain."

Meg started trying the keys. "This thing is so heavy. It must be a workout just to carry it around."

The older woman chuckled. "Actually, I use it as a weapon. Two years ago, I used it on a would-be mugger in the park. He ended up with ten stitches over one eye and three months in the can."

"That'll teach them to mess around with you."

"You've got that right. They even wanted me to go on one of those late night shows when it happened." Eve nodded proudly. "But you were telling me about yourself."

Meg sped up her efforts with the keys. "Well, there really isn't much to say."

"I believe that comes under the category of 'bullshit'."

Meg couldn't stifle her laugh.

"Hah! I got you. You didn't think little old ladies in white sneakers could swear, did you?"

She shook her head and for the first time met Eve's intensely green eyes.

"That's the right key."

Meg turned her attention back to the door and the key that had turned in the lock.

"Is it?" she murmured quietly.

Eve pushed the door open and Meg followed her into an open and empty foyer.

"Don't mind the lack of furniture. I'm told it's coming, and an old woman can only complain so much."

Meg just nodded absently as she walked slowly through the foyer and into a huge, high-ceilinged living room. Beyond a pair of open French doors, she could see an empty dining room. With the exception of floor to ceiling bookcases, already lined with books, and couple of gorgeous oriental rugs on the parquet floor, there was hardly a stick of furniture in sight anywhere. But with the afternoon sun pouring in the large, arched windows, everything looked absolutely perfect.

Meg heard Eve disappear through a set of double doors into a corridor. She wondered briefly just how big this apartment must be.

"How about some tea?" Eve called from down the hall.

"That would be wonderful," Meg called over her shoulder. "Need some help?"

"No, thanks."

Dropping her briefcase against a wall, Meg wandered over to the door-sized windows. Outside was a stretch of balcony overlooking Central Park.

It was so beautiful here. So peaceful. Glancing around at the spacious room, Meg's mind was suddenly filled with images of Evan and the night of the ball at Rosecliff. She could just see him, dressed in his black tuxedo, gliding through this room. She could see him standing by the marble trimmed fireplace. He was made for a place like this. It would suit him. Money, elegance, charm.

The sound of something scraping across the wood floor whipped Meg's head around. She caught sight of Eve dragging two Windsor chairs into the living room. She quickly went to older woman's aid.

"Please, Eve. Let me help with these."

"Sorry, these were the only things I could find for us to sit on."

"They'll be just perfect." Meg arranged the chairs close to each other, facing the windows and looking out on the park.

"And as far as tea, I'm afraid I'm out of tea bags."

"I really didn't want one, anyway. I was just trying to keep you company." Meg followed Eve's lead and sat down.

"You're a very good-natured person, Meg Murphy. I like you."

Meg felt a blush creep into her cheeks. "Thank you, Mrs. Stenerud. I like you too."

"Eve. Call me Eve."

"Yes. Eve."

"So you're widowed," the older woman said without a pause.

Meg immediately felt the hackles on her neck go up. "How did you know I was widowed?"

"The ring." Eve's intense green eyes were on her wedding ring. Angry with herself, Meg unconsciously fisted her hands. She'd gotten rid of nearly all the excess reminders of Robert in her living arrangements, but her wedding ring had totally escaped her mind.

"In some ways, dear, we women—all of us—are very

predictable." The older woman fingered a wedding ring on her own hand. "If you were married, then you'd have already mentioned your husband. As in, 'My husband will be waiting for me in Boston.' If you were divorced, you wouldn't be wearing the ring. But the fact that you're still wearing it says *widow*."

"He died five years ago," Meg said quickly. "But I'm determined to let go and move on."

"That's a good thing. We all have to, sooner or later. I was married twice myself. And after my first husband died, there was a period of time when I even felt guilty for surviving him. But you know the clichés about time and healing. I suppose it's true. All I know is that our heart lets us know when we can love again."

A comfortable silence descended on the two women for a moment, but the sound of a knock at the door brought them both quickly to their feet.

"Oh. My groceries," she explained with a cheerful smile. "I asked the doorman to have them brought up the front way. Excuse me, won't you?"

Meg nodded absently and looked down at her left hand.

It was time to discard this last symbol of her past with Robert. Pulling the ring slowly off her finger, she walked to the closest window. It opened inward, and she stepped through onto the balcony. Ten floors beneath her, a narrow strip of evergreen trees hugged the front of the building.

She gave the gold band one last look. Until death...

"Goodbye, Robert," she whispered as she dropped her wedding ring. "I'm letting you go."

This was the end. She never wanted to erase him from her past. But from this time forward, a new life would pulse in her veins, and she could feel her spirit grow with every breath she took.

"Goodbye."

Her voice drifted away on the breeze, and Meg remained

there for a moment, breathing in the crisp autumn air and feeling it cleanse her soul.

The chapter had ended. The page had been turned. The book —complete now—was tucked away on the shelf.

She stepped back into the room and slowly closed the window. When she turned to the foyer, though, her heart stopped.

Evan.

"You look great. Cut your hair?"

She had. Rebekah had made her. He'd noticed.

She forced herself not to meet his gaze. And she forced herself not to voice her concern over the weight that he had lost. Most of all, though, she tried not to take the dozen steps that would carry her across the room and into his arms. She had missed him.

Instead, her eyes searched the foyer beyond where Evan stood leaning against the arched entryway.

"Where is Eve? I mean, Mrs. Stenerud?"

"My grandmother had some things to do."

Uncontrollably, Meg's eyes moved to his face. "Your...your grandmother?"

He nodded. "She lives down on the eighth floor. She said was waiting for some groceries or something. I told her I could take it from here."

Meg's emotions were holding Highland games in her stomach. She let her eyes again travel through the empty room.

"And this apartment?"

"It's mine. I bought it a couple of years ago, at her suggestion. But I've never gotten around to decorating it. I'm kind of glad now that I didn't."

He straightened where he stood, and Meg wrapped her arms around her middle—as if by that small gesture, she could block the entrance to her heart.

It's too late, she heard her heart tell her. *He is already there. And no matter what you do, it's too late to push him away.*

"I heard you've had a full day."

She took a step aside and stood behind one of the chairs. "And how do you know about my day?"

"Let's see." He ran a hand over his chin. "Fred thought he had you sixty percent convinced. And John thought he had you ready to sign before he mentioned my name. But Eve was the only one who thought she had you all the way."

Her hands reached out and grabbed the back of the chair as she felt her temper suddenly bubbling to the surface.

"Are you telling me you had those interviews arranged?"

"Yes. That's exactly what I'm telling you."

"You had no right to."

"I had every right," he replied. "I couldn't let you throw my love back in my face because of some stunts on the part of your creative and very dead husband."

"But you don't understand."

"But I do."

"You can't. Robert *did* plan the whole thing."

"I believe you."

She shook her head. "He thought he was doing it for my good. But he never thought of you or your future."

"I believe you."

"We met because he *wanted* us to meet," she cried out desperately. "You had no say in this."

He started toward her. "Meg, I believe you."

Suddenly, his words started to sink in. "What did you say?"

He reached the chair that stood between them. "I said I believe you."

She looked up into a face hardened with resolve, into eyes that showed a spirit dogged and determined.

"But if you know, then why?"

"Because Robert didn't force me to love you. With all his tricks, all he could really do was arrange for us to meet. That's it,

Meg. Just meet. The rest of it was left to us. Pure and simple. Everything else was up to the two of us."

Every shred of emotion in her body was knotted in her throat.

"Meg, I need to know how you feel about me."

She bit her lip. She couldn't let him become more of a victim than he was by confessing her feelings.

He took the chair out of her grip and pushed it aside. In an instant, she felt his hands on her shoulders, his head down as he looked directly into her eyes.

"How do you feel about me, Meg?"

As hard as she tried, she couldn't hold back the words.

"I love you." Her voice cracked. "But that doesn't mean—"

"It sure as hell does," he growled. She could see the glow of life deep in his eyes. "You love me, Meg, and I love you. And nothing in this world—and no one in the next—can change how we feel about each other."

She closed her eyes as his arms tightened around her. She shivered at the feel of his warm breath on her ear.

"I don't know, Evan," she whispered stubbornly. "I just can't help but think if it weren't for Robert—"

"No, Meg. If it weren't for *me*."

She opened her eyes and looked up.

"If it weren't for me, you wouldn't have come to New York today. If it weren't for me, Morgan Publishing wouldn't have called you with a second interview offer, though they *did* call you with the first. If it weren't for me, neither John nor Eve—"

"You still had no right."

"I did, love. I did." He ran a finger across her trembling lips. "Your dead husband is not the only one who can play matchmaker. I can, too. And I had to, in order to make you see. In order to make you understand that how much I love you and need you. I won't let you go. Not without a fight. Not before I use every earthly trick that I can think of."

As twisted as it sounded, all of the sudden everything started to make sense. She actually began to see the logic in it.

"When it comes to you, there is no end to what I'll do, Meg. Robert may have opened my eyes and made me realize how empty my life is without you, but now I'm prepared to go any distance and do any crazy stunt to make you believe in me. Setting up job interviews would have been only the beginning."

She brushed away the tears that were coursing down her face and smiled up at him. "I love you, Evan. I love you so much that it hurts."

"It doesn't have to hurt, sweetheart." He brushed his lips across her wet cheek. "It doesn't have to hurt anymore."

"I want you to know, I've made my peace with Robert." She placed her hand on his chest. His heart was beating, strong and sure. "And for the first time since he died, I feel that he is truly gone."

"I'm glad to hear that. It means he took me up on my suggestion."

His lips silenced her before she could ask the next question. Each of them, famished from being so long apart, devoured the other.

Before she knew it, they were on their knees and hurriedly pulling at each other's clothes.

"Your suggestion?" she whispered raggedly. "What did you tell Robert?"

"That I'll love you. Cherish you. Marry you."

She helped him pull his shirt over his head. "He's a shrewd negotiator."

"He also wants a press release that publicly acknowledges that ours was a match made in heaven."

Lying beside him on the floor, Meg gazed into Evan's eyes.
"Very shrewd."

"But that wasn't all of it." He leaned over and kissed her. "He wants us to name our first son Robert."

"Our first son."

Evan nodded, his eyes sparkling with mischief. "Meg, I don't have any condoms."

"Our first son." She smiled, pulling him closer. "Imagine that, naming our first son Robert."

Two years later

THERE WERE ABOUT three dozen people or so, all with young children, lined up for Kay Wilson's book signing when Evan and Meg pushed the baby's carriage into the Manhattan bookstore.

Sensing his wife's excitement, he took a place in line and immediately drew Meg tightly to his side.

"Still don't want to tell her?"

She shook her head, but her eyes proudly scanned the small crowd and rested on the white-haired woman sitting behind a little table. Copies of her bestselling children's book were stacked up around her.

He placed a kiss on her temple. "Have I told you lately how much I love you?"

A pretty blush covered her face as she looked up and met his gaze.

"You did. We both did. About an hour ago while Robert was napping. In the small pantry, if you recall." She giggled and rested her head against his shoulder. "And I'm sure we both have the bruises to prove it."

"Oh, yeah." He ran a hand suggestively down the backside of her jeans. "But you dared me to follow you in there."

"Dared you?" she whispered teasingly. "The way I remember it, *you* decided that I'd worked you too hard at your writing today. I believe you said we needed a break, and since we hadn't tried out the pantry…"

A happy screech from the baby immediately drew their attention to the high-energy bundle of waving arms and kicking legs.

Meg unsnapped Robert's seatbelt as Evan brought the baby to his shoulder. A sloppy kiss of mouth and tongue on his jaw was Evan's reward for being an adoring father. And he loved it.

As they moved forward in the line, Meg took a set of plastic keys from her tote bag and handed them to Robert.

"I hope Eve is not going to too much trouble for this party today. It didn't matter what I said, she was bound and determined to do the whole thing by herself."

"Seeing her great grandson turn one has given her all the energy she needs. She seems younger now than when she was raising me."

"You as a baby…" Meg wrapped an arm around his waist, placed a kiss on the baby's cheek, and then one on Evan's lips. He was slow to let her draw away.

"Oh, I did tell you I sent a car to the airport to pick up your mom."

"You did. Thanks." Meg smiled. "I've seen her more this past year than I have for a long time. Must be you and your charm."

He adjusted the baby in his arm. "I guess I can't take all the credit. Now can I, Robert?"

The baby mouthed him again, this time on his nose, as they moved forward a few more steps.

"Jada and Ted are arriving on the two o'clock train. You know, she's really excited about starting college in the fall. She said she already found a daycare right on campus. She said she'll give us all the details when she gets in."

Evan watched as his wife's eyes again focused on the signing author. Meg beamed as a fan gushed loudly about the book.

"Phil and Rebekah should arrive this afternoon too. But I think they're driving."

Meg's eyes snapped back to his face. "They're coming together? Weren't Rebekah's exact words, Phil could be the last man on earth, and she still wouldn't be caught dead...?"

"I'm sure we'll get all the gory details."

"Yeah. Can't wait." Meg caught the keys as the baby tried to fling them at the woman in front of them. She handed them back to him.

They were one person away from the author, and Evan could see Meg's anticipation building. She turned abruptly, though, and their eyes met. He saw the tears welling up in her glistening brown eyes.

"I love you," she whispered quietly.

"I'm proud of you," he whispered back.

They came flush against the table and when Meg hesitated, Evan spoke up.

"Would you mind autographing a book for us?"

"I'd be delighted." The gray-haired woman beamed up at all of them. "Whom should I make it to?"

Meg leaned forward and smiled. "To Robert, Evan, and Meg."

"Oh. How nice! You know, I dedicated this book to a woman named Meg. Though we've never met, she was the one..."

Evan continued to gaze at his wife. At the mother of his child. At the love of his life.

Thanks, Robert, he thought, sending the words silently heavenward.

Thank you for taking time to read *Made in Heaven*. If you enjoyed it, please consider telling your friends or posting a short review. Word of mouth is an author's best friend...and much appreciated.

And please read the preview of *Thanksgiving in Connecticut* included at the end of this book.

THANKSGIVING IN CONNECTICUT

"IN TRUE MAY MCGOLDRICK STYLE, A TIMELY AND HEARTWARMING STORY FOR THE HOLIDAYS!"

"Former flames get a second chance at love. You can feel yourself a part of the crazy chaotic nature of their Thanksgiving gathering."
- Amazon Review

Paige Coleman has stayed away from her beloved seaside home in the Connecticut village of Stonington ever since being mortified by the 'viral' YouTube video that captured her in the buff at the top of a whaling ship at Mystic Seaport.

Now, four years later, Paige decides that the time has come to face up to her past when her quirky, eighty-six year old grandmother throws the mother of all Thanksgivings to celebrate her recent marriage to 'younger man' Ed Fenwick. But with hometown god and former flame Stanley Fenwick, grandson of the groom, sure to be a part of every event, Paige must now protect her heart as well as retain her sanity, even as her cougar-turned-matchmaker grandmother uses every resource at her disposal to rekindle old fires of passion.

As Thanksgiving dinner looms, Paige must decide if the sacrifice of a little dignity is worth the New England home and family she has missed so much.

Get THANKSGIVING IN CONNECTICUT from your favorite retailer.

AUTHOR'S NOTE

For those readers who have been following our stories, you're probably surprised that this story is set in Newport, Rhode Island, rather than in the medieval Highlands or Regency-era England or Scotland. In fact, this was a very early work of ours. In many ways, it's sort of a 'historical' novel at this point. Hope you enjoyed it. And be sure to check out our holiday novella, *Thanksgiving in Connecticut*.

For new readers, since writing this story we've been busy creating an entire world of interconnected historical romances involving the Macpherson Clan and the Pennington family. Please take a look at our May McGoldrick website for our current releases. And if you prefer a series of contemporary suspense thrillers, check out our Jan Coffey website.

As authors, we work hard to write stories that you will cherish and recommend to your friends. If you liked *Made in Heaven*, be sure to leave a review. For news updates sign up for our newsletter and follow us on BookBub.

Peace and Health!

PREVIEW OF THANKSGIVING IN CONNECTICUT

Connecticut
Saturday, November 17th

"Should Bob take the exit for Mystic?" Ryan asked, sending the driver a sly look. "We can drive to the Borough along the water."

"No!" Paige croaked at her younger brother from the back seat. Her yogic breathing had quickly devolved into hyperventilation when she saw the highway sign for "Tall Ships and Mystic Seaport." She closed her eyes to the scenic panorama of crystal-clear water and quaint cottages.

Just ten minutes past Mystic and they'd be in Stonington Borough, the homey little village situated on a narrow, mile-long peninsula jutting into Fisher's Island Sound. From the old stone lighthouse at the Point, visitors could see Connecticut, Rhode Island, and New York. A couple of blocks away, the last commercial fishing fleet in the state still brought in fresh lobster, scallops, and flounder to the Town Dock.

Paige loved the Borough. She'd grown up here. But she felt a lot different about the place since "The Incident" four years ago.

"Twelve million, three hundred thousand, forty-five views."

Ryan's announcement sliced through Paige's brief moment of nostalgia.

"I may have to kill you," she whispered.

"Seriously, Paige. That's really impressive." Bob was looking at her in the rearview mirror. "My producer would cheerfully sacrifice a choice part of his anatomy for that kind of coverage on YouTube."

Bob Morse was a famous celebrity chief on the Cooking Channel. Paige Coleman was a hard-to-make-ends-meet photographer who, because of this video, had been too embarrassed to come back to the only place she considered home.

As they passed the exit for Mystic, she turned her gaze away from the view of the seaport and the masts of the tall ships down the river. But she couldn't stop her mind from recalling that disastrous ten-year high school reunion four years ago.

Always a bit of an outsider at school, Paige didn't know what possessed her to go solo to the reunion they held at Mystic Seaport the Friday of that Thanksgiving weekend. What made things worse was drinking way too much and falling prey to a prank her classmates played on her.

Naturally, the fuzzy YouTube video showing Paige climbing butt-naked up the rigging of the whaling ship *Charles W. Morgan*, and carrying their class banner, was a hit.

Even more horrible, ten seconds after reaching the very top, she'd suddenly remembered her fear of heights. Screaming, crying, and begging for help only made for better entertainment, of course, and the cell phone video continued to capture the pathetically frantic, comically naked creature clinging to the mast.

Four years later, she still had splinters in her thighs.

The four-minute, nineteen-second video had gone viral after being posted. No names, no location, no close-up of her face, nothing that categorically tied Paige to the incident, but somehow, everyone in the world seemed to know.

The greatest personal embarrassment for Paige wasn't even

captured on video. After what felt like an eternity, Stanley Fenwick had left his gorgeous girlfriend on the dock, climbed the rigging, pried Paige's fingers and legs off the mast, tucked her under one arm, and carried her sobbing and slobbering to the dock.

She was *such* an idiot.

Paige had given away her virginity to Stanley Fenwick the night they'd graduated from high school. She'd been totally in love with him for as many years as she cared to remember.

But what good is it having a 'knight in shining armor' when you can never bring yourself to look him in the face again?

"Okay, we're almost there," Ryan warned.

Paige realized they had already exited the highway. She glanced at the familiar stone walls lining the country road leading to the Borough.

Trying to fight the rising panic, she envisioned her grandmother's face.

Tough, quirky, full of life and surprises, Grandma Shirley was Paige's absolute favorite person in the world. She idolized the old woman for the way she lived her life. She had no fear. Nothing embarrassed her. Clichéd or not, "Live every day to the max!" was her mantra—and be remembered for the love you have for everyone and everything.

Getting the call last month that her eighty-six-year-old grandmother was eloping to Vegas with her "younger" man, a seventy-six-year-old retired minister from Stonington, was hardly a shocker. It was right in line with Shirley's personality. The only problem was that the groom was Edward Fenwick, Stanley's grandfather.

Now Shirley planned to have a weeklong post-wedding celebration at Thanksgiving to celebrate the union. As the *only* granddaughter of the older woman, Paige was given no choice. The same way that she wasn't given an option as to where she stayed. The whole family had to room at the house on Fenwick Point.

Minutes later, they were driving down the causeway that connected Fenwick Point to Stonington Borough. Paige picked up the camera from the seat next to her and held it against her as a shield. The old house, sitting solidly among the storm-battered oaks and maples, loomed over the sparkling waters of the Sound.

Paige suppressed a shudder. Acrophobia might be her number one fear, but right now she'd consider jumping off the Woolworth Building rather than getting out of the car.

Flinging her arms around Paige, Shirley held onto her grand-daughter as if she hadn't seen or talked to her for a lifetime. Paige hugged her, too, enjoying the embrace. This was the way it always was with them. They were the only two in their family who didn't mind showing their affection.

They didn't have to say anything. No small talk about how they looked. Or about sleeping enough. Or about what's good or bad with life. Shirley's hug made everything seem right. Of course, it was always a contest as to who would hold on longer to the other. Paige always lost.

"Okay, that's enough. I'm here, too, Gram," Ryan interrupted.

The corners of Shirley's warm blue eyes crinkled as she smiled, but as she drew back, her face took on an "I'm here for you" look.

"Get it over with now, honey, and you'll be okay."

Puzzled, Paige stared at her for a moment. Shirley cocked an eyebrow, and the significance of the look and the whispered words hit Paige. Her gaze drifted over the shoulder of her grand-mother to the person coming out the front door to join them on the gravel driveway.

Stanley.

Paige's arms turned to rubber and dropped to her sides, her heart kicking into double-time. Her face was suddenly on fire. In spite of herself, she thought of how she'd left New York with no makeup and her long brown hair pulled back in a simple ponytail. Faded skinny jeans, an old sweater, and knockoff Doc Martens.

She hadn't rehearsed what to say or how to act. She hadn't even practiced digging a hole to bury her head in.

He was looking at her, a full-body scan, starting with her hair and then taking in the whole picture. If he broke out laughing, she might just crawl back to New York.

Paige was certain she'd clipped the wings of every one of those "crazy-in-love-with-Stanley-Fenwick" butterflies years ago. Only maimed, apparently, they were back at full strength in her gut now, and making sure she knew it, too.

She smiled weakly as Shirley moved around her to greet Ryan and Bob. Thankfully, Ed Fenwick stepped in, momentarily blocking her.

"Paige. Welcome. It's so good to see you." The retired minister gave her a quick peck on the cheek and then looked past her. "I see I'll have to talk to you later. Right now, I have to make sure my wife doesn't run off with your handsome friend."

And then it was just Stanley. When it came to looks, Paige could honestly think of only a few men who were touched by the hand of God. The last time she saw him—four years ago—he'd been at the top of that ladder. He now shattered the ceiling. Stanley only seemed to become more handsome with age. Damn him.

He was wearing his dark hair shorter. There were just a few more lines defining his chiseled face. Dressed in jeans and a dark green sweater that matched the color of his eyes, he took a step forward to greet her. A hug? A friendly kiss? A handshake? Like a dork, she stuck out her hand about an hour before he reached her.

His large, warm hand enveloped her icy fingers, holding her captive for a few heartbeats before letting go. "Been a long time, Paige. How have you been?"

Some bullfrog seemed to be drowning out her reply, but Paige quickly realized the croaking was coming from her. She tried again. "Great. Busy. You?"

"The same."

She searched for something to say. "Are your parents here already?"

"No, they're in Florida. Flying in Wednesday. How about yours?"

"California. They're coming on Wednesday, too."

They were both doing a great job with the small talk. She noticed that Stanley's gaze moved a couple of times to the commotion that was taking place behind her. Shirley was an entertainer by nature, and it was obvious that Bob was being made to feel right at home.

Seizing the opportunity, she turned around and Ryan pushed past her. He wasn't standing on ceremony and gave Stanley a man-hug before exchanging friendly greetings with him.

As townies, the Colemans and the Fenwicks were never part of the summer-only crowd. Their families—and the three of them —were all socializing long before the kids hit those awkward teenage years. And long before Paige developed a secret crush on the popular captain of the rowing team. But when her feelings suddenly changed, it hit her hard. Even now, an ache of longing burned in her chest, thinking of their time together. Ice skating every winter and laughing as they huddled by the bonfires they'd build by the frozen pond. And all those golden summer evenings on the beach, sitting together after swimming, talking about everything as the sun went down. She could still recall the glint of sunlight in his gorgeous green eyes.

That crush survived a veritable parade of his girlfriends, but it wasn't until a month before their graduation that Stanley noticed her as anything other than a "buddy" he liked to hang out with. Ryan and Stanley's relationship, on the other hand, had remained unchanged. Through the Dark Ages of high school and the occasional bullying that took place there, Ryan grew up safe and free under Stanley's ever-protective wing.

"Come on, Gram. You have Bob for the entire week," Ryan

said, walking back to the trunk of the car to get their luggage. Their guest hadn't been able to move two steps from the driver's door.

Stanley stood next to her, eyeing the television chef.

"New boyfriend?" he asked quietly.

"Not too new. But . . . yes," Paige answered.

"I never took you for one who would give the time of day to a celebrity." Stanley realized he was glaring.

"What? Oh, but—"

Before Paige finish, though, Bob broke free of Shirley and walked over to them.

"Paige, sweetie, you look exhausted. Why don't you go on in? Ryan and I can bring in the luggage," he said, affectionately tucking a loose strand of hair behind her ear. He turned to Stanley. "Hi. I'm Bob Morse. You must be Stanley Fenwick. I've heard so much about you."

"I wish I could say the same thing, Bob," Stanley replied, nodding curtly before stepping around them to help Ryan with the luggage.

The sudden stab of irritation was as surprising as it was sharp. Part of Stanley's job involved dealing with superstar athletes and celebrities. Big egos and center stage personalities didn't bother him in the least.

But Bob Morse bothered him.

"So are you staying for the week, too?" Ryan asked, handing Stanley a suitcase and a duffel bag.

"I'll be in and out. Mostly day trips. We're trying to close a big deal before Thanksgiving."

"Yeah, I've been reading up on what you've been doing with your aviation company since you took over from your father. Pretty impressive. Who knew you could carve such a profitable niche in sports team transportation?" He dragged the last of their luggage out of the trunk. "Of course, you knew. That was a nice write-up in the *Wall Street Journal* a few months ago."

Fenwick Charter Air was doing great. But Stanley felt he deserved no bragging rights. His father had built the company from nothing into a lucrative business. When he'd started running the show, Stanley had access to enough cash to make things happen. So he'd made some acquisitions and they had paid off. The timing had been right.

"How's the advertising business these days?" Stanley asked, trying to change the subject.

"Good. Busy, despite the fact that people say the magazine business is dead. There's still plenty of advertising money coming our way, and it pays the rent. It's nice to have a steady paycheck, considering my housemate works on commission."

Stanley looked in the direction Ryan motioned and saw Paige huddled with her grandmother. The familiar look about her had blown him away. Her hair, the clothes, the dark, beautiful eyes and long lashes that he could get lost in. Her skin glowing in the November air. She'd materialized before him, looking just as he had her etched in his memory.

"You and Paige live together?"

"We've been sharing an apartment for a while. It's been good for both of us. But all good things have to come to an end."

Being an only child, Stanley had always envied the bond between Paige and Ryan. They were fiercely protective of each other, but they'd always allowed him to be part of the pack, and their times together were still his favorite childhood memories.

"I think we're going to be trying out some new living arrangements next year," Ryan continued, his grin widening. "And I think Bob is going to figure into the plans."

"Is that right?" Stanley attempted to keep the flatness out of his voice and ignore the tightening in his chest.

"Those are Paige's." Ryan nodded at the bags Stanley was

carrying. "Gram has already decided that Princess Paige deserves privacy and gets the boathouse all to herself."

Privacy was good, Stanley decided, thinking darkly of Chef Bob. *Very* good.

Get THANKSGIVING IN CONNECTICUT from your favorite retailer.

USA Today Bestselling Authors Nikoo and Jim McGoldrick have crafted over fifty fast-paced, conflict-filled novels, along with two works of nonfiction, under the pseudonyms May McGoldrick, Jan Coffey, and Nik James.

These popular and prolific authors write historical romance, suspense, mystery, historical Westerns, and young adult novels. They are four-time Rita Award Finalists and the winners of numerous awards for their writing, including the Daphne DeMaurier Award for Excellence, the *Romantic Times Magazine* Reviewers' Choice Award, three NJRW Golden Leaf Awards, two Holt Medallions, and the Connecticut Press Club Award for Best Fiction. Their work is included in the Popular Culture Library collection of the National Museum of Scotland.

facebook.com/MayMcGoldrick

twitter.com/MayMcGoldrick

instagram.com/maymcgoldrick

bookbub.com/authors/may-mcgoldrick

www.ingramcontent.com/pod-product-compliance
Lightning Source LLC
Chambersburg PA
CBHW050007120726
47903CB00006B/1676